From #1 **New York Times** *bestselling author Nora Roberts, writing as J. D. Robb, comes a tantalizing new novel in the futuristic series. . . . This time, Lieutenant Eve Dallas is searching for a Casanova killer with a deadly appetite for seduction. . . .*

SEDUCTION IN DEATH

Dante had been courting his victim in cyberspace for weeks before meeting her in person. A few sips of wine and a few hours later, she was dead. The murder weapon: a rare, usually undetectable date-rape drug with the street value of a quarter of a million dollars.

Lieutenant Eve Dallas is playing and replaying the clues in her mind. The candlelight, the music, the rose petals strewn across the bed—a seduction meant for his benefit, not hers. He hadn't intended to kill her. But now that he has, he is left with only two choices: He can either hole up in fear and guilt, or he can start hunting again. . . .

"So certain is Robb at maintaining an atmospheric setting for this well-paced and expertly rendered series, followers will feel as if they have gone home to the future."
—*Publishers Weekly*

continued on next page . . .

The bestselling series featuring Eve Dallas . . .

NAKED IN DEATH

Breaking every rule, Eve gets involved with Roarke, a suspect in her latest murder case. . . .

"Danger, romance . . . a masterpiece of fine writing."

—*Rendezvous*

GLORY IN DEATH

In Eve's latest case, two murder victims have one connection: Eve's lover, Roarke. . . .

"Ms. Robb's brilliant talent for creating fresh, innovative plots . . . is unsurpassed."

—*Rendezvous*

IMMORTAL IN DEATH

A top model is dead—and the suspect is none other than Eve's best friend. . . .

"Wonderful . . . If ever there was a book for all tastes, this is the one."

—*Affaire de Coeur*

RAPTURE IN DEATH

Three apparent suicides draw Eve into the world of virtual reality—where the mind can be a deadly weapon. . . .

"Sure to leave you hungering for more."

—*Publishers Weekly*

CEREMONY IN DEATH

Every step Eve takes brings her closer to a confrontation with humanity's most seductive form of evil. . . .

"Explosive . . . [A] spectacular sizzler."

—*Romantic Times*

VENGEANCE IN DEATH

A madman brutally murders two men—both with ties to an ugly secret shared by Eve's new husband. . . .

"The publishing world might be hard-pressed to find an author with a more diverse style or fertile imagination than Nora Roberts, writing here as J. D. Robb."

—*Publishers Weekly*

HOLIDAY IN DEATH

In a future when computer technology brings lovers together, dating can be a deadly game....

"One of the best futuristic mystery series on the market today."
—*Without A Clue*

CONSPIRACY IN DEATH

The pursuit of a serial killer leaves Eve Dallas's job on the line....

"Masterful ... I stand in absolute awe of J. D. Robb's talent."
—*The Romance Reader*

LOYALTY IN DEATH

Eve Dallas returns to face her most ingenious foe, a "secret admirer" who taunts her with letters—and kills without mercy....

"This series gets better with each book." —*Publishers Weekly*

WITNESS IN DEATH

Eve Dallas is thrust into the spotlight when she becomes the key witness in the brutal murder of a famous actor....

"Sexy, gritty, richly imagined." —*Publishers Weekly*

JUDGMENT IN DEATH

When a cop killer cuts loose in a club called Purgatory, Detective Eve Dallas descends into an underground criminal hell....

"Electrifying suspense and hot, hot passion." —*Romantic Times*

BETRAYAL IN DEATH

Eve is up against a hit man for the elite, whose next target may be her own husband, Roarke....

"Robb [gets] into the minds and souls of her characters."
—*The Romance Reader*

Turn the page for a complete list of titles by Nora Roberts and J. D. Robb from The Berkley Publishing Group ...

SEDUCTION IN DEATH

J. D. Robb

BERKLEY BOOKS, NEW YORK

This is a work of fiction. Names, characters, places, and incidents are either the product of the author's imagination or are used fictitiously, and any resemblance to actual persons, living or dead, business establishments, events, or locales is entirely coincidental.

SEDUCTION IN DEATH

A Berkley Book / published by arrangement with
the author

PRINTING HISTORY
Berkley edition / September 2001

Visit our website at
www.penguinputnam.com

ISBN: 0-425-18146-4

BERKLEY®
Berkley Books are published by The Berkley Publishing Group,
a division of Penguin Putnam Inc.,
375 Hudson Street, New York, New York 10014.
BERKLEY and the "B" design
are trademarks belonging to Penguin Putnam Inc.

PRINTED IN THE UNITED STATES OF AMERICA

10 9 8 7 6 5 4 3 2 1

SEDUCTION
IN
DEATH

True, I talk of dreams,
Which are the children of an idle brain,
Begot of nothing but vain fantasy.

—William Shakespeare

Yet each man kills the thing he loves,
By each let this be heard,
Some do it with a bitter look,
Some with a flattering word.
The coward does it with a kiss,
The brave man with a sword!

—Oscar Wilde

Chapter 1

Death came in dreams. She was a child who was not a child, facing a ghost who, no matter how often his blood bathed her hands, would not die.

The room was cold as a grave, hazed by the red light that blinked, on and off, on and off, against the dirty window glass. The light spilled over the floor, over the blood, over his body. Over her as she huddled in the corner with the knife, covered with gore to the hilt, still in her hand.

Pain was everywhere, radiating through her in stupefying waves that had no beginning or end, but circled, endlessly circled, into every cell. The bone in her arm he'd snapped, the cheek where he'd backhanded her so carelessly. The center of her that had torn, again, during the rape.

She was smothered by the pain, coated with shock. And washed with his blood.

She was eight.

She could see her own breath as she panted. Little ghosts that told her she was alive. She could taste the blood inside her mouth, a bright and terrible flavor, and smell—just under the ripeness of fresh death—the stink of whiskey.

She was alive, and he was not. She was alive, and he was not. Again and again she chanted those words in her head, and her mind tried to make sense of them.

She was alive. He was not.

And his eyes, open and staring, fixed on her.

Smiled.

You can't get rid of me so easy, little girl.

Her breath came faster, in hitching gasps that wanted to gather into a scream. That wanted to burst out of her throat. But all that came was a whimper.

Made a mess of things, haven't you? Just can't do what you're told.

His voice was so pleasant, bright with that grinning humor she knew was the most dangerous of all. While he laughed, blood poured out of the holes she'd hacked into him.

What's the matter, little girl? Cat got your tongue?

I'm alive and you're not. I'm alive and you're not.

Think so? He wiggled his fingers, a kind of teasing wave that made her moan in terror as wet red drops flicked from the tips.

I'm sorry. I didn't mean it. Don't hurt me again. You hurt me. Why do you have to hurt me?

Because you're stupid. Because you don't listen! Because—and here's the real secret—I can. I can do what I want with you and nobody gives a stinking rat's ass. You're nothing, you're nobody, and don't you forget it, you little bitch.

She began to cry now, thin cold tears that tracked through the mask of blood over her face. Go away. Just go away and leave me alone!

I'm not going to do that. I'm never going to do that.

To her horror, he pushed himself to his knees. Crouched there like some nightmarish toad, bloody and grinning. Watching her.

I got a lot invested in you. Time and money. Who puts

a fucking roof over your head? Who puts food in your belly? Who takes you traveling all over this great country of ours? Most kids your age haven't seen shit, but you have. But do you learn? No, you don't. Do you pull your weight? No, you don't. But you're gonna. You remember what I told you? You're gonna start earning your keep.

He got to his feet, a big man with his hands slowly balling into fists at his side.

But now, Daddy has to punish you. He took a shambling step toward her. *You've been a bad girl.* And another. *A very bad girl.*

Her own screams woke her.

She was drenched in sweat, shuddering with cold. She fought for breath, wildly struggled to tear away the ropes of sheets that had wrapped around her as she'd thrashed through the nightmare.

Sometimes he'd tied her up. Remembering that, she made small, animal sounds in her throat as she tore at the sheets.

Freed, she rolled off the bed, crouched beside it in the dark like a woman prepared to flee or fight.

"Lights! On full. God, oh God."

They flashed on, chasing even a hint of shadow out of the huge, beautiful room. Still, she scanned it, every corner, looking for ghosts as the nasty edge of the dream jabbed through her gut.

She forced back the tears. They were useless, and they were weak. Just as it was useless, it was weak, to let herself be frightened by dreams. By ghosts.

But she continued to shake as she crawled up to sit on the edge of the big bed.

An empty bed because Roarke was in Ireland and her experiment of trying to sleep in it without him, without dreams, had been a crashing failure.

Did that make her pitiful? she wondered. Stupid? Or just married?

When the fat cat, Galahad, bumped his big head against her arm, she gathered him up. She sat, Lieutenant

Eve Dallas, eleven years a cop, and comforted herself
with the cat as a child might a teddy bear.

Nausea coated her stomach, and she continued to
rock, to pray she wouldn't be sick and add one more mis-
ery to the night.

"Time display," she ordered, and the dial of the bedside clock blinked on. *One-fifteen*, she noted. Perfect.
She'd barely made it an hour before she'd screamed herself awake.

She set the cat aside, got to her feet. As carefully as an
old woman she stepped down from the platform, crossed
the room, and walked into the bathroom.

She ran the water cold, as cold as she could stand, then
sluiced it onto her face while Galahad wound himself like
a plump ribbon between her legs.

While he purred into the silence, she lifted her head,
examined her face in the mirror. It was nearly as color-
less as the water that dripped from it. Her eyes were
dark, looked bruised, looked exhausted. Her hair was a
matted brown cap, and her facial bones seemed too
sharp, too close to the surface. Her mouth was too big,
her nose ordinary.

What the hell did Roarke see when he looked at her?
she wondered.

She could call him now. It was after six in the morning
in Ireland, and he was an early riser. Even if he were still
asleep, it wouldn't matter. She could pick up the 'link and
call, and his face would slide on-screen.

And he'd see the nightmare in her eyes. What good
would that do either of them?

When a man owned the majority of the known universe, he had to be able to travel on business without
being hounded by his wife. In this case, it was more than
business that kept him away. He was attending a memo-
rial to a dead friend, and didn't need more stress and
worry heaped on him from her end.

She knew, though they'd never really discussed it,
that he'd cut his overnight trips down to the bone. The

nightmares rarely came so violently when he was in bed beside her.

She'd never had one like this, one where her father had spoken to her *after* she'd killed him. Said things to her she thought—was nearly sure—he'd said to her when he'd been alive.

Eve imagined Dr. Mira, NYPSD's star psychologist and profiler, would have a field day with the meanings and symbolism and Christ-all.

That wouldn't do any good either, she decided. So she'd just keep this little gem to herself. She'd take a shower, grab the cat, and go upstairs to her office. She and Galahad would stretch out in her sleep chair and conk out for the rest of the night.

The dream would have faded away by morning.

You remember what I told you.

She couldn't, Eve thought as she stepped into the shower and ordered all jets on full at a hundred and one degrees. She couldn't remember.

And she didn't want to.

She was steadier when she stepped out of the shower, and however pathetic it was, dragged on one of Roarke's shirts for comfort. She'd just scooped up the cat when the bedside 'link beeped.

Roarke, she thought and her spirits lifted considerably.

She rubbed her cheek against Galahad's head as she answered. "Dallas."

Dispatch. Dallas, Lieutenant Eve . . .

Death didn't only come in dreams.

Eve stood over it now, in the balmy early morning air of a Tuesday in June. The New York City sidewalk was cordoned off, the sensors and blocks squaring around the pavement and the cheerful tubs of petunias used to spruce up the building's entrance.

She had a particular fondness for petunias, but she didn't think they were going to do the job this time. And not for some time to come.

The woman was facedown on the sidewalk. From the angle of the body, the splatter and pools of blood, there wasn't going to be a lot of that face left. Eve looked up at the dignified gray tower with its semicircle balconies, its silver ribbon of people glides. Until they identified the body, they'd have a hard time pinning down the area from which she'd fallen. Or jumped. Or been pushed.

The one thing Eve was sure of: It had been a very long drop.

"Get her prints and run them," she ordered.

She glanced down at her aide as Peabody squatted, opened a field kit. Peabody's uniform cap sat squarely on her ruler-straight dark hair. She had steady hands, Eve thought, and a good eye. "Why don't you do time of death."

"Me?" Peabody asked in surprise.

"Get me an ID, establish time of death. Log in description of scene and body."

Now, despite the grisly circumstance, it was excitement that moved over Peabody's face. "Yes, sir. Sir, first officer on-scene has a potential witness."

"A witness from up there, or down here?"

"Down here."

"I'll take it." But Eve stayed where she was a moment longer, watching Peabody scan the dead woman's fingerprints. Though Peabody's hands and feet were sealed, she made no contact with the body and did the scan quickly, delicately.

After one nod of approval, Eve strode away to question the uniforms flanking the perimeter.

It might have been nearly three in the morning, but there were bystanders, gapers, and they had to be encouraged along, blocked out. News hawks were already in evidence, calling out questions, trying to snag a few minutes of recording to pump into the airwaves before the first morning commute.

An ambitious glide-cart operator had jumped on the opportunity and was putting in some overtime selling to the crowd. His grill pumped out smoke that spewed the scents of soy dogs and rehydrated onions into the air.

He appeared to be doing brisk business.

In the gorgeous spring of 2059, death continued to draw an audience from the living, and those who knew how to make a quick buck out of the deal.

A cab winged by, didn't bother to so much as tap the brakes. From somewhere farther downtown, a siren screamed.

Eve blocked it out, turned to the uniform. "Rumor is we've got eyes."

"Yes, sir. Officer Young's got her in the squad car keeping her away from the ghouls."

"Good." Eve scanned the faces behind the barrier. In them she saw horror, excitement, curiosity, and a kind of relief.

I'm alive, and you're not.

Shaking it off, she hunted down Young and the witness.

Given the neighborhood—for in spite of the dignity and the petunias, the apartment building was right on the border of midtown bustle and downtown sleaze—Eve was expecting a licensed companion, maybe a jonesing chemi-head or a dealer on the way to a mark.

She certainly hadn't expected the tiny, snappily dressed blonde with the pretty and familiar face.

"Dr. Dimatto."

"Lieutenant Dallas?" Louise Dimatto angled her head, and the ruby clusters at her ears gleamed like glassy blood. "Do you come in, or do I come out?"

Eve jerked a thumb, held the car door wider. "Come on out."

They'd met the previous winter, at the Canal Street Clinic where Louise fought against the tide to heal the homeless and the hopeless. She came from money, and her bloodline was blue, but Eve had good reason to know Louise didn't quibble about getting her hands dirty.

She'd nearly died helping Eve fight an ugly war during that bitter winter.

Eve skimmed a look over Louise's stoplight-red dress. "Making house calls?"

"A date. Some of us try to maintain a healthy social life."

"How'd it go?"

"I took a cab home, so you be the judge." She skimmed back her short, honeycomb hair with her fingers. "Why are so many men so boring?"

"You know, that's a question that haunts me day and night." When Louise laughed, Eve smiled in response. "It's good to see you, all things considered."

"I thought you might drop by the clinic, come see the improvements your donation helped implement."

"I think it's called blackmail in most circles."

"Donation, blackmail. Let's not split hairs. You've helped save a few lives, Dallas. That's got to be nearly as satisfying to you as catching those who take them."

"Lost one tonight." She turned, looked back toward the body. "What do you know about her?"

"Nothing, really. I think she lives in the building, but she's not looking her best at the moment, so I can't be sure." After a long breath, Louise rubbed the back of her neck. "Sorry, this is more in your line than mine. It's my first experience nearly having a body fall in my arms. I've seen people die, and it's not always gentle. But this was . . ."

"Okay. You want to sit back down? Want some coffee?"

"No. No. Let me just tell it." She steadied herself, a subtle squaring of the shoulders, stiffening of the spine. "I ditched the date from tedium, grabbed a cab. We'd gone to dinner and a club uptown. I got here about one-thirty, I suppose."

"You live in this building?"

"That's right. Tenth floor. Apartment 1005. I paid the cab, got out on the curb. It's a pretty night. I was thinking, It's a beautiful night, and I just wasted it on that jerkoff. So I stood there for a couple minutes, on the sidewalk, wondering if I should go in and call it a night, or take a walk. I decided I'd go up, fix a nightcap, and sit out on my balcony. I turned, took another step toward the doors. I don't know why I looked up—I didn't hear anything. But I just looked up, and she was falling, with her hair spread out like wings. It couldn't have been more than two or three seconds, I'd barely had time to register what I was seeing, and she hit."

"You didn't see where she fell from?"

"No. She was coming down, and fast. Jesus, Dallas." Louise had to pause a moment, rub the image from her eyes. "She hit so hard, and with a really nasty sound I'm going to be hearing in my sleep for a long time. It couldn't have been more than five or six feet from where I was standing."

She drew another breath, made herself look over at the body. Now there was pity over the horror. "People think they've reached the end of their ropes. That there's nothing left for them. But they're wrong. There's always more rope. There's always something left."

"You think she jumped?"

Louise looked back at Eve. "Yes, I assumed . . . I said I didn't hear anything. She didn't make a sound. No scream, no cry. Nothing but the flutter of her hair in the wind. I guess that's why I looked up." She thought now. "I did hear something after all. That flutter, like wings."

"What did you do after she hit?"

"I checked her pulse. Knee-jerk," Louise said with a shrug. "I knew she was dead, but I checked anyway. Then I took out my pocket-link and called nine-one-one. You think she was pushed? That's why you're here."

"I don't think anything yet." Eve turned back toward the building. Some lights had been on when she'd arrived, and there were more now so that it looked like a vertical chessboard in silver and black. "Homicide gets tagged on leapers like this. It's standard. Do yourself a favor. Go in, take a pill, zone out. Don't talk to the press if they wheedle your name."

"Good advice. Will you let me know when . . . when you know what happened to her?"

"Yeah, I can do that. Want a uniform to take you up?"

"No, thanks." She took one last look at the body. "As bad as my night was, it was better than some."

"I hear you."

"Best to Roarke," Louise added, then walked toward the doors.

Peabody was already standing, her palm-link in hand. "Got an ID, Dallas. Bryna Bankhead, age twenty-three, mixed race. Single. Residence apartment 1207 in the building behind us. She worked at Saks Fifth Avenue. Lingerie. I established time of death at oh-one-fifteen."

"One-fifteen?" Eve repeated, and thought of the read-out on her bedside clock.

"Yes, sir. I ran the measurements twice."

Eve frowned down at the gauges, the field kit, the bloody pool under the body. "Witness said she fell about one-thirty. When was the nine-eleven logged?"

Uneasy now, Peabody checked her 'link for the record. "Call came in at oh-one-thirty-six." She heaved out a breath that fluttered her thick, straight bangs. "I must've screwed up the measurements," she began. "I'm sorry—"

"Don't apologize until I tell you you've screwed up." Eve crouched, opened her own field kit, took out her own gauges. And ran the test a third time, personally.

"You established time of death accurately. For the record," she continued. "Victim, identified as Bankhead, Bryna, cause of death undetermined. Time of death oh-one-fifteen. TOD verified by Peabody, Officer Delia, and primary investigator Dallas, Lieutenant Eve. Let's roll her, Peabody."

Peabody swallowed the questions on her tongue, and the quick rise of her own gorge. For the moment she blanked her mind, but later she would think it had been like rolling over a sack full of broken sticks swimming in thick liquid.

"Impact has severely damaged victim's face."

"Boy," Peabody breathed through her teeth. "I'll say."

"Limbs and torso also suffered severe damage, rendering it impossible to determine any possible premortem injury from visual exam. The body is nude. She's wearing earrings." Eve took out a small magnifier, peered through it at the lobes. "Multicolored stones in gold settings, matching ring on right middle finger."

She eased closer until her lips were nearly on the victim's throat—and Peabody's gorge tried a second rising. "Sir . . ."

"Perfume. She's wearing perfume. You walk around your apartment at one in the morning, Peabody, wearing fancy earrings and fancy perfume?"

"If I'm awake in my apartment at one in the morning, I'm usually in my bunny slippers. Unless . . ."

"Yeah." Eve straightened. "Unless you've got company." Eve turned to the crime scene tech. "Bag her. I want her tagged for priority with the ME. I want her checked for recent sexual activity, and any injuries that are premortem. Let's have a look at her apartment, Peabody."

"She's not a leaper."

"Evidence is pointing to the contrary." She strode into the lobby. It was small and quiet, and security cameras swept the area.

"I want the discs from security," she told Peabody. "Lobby level, and twelfth floor to start."

There was a long pause as they stepped into the elevator and Eve called for the twelfth floor. Then Peabody shifted her weight, trying for casual. "So . . . are you going to bring in EDD?"

Eve stuck her hands in her pockets, scowled at the blank, brushed metal doors of the elevator. Peabody's romantic liaison with Ian McNab, Electronics Detective Division had recently detonated. *Which, if anyone had listened to me*, Eve thought bitterly, *wouldn't be in many ugly pieces because it never would have existed in the first place.*

"Suck it in, Peabody."

"It's a reasonable question on procedure, and has nothing whatsoever to do with anything else."

Peabody's tone was stiff enough to communicate insult, hurt feelings, and annoyance. She was, Eve thought, good at it. "If during the course of this investigation, I, as primary investigator, deem EDD is needed for consult, I will so order."

"You could also request someone other than he who shall not be named," Peabody muttered.

"Feeney runs EDD. I don't tell Feeney which of his people to assign. And damn it, Peabody, this case or another, you're going to end up working with McNab, which is why you should never have let him bang you in the first place."

"I can work with him. It doesn't bother me a bit." So saying, she stomped off the elevator onto the twelfth floor. "I'm a professional, unlike some others who are always cracking wise and coming to work in weird getups and showing off."

At the door of Bankhead's apartment, Eve lifted her eyebrows. "You calling me unprofessional, Officer?"

"No, sir! I was . . ." Her stiff shoulders loosened, and humor slid back into her eyes. "I'd never call your getups weird, Dallas, even though I'm pretty sure you're wearing a guy's shirt."

"If you're finished with your snit, we'll go back on record. Using master to gain entrance to victim's apartment," Eve continued, and coded through the locks. She opened the door, examined it. "Interior chain and snap bolt were not in use. Living area lights are on dim. What do you smell, Peabody?"

"Ah . . . candles, maybe perfume."

"What do you see?"

"Living area, nicely decorated and organized. The mood screen's on. Looks like a spring meadow pattern. There are two wineglasses and an open bottle of red wine on the sofa table, indicating the victim had company at some point in the evening."

"Okay." Though she'd hoped Peabody would take it a little further, Eve nodded. "What do you hear?"

"Music. Audio system's playing. Violins and piano. I don't recognize the tune."

"Not the tune, the tone," Eve said. "Romance. Take another look around. Everything's in place. Neat, tidy, and as noted, organized. But she left a bottle of wine sitting open, and used glasses sitting out? Why?"

"She didn't have a chance to put them away."

"Or turn off the lights, the audio, the mood screen." She stepped through, glanced into the adjoining kitchen. The counters were clean, and empty but for the corkscrew, the wine cork. "Who opened the wine, Peabody?"

"The most likely conclusion would be her date. If she'd opened it, she would have, giving the indication of the apartment, put the corkscrew away, dumped the cork in her recycler."

"Mmm. Living area balcony doors closed and secured from inside. If this was self-termination or an accidental fall, it wasn't from this point. Let's check the bedroom."

"You don't think it was self-termination or an accident."

"I don't think anything yet. What I know is the victim was a single woman who kept a very neat apartment and that evidence indicates she spent at least a portion of this evening at home with company."

Eve turned into the bedroom. The audio played here as well, dreamy, fluid notes that seemed to drift on the breeze fluttering through the open balcony doors. The bed was unmade, and the disordered sheets were strewn with pink rose petals. A black dress, black undergarments, and black evening shoes were piled beside the bed.

Candles, guttering fragrantly in their own wax, were set around the room.

"Read the scene," Eve ordered.

"It appears as if the victim engaged in or was about to engage in sexual intercourse prior to her death. There are no signs of struggle here or in the living area, which indicates the sex, or plans for the sex, were consensual."

"This wasn't sex, Peabody. This was seduction. We're going to need to find out who seduced who. Record the scene, then get me those security discs."

With a sealed finger, Eve eased open the drawer of the bedside table. "Goodie drawer."

"Sir?"

"Sex drawer, Peabody. Single girl provisions, which in this case includes condoms. Victim liked men. Couple bottles of tasty body oils, a vibrator for when self-servicing is necessary or desired, and some vaginal lubricant. Fairly standard, even conservative and straight goodies. No toys or aids here to indicate victim leaned toward same-sex relationships."

"So her date was a man."

"Or a woman hoping to broaden Bankhead's horizons. We'll nail that down with the discs. And maybe we get lucky with the ME's report and find some little soldiers in her."

She stepped into the adjoining bath. It was sparkling clean, the ribbon-trimmed hand towels perfectly aligned. There were fancy soaps in a fancy dish, perfumed creams in glass-and-silver jars. "My guess is her bed partner didn't hang around and wash up. Get the sweepers up here," she ordered. "Let's see if our Romeo left anything behind."

She opened the mirror on the medicine cabinet, studied the contents. Normal over-the-counter meds, nothing heavy. A six-month supply of twenty-eight day contraceptive pills.

The drawer beside the sink was packed, and meticulously organized, with cosmetic enhancers. Lip dyes, lash lengtheners, face and body paints.

Bryna had spent a lot of time in front of this mirror,

Eve mused. If the little black dress, the wine, the candle-light were anything to go by, she'd spent considerable time in front of it tonight. Preparing herself for a man.

Moving to the bedroom 'link, Eve played back the last call and stood, listening to Bryna Bankhead, pretty in her little black dress, talk of her big plans for the evening with a brunette she called CeeCee.

I'm a little nervous, but mostly I'm just excited. We're finally going to meet. How do I look?

You look fabulous, Bry. You just remember real-life dating's different from cyber-dating. Take it slow, and keep it public tonight, right?

Absolutely. But I really do feel like I know him, CeeCee. We've got so much in common, and we've been e-mailing for weeks. Besides, it was my idea to meet— and his to make it drinks in a public place so I'd feel more at ease. He's so considerate, so romantic. God, I'm going to be late. I hate being late. Gotta go.

Don't forget. I want all the deets.

I'll tell you all about it tomorrow. Wish me luck, CeeCee. I really think he could be the one.

"Yeah," Eve murmured as she shut off the 'link. "So do I."

Chapter 2

In her office at Cop Central, Eve reviewed the security discs of the apartment building on the day of the murder. People came, people went. Residents, visitors. She pegged slinky twin blondes who strolled across the lobby in tandem as licensed companions. *Double your pleasure*, she thought as she watched one setting up the next job on her pocket-link while the other noted down the split in her daybook.

Bryna Bankhead rushed in at six-forty-five, a couple of shopping bags in tow and a pretty flush on her cheeks.

Happy, Eve thought. *Excited. She wants to get upstairs, take out her new stuff and play with it. Groom herself, primp, change her mind about her outfit a few times. Maybe fix a quick bite to eat so her stomach won't be too nervous.*

Just a typical single woman anticipating a date. Who doesn't know she'll be a statistic before it's over.

She watched Louise come in just before seven-thirty. She moved quickly, too, but then she always did. There was no light of adventure or anticipation on her face, Eve mused. She looked distracted, a little tired.

No shopping bags for Dr. Dimatto, Eve noted. Just her medical kit and a handbag as big as Idaho.

A not-so-typical single woman, Eve thought, who looks as if she's already decided she isn't going to enjoy the evening ahead of her.

And who doesn't know she'll end it with a body broken at her feet.

Louise was quicker than Bryna. She was striding out of the elevator, slicked into her killer red dress, at eight-forty. Polished, she didn't look like the dedicated, overworked and steely minded crusader.

She looked sharp, sexy, female.

The guy coming in as she was going out obviously agreed. He took a good long look at her ass as Louise zipped out. She either didn't notice or didn't give a damn as she didn't so much as glance back at him.

A kid of about eighteen swaggered out of the elevator. He was dressed in solid black leather, tip to toe, and carted an air scooter under his arm. He swung it down as he shoved open the doors, leaped on with an agility and flash Eve had to admire, and winged off into the night.

She sipped coffee as she watched Bryna exit the building just before nine P.M. Nearly running, Eve thought, risking a turned ankle in her date shoes because she didn't want to be late. Her hair was styled in a glossy up-do, like an ebony tower. Her face, a delicate caramel color, was flushed with anticipation and nerves. She carried a small evening bag and wore the pretty, flashing earrings.

"Check cab pick ups within a block radius of the building, Peabody. She's in a hurry, so unless she's meeting the guy closeby, she'd spring for a cab." She frowned as she zipped through time, slowing whenever someone came in or out of the building.

"She was a good-looking woman," Eve commented. "Seemed reasonably smart, had her own place, decent job. Why does someone like that go fishing in the cyberpool for a date?"

"Easy for you to say," Peabody muttered and earned a narrowed stare. "Well, jeez, Dallas, you're *married*. For the rest of us, it's a jungle out there, full of apes and snakes and baboons."

"You ever do the cyber-thing?"

Peabody shuffled her feet. "Maybe. And I don't want to talk about it."

Amused, Eve started the scan again. "I was single a hell of a lot longer than I've been married. I never stooped to cyber-world."

"Big deal when you're tall and thin with jungle-cat eyes and have a sexy little dent in your chin."

"You coming onto me, Peabody?"

"My love for you is a fearsome thing, Dallas. But I've given up dating cops."

"Good policy. Ah, here they come. Freeze screen."

The time read twenty-three thirty-eight. In two hours plus, Bryna had obviously gotten very cozy with her cyber date. They came in with their arms snugged around each other's waists, and laughing.

"He looks great," Peabody decided as she leaned closer to the monitor. "Answer to a maiden's prayer kind of thing. Tall, dark, and handsome."

Eve grunted. She judged the man to be about six one, running to about one-ninety. His dark hair was swept back in a tightly curled mane that spilled over his shoulders. His skin was poetically pale, and set off by glinting emerald studs at the corner of his mouth and the high point of his right cheekbone. His eyes were the same vivid green. A thin line of beard ran vertically from just below center of his bottom lip to his chin.

He wore a dark suit with a shirt, in that same jewel green, open at the collar. He carried a black leather bag from a strap on his shoulder.

"Nice-looking couple," Peabody added. "She looks like she's knocked back a few alcoholic beverages."

"More than cocktails," Eve corrected, then ordered the computer to zoom in on Bryna's face. "She's got a chemical gleam in her eye. Him?" She zoomed onto the man's face. "He's stone sober. Contact the morgue. I want a priority put on her tox screen. Computer?"

Working . . .

"Yeah, yeah, let's try a little multitasking." Since, at long last, she had a new unit, she had hope. "Run current image of male on-screen through identification banks. I want a name."

OPENING IDENTIFICATION BANKS. REQUEST FOR CITYWIDE, STATE, NATIONAL, GLOBAL?

Eve patted the side of the machine. "Now, that's what I like to hear. Begin with New York City. Continue disc run, normal view.

WORKING . . .

The computer hummed quietly, and the image on-screen began to move again. Outside the elevator, the man lifted Bryna's hand, pressed his lips to the palm.

"End run, begin run on elevator two, twenty-three forty."

The image flashed off, the next flashed on. Eve watched the mating process continue on the ride to the twelfth floor. The man nibbled on her fingers, leaned in to whisper something in her ear. It was Bryna who made the advances, pulling him against her, aggressively pressing her body, her lips to his.

It was her hand that moved between their bodies, groping.

When the doors opened, they circled out, still locked together. Once again Eve ordered a disc change and studied the couple as they walked to her apartment door. Bryna fumbled a bit as she uncoded her locks. She lost her balance slightly, swayed against him. When she stepped inside, he stood at the threshold.

The perfect gentleman, Eve mused. He had a warm

smile on his face, a question in his eyes. *Are you going to ask me in?*

She watched Bryna's arm shoot out, watched her hand fist in the man's jacket. She pulled him inside, and the door shut behind them.

"She was making the moves." Peabody frowned at the empty hallway now on-screen.

"Yeah, she was making the moves."

"I don't mean she deserved to die. I just mean he wasn't pushing. Even when she got aggressive in the elevator, he didn't push. A lot of guys—hell, most guys—would've had a hand under her skirt at that point."

"Most guys don't sprinkle rose petals over the sheets." She fast-forwarded, ordered full-stop when Bryna's apartment door opened.

"Note time unidentified male exits victim's apartment. Oh-one thirty-six. Same time the nine-eleven's logged. Louise said she checked for a pulse. Give her a few seconds for shock, a few seconds to run to the body, then check the pulse, then get her pocket-link out and make the call. And that's all the time it took him to walk away from the balcony, move through the apartment and out the door. Computer, continue run."

"He's shaking," Peabody murmured.

"Yeah, and he's sweating." *But he didn't run*, Eve noted. His eyes darted right, left, right as he hurried down the hall to the elevator. But he didn't run.

She watched him ride down, his back pressed to the wall, the leather bag clutched against his chest. But he was thinking, she mused. Thinking carefully enough to take the elevator to the basement instead of the lobby, to exit the building by the delivery port instead of the front doors.

"There was no sign of struggle in the apartment. And between time of death, and the time she hit, no time for him to put it back to rights if there had been a fight. But she was dead before she went over. Before he threw her over," Eve added. "She'd been using illegals, but there were no illegals in her apartment. Let's put a bug in the lab's ear on the contents of the wine bottle and glasses. Then go home, catch some sleep."

"You're going to call Feeney? You need EDD to walk through her computer and find the e-mails she and the suspect exchanged, trace the account."

"That's right." Eve rose, and though she knew it was a mistake, ordered one more cup of coffee from her AutoChef. "Put the personal garbage in the recycler, and do the job."

"I'd appreciate it if you'd give McNab that same order. Sir."

Eve turned back. "He hassling you?"

"Yes. Not exactly." She huffed out a breath. "No."

"Which is it?"

"He just makes sure I know about all the hot women he's sleeping with, and how he's practically doing hand-springs since I cut him loose. And he doesn't even have the decency to do it to my face. He just makes sure I hear about it."

"It sounds like he's moved on. You did cut him loose, Peabody. And you're hanging with Charles."

"It's not like that with Charles," Peabody insisted, speaking of the sexy licensed companion who'd become her friend. And had never been her lover. "I told you."

"But you didn't tell McNab. Your business," Eve said quickly when Peabody started to speak. "And I don't want any part of it. McNab wants to screw every female in the five boroughs, and it doesn't interfere with the job, it's none of my business. And none of yours. Leave the priority requests for the morgue and the lab, then go home. Report in at eight hundred hours."

Alone, Eve sat back at her desk. "Computer, status on identification search."

SEARCH EIGHTY-EIGHT-POINT-TWO PERCENT COM-PLETE. NO MATCHES.

"Expand search statewide."

AFFIRMATIVE. WORKING . . .

Eve sat back with her coffee, and hoped for a name. Hoped for quick justice for Bryna Bankhead.

Despite the caffeine, Eve managed a more restful sleep on her office floor than she had in the big, empty bed at home. When she woke, she widened the thus far negative identity search. Taking yet another cup of coffee with her into the locker room, she washed up, finger-combed her hair, and rolled up the sleeves of Roarke's shirt.

It was just after eight when she walked into Captain Feeney's office in EDD. He was standing at his own AutoChef with his back to her. Like Eve, he was in his shirtsleeves, with his weapon harness in place. His wiry, ginger-colored hair had probably seen a comb that morning, but looked no tidier than hers.

She stepped in, sniffed the air. "What's that smell?"

He whirled around, his long, basset hound face covered with surprise. And, she thought, guilt.

"Nothing. What's up?"

She sniffed again. "Doughnuts. You got doughnuts in here."

"Shut up, shut up." He stalked by her to shut the door. "You want the whole squad pouring in here?" Knowing a closed door wouldn't be enough, he locked it. "What do you want?"

"I want a doughnut."

"Look, Dallas, the wife's gone on some health kick. You can't get a decent bite to eat in my house these days with all the tofu this and rehydrated vegetable that. A man's gotta have some fat and sugar once in awhile or his system suffers for it."

"I'm with you, so's the crowd. Gimme a doughnut."

"Goddamn it." He strode over to the AutoChef, popped it open. Inside were a half dozen doughnuts, fragrant in the low heat.

"Holy shit. *Fresh* doughnuts."

"Bakery down the block does a few dozen reals every morning. You know what they charge for one of these bastards?"

Quick as a whiplash, Eve reached in, snagged one, bit in. "Worth it," she said around a mouthful of fat and cream.

"Just keep it down. You start making yummy noises, they'll beat the door in." He took a doughnut and blissfully chewed the first bite. "Nobody wants to live forever, right? I tell the wife, hey, I'm a cop. Cops face death every day."

"Damn straight. You got jelly, too?"

Before she could reach in, he closed the AutoChef. Smartly. "So, being a cop, facing death, all that, who gives a horse's ass about pumping a little fat into the arteries?"

"Really superior fat, too." She licked sugar off her fingers. She could've blackmailed him into a second doughnut, but figured she'd just get sick off it. "Got a sidewalk splat last night."

"Leaper?"

"Nope. Already dead when she went off. I'm waiting for the ME and some lab reports, but it looks like sexual homicide. She had a date with a cyber-guy, e-mail lovers. I got a visual of him going in and out of her place, but the ID search hasn't hit a match. I need you to track him through her computer."

"You got the unit?"

"Yeah. I'm holding it in Evidence. Victim's Bankhead, Bryna. Case-file H-78926B."

"I'll get somebody on it."

"Appreciate it." She paused at the door. "Feeney, if you bring McNab in, maybe you could ask him to, I don't know, tone it down around Peabody."

The glow the doughnut brought to his face faded into painful embarrassment. "Aw, jeez, Dallas."

"I know, I know. But if I have to deal with her, you've got to deal with him."

"We could lock them in a room together, let them hash it out."

"We'll keep that as an option. Let me know as soon as you find something on the victim's unit."

The search wasn't getting anywhere. Without much hope, Eve bumped it up to global. She wrote and filed her preliminary report for her commander, then shot it off through the interoffice system. After ordering Peabody to keep pushing on the lab and morgue, she headed to the courthouse to give her testimony in a case on trial.

Two and a half hours later, she stormed out, damning all lawyers. She flipped on her communicator and tagged Peabody. "Status."

"Test results still pending, sir."

"Fuck that."

"Rough day in court, Dallas?"

"Defense council seems to think the NYPSD splattered the victim's blood all over his innocent client's hotel room, clothes, person just to give psychopathic tourists who stab their wives a couple dozen times during a marital spat a bad name."

"Well, it is tough on the Chamber of Commerce."

"Ha-ha."

"We have identified the woman Bankhead spoke with on the 'link the night she died. CeeCee Plunkett. She worked with the victim in the lingerie department at Saks."

"Grab transpo. Meet me there."

"Yes, sir, and may I suggest their lovely sixth-floor café for lunch? You need protein."

"I had a doughnut." With an evil smile, Eve broke transmission on Peabody's shocked and envious gasp.

Being caught in the hell of lunch-shift traffic did little to improve her mood. Cars bumped and churned in place for so long she considered the possibility of just leaving her vehicle where it was and hoofing it across town.

Until she studied the jammed sidewalks.

Even the sky was packed—ad blimps, airbuses, tourist trams vying for air space. The noise was ridiculous, but for some reason, the sheer weight of sound smoothed out the rough edges. So much so that when she was trapped at a light at the corner of Madison and Thirty-ninth, she leaned out the window and spoke pleasantly to the glide-cart operator.

"Give me a tube of Pepsi."

"Small, medium, or large, fair lady?"

Her eyebrows lifted, disappeared under her fringe of bangs. An operator that friendly was either a droid or new. "Make it large." She dug in her pocket for loose change.

When he leaned down to make the exchange, she saw he was neither droid nor new. She pegged him at a well-tended ninety, and his smile showed an appreciation of dental hygiene far superior to most glide-carters.

"Beautiful day, isn't it?"

She looked at the traffic, at the knots of vehicles that were all but blocking out the sky in this sector. "You gotta be kidding."

He only smiled again. "Every day you're alive's a beauty, miss."

She thought of Bryna Bankhead. "Guess you're right."

She popped the tube, sucked on it contemplatively as she inched her way up Madison. At Fifty-first, she cut over, double parked, and engaged her ON DUTY sign.

And girding her loins, strode into Saks and the gauntlet of cosmetic shills.

High-fashion droids glided by the doors in a pattern designed to dazzle the eye, and make it impossible to break through unscathed. Backing them up were human consultants who manned booths, counters, or patrolled the aisle looking, in Eve's opinion, for escapees. The air was choked with scent.

A female droid with a starburst of magenta hair slithered across the floor to block Eve's forward progress.

"Good afternoon, and welcome to Saks. Today our premiere fragrance—"

"One drop goes on me, just one, and I'll ram that

spritzer down your throat," she warned as the droid moved in for the kill.

"Indeed, madam, it only takes a drop of Orgasma to entice the lover of your dreams."

Eve flipped her jacket aside, tapped her fingers on her weapon. "It only takes one blast of this to put you in the recycle bin, Red. Now back off."

The droid backed off, with satisfying speed. Eve heard the call go up for Security as she plowed through the wall of customers and consultants. She flipped out her badge as a pair of uniformed droids rushed toward her.

"NYPSD. Official business. Keep those damn smell pushers off me."

"Yes, Lieutenant. May we be of some assistance?"

"Yeah." She tucked her badge in her pocket. "Where's the lingerie department?"

At least, Eve thought as she got off on the proper floor, nobody up here rushed you waving underwear. Still, selling sex seemed to be the order of the day as model droids roamed the department in foundation garments or nightwear. Human clerks, at least, wore real clothes.

She spotted CeeCee Plunkett immediately and waited until the woman completed bagging up a sale.

"Ms. Plunkett?"

"Yes, may I help you?"

Eve took out her badge again. "Is there a place we can speak privately?"

She had rosy cheeks, and they went white. She had pretty blue eyes, and they went wide. "Oh God. Oh God, it's Bry. Something's happened to Bryna. She didn't come into work, she doesn't answer her 'link. She's been hurt."

"Is there somewhere we can talk?"

"I—yes." Pressing a hand to her temple, CeeCee looked around. "The—the dressing area, but I'm not supposed to leave my station. I . . ."

"Hey." Eve snagged a droid in a sheer black bra and

panties. "Take over here. Which way?" she asked CeeCee and came around the counter to take her arm.

"Back here. Is she in the hospital? Which hospital? I'll go see her."

Inside one of the small changing cubes, Eve closed the door. There was a tiny padded stool in the corner, and she guided CeeCee to it. "Sit down."

"It's bad." She gripped Eve's arm. "It's very bad."

"Yes, I'm sorry." There would never be an easy way. There was only the fast way—a quick stab to the heart rather than slicing inch by inch. "Bryna Bankhead was killed early this morning."

CeeCee shook her head, kept shaking it slowly as the first tear trickled down her cheek. "She had an accident?"

"We're trying to determine what happened."

"I talked to her. I talked to her yesterday, last night. She was going out on a date. Please tell me what happened to Bry."

The media had already reported the death, and the circumstances, so far as they were known. If they hadn't ferreted out the name by now, Eve thought, it wouldn't take them much longer.

"She . . . fell from her balcony."

"Fell?" CeeCee started to surge to her feet, but only sank back down again. "That can't be. That just can't be. There's a safety wall."

"We're investigating, Ms. Plunkett. You'd help a great deal if you'd answer some questions for me. On record?"

"She wouldn't have fallen." There was anger now, and insult, pricking through the shock. "She wasn't stupid or clumsy. She wouldn't have fallen."

Eve took out her recorder. "I'm going to find out what happened. My name is Dallas. Lieutenant Eve Dallas," she said for CeeCee, and the record. "I'm primary investigator in the matter of the death of Bryna Bankhead. I'm interviewing you, CeeCee Plunkett, at this time, because you were a friend of the deceased. You had a conversation with her via 'link last night, a few minutes before nine o'clock, just before she left her apartment."

"Yes. Yes. She called me. She was so nervous, so excited." Her voice went thick. "Oh, Bry."

"Why was she nervous and excited?"

"She had a date. Her first date with Dante."

"What's his full name?"

"I don't know." She dug in her jacket pocket for a tissue, then tore it to pieces rather than mopping her face. "They met online. They didn't know each other's last names, that's part of the deal. It's for safety."

"How long had she been in contact with him?"

"Maybe three weeks now."

"How did they meet?"

"A poetry chat room. There was this discussion of great romantic poetry through the centuries and . . . Oh God." She leaned forward, buried her face in her hands. "She was my best friend. How could this happen to her?"

"Would she confide in you?"

"We told each other everything. You know how it is with girlfriends."

More or less, Eve thought. "This was, to your knowledge, her first date with Dante?"

"Yes. That's why she was so excited. She bought a new dress, and shoes. And these great earrings . . ."

"And would it be usual for her to bring a first date back to her apartment for sex?"

"Absolutely not." CeeCee gave a watery laugh. "Bry's got too many old-fashioned hang-ups about sex and relationships and stages. A guy had to pass what she called the Thirty Day Test before she'd go to bed with him. I used to tell her nothing stays fresh for a month, but she . . ." CeeCee trailed off. "What are you saying?"

"I'm only trying to get a picture. Did she do illegals?"

Though tears were still glistening in them, CeeCee's eyes went hard. "I don't like your questions, Lieutenant."

"They have to be asked. Look at me. Look at me," Eve

repeated. "I don't want to hurt her, or you. I have to know who she was, to do right by her."

"No, she didn't do illegals," CeeCee snapped. "She took good care of herself, inside and out. That's the way she was. She was smart and she was fun and she was decent. And she did *not* get crazy on illegals and fall off her goddamn balcony. She didn't jump either, so don't even think about trying to pass this off as suicide. If she went off that balcony, it's because somebody pushed her off. It's because . . ."

As her own words sank in, CeeCee's anger flared. "Someone killed her. Someone killed Bry. That—that Dante. He, he followed her home after their date. And he got into her apartment somehow, and he killed her. He killed her," she repeated and dug her fingers into Eve's wrist. "You find him."

"I'll find him," Eve promised. "CeeCee, I don't know all the facts yet, but I will. Tell me what you can about this man she knew as Dante. Everything you remember Bryna told you."

"I can't take it in. I'm sorry, I just can't." She rose, walked slowly to the pitcher of ice water on the dressing room table. When the pitcher shook and sloshed, Eve went over, poured the glass.

"Thanks."

"Take a minute. Sit down, drink your water, and take a minute."

"I'm okay. I'll be okay." But she had to hold the glass with both hands to drink. "He was supposed to own his own business. He was rich. She said he didn't brag about it, but she could tell from the little things he said. Places he'd been, like Paris and Moscow, the Olympus Resort, Bimini, I don't know."

"What kind of business?"

"They didn't get into specifics about that. Just like he wasn't supposed to know she worked here. But he did."

Eve's gaze sharpened. "How do you know that?"

"Because he sent her pink roses here last week."

Pink roses, Eve thought. *Pink rose petals.*

"What else?"

"He spoke Italian, and um, French and Spanish. Romance languages," she added, smearing tears and mascara with the backs of her hands. "Bry was all caught up in the romance of it. She said he had the most romantic soul. And I'd say, well great, but what about his face? She'd just laugh and say that appearances didn't matter when hearts spoke to each other. But it wouldn't hurt her feelings any if he looked as good as he sounded."

Steadier, she turned the glass in her hands. "Lieutenant . . . Did he rape her?"

"I don't know." Eve drew out a picture she'd printed off disc. "Do you recognize this man?"

CeeCee studied Dante's face. "No," she said, wearily now. "I've never seen him before. This is him, isn't it? Well. Well. I guess he looked as good as he sounded. The son of a bitch. The vicious son of a bitch." She began shredding the photo, and Eve did nothing to stop her.

"Where were they meeting for drinks last night?"

"The goddamn Rainbow Room. Bry picked it out because she thought it was romantic."

When Eve came out of the dressing area, she found Peabody staring, a bit wistfully, at a display of lacy bodysuits.

"Those wouldn't be comfortable for more than five minutes," Eve pointed out.

"If it works, you wouldn't have it on over five minutes. Droid said you were back in the dressing area with Plunkett."

"Yeah. Dude goes by the name of Dante, heavy on the poetry and pink rosebuds. I'll fill you in."

"Where are we going?"

"The morgue, by way of the Rainbow Room."

"That sounds so . . . weird."

It was, if you compared the chrome and marble temple of one with the dingy white box of the other. But the best

Eve could get from the landmark lounge was the names and addresses of the waitstaff on duty the night before.

She had more immediate luck at the dead house.

"Ah, my favorite cop come to scold me." Morris, Chief Medical Examiner, switched off his laser scalpel and beamed. He wore his long, dark hair in a half dozen braids, covered now with a clear surgical cap. A natty plum-colored shirt and slacks were protected from distressing splashes of body fluids by a transparent lab coat.

"That's not my case you're slicing up there, Morris."

"No, more's the pity." He glanced down at the body of a young black man. "This unfortunate fellow appears to have backed into—numerous times—a sharp, long-bladed instrument. You'd think he'd have stopped after the first, but no. He just continued to ram himself back into the knife until he keeled over dead."

"Slow learner." She pursed her lips as she studied the corpse's very impressive hard-on. "From the looks of that boner he's carrying, I'd make an educated guess that he'd popped some Exotica laced with Zeus. The combo can make a guy's tool stay in use long after he's gone flat otherwise."

"I tend to agree, particularly since your associate Detective Baxter reports that our recently deceased was employing that tool enthusiastically on his brother's wife."

"Oh yeah? And I guess he just decided to stop fucking and dance into a knife as a change of pace."

"According to his brother, and the wife who is still among the living and recovering from a nasty fall that broke her jaw."

"Takes all kinds. If Baxter's got the brother in custody, and you've got cause of death, why aren't you working on my case?"

"Come with me." Morris crooked a finger and walked through a set of swinging doors into another autopsy room. What was left of Bryna Bankhead was the single occupant. She was laid on a stainless steel slab with a thin green sheet covering her to the neck.

That would have been Morris's touch, Eve thought. He could be very respectful with the dead.

"I imagine she was an attractive young woman once."

Eve stared down at the ruined face. She thought of the bathroom mirror, the ruthlessly organized drawer of enhancements. "Yeah. Tell me how she died, Morris."

"I think you know. Your time of death measurement was accurate. She was spared the fear of falling, the insult of the pavement, even the knowledge that she was dying." He touched sealed fingertips, very gently, to her hair. "She'd ingested, over a period of two and a half to three hours, more than two ounces of the synthetic hormonibital-six, an expensive and very difficult to acquire controlled substance."

"Street name Whore. An inhibition blocker," Eve murmured. "Commonly used in date rape once upon a time."

"Not commonly," Morris corrected. "Its derivatives are more common, and much less potent and effective. What she had in her was pure. Two ounces, Dallas, would have a street value of more than a quarter million. If you could find it on the street, which you can't. I haven't come across traces of it in a body for more than fifteen years."

"I heard about it when I was in school. Mostly urban legend shit."

"And most of it was urban legend shit."

"Did it kill her? An OD?"

"Not by itself. The combination with alcohol was dangerous, but not fatal. But our hero went overboard. Half the amount he slipped her would've been enough to ensure her full cooperation. What she had in her would, most likely, have kept her under for eight, maybe ten hours. And she'd wake up with the mother of all hangovers. Headache, vomiting, the shakes, blackouts, lost time. It would take up to seventy-two hours to purge her system."

It made Eve sick to think it. "She was spared that, too. How?"

"He gave her too much. It would make her lethargic. I'm assuming he wanted a more active fuck because he doctored the last glass of wine with a little cocktail of aneminiphine-colax-B. Wild Rabbit."

"Covered his bases, didn't he?" she said quietly.

"It bombards the nervous and respiratory systems, and hers was already compromised. The combination over-taxed her heart. It gave out on her within twenty minutes of ingestion. She'd have been too doped by the earlier doses of Whore to know what was happening."

"Could she have taken it willingly at that point?"

Gently, Morris lifted the sheet over Bryna's face. "After the first ounce of inhibition blocker, nothing this girl did was willing."

"He drugged her, he raped her, and the combination killed her," Eve said. "Then he tossed her out the window like a used doll in an attempt to cover up what happened."

"In my esteemed and renowned medical opinion, that's the scenario."

"Now make my day, Morris, and tell me he left sperm in her. Tell me you got his DNA."

Morris's face went bright as a boy's. "Oh yeah, I got it. You bring him in, Dallas, and I'll help you lock the cage."

Chapter 3

"Sick bastard creep ought to have his balls scooped off with a rusty spoon."

Eve settled back in her car. "Don't hold back, Peabody. Tell me how you really feel."

"Goddamn it, Dallas, it got to me in there, looking at her on that slab, remembering how pretty she was, how excited when she called her pal about going out to meet this fuckhead. Thinking she was meeting someone romantic and, damn it, nice. Someone nice and the whole time he's planning to . . ."

"Fuck her to death? I don't know that he planned that going in, but that's how it worked out. Could be we get him on Murder One, using the illegals as the murder weapon. More likely, it's going to be Second Degree. And don't blow your cortex, Peabody, we wrap him on that, add in the sexual assault and his attempt to dispose of the evidence, he's not going to see daylight again."

"It's not enough." She shifted in her seat, appalling them both because there were tears in her eyes. "Sometimes it doesn't seem to be enough."

Eve stared through the windshield to give them both

time for Peabody to pull herself together. A pack of kids, sprung from school, were cruising over the crosswalk on airboards, wreaking havoc on the bipeds they wove through.

There was something painfully innocent, painfully alive about the flash and color of them, a half a block away from a house of dead.

"It's enough," Eve said, "because it's what we can do. Our job is to stand for Bryna Bankhead and bring in the man who killed her. After that . . ." She remembered her session in court, the defense attorney's slippery twist on the law. "After that, we trust the system to give her justice, and we put it away. You don't put it away, they pile up. The dead pile up," she added when Peabody stared at her, "until you can't see past them, and you can't do the job."

"Do you put it away? Can you?"

It was a question Eve tried not to ask herself—and asked herself too often. "A lot of murder cops, they've only got so many years in them. So many dead. Then it starts eating at them until they're used up. I can't do anything else but this, so it's not going to use me up." She let out a long breath. "But in a perfect world, we'd have the rusty spoon option."

"When I started working with you, I thought Homicide was the most important thing I could do. It's been about a year now. I still think that."

"Okay." She jammed her way into traffic like a battering ram. "I need to make a stop down at the Canal Street Clinic. Let's see if the boys in EDD have made any progress."

She used the in-dash 'link to contact Feeney's office, and felt Peabody stiffen when McNab's pretty face appeared on-screen.

"Hey, Lieutenant." Eve watched his gaze shift over, saw his lips stretch into a smile every bit as stiff as Peabody's shoulders. "Peabody."

"I need your captain," Eve told him.

"He just stepped out."

"Tell him to tag me as soon as he comes back."

"Hold it, hold it, hold it." His face filled the screen as he leaned in. "Don't eject till you hear the tune. The captain put me on your electronic account search."

Eve punched her vehicle through a narrow opening, switched lanes, and gained half a block. "Pretty basic e-work for a hotshot, isn't it?"

"Yeah, well, it got bumped up to hotshot level when the tech ran into some snags. Your cyber-Casanova put in some blocks and walls. I scaled them, being a hotshot, and came up with an address."

"Are you going to stop bragging long enough to give it to me?"

"I would, Lieutenant, but you'd be wasting your time. Address is in the Carpathian Mountains."

"Where the hell is that?"

"Mountain range, Eastern Europe. I know," McNab said, with a frisky toss of his long blond ponytail, "because I looked it up. And before you ask me what the hell our perp's doing on a mountain in Eastern Europe, he's not. It's a dummy. Address is bogus as my cousin Sheila's tits."

"It doesn't sound like you scaled a wall to me, McNab."

"Dallas, I scaled a fucking mountain here. I got a bounce from the fake address, and I'm following the echo. Should have it nailed in another hour."

"Then don't talk to me until you set down the hammer. And McNab? Any guy who knows anything about his cousin's tits is a perv."

She broke transmission on his hoot of laughter. "He may be irritating," Eve said to Peabody, "but he's good. He'll nail it. And if it's taking him this long, that tells me our suspect is an above-average hacker. He protected himself going in, which in court will be, to overuse an image, another nail in his coffin."

She glanced at Peabody's profile. "Don't sulk."

"I'm not sulking."

Hissing, Eve flipped down the passenger visor so the mirror dropped down. "Look at your face. You want him to know you get bent when you have to deal with him? Snag a little pride, Peabody."

Studying herself, Peabody saw sulk move into pout mode at Eve's words. She flipped the visor back up. "I was just thinking, that's all."

Eve made the swing onto Canal, pitching through its bazaarlike sector where the offerings were plentiful and cheap and the Black Market did the lion's share of business. Tourists were routinely scammed, then they filed complaints against shops that changed venues more often and with greater efficiency than a tent circus.

Then again, Eve figured if you were stupid enough to believe you could buy a Rolex for the same price as a large pizza, you deserved the skinning.

Within a few blocks, the carnival gave way to the dumping ground for the homeless and the disenfranchised. Sidewalk sleepers erected their boxes and tents in pitiful little communities of despair. Those with beggar's licenses, and many without them, wandered across town to shill enough credit tokens to buy a bottle of home brew to get them through another night.

Those who didn't make it through the night would be transported to the morgue by the NYPSD unit not-so-affectionately known as the Sidewalk Scoopers.

No matter how many were loaded up, cremated at city expense, more came to replace them.

It was a cycle no one, particularly the city fathers, seemed to be able to break. And it was here, in the midst of the filth and despair, that Louise Dimatto ran the Canal Street Clinic. *She didn't break the cycle either,* Eve thought, *but she made the spin on it a little less painful for some.*

In an area where the shoes on your feet were considered fair game, it was a risky business to park a car unless you then surrounded it by droids wearing body armor and hefting rocket lasers. Patrol cars were manned by exactly that.

The good news was, parking places were plentiful.

Eve pulled to the curb behind what might have been a sedan at one time. But since all that was left of it was part of a chassis and a broken windshield, she couldn't be sure.

She stepped out, and in the hot, stinking steam that gushed up from a subway vent, engaged all locks, activated all alarms. Then she stood on the sidewalk, scanned the street in all directions. There were a few loiterers hulking in doorways and one pitifully skinny street LC trying to drum up customers.

"I'm Lieutenant Dallas, NYPSD." She didn't shout it, but raised her voice enough to cause faces to shift in her direction. "This piece of shit is my official city vehicle. If said piece of shit is not in this exact spot, in this exact condition when I come back, I'll bring a squad of doorbangers down here to roust every living soul in a five-block radius, along with illegals-sniffer dogs who will find and confiscate all the goodies you've got stashed. I guarantee it will be a very unpleasant experience."

"Bitch cop!"

Tracking the direction of the comment, Eve lifted her gaze to a third-floor window in a building across the street. "Officer Peabody, will you verify the asshole's opinion?"

"Yes, sir, Lieutenant, the asshole is correct. You are the supreme bitch cop."

"And what will happen if anyone lays hands on my vehicle?"

"You will make their life a living hell. You will make their friends' lives a living hell, their family's lives a living hell. And, sir, you will make people's lives who are complete strangers to them a living hell."

"Yes," Eve said with a cold and satisfied smile. "Yes, I

will." She turned away and walked to the door of the clinic.

"And you'll enjoy it."

"Okay, Peabody, point made." She pulled open the door, stepped inside.

For an instant she thought she'd walked into the wrong door. From her visits over the past winter, she remembered the jammed waiting room, the dingy walls, the tattered, inadequate furniture. Here instead was a wide space partitioned by a low wall where glossy green plants thrived in simple clay pots. Chairs and sofas were ranged on either side, and though nearly every seat was taken, there was a sense of order.

The walls were a pale, pretty green decorated with framed pictures obviously drawn by children.

There was the hacking, wheezing, the soft whimpering of the ill and the injured. But there was not, as there had been the previous winter, an underlying sense of anger and hopelessness.

Even as she scanned the room a woman in a jumpsuit the same color as the walls came through a doorway. "Mrs. Lasio, the doctor will see you now."

At the shift in patients, Eve crossed over to the reception window. Through it she could see updated equipment and the same sense of ordered efficiency that permeated the waiting areas.

There was a young man at the station with a face as cheerful and harmless as a daisy. He couldn't have been more than twenty, Eve thought as he beamed up at her.

"Good afternoon. How can we help you today?"

"I need to see Doctor Dimatto."

"Yes, ma'am. I'm afraid Doctor Dimatto is fully booked for the rest of this afternoon. If this is a medical emergency—"

"It's personal business." Eve laid her badge on the counter. "Official business. If she's tied up, have her contact me when she's free. Lieutenant Dallas, Cop Central."

"Oh, Lieutenant Dallas. Doctor Dimatto said you might come by. She's with a patient, but if you don't mind waiting just a few minutes? You can wait in her office, and I'll tell her you're here."

"Fine."

He buzzed her through the door. She saw what she assumed were examining rooms on either side of a hallway, and the hallway opened into a wide pass-through where lab equipment stood on counters. From somewhere nearby, she heard a child laughing.

"You guys expanded."

"Yes. Dr. Dimatto was able to purchase the building that adjoined the original clinic." Still beaming smiles he led them across the pass-through, into another hallway. "She expanded and updated the clinic and its services and added pediatrics. We have six doctors now, two full-time and four on rotation, and a fully equipped lab."

He opened a door. "Doctor Dimatto is the angel of Canal Street. Please, help yourself to the AutoChef. She'll be with you as soon as she can."

Louise's office hadn't changed much, Eve noted. It was still small, still cramped, still crowded. And reminded Eve very much of her own space at Central.

"Jeez, she's really done something here," Peabody commented. "It had to run her a couple million."

"I guess." And since Eve had only donated—okay, bribed Louise with—a half a million for the clinic, she figured the angel of Canal Street had done some very intense, very successful fund-raising in a very short amount of time.

"This place is better equipped, and I bet better run, than my local health center." Peabody pursed her lips. "I might switch."

"Yeah, well." To Eve's mind one health facility was the same as another. They were all voids of hell. "You got an e-memo on you? We'll just leave the doctor a message. I want to get back to Central."

"Maybe. Somewhere." And as Peabody dug into her pockets, Louise rushed in.

"Got five. Need coffee." She made a beeline for the AutoChef. "Fill me in while I refuel."

"Did you know Bryna Bankhead?"

"No."

"Picture Peabody." Eve took the ID photo Peabody took from her file bag, held it out. "Recognize her?"

Louise drank coffee with one hand, dragged her other through her hair as she frowned at the image. A stethoscope and a red lollipop peeked out of her lab coat pocket. "Yes. I'd ridden in the elevator with her now and again, seen her in the local markets where I shop. I suppose I might have spoken to her, the way you do with neighbors you don't have time to know. Was she murdered?"

"Yeah." Eve held out a copy of the suspect's image. "Recognize him?"

"No." Louise set down her coffee, took the photo for a closer look. "No, I've never seen him before. He killed her? Why?"

Eve handed the photos back to Peabody. "You ever treat anybody for sex-inducement drugs? Whore, Rabbit?"

"Yes. In my ER rotation we'd have somebody coming down off Rabbit a few times a month. Mostly Rabbit clones, or Exotica/Zeus combo, because the real's so pricey. I never dealt with Whore, don't know anybody who has. You study it, and its derivatives in illegals training, but it's on the inactive list."

"Not anymore."

"Is that what he did to her? Doped her with Whore? Whore *and* Rabbit. Jesus Christ." She rubbed her hands over her face. "Mixed with alcohol, I take it. Why didn't he just blast her brains out with a laser?"

"Maybe you could poke around, ask some of your doctor friends if they've seen any re-emergence of Whore."

"I can do that. You know, a man had to come up with the street name for that crap. You know how it started?"

"No, how?"

"As an experimental treatment for phobias and conditions like social anxiety disorder. It was a little too good at it."

"Meaning?"

"It also had an affect on the hormones. It was discovered that it worked more effectively as an aid in sexual disorders. In diluted and carefully monitored doses, it could and did enhance sexual desire and function. From there, it went into use as an aide for training licensed companions. Though nonaddictive, it was soon found to be dangerously unstable. Which, naturally, meant it became desirable on the street, particularly among your more well-heeled college boys and junior execs who would slip a dose into their dream girl's drink to loosen her up." She washed the rising rage back down her throat with coffee.

"That's how it got its name," she continued, "as mixed with alcohol it tends to loosen the system up enough so the ingestor would be amenable to being fucked naked on the ice rink at Rockefeller Center. The ingestor wouldn't necessarily have the motor coordination left to actively participate, and would unlikely remember doing so, but she'd be damn amenable to suggestion."

"Add Rabbit?"

"Oh, she'd participate with the entire U.S. Marine Corps, until she passed out cold, until her heart rate went off the charts and her brain-wave pattern flattened."

"A doctor would know that," Eve prompted. "A chemist, pharmacist, nurse, med tech, anyone with a working knowledge of pharmaceuticals would know the combination was fatal?"

"Yeah, anyone should. Unless he or she is a moron, or just didn't give a shit as long as it was fun while it lasted."

"Okay, ask around. If anything strikes you, get in touch."

"You can bank on it."

"You did a nice job around here," Eve added.

"We like to think so." Louise finished off the coffee, two-pointed the cup in the recycle bin. "Your three million went a long way."

"Three million?"

"I was ready to dive into the half million we agreed on. Didn't expect the bonus."

"When . . ." Eve ran her tongue around her teeth. "When did I give you the bonus?"

Louise opened her mouth, closed it again. Smiled. "Now why do I think you don't have a clue?"

"Refresh me, Louise. When did I give you three million dollars?"

"Never. But your rep did, late February."

"And my rep would be?"

"Some slick suit named Treacle, of Montblanc, Cissler and Treacle. Issued in two installments—the half mil as agreed, and another two point five if I contracted to donate my services to *Dochas*, a newly established abuse center for women and children on the Lower East Side. *Dochas*," she said, still smiling, "is, I'm told, Gaelic for *hope*."

"Is that so?"

"Yeah. You've got a hell of a man there, Dallas. You ever get tired of him, I'll take him off your hands."

"I'll keep that in mind."

"You gave her the money for all that?" Peabody demanded as she hustled out after Eve.

"No, I didn't give her the money because it's not my money, is it? It's Roarke's money. I'm a cop, goddamn it. A cop doesn't have space stations full of money to make grand gestures with."

"Yeah, but still. Does that piss you off?"

Eve stopped on the sidewalk, took a long breath. "I don't know if it pisses me off." But she kicked the base of a street lamp just in case she was. "He could tell me about this stuff, couldn't he? He could keep me in the loop so I wouldn't go into this sort of situation and come out feeling like an idiot."

Peabody looked back at the clinic, her soft heart going to goo stage. "I think it was a beautiful gesture."

"Don't contradict me, Peabody. Do you forget I am the supreme bitch cop?"

"No, sir. And as your vehicle is in the same spot and the same condition as you left it, the neighborhood didn't forget that either."

"Too bad." A bit wistful, she looked around. "I'd've enjoyed busting some ass."

Back at Central, Eve snagged a candy bar in lieu of lunch, brooded, called up data on the chemicals pertinent to the Bankhead homicide, brooded some more, then called to harass McNab.

"I want an address."

"Would you settle for twenty-three of them?"

"What the hell does that mean?"

"Look, I'm going to snag a conference room, your office is a box. Your level," he said, working a keyboard to his left manually as he spoke. "Ah ... Room 426. I'm using your name to finesse it."

"McNab—"

"Easier, quicker to explain this face-to-face. Give me five."

He broke transmission on her snarl, which gave her no choice but to finish her snarl at Peabody. "Conference room 426. Now," she ordered.

She stormed out of her office, through the detective's bullpen where the kill lights in her eyes discouraged any of her associates from speaking to her. By the time she shoved into the conference room she'd worked up a fine head of steam and only required a handy target to spew it on.

To his misfortune, Feeney strolled in first.

"What the hell kind of division are you running up

there?" she demanded. "McNab's giving me orders now? Hanging up on me? Booking rooms in *my* name on his own initiative, and . . . *and* refusing to give me data when ordered."

"Hold on now, Dallas. I'm an innocent bystander."

"Too bad, 'cause they're the ones who usually end up bloody."

With a little shrug, Feeney rattled the bag of nuts weighing down his pocket. "All I know is the kid tagged me, asked me to swing by here so he could fill us both in at once."

"I'm primary on this case. EDD was requested to assist and consult. I have not yet formed a task force in this matter, nor have I been authorized by the commander to do so. Until I say different McNab's a drone and nothing more."

Feeney stopped rattling the bag, angled his head. "That go for me, too? Lieutenant?"

"Your rank doesn't mean dick when I'm primary. If you can't teach your subordinates proper pecking order and procedure, then maybe your rank doesn't mean dick in your own division."

He stepped in until the tips of his shoes bumped her boots, leaned in until the tip of his nose bumped hers. "Don't you tell me how to run my division. I trained your ass and I can still kick it, so don't you start thinking you can tear a strip off mine."

"Back off."

"Fuck that. *Fuck* that, Dallas. You got a problem with my command style, you spit it out. Chapter and verse."

Something in her head wanted to explode. Why hadn't she felt it? Something in her heart was screaming. But she hadn't heard it. So it was she who backed off, one cautious step. "He drugged her with Whore and Rabbit. He covered the bed with rose petals and fucked her on them until she died. Then he tossed her out the window so she lay broken and naked on the sidewalk."

"Oh Jesus." Pity edged his voice.

"I guess it's been stuck in my throat since Morris told me. I'm sorry I slapped at you."

"Forget it. Sometimes you catch one that hits you harder than others. You gotta slap at somebody."

"I've got his face, I've got his DNA, I've got his transmissions. I know the table in the club where he fed her the first of the Whore in drinks that she paid for with her own debit card. But I don't have him."

"You will." He turned as Peabody strode in a step in front of McNab. Both of them had flushed faces. "Detective, did you request permission from the primary to convene in this room?"

McNab blinked. "I needed to—"

"Answer the question."

"Not exactly, Captain." He didn't need to see Peabody smirk to know she did. "I apologize for overstepping, Lieutenant Dallas. I believe the information I have to, ah, impart, is important to the investigation and is better served in person than interoffice transmissions."

The dull flush burning up his throat was enough to satisfy her. "Then impart it, McNab."

"Yes, sir." It was difficult to look stiff and cold while wearing cherry red trousers and a skin-tight sweater the color of daffodils. But he nearly managed it. "In tracing the suspect's account from the fraudulent source location, I was able to ascertain the name used to register the account. It purports to be a business called La Belle Dame."

"Purports to be," Eve said.

"Yes, sir. There is no firm or organization by that name doing business in the state of New York. The address given for the company is, in fact, Grand Central Station."

"And I'm to be excited about this because . . . ?"

"Well, I kept separating layers and hit on sources for the actual transmissions. The locations they were sent out from. So far, I've hit twenty-three spots. All public cybercafés and clubs, in Manhattan, Queens, and Brooklyn. So far," he repeated. "He moves around, sends and receives from ports in public venues. The only e-mail sent or received from that screen address was to and from Bryna Bankhead."

"He created it for her," Eve murmured.

"The umbrella account could have other screen names," McNab went on. "I haven't been able to break through the blocks. Yet. Whoever created the account knows his cyber-shit. I mean, he's good, and he's careful."

"Her best friend didn't recognize him. So far none of the door-to-doors on the building have turned up any neighbors who recognized him." Eve paced. "If Bankhead didn't know him, if he wasn't seen in or around her building before the night of the murder, then we have to assume he targeted her from the chat room."

"He knew where she worked," Peabody put in.

"But she didn't make him, and neither did her friend who works the same department. So he's maybe a casual customer. If he was a regular or an employee who spent any time in their department, they'd have noticed. You still notice guys who hang out where they sell women's underwear. But we'll run his picture through their human resources division.

"So he uses public venues. He either likes to socialize or he's hiding in plain sight. Maybe both. We circulate his picture at the cyber-spots."

"Lieutenant?" McNab wagged his fingers. "Do you know how many cyber-venues there are in New York?"

"No, and I don't want to know. But you can start counting them off as you visit them." She looked at Feeney. "You in if Whitney authorizes?"

"I'd say we're already in."

"Generate a list," she told McNab. "We'll split it up, work in pairs for now." She gave a soft sigh. "McNab and Feeney are the experts in this area. I'm only going to ask this once, in this room. Does anyone here have a problem working with anyone else on this team?"

McNab stared at the ceiling as if fascinated by the dull white tone of the paint. Peabody simply frowned at her shoes.

"I take that as a no. Peabody, you're with McNab; Feeney, you're with me. Start on the West Side; we'll take the East. We'll do as many venues as possible until . . ." She checked her wrist unit, calculated. "Twenty-one hundred. We'll meet at my home office tomorrow, oh eight hundred for a full briefing. Feeney, let's pitch this to Whitney."

Feeney strolled out after her, whistling. "You could've split us up another way."

"Yeah." She glanced back down the corridor and hoped she wasn't making a mistake. "But I'm thinking this way maybe the two of them will duke it out and we can all get back to normal."

He considered that as they hopped on a glide. "I got twenty on Peabody."

"Shit." She jammed her hands in her pockets. "Okay, but if I've got to lay down on McNab's bony ass, I want odds. Three to five."

"Done."

Back in the conference room, Peabody and McNab sat just as they were.

"I've got no problem working with you," McNab said.

"Why should you? I haven't got one working with you either."

"Good."

"Good."

They stared, ceiling and shoes, for another twenty seconds. McNab broke first. "You're the one who's been avoiding me anyway."

"I have not. Why should I? We are so over."

"Who said anything different?" And it burned him that she could say it, just that coolly, when he thought about her all the time.

"And you wouldn't think I'd been avoiding you if *you* hadn't been trying to get my attention."

"Shit. For what? I'm a busy boy, She-Body. Too busy to worry about some stiff-necked uniform who spends her off-time playing with LCs."

"You leave Charles out of this." She leaped to her feet, rage boiling in her blood. And a new little tear in her heart.

"Me, I don't have to hunt up pros. I got all the amateurs I can handle." He kicked out his legs, worked up a sneer. "But that's neither here nor there, right? We got the job, and that's it. If you can handle it."

"I can handle anything you can. More."

"Fine. I'll put the list together, and we'll get started."

Chapter 4

"You don't have his face."

Eve scowled at Dickie Berenski, the chief lab tech. He might have had a smarmy smile, an attitude that had earned him the not-so-affectionate nickname of Dickhead and a personality defect that deluded him into thinking of himself as a ladies' man, but he was a genius in his little world of fibers, fluids, and follicles.

"You called me out of the field to tell me I don't have his face?"

"Figured you'd want to know." Dickie pushed himself away from the station, sent his chair spinning toward another monitor. His spidery fingers danced over a keyboard. "See that there?"

Eve studied the color-washed image on monitor. "It's a hair."

"Give the lady a prize. But what kinda hair, you might ask, and I'm here to tell you. This didn't come out of your perp's head, it didn't come out of your victim's head, or any other area of their bodies. Came out of a wig. Expensive, human hair wig."

"Can you track it down?"

"Working on it." He scooted his chair to yet another post. "Know what this is?"

There were colored shapes and circles and formulas on the monitor. Eve blew out a breath. She hated the guessing games, but knew her job when it came to Dickie. "No, Dickie, why don't you tell me what it is?"

"It's makeup, Dallas. Base cream number 905/4. Traces of it found on the bed linens. And it don't match what was on the dead girl. Got more." He switched the image. "We got here traces of face putty. Stuff people use to give 'em more chin or cheekbone, whatever, if they don't want to go for permanent face sculpting and shit."

"And she wasn't using any face putty."

"Another prize for the little lady! Guy was wearing a wig, face putty, makeup. You don't have his face."

"Well, this is just wonderful news, Dickie. You got any more?"

"Got a couple of his pubic hairs. The real thing—medium brown. Be able to give you more on him from that before we're finished. Got his fingerprints on the wineglasses, on the bottle, on the body, balcony doors, and rail. And here and there. You find him, we'll box him up real pretty."

"Send me what you've got. Track down those brand names. I want that data by morning."

"Hey!" he shouted as she strode out. "You could say thanks."

"Yeah. Thanks. Goddamn it."

She let it play through her head all the way home, trying to see what kind of man lived inside her killer. She was afraid she did see. He was smart—smart enough to change his appearance so the security cameras and Bryna Bankhead wouldn't identify him. But he hadn't taken her out, or gone back to her apartment with the idea of killing her. Eve was sure of it.

He'd gone to seduce her.

But things had gotten out of hand, she mused, and

he'd found himself with a dead woman on his rose petals. He'd reacted, panicked or angry, and had tossed her. *Panicked* rang with her. It hadn't been temper on his face when he'd come out of the apartment.

He had money, or access to it. After more than a year with Roarke she knew the signs. She'd recognized the exclusive cut of the killer's suit, even the pricey gleam of his shoes.

But he'd let Bryna pay for the drinks. *A two for one*, Eve thought. No paper trail, and a boost to his ego by having the woman pay for him.

He had solid tech skills and a knowledge of chemistry. Or again, access to that knowledge and skill.

He was sexually twisted. Perhaps inadequate, even impotent under normal circumstances. He'd be single, she decided as she approached the gates of home. Unlikely to have had any long-term or healthy relationships in his past. Nor had he been looking for one. He'd wanted complete control. The romantic trappings had been for his benefit, not hers.

An illusion, she decided, *his fantasy.* So that he could envision himself as lover.

Now that he'd achieved that control, he would do one of two things. He'd hole up in fear and guilt over what he'd done. Or he'd start hunting again.

Predators, in Eve's experience, rarely stopped at one.

The house loomed into view, with all its fanciful and elegant angles softened by twilight. Lights glowed richly against too many windows to count. Ornamental trees and shrubs she couldn't name were in wild bloom, perfuming the air so delicately, so completely, you could almost forget you were in the city.

Then again, sometimes she thought of this strange and perfect space behind stone walls and iron gates as its own country. She just happened to live in it.

She'd come to love the house. Even a year before she wouldn't have believed that possible. She'd admired it, certainly. Been both intimidated and fascinated by its sheer beauty, its amazing warren of rooms and treasures. But the love had caught her, and held her. Just as love for the man who owned it had caught her. Had held her.

Knowing he wasn't inside tempted her to turn around and drive away again. She could spend the night at Central.

Because the idea depressed her, because it reminded her of what she might have done before her life had opened to Roarke, she pulled to a stop in front of the house.

She climbed the old stone steps, pulled open the grand front door, and stepped out of the dusk into the glamorous light of the entrance foyer.

And Summerset, a skinny crow in his habitual black, stood waiting. His stony face matched his stony voice.

"Lieutenant. You left the premises in the middle of the night and failed to inform me of your schedule or your expected return."

"Gee, Dad, am I grounded?"

Because it would irritate him, and irritating Roarke's majordomo was one of life's guaranteed pleasures, she stripped off her jacket and tossed it on the polished newel of the main staircase.

Because it would irritate her, and irritating Roarke's cop was one of Summerset's pleasures, he lifted the scarred leather jacket with two thin fingers. "Informing me of your comings and goings is a basic courtesy, which naturally you're incapable of understanding."

"Ice. We understand each other. Anyway, I was out partying all night. You know, while the cat's away." She wanted to ask, and couldn't bring herself to ask, if he knew when Roarke was expected back.

He'd know, she thought as she started upstairs. He knew every fucking thing. She could call Roarke herself, but that would make her feel nearly as stupid. Hadn't she talked to him twenty-four hours ago? Hadn't he said he hoped to wrap things up and be home in another couple of days?

She walked into the bedroom, thought about a shower,

thought about a meal. And decided she wasn't in the mood for either. Better to go up to her office, run some probabilities, read through her case notes. She removed her weapon harness, rolled her shoulders. And realized work wasn't the answer either.

What she needed was some thinking time.

It was a rare thing for her to go up to the roof garden. She didn't like heights. But despite the sprawling space of the house, being inside made her feel closed in. And maybe the air would clear her head.

She opened the dome so starlight sprinkled down on the dwarf trees, the lush blooms that speared and spilled out of pots. A fountain gurgled into a pool where exotic fish flashed like wet jewels.

She took her time walking to the wall, carved with winged fairies, that circled this section of the roof.

They'd entertained up here a few times, she remembered. For a man in Roarke's position, entertaining was a job. Though, for reasons that escaped her, it was something he actually enjoyed.

She couldn't recall ever coming up here alone before, or for that matter, ever coming up with just Roarke. And she wondered who the hell tended the masses of flowers and plants, fed the fish, kept the tiles gleaming, made certain the seats and tables and statuary were clean.

It was rare to see any sort of servant, human or droid, in the house other than Summerset. But then, she'd learned that people who held great wealth, great power, could easily command silent and nearly invisible armies to handle the pesky details of life.

Despite that wealth and that power, Roarke had gone personally to handle the final details of a friend's death.

And she spent her days handling the details of the deaths of strangers.

She let her mind clear, then filled it with Bryna Bankhead.

Young, eager, romantic. Organized. She'd surrounded herself with attractive things displayed in an attractive manner. Her closet had been full of stylish clothes, with everything hung neatly.

Both the dress and the shoes she'd worn on her fatal date had been new, with the debits efficiently listed in her log book. She'd gotten a manicure and had a facial as well, had put on pretty earrings purchased the afternoon of her date.

A very female woman, Eve mused. One who read and enjoyed poetry.

Which meant the killer had hunted the young, the romantic, the particularly female.

She had two bottles of wine in her kitchen, one white, one red. And neither approaching the label or price range of the bottle on the table. Had he brought it with him, in his black leather bag, along with the illegals, the rose petals, the candles?

She'd kept condoms in her goodie drawer, but the killer hadn't used one. Bryna had been too high on illegals to insist on such defenses, which meant the killer hadn't been concerned about protection, or leaving DNA evidence.

Because, had she lived, she wouldn't have been able to identify him by description. More, Eve thought, she wouldn't have been sure what had happened. They'd had drinks in public, where, according to the server Eve had interviewed that evening, she had been very cozy with her date. Hand-holding, kisses, quiet laughter, long, soulful looks. The server, according to his statement, had assumed they were lovers.

The security cameras would not only follow that theme but add to it. She'd not only let him into her apartment, she'd pulled him inside.

That had been clever of him, Eve thought now. Waiting, letting her make the move. For the record.

If she'd lived, he'd have gotten away clean.

She wondered now if he'd done it before.

No, no. She began to pace along the wall. If he had, why would he make the mistake of overdosing her? It seemed like a first time. But she'd run a probability on that.

If there were another it was another channel to explore, another route to tracking him. To stopping him.

Pulling out her memo book, she plugged in key words.

> *Chat rooms*
> *Poetry*
> *Rare, expensive illegals*
> *Wig, cosmetic enhancements*
> *Pink roses*
> *Pinot Noir '49*
> *Sexual deviant*
> *Tech skills*
> *Chemistry knowledge*

After scanning her own words, she tucked the book back in her pocket. Maybe she'd have that shower, that meal, and work after all.

And turning, she saw Roarke.

It didn't matter that they'd been together more than a year. It occurred to her that she would, very likely, have this leap of heart, this dazzling rush, every time she saw him for the rest of her life.

Eventually, it might stop embarrassing her.

He looked like something fashioned from fantasy. The long, rangy body clad in black, would have looked just as natural in a billowing cape or tarnished armor.

His face, framed by that silky sweep of black hair, would have suited either poet or warrior with its chiseled bones and full sensuous mouth. His eyes, that wild and wonderful blue, still had the power to weaken her knees.

No, she realized, it would never stop embarrassing her. It would never stop thrilling her.

"You're back early."

"A bit. Hello, Lieutenant."

At the sound of his voice, that subtle and rich lilt of Ireland, everything inside her tumbled. Then he smiled, just the faintest curve of his lips, and she took a step toward him. By the second she was running.

He caught her halfway, lifted her right off her feet even as his mouth found hers.

There was heat, one quick flash, and warmth beneath it, a spreading, settled warmth that reached down to the marrow.

Home, he thought as the taste of her coated over the grief and fatigue of the last days. Home at last.

"You failed to inform me of your schedule," she said in a reasonably accurate mimic of Summerset. "Now I guess I have to cancel the hot date I lined up with the lap-dancing twins."

"Ah, Lars and Sven. I've heard they're very inventive." He rested his cheek against hers as he set her on her feet again. "What are you doing up here?"

"I don't know exactly. Couldn't settle, wanted air." She eased back to study his face. "You okay?"

"Yes."

But she angled her head, took his face in her hands. "Are you okay?" she repeated.

"It was difficult. More than I expected it to be. I thought I'd put it away."

"He was your friend. Whatever else, he was your friend."

"One who died so I didn't. I've resolved that." He laid his brow on hers. "Or thought I had. This wake Brian wanted, the gathering of so many from my past, then seeing where Mick had been put in the ground . . . it was difficult."

"I should have gone with you."

He smiled a little. "Some of the mourners might have been a little uneasy with a cop in the midst. Even my cop. Still, I've a message from Brian for you. As he stood behind his bar at the Penny Pig he asked that I tell you when you've come to your senses and shed yourself of the likes of me, he'll be waiting for you."

"It's always good to have backup. You have dinner?"

"Not yet, no."

"Why don't we try a little role reversal? I'll make you eat, sneak a soother in your food, then tuck you into bed."

"You've shadows under your eyes, so it seems to me you're the one in need of food and bed. Summerset said you were out all night."

"Summerset is a big, fat tattletale. I caught a case last night."

He feathered his long fingers through her hair, letting all those shades of brown and blonde spill through. "Want to tell me about it?"

She could have said no, and he'd have wheedled it out of her. "Later." She eased back into his arms, held on.

"I missed you, Eve. Missed holding you like this. Missed the smell of you, the taste."

"You could make up for it." She turned her head so that her lips skimmed over his jaw.

"I intend to."

"Intentions are easy." Now she used her teeth. "I prefer action. Right here, right now."

He let her back him toward a long, padded chaise. "What about Lars and Sven?"

"I'll take care of them later."

He grinned, spun her around so she hit the chaise first. "I think you're going to be much too tired for a lap dance."

"I don't know. I'm feeling pretty energetic." She shifted to cradle him between her thighs. And her eyebrows winged up. "Hey, you, too."

"I seem to have caught my second wind." He opened the first button on her shirt, paused. "Isn't this my shirt?"

She winced before she could stop herself. "So?"

"So." Touched, amused, he dispatched the rest of the buttons. "I'm afraid I'll have to have it back."

"Yeah, like you don't already have about five hundred . . ." She trailed off when his fingers traced over her breasts. "Okay, if you want to be that way about it."

"I do." He touched his lips to hers.

He sank into her, layer by layer. The taste of her mouth, her skin, and the texture of both, aroused, soothed, seduced. The shape of her—the long legs, the narrow torso, the small, firm breasts—were an unending delight.

She tugged at the shirts, the one he wore, the one she'd borrowed, and flesh met flesh. She arched; he burrowed.

The night air cooled around them, but blood heated. She sighed as their mouths met again, as lips parted, as tongues slicked in a long wet kiss that slipped from gentle to urgent.

And her sigh was a moan as his mouth began to move restlessly down her body.

More. All. Everything, he thought. Then stopped thinking.

Her throat, her shoulders, the lines and curves of them. He fed on them, then hungrily on her breasts until it seemed he fed on her heart as well.

Shuddering, she bowed to him, offering more while her hands streaked over him to take.

He made her want more than she'd known there was to have. It was always the same. And when his mouth, his hands stroked down her, she gripped the side of the chaise and rode the ferocious storm of pleasure.

She saw the stars wheeling in the sky overhead, felt others explode inside her body. She went limp, she went liquid, and moved against him now in a slow, sinuous rhythm.

Urgency mellowed toward tenderness. A caress, a whisper, a gentle shift, body to body.

Her fingers stroked through his hair. Her lips found the curve of his throat, nuzzling against the pulse that beat for her. When he slipped inside her, she opened her eyes to find him watching her.

No one, she thought as the breath trembled through her lips, no one had ever looked at her as he did. In a way that told her she was the center.

She rose to him, fell away, rose again in a dance that was both patient and pure. The rhythm stayed slow, silky and slow as their lips met again.

She heard, felt him say her name. "Eve."

She wrapped her arms around him, held him close, as they slipped home together.

He unearthed robes from somewhere. Eve sometimes wondered if he had some factory of silkworms buried in the house as he never seemed to run out of silk robes. These were black and just weighty enough to keep a body comfortable on a warm spring night while dining alfresco.

She decided it was hard to beat eating rare steak, from actual cows, drinking a full-bodied red wine at a candle-lit table on the roof garden. And all this after stupendous sex.

"It's a pretty good deal," she said between bites.

"What is?"

"Having you back. No fun having a fancy dinner by yourself."

"There's always Summerset."

"Now you're going to spoil my appetite."

He watched her plow through the steak. "I think not. Haven't you eaten today?"

"I had a doughnut, and don't start. What's Pinot Noir forty-nine run?"

"What label?" he retorted just as casually as she had asked.

"Ahh, shit." She closed her eyes until she had the image of the bottle in her head. "Maison de Lac."

"Excellent choice. About five hundred a bottle. I'd have to check to be certain, but that's close."

"One of yours?"

"Yes. Why?"

"It's one of the murder weapons. Do you own the apartment building on Tenth Street?"

"Which apartment building on Tenth Street?"

She hissed, rifled through her mental files, and gave him the address.

"I don't believe I do." He smiled easily. "Now how did I miss that one?"

"Very funny. Well, it's nice to know I can catch a murder someplace in the city you don't own."

"How is a five-hundred-dollar bottle of very nice wine used as a murder weapon? Poison?"

"In a way." She debated about five seconds, then told him.

"He courts her through e-mail," Roarke said. "Romances her with poetry, then slips two of the most despicable illegals ever devised into her drink."

"Drinks," Eve corrected. "He was plying her through the evening."

"And sets the stage—romance, seduction—and uses her. Uses her up," he said softly. "All the while telling himself, I'd think, that she was enjoying it. That it wasn't rape, but again, seduction, romance. Nonviolent, erotic, and mutually satisfying."

Eve set down her fork. "Why do you say that?"

"You said he was disguised. Once he was in her apartment, and she was already under the influence, he could have done what he wanted with her. If he'd wanted to hurt her, if violence was part of his turn-on, he could have done so. But he added candlelight, music, flowers. And gave her a drug designed to make her aggressive and needy sexually. The illusion that she was not only willing, but passionate. Did he need that for his ego, to be able to perform physically? Or both?"

"That's good. That's good," she said again with a nod. "I haven't been thinking enough like a guy. The disguise is part of the seduction, too. The expensive clothes, the hair and makeup. He wanted to look like . . ."

She stopped, stared at the exceptional specimen across from her.

"Oh shit, he wanted to look like you."

"Excuse me?"

"Not *you* you—he went for really long, curly hair and green eyes. But you as a type. The perfect fantasy."

"Darling, you'll embarrass me."

"Fat chance. What I'm saying is the look was part of *his* fantasy, too. He wants to be the great lover, the irresistible image. How he looks and what he is, or pretends to be. Rich, traveled, well-read, sophisticated yet hopelessly romantic at the core. There's a certain type of woman who's prime target for that kind."

"But not you, Lieutenant," he said with a smile.

"I just married you for the sex." She picked up her fork again. "And the regular servings of red meat. Which brings me to a little sidebar here. Louise Dimatto lives in the same apartment building."

"Does she?"

"And she was standing on the sidewalk when Bankhead hit the pavement."

He topped off their glasses. "I'm sorry to hear that."

"I swung by the clinic today to bring her up to date. Lot of changes around there."

"Hmm."

"Yeah, hmmm. Why didn't you tell me you'd given the clinic three million dollars?"

He lifted his glass, sipped. "I make quite a number of charitable donations I don't tell you about." He offered a smile. "Would you like to be copied on the data in the future?"

"Don't get smart with me, ace. I'd like to know why you went around me and gave her five times the amount agreed on. I'd like to know why you didn't tell me about this shelter you asked her to give time to."

"I liked the work she was doing."

"Roarke." She laid her hand over his. Firmly. "You started this shelter for me. Did you think I'd be upset, or pissed off or what if you told me about it?"

"I implemented plans for the shelter several months ago. For you," he said and turned his hand over hers so that their fingers linked. "For myself. We had nowhere to go, did we, Eve? And if I had, I wouldn't have gone. Too tough, too angry. Even bleeding from the ears from the last beating, I'd not have gone. But others will."

He lifted their joined hands, studying the way they fit. The way they held. "Still, I'm next to certain I wouldn't have thought to do this thing if it hadn't been for you."

"But you didn't tell me."

"The shelter's not altogether finished," he began. "It's open, and they've taken in what they're calling guests. But there are still details to be completed, some programs that are yet to be fully implemented. It should be—" He broke off. "No, I didn't tell you. I don't know whether I intended to or not because I couldn't be sure if it would please you or distress you."

"The name pleases me."

"Good."

"And what distresses me, though that's a wimpy word, is that you didn't tell me about something you're doing that makes me really proud of you. I wouldn't have gone to one of those places either," she continued when he only looked at her. "Because he had me so scared of them, because he made them sound like big, dark pits and I was as afraid of the dark as I was of him. So I wouldn't have gone. But others will."

He lifted her hand to his lips. "Yes."

"Now look at you, Dublin's bad boy. Pillar of the community, philanthropist, a leading social conscience of the city."

"Don't *you* start."

"Tough guy with a big, gooey heart."

"Don't make me hurt you, Eve."

"Hear that?" She cocked her head. "That's the sound of my knees knocking." She sat back, satisfied the sadness she'd seen lingering on his face when he'd first come home was gone. She was really starting to nail this wife thing.

"Okay, now that I've let you fuck me and feed me,

thereby satisfying all immediate appetites, I've got work."

"I beg your pardon, but I seem to recall someone promising to tuck me into bed."

"That'll have to wait, ace. I want to run some probabilities, and see if I can get a line on the umbrella account this guy uses. French deal. La Belle Dame."

"Keats."

"What's that?"

"Not what, you plebeian, who. John Keats. Classic poet, nineteenth century. The poem is 'La Belle Dame Sans Merci.' The beautiful woman without mercy."

"How come you know all this stuff?"

"Amazing, isn't it?" He laughed as he pulled her to her feet. "I'll get you the poem, then we can get to work."

"I don't need—"

He shut her up with a quick, hard kiss. "How about this? Let's pretend you argued about not needing or wanting civilian help or interference, then I pointed out all the very sane and reasonable advantages of same. We wrangled about it for twenty minutes, then admitting that I can find data more quickly than you, and two heads are better than one, and so on and so forth, we got to work. That'll save some time."

She hissed out a breath. "Okay, but if I catch you looking smug, I'm kicking your ass."

"Darling, that goes without saying."

Chapter 5

They didn't have his face. Whenever fear tried to creep under his skin like hot ants, he repeated that single and most essential fact.

They did not have his face, so they could not find him.

He could walk the streets, ride in a cab, eat in a restaurant, cruise the clubs. No one would question him or point fingers or run to find a cop.

He had killed, and he was safe.

In its most basic sense, his life hadn't changed. And still, he was afraid.

It had been an accident, of course. Nothing more than an unfortunate miscalculation caused by a perfectly understandable excess of enthusiasm. Actually, if one looked at the overall picture, it had been as much the woman's fault as his.

More, really.

When he said as much, again, while gnawing viciously on his thumbnail, his companion sighed.

"Kevin, if you must pace and repeat yourself do it elsewhere. It's very annoying."

Kevin Morano, a tall, trim young man of twenty-two,

threw himself down, drummed his well-manicured fingers on the buttery leather arm of a wingback chair. His face was unlined, his eyes a quiet, unremarkable blue, his hair a medium brown of medium length.

His looks were pleasant if ordinary, marred only by his tendency to sulk at the slightest hint of criticism.

He did so now as he watched his friend, his oldest and most constant companion. From that quarter, at least, he felt he deserved some sympathy and support.

"I think I have some cause to be concerned." There was petulance in his voice, a whine for sympathy. "It all went to hell, Lucias."

"Nonsense." The word was more command than comment. Lucias Dunwood was used to commanding Kevin. It was, in his opinion, the only way they got anything done.

He continued to work on his calculations and measurements in the expansive laboratory he'd designed and equipped to suit both his needs and his wants. As always, he worked with confidence.

As a child he'd been considered a prodigy, a pretty boy with red curls and sparkling eyes with a stunning talent for math and science.

He'd been pampered, spoiled, educated, and praised.

The monster inside the child had been very sly, and very patient.

Like Kevin, he'd been raised in wealth and in privilege. They'd grown up almost like brothers. In a very real sense, as they'd been created in much the same way, for much the same purpose, they considered themselves even more than brothers.

From the beginning, even as infants, they had recognized each other. Had recognized what hid beneath those small, soft bodies.

They'd attended the same schools. Had competed academically, socially, throughout their lives. They fed each other, and found in each other the only one who understood that they were beyond the common and ordinary rules that governed society.

Kevin's mother had birthed him, then turned him over to paid tenders so that she could pursue her own ambitions. Lucias's mother had kept him close, and found in him her only ambition.

And both had been smothered with excesses, indulged in every whim, directed to excel, and taught to expect nothing less than everything.

Now they were men, Lucias was fond of saying, and could do as they pleased.

Neither worked for a living, nor needed to. They found the idea of contributing to a society they disdained laughable. In the town house they'd bought together, they'd created their own world, their own rules.

The primary rule was never, never to be bored.

Lucias turned to a monitor, scanning the various components and equations that rushed over the screen. *Yes,* he thought, *yes.* That was correct. That was perfect. And satisfied, he strolled over to the bar, a gleaming antique from the 1940s, and mixed a drink.

"Whiskey and soda," he said. "That'll set you right up."

Kevin only waved a hand, sighed heavily.

"Don't be tedious, Kev."

"Oh pardon me. I'm just a bit out of sorts because I killed someone."

Chuckling, Lucias carried the highball glasses across the room. "It doesn't matter. If it did, I'd be very angry with you. After all, I was very clear on the dosage, and the choice. You weren't to mix the two solutions, Kevin."

"I know it." Irritable, Kevin took the glass, frowned into it. "I got carried away with the whole thing. I've never had a woman so completely under my spell. I didn't know it could be that way."

"That was the point of the game, wasn't it?" Smiling, Lucias lifted his glass in toast, drank. "Women have never

been what we wanted them to be for us. Christ, look at
our mothers. Mine's spineless and yours is bloodless."

"At least yours shows an interest in you."

"You don't know how lucky you are." Lucias gestured
with his glass. "The bitch would hang around my neck
like a pendant if I didn't keep away from her. Small wonder dear old Dad spends the majority of his time out of
town."

Lucias stretched out his legs. "In any case, back to the
point. Women. If they were interested in either of us, they
were usually dull intellectuals or brainless money-
grubbers. We deserve better, Kevin. We deserve exactly
the women we want, as many as we want, and in precisely the way we want them."

"We do. Of course we do. But God, Lucias, when I realized she was dead—"

"Yes, yes." Lucias sat in the matching chair, leaned
forward eagerly. "Tell me again."

"She was so sexy. Beautiful, exotic, confident. The
kind of woman I've always wanted. And she couldn't
keep her hands off me. I could've had her in the cab, in
the elevator. I scored a hell of a lot of points even before
we were in her apartment."

"We'll tally them up shortly." Lucias gave an impatient wave. "Go on."

"I had to keep slowing her down. I didn't want it to be
over too quickly. I wanted the romance of it, for both of
us. The slow steps of seduction. And of course . . ." The
first hints of amusement crossed his face. "To continue to
rack up as many points as possible during the allotted
time period."

"Naturally," Lucias agreed, and toasted.

"It was working. She let me do whatever I wanted.
She enjoyed it."

"Yes. Yes. Then?"

"I told her to wait so I could set the scene in the bedroom. Just as I'd planned. It was perfect. It was all perfect. The lighting, the music, the scent of the air."

"And she surrendered to you."

"Yes." Kevin sighed, letting it come flooding back. "I carried her into the bedroom. I undressed her, so slowly, while she trembled for me. She whimpered for me. But then, she became lethargic."

Lucias rattled the ice in his glass. "You'd given her too much."

"I know it, but I wanted more, damn it." His mouth turned down, his voice was edged with temper. "It wasn't enough for her to lie there like a droid. I wanted her hot, out of control. I deserved that after all I'd done."

"Of course you did. So you gave her the Rabbit."

"I should have diluted it. I know. But I was careful, just a few drops on her tongue. Lucias . . ." He wet his lips. "She went wild. Hot and screaming. Begging me to take her. She begged me, Lucias. We coupled like animals. Romance to seduction to the primitive. I've never felt like that. When I came it was like being born."

He shuddered, sipped. "When it was over I lay there, spent, drifting with her under me. I kissed her, caressed her so she'd know she'd pleased me. Then I looked down at her. She stared up at me. Just stared and stared. I didn't understand at first, but then . . . I knew she was dead."

"You were born," Lucias said, "and she died. The ultimate in experiences." He sipped and considered. "Think of it, Kevin. She died much the same way as we were conceived. From a frantic coupling induced by chemicals. One an experiment with superior results. If we do say so ourselves."

"And we do," Kevin agreed with a laugh.

"The other a game. A game well played, for the first round. Now it's my turn."

"What are you talking about?" Kevin leaped to his feet as Lucias rose. "You can't be serious. You can't go through with it."

"Of course I can. Why should you have all the fun?"

"Lucias, for God's sake—"

"It was stupid of you to throw her out the window. If

you'd just left her there, walked out, it would have taken more time for them to find her. Deduction in points for poor strategy. I won't make that mistake."

"What do you mean?" Kevin gripped his arm. "What are you going to do?"

"Kev, we're in this together. Planning and execution. When we started we considered this a bit of recreation, a kind of interlude where we'd expand our sexual experiences. And at a dollar a point, a kind of casual competition to keep us entertained."

"No one was supposed to be hurt."

"And you're not," Lucias pointed out. "Who else matters? It's our game."

"Yes." It was unarguable logic, and calmed him again. "That's true."

"And now, think of it." Lucias spun away, threw out his arms. "In a way it's the most fascinating circle. Birth to death. Don't you see the irony, the beauty of it? The very drugs that were used to help us come into existence are the ones you used to end someone else's existence."

"Yes . . ." Kevin could feel himself being pulled into the thrill of it. "Yes, but—"

"The stakes are higher, and so much more interesting." Lucias turned back and gave Kevin's arm a manly and congratulatory squeeze. "Kevin, you're a murderer."

He paled, but the gleam of respect in Lucias's eyes made him want to preen. "It was an accident."

"You're a murderer. How can I be less?"

"You mean to . . ." Excitement began to ball in his belly. "Deliberately?"

"Look at me. Tell me, and you know you can't lie, not to me, if her death at your hands wasn't part of the thrill. Wasn't, in fact, the biggest part of it?"

"I . . ." Kevin grabbed his drink, gulped whiskey. "Yes. God, yes."

"Would you deny me the same experience?" He draped an arm around Kevin's shoulders, led him to the elevator. "After all, Kev, they're only women."

• • •

Her name was Grace. Such a sweet, old-fashioned name. She worked as a page in the New York City library, delivering discs and precious books to patrons who settled into the reading rooms to study or research or simply pass the time with literature.

She loved poetry.

She was twenty-three, a pretty, delicate blonde with a shy nature and a generous heart. And she was already in love with the man who called himself Dorian and wooed her in the safe world of cyber-space.

She'd told no one about him. It made it more special, more romantic that no one knew. For their first date, she bought a new dress with a long, flowing skirt in blending pastels that made her think of rainbows.

When she left her little apartment to ride the subway uptown, she felt very daring, very adult. Imagine having drinks at the Starview Lounge with the man she was convinced she would marry.

She was certain he'd be handsome. He just had to be. She knew he was rich and articulate and a great traveler, a man who loved books and poetry as she did.

They were soul mates.

She was too happy to be nervous, too sure of the outcome of the evening to have a single doubt.

She would be dead before midnight.

Her name had been Grace, and she had been his first. Not just his first kill, but his first woman. Even Kevin didn't know that he had never been able to complete the sexual act. Until tonight.

He had been a god in that narrow bed in the pathetic little apartment. A god who had made the woman beneath him cry out and weep and beg for more. She had babbled her love for him, had agreed to every demand. And her glassy, drugged eyes had clung adoringly to his face no matter what he'd done to her.

He'd been so surprised she'd been a virgin he'd come

too quickly the first time. But she'd said it had been wonderful, she said she'd been waiting for him all her life.
She had saved herself for him.

And his very disgust with her aroused him.

When he took the last vial out of his bag, he showed it
to her so that the glass and liquid glinted in the candlelight. When he told her to open her mouth, she did so,
like a little bird waiting for a worm.

Pounding himself into her, he felt her heart gallop. He
felt it burst. And he knew Kevin had been right. It was
like being born.

He studied her after she was used up, when her body
grew colder on the tangled sheets and rose petals. And
knew one thing more. This had been his right. She was
every girl who had ever ignored his needs, or turned away
when he was unable to perform. Everyone who'd ever refused him, denied him, smirked at him.

She was, in essence, nothing.

He dressed, brushed at the sleeves of his suit jacket,
shot his cuffs. Leaving the candles burning, he strolled
out. He couldn't wait to get home and tell Kevin.

Eve felt fabulous. Sex and sleep, she decided. It was hard
to beat the combo. Then when you started the day with a
quick swim, a monster cup of real coffee strong enough
to break bricks, you were in fat city.

The way she was feeling, she figured the bad guys had
best take a day off.

"You look rested, Lieutenant." Roarke leaned on the
jamb of the doorway between their home offices.

"Ready to rock," she said, watching him over the rim
of her coffee cup. "I guess you've got a lot of catching
up to do."

"I made a pretty good start on that."

She snorted. "Yeah, not bad, but I was thinking of work."

"Ah. I've made a start on that as well." He crossed
over, caged her in between his body and the desk. Lean-

ing over, he stroked the cat who'd draped himself over the 'link like a rag.

"You're crowding me, pal, and I'm on the clock here."

"Not for five minutes yet."

She angled her head to look at her wrist unit. "You're right. Five minutes." She slid her arms around his waist. "We ought to be able to . . ." Just as she caught his bottom lip between her teeth, she heard the approaching footsteps, the unmistakable clomp of cop shoes. "Peabody's early."

"Let's pretend we didn't hear her." Roarke nibbled at her mouth. "That we can't see her." Traced it with his tongue. "That we don't even know her name."

"That's a good plan except—" When he put sincere effort into the kiss, she was pretty sure she could feel her heart melting. "Down boy," she murmured just as Peabody strode into the room.

"Oh. Um. Ahem."

Roarke turned, picked up Galahad to scratch his ears. "Hello, Peabody."

"Hi. Welcome home. Maybe I'll just go in the kitchen there and get some coffee . . . and stuff."

But when she started by, Roarke reached out, lifted her chin with a finger, and studied her face. It was pale, the eyes heavy and chased by shadows. "You look tired."

"Guess I didn't sleep very well." She muttered, "Need that coffee." Then she hurried away.

"Eve."

"Don't." She held up a finger at Roarke's quiet tone. "I don't want to talk about that now. I don't ever want to talk about it, but I especially don't want to talk about it now. And if anybody had listened to me when I said she and McNab getting tangled was going to screw things up, we wouldn't *have* to talk about it, would we?"

"Correct me if I'm wrong, but I think you're talking about it."

"Oh, shut up. All I know is she's going to suck it in

and do the job, and so is he." She gave the desk one bad-tempered little kick before walking around behind it. "Now go away."

"You're worried about her."

"Damn it, you think I can't see she's hurt? That it doesn't get to me?"

"I know you can, and I know it does."

She opened her mouth, then heard more footsteps in the hallway. "Let it go," she muttered. "Peabody." She lifted her voice. "Feeney's here. Coffee light and sweet."

"How'd you know it was me?" Feeney demanded as he came inside.

"You shuffle."

"Hell I do."

"Hell you don't. You shuffle, Peabody clomps, McNab prances."

"If I wore some of the shoes he does, I'd prance, too. Hey, Roarke, didn't know you were back."

"Just. I'll be working at home for another hour or so," he told Eve. "Then I'll be in the midtown offices. The book stays here," he added. "You're welcome to take it on disc if you need it."

"What book?" Feeney asked.

"Poetry. Seems our guy took his umbrella name from a poem some guy named Keats wrote a couple hundred years ago."

"Bet it doesn't even rhyme. You take Springsteen, McCartney, Lennon. Those boys knew how to rhyme. Classic shit."

"Not only doesn't it rhyme, but it's weird and depressing and mostly stupid."

"With that canny analysis, I'll leave you to work." Carrying the cat, Roarke started toward his office. "I believe I hear McNab's prance."

He might have been wearing candy-apple red airboots, but he didn't look any perkier than Peabody. Doing her best to ignore it, Eve sat on the edge of her desk and updated them.

"That explains why we didn't have any luck at the cyber-joints either," McNab put in. "It didn't make sense that nobody'd seen this dude."

"We can do some morphing probabilities," Feeney mused. "Most possible face structures, colorings, combos. But basically we'll be working without a visual ID."

"I ran some probabilities myself. It's most likely we're looking for a single male between twenty-five and forty. Upper income bracket, advanced education, with some sort of sexual dysfunction or perversion. It's most probable he lives in the city. Feeney, where'd he get the high-priced illegals?"

"Dealers with Rabbit cater to a small, exclusive clientele. Aren't that many of them. Only one in the city I know of, but I can check with Illegals to see if there's more. Nobody deals in Whore that I know of. Just isn't cost effective."

"But at one time it was used in sex therapy, and for LC training?"

"Yeah, but the price tag was too high, and the substance too unpredictable."

"Okay." But it gave her more threads to pull. "We'll back off the cyber-joints for now. McNab, start on the morphings. Feeney, see what you can find out from Illegals. Once I hammer Dickhead into identifying brands of the putty and enhancers, the wig, we'll have that trail to follow. I got a tag on the wine. My source tells me there were three thousand and fifty bottles of that label and vintage sold in this borough. Peabody and I will run that down, and we'll see if we can nail down the pink roses. The guy spends money—wine, flowers, enhancements, illegals—then he's left a trail. We're going to find it. Peabody, you're with me."

When they were in the car, Eve took a long breath. "If you're having trouble sleeping, take a pill."

"That's some advice coming from you."

"Then consider it an order."

"Yes, sir."

"This is really pissing me off." Eve punched it, roared up the drive.

Peabody's chin jutted out so far, Eve was surprised it didn't spear through the windshield. "I apologize if my personal difficulties are an annoyance to you, Lieutenant."

"If you can't do better sarcasm than that, give it up." She swung through the gates, then slammed on the brakes. "Do you want time off?"

"No, sir."

"Don't *sir* me, Peabody, in that tone or I'll kick your ass right here and now."

"I don't know what's wrong with me." Her voice went watery. "I don't even *like* McNab. He's annoying and he's a jerk and he's *stupid*. So what if the sex was great? And maybe we had some laughs. Big deal. It's not like we were serious or anything. It's not like it gives him the right to give me ultimatums or make insulting comments and draw asshole conclusions."

"Have you slept with Charles yet?"

"What?" Peabody actually blushed. "No."

"Maybe you should. Maybe, I can't believe I'm having this conversation, maybe if you relieved some stress in that area you'd get your head settled right. Or something."

"We're . . . Charles and I are friends."

"Yeah. You're friends with a very high-priced sexual professional. Seems to me he'd be willing to help you out."

"It's not the same as loaning me twenty till payday." Then she sighed. "But maybe I should think about it."

"Think fast. We're going to see him."

Peabody came straight up out of the seat. "What? Now?"

"Officially," Eve said and started the car again. "He's an expert on sex, right? Let's see what the expert knows about sexual illegals."

The sexual expert had the morning off. He answered the door wearing blue silk pajama bottoms.

As man-candy went, he was a caloric binge. Eve thought it was easy to see why he had so many clients paying for a nibble.

"Lieutenant, Delia. What an attractive sight to wake up to."

"Sorry to roust you," Eve told him. "Got a minute?"

"For you, Lieutenant Sugar, I have hours." He stepped back to let them in. "Why don't we have breakfast? I've got crêpes stocked in the AutoChef."

"Rain check," Eve said before Peabody could even nod. "You alone or do you have a client sleeping you off?"

"All alone." The sleepiness began to clear. "Is this official?"

"We're on a case, and I think you may be helpful in certain aspects of it."

"Was it anyone I knew?"

"Bankhead, Bryna. Downtown address."

"The woman who jumped out of her window? Wasn't that suicide?"

"Homicide," Eve corrected. "The media will have that this morning."

"Why don't you sit down? I'll make coffee."

"Peabody, why don't you make it?" Eve chose a seat in the well-appointed living area. Sex, when it was done right, paid well. "The questions I ask you, any portion of this investigation I may discuss with you, is confidential."

"Understood." He sat across from her. "I take it I'm not a suspect this time."

"I'm considering you an expert civilian consultant." She took out her recorder. "Officially."

"Then I assume sex reared its ugly head."

"Consult with Monroe, Charles, licensed companion," Eve announced. "Initiated by Dallas, Lieutenant Eve, and on her authority as primary of casefile H-78926B. Also attending, Peabody, Officer Delia. Mr. Monroe, are you willing to consult in this matter?"

He managed to keep his face nearly sober. "Whatever I can do to help as a concerned citizen."

"What do you know about the illegal substance known on the street as Whore?"

Instantly his expression changed. "Did someone use Whore on that poor woman?"

"The question, Charles?"

"Christ." He got to his feet, was pacing as Peabody came back with a coffee tray. "Thanks, honey." He took a cup, drank slowly. "It was already illegal by the time I started training," he continued. "But I heard plenty about it. I took a seminar in my early days. Sexual Deviants: Dos and Don'ts. That kind of thing? Illegals of any kind were a big don't. You can get your license pulled. Of course, that doesn't mean that certain . . . aids aren't employed by some LCs or clients. But not this one."

"Why?"

"First, since it was once used to make trainees more malleable, we'll say, it has a very bad rep in my business. The sex-slave gambit is fine as a role-playing game, but not in reality. We're professional sexual companions, Dallas. We're not whores or puppets."

"You've never known anyone who used it?"

"Some of the older pros. You hear stories, and most of them involve abuse of one kind or another. Experimentation. Dose the LC trainee with it, then bang away. Like we were goddamn guinea pigs," he said in disgust.

"Still, it's an elitist substance. Any connoisseurs you know of?"

"No, but I can check around."

"Carefully," Eve warned. "What about Rabbit?"

He lifted one shoulder, rather elegantly. "Only amateurs and perverts use Rabbit, on themselves or a partner. In my circle it's considered both tacky and insulting."

"Dangerous?"

"If you're stupid or careless, certainly. You don't mix it with alcohol or any other stimulant. And you don't want to overdose. ODs are extremely rare because the shit costs more than liquid gold."

"You know dealers who handle it? Clients who use it?"

He stared, then looked pained. "Jesus, Dallas."

"I won't use your name."

He shook his head, then walked to the window, lifted the privacy shade. Light washed in.

"Charles, it's really important." Peabody stepped up to him, touched his arm. "We wouldn't ask if it wasn't."

"I don't do illegals, Delia. You know that."

"I know."

"It's not up to me to judge clients who do. I'm no one's moral center."

Eve leaned over, switched off the recorder. "Off the record, Charles. And my word no charges will be brought against your client for illegals use."

"I'm not giving you her name." He turned back. "I'm not violating that trust. But I will talk to her myself. I'll get the name of her dealer. And that I'll give you."

"I appreciate it." Her communicator beeped. "I'm going to take this in the kitchen."

"Charles." Peabody rubbed his arm when Eve left the room. "Thanks. I know we put you in a sensitive position."

"Sensitive positions are my specialty." He grinned. "You look tired, Delia."

"Yeah. I've been hearing that."

"Why don't I fix you dinner one night this week? A nice, quiet evening. I'll check my book."

"That'd be great."

When he leaned down to brush his lips over hers, she closed her eyes, waited for the thrill. And wanted to scream when it didn't come. It was, she thought, like kissing her brother. If any of her brothers happened to be gorgeous as sin.

"What's troubling you, sweetheart?"

"Bunch of stuff." She grumbled. "Bunch of stupid stuff. I'm working it out."

"If you want to talk about it, you know I'm here."

"Yeah. I know."

Eve came out of the kitchen and headed straight for the door. "Let's move, Peabody. Get me a name, Charles, soon as you can."

"Dallas?" With a quick, apologetic glance at Charles, Peabody ran to catch up. "What is it?"

"We've got another one."

Chapter 6

He'd left her on the bed, her legs obscenely spread, her eyes gaping. Some of the pink petals stuck to her skin. Candlewax had spilled and hardened into cold pools over the holders onto the table, the little dresser, the floor, and the cheap, colorful rug.

It was a tiny efficiency apartment that the young woman named Grace Lutz had tried to make cheerful and cozy with frilled curtains and inexpensive prints in inexpensive frames.

Now it stank of death, stale sex, and scented candles.

There was a wine bottle, this time a cabernet. And this time nearly empty. The music came from a cheap audio unit beside the convertible sofa that served as a bed.

There was no mood screen, no video screen, and only a single 'link. But there were books, carefully tended and set proudly on the painted shelf along one wall. There were photographs of Grace with a man and woman Eve took to be her parents. There was a small glass vase filled with spring daisies that were shedding their petals on the dresser top.

The kitchen was no more than a corner with a two-

burner stove, a stingy sink, and a minifridge. Inside the
fridge were a carton of egg substitute, a quart of milk,
and a small jar of strawberry jam.

There were no bottles of wine but the one that had
killed her.

Grace hadn't spent money on things, Eve mused. Nor
on fashion if the contents of her closet were any indication. But, though she'd worked in a library, she'd spent it
on books.

And on what looked to be a new dress, now carelessly
heaped on the floor.

"He knew what he was doing this time. There's no
panic here. What there is, is deliberation."

"Physically they're very different types," Peabody
pointed out. "This girl's white bread, sort of tiny. Nails
are short and neat and unpolished. Nothing slick or flashy
about her."

"Yeah, economically they're from different brackets.
Socially, too. This one was a stay-at-home." She looked
at the dried blood on the sheets, the smears of it on the
victim's inner thighs. "The ME's going to confirm she
was a virgin." She bent down. "She's got bruising, thighs,
hips, breasts. He was rough with this one. Check the security, Peabody, see what we've got to work with."

"Yes, sir."

Why did he hurt you? Eve wondered as she studied the
body. Why did he want to?

Crouched there beside the dead, she saw herself huddled in the corner. Broken, bruised, bloody.

Because I can.

She shoved the image away as she got to her feet. Pain
could be sexual, it could be a kind of seduction. But it
wasn't romantic. Yet he'd still set the stage with rose
petals and candlelight, with wine and music.

Why did this stage seem to be a mockery of romance
rather than a clichéd attempt at it? Too much wine had
been drunk, and some of it spilled on the table and rug.

The candles had been allowed to spread into messy drips and pools. The sleeve of her new dress had been torn.

There was a violence here, an underlying meanness that had been absent from the first murder. Was he losing control? Had he found the killing more exciting than the sex?

Peabody came back in. "Security at the front entrance only. I've got the disc from last night. No cams in corridors or elevators."

"Okay. Let's talk to the neighbor."

Notifying next of kin never got easier. It never became routine. Eve stood with Peabody on the small square stoop outside the small square duplex. There were red and white geraniums arranged in a cheerful chorus line on either side of the entrance and a frill of white curtains framing the front window.

Behind them, the neighborhood was quiet as a church with its green-leafed trees and little gardens and narrow, tidy streets.

She didn't understand the suburbs with their regimental order and boxy yards and useless fences. Nor did she understand why so many considered a house in the 'burbs as a kind of mecca they would someday reach.

In her mind, everyone would someday reach a coffin, too.

She rang the bell and heard the three chimes that echoed inside. When the door opened and she said what needed to be said, nothing would ever be the same in this house again.

The woman who answered was pretty and blonde. It was the woman from the dresser photograph. Must be the mother. Eve saw the resemblance immediately.

"Mrs. Lutz?"

"Yes." Though she smiled, it was a quick reflex action, and her eyes were both puzzled and distracted. "May I help you?"

"I'm Lieutenant Dallas." Eve offered her badge. "NYPSD. This is my aide, Officer Peabody. May we come in?"

"What's this about?" The woman lifted a hand to brush at her hair, and the first sign of nerves showed in the faint tremor.

"It's about your daughter, Mrs. Lutz. It's about Grace. May we come in?"

"Gracie? She's not in any trouble, is she?" The smile tried to spread, but only fell away from her face. "My Gracie's never in trouble."

So it had to be done in the doorway, with the bright flowers a soldier's guard. "Mrs. Lutz, I'm sorry to tell you Grace is dead."

Her eyes went blank. "She is not." There was a crack of irritation in her voice. "Of course she's not. What a terrible thing to say. I want you to go away right now. I want you to go away from here."

Eve braced a hand on the door before it closed in her face. "Mrs. Lutz, Grace was killed last night. I'm the primary investigator, and I'm very sorry for your loss. You need to let us in now."

"My Grace? My baby?"

Eve said nothing now, but slid an arm around the woman's waist. The door opened into the living area with a plump blue sofa and two sturdy chairs. Eve led her to the sofa, sat beside her.

"Is there someone we can call for you, Mrs. Lutz? Your husband?"

"George. George is at school. He teaches at the high school. Grace." She looked around blindly as though her daughter might walk into the room.

"Peabody, make the call."

"You've made a mistake, haven't you?" Mrs. Lutz gripped Eve's hand with frozen fingers. "That's all. You've just made a mistake. Grace works in the city, at the library on Fifth Avenue. I'll just call her and we'll all feel much better."

"Mrs. Lutz. There's no mistake."

"There *has* to be. George and I went into the city only Sunday and took her to dinner. She was fine." The anger and shock were breaking down so tears flooded through them. "She was *fine*."

"I know. I'm sorry."

"What happened to my baby? Was there an accident?"

"There wasn't an accident. Grace was murdered."

"It's just not possible." Her head shook, as if gently tugged side-to-side with invisible strings. "It's just not possible."

Eve let her weep. She knew that first roll of grief flattened everything else.

"He's on his way," Peabody murmured.

"Good. Get her some water or something."

She sat beside the sobbing woman, scanning the living area. There were books here, displayed like treasures on shelves. There was a quiet order to everything, and the sturdiness of solid middle-class living. A framed hologram of Grace stood on a table.

"What happened to my baby?"

Eve shifted, looked into Mrs. Lutz's shattered face. "Last night Grace met a man she'd been corresponding with by e-mail and in chat rooms. We believe this man doctored her drink or drinks during the evening with a substance known to be used in date rapes."

"Oh God." Mrs. Lutz wrapped her arms around her belly and began to rock. "Oh my God."

"Evidence indicates that he returned with her to her apartment, continued to give her illegals until she overdosed."

"She would never take illegals."

"We don't believe she was aware, Mrs. Lutz."

"He gave them to her because he wanted to . . ." She pressed her lips together in a tight white line. Then breathed out, one long ragged sound. "He raped her."

"We suspect that's true. I . . ." How far did you go? Eve wondered. How much could you help? "Mrs. Lutz, if it's any comfort to you, Grace wouldn't have been afraid. She wouldn't have been in pain."

"Why would anyone hurt her? What kind of person does that to an innocent young girl?"

"I can't tell you, but I can tell you I'll find him. I need you to help me."

Mrs. Lutz laid her head back. "What can I do if she's gone?"

"Did she have any boyfriends?"

"Robbie. Robbie Dwyer. They dated in high school, and a bit in the first few semesters of college. He's a nice boy. His mother and I belong to the same book club." Her voice wavered. "I suppose we'd hoped more would come of it, but it was more friendship than romance. Grace wanted to move to the city, and Robbie got a job teaching here. They drifted apart."

"How long ago did they drift?"

"If you're thinking Robbie would do this, anything like this, you're wrong. I've known him since he was a baby. Anyway, he's seeing a very nice girl now."

"Did she ever talk about anyone she was interested in, or who was interested in her? In the city?"

"No, not really. She worked very hard, and she was studying as well. She's shy. My Gracie's shy. It's hard for her to meet new people. That's why I encouraged her to move to . . ." She broke down again. "George wanted her to stay here, to teach and stay in the nest. I pushed her out, just little nudges, because I wanted her to fly. Now I've lost her. Will you take me to her? When George gets here, will you take us to our baby?"

"Yes. I'll take you to her."

Commander Whitney was on the 'link when he motioned Eve into his office. He didn't gesture to a chair, nor did she make any move to sit. His wide face was creased with lines, a map that showed the routes of stress, battles, and authority. His suit was a rich coffee color, nearly the same tone as his skin. In it he looked both beefy and tough. A combination, Eve had always thought, that made him appear as natural behind a desk as he did in the field.

A fluted bowl sat on the right corner of his desk. It was filled with cerulean water with smooth, colored stones shimmering in the base. While she puzzled over it, she caught the quick flash of scarlet.

"My wife," Whitney said when he ended the call. "She thinks it cheers up the office. Supposed to relax me. What the hell am I supposed to do with a damn fish?"

"I couldn't say, sir."

For a moment both of them studied the red streak that circled the bowl. Knowing the commander's wife was keen on fashion and decor, Eve searched for a polite comment.

"It's fast."

"Crazy thing spins around like that most of the day. I get tired just looking at it."

"At that rate it'll probably wear itself out and die within a couple weeks."

"Your mouth to God's ear. Where's your aide, Lieutenant?"

"I've got her running cross-checks on the two victims. We've found no evidence to support a relationship between them. They both liked books, poetry in particular. Both spent time in cyber-rooms. At this point we can't place them in the same chat or club at the same time."

He sat back. "What have you got?"

"The across-the-hall neighbor of Lutz's, Angela Nicko, found the body this morning. They had a regular morning coffee date, and when Lutz didn't show, didn't answer her door, Ms. Nicko was concerned enough to open the door with her spare key. Nicko is a retired librarian, well into her nineties."

And had cried, Eve thought wearily, cried silent tears while she'd given her statement.

"At this point she appears to be the only resident of the apartment building the victim had regular contact with. Lutz is described as a quiet, polite young woman who rarely varied her routine. She went to work, she came home. Twice a week she stopped in the neighborhood market for supplies. Other than Nicko, she had no close friends, no lovers. She was doing a part-time, in-home course to get her degree in library science."

"The security cams?"

"One, at entrance. As trace evidence at the first scene confirmed, the suspect wears a disguise, we're assuming he was doing so again. I'm waiting for lab reports. His appearance was markedly different in the second murder. Short, straight blonde hair, lantern-jaw, wide brow, dark brown eyes, pale gold complexion."

Eve stared at the fish. It was making her dizzy, but she couldn't look away. "There was a different attitude, as well. A deliberation, and a pleasure in the violence that wasn't apparent in the first killing. We're working to trace the first wig, the enhancements. We're also pursuing the cyber-angle, and continue to look for another connection between the victims. I've requested a consult with Dr. Mira, and am copying her all files and reports to date."

"The media hasn't yet sniffed out the connection, but we won't keep it that way for long."

"In this case, sir, the media might be an advantage. If women are made aware of the potential dangers, the suspect's pool gets shallow. I'd like to leak some of the data to Nadine Furst at Channel Seventy-five."

He pursed his lips. "Make sure the leak doesn't become a flood before we're ready for it."

"Yes, sir. I have some more sources on the illegals angle, and I've asked Feeney to use his contacts within the department in that area. Neither drug is common. When I find the supplier, I may need room to deal."

"We'll work that out when you find the supplier. But I can tell you there won't be much room. Politically, these illegals are a hot button. We go soft on a supplier, we'll have feminist's organizations, social balance, and moral watchdog groups taking numbers to kick us in the teeth."

"And if dealing with the supplier saves lives?"

"For a lot of these people, that won't matter. They deal in principles, not individuals. Work the angles, Lieutenant, do the checklist and get this bastard before we have more dead. And a public relations nightmare."

Eve didn't give a rat's skinny ass about public relations. Since this wasn't a well-kept secret, it was no surprise that Nadine expressed some suspicion at being offered inside data.

"What kind of happy bullshit is this, Dallas?"

Eve had waited, deliberately, until she was home rather than at Central to contact Nadine. It seemed to her that made the exchange friendly rather than official.

"I'm doing you a favor."

Nadine, already polished for an on-air segment, lifted one perfectly arched brow, let her coral-slicked mouth curve. "You, Lieutenant Locked Lips, are going to, of your own free will and out of a sense of camaraderie, give me data on an ongoing investigation."

"That's right."

"Just a minute." Nadine's face disappeared from the 'link screen for ten seconds. "Just wanted to check with the meteorologist. It appears, despite indications to the contrary, hell has not frozen over."

"Pardon me while I fall into an uncontrollable fit of giggles. You want the data or not?"

"Yeah, I want it."

"A top police source confirms that the investigations of the Bryna Bankhead and the Grace Lutz cases are linked."

"Hold on." Everything about Nadine sharpened as she leaped into full reporter mode. "There's been no confirmation to this point as to whether the Bankhead death was accidental, self-termination, or homicide."

"It's homicide. Confirmed."

"My information is that the Lutz murder was sexual homicide." Nadine's voice was brisk now. All business. "Is that the case in the Bankhead homicide? Did the victims know each other, and are we dealing with one suspect?"

"Don't interview me, Nadine. This isn't a one-on-one. Both victims were young, single women who, on the night of their deaths, met with an individual they had corresponded with via e-mail and online chat rooms."

"What kind of chat rooms? Where did they meet?"

"Shut up, Nadine. Evidence indicates that both victims were given an illegal substance, possibly without their knowledge, during the evening."

"A date rape drug?"

"You're quick. Your source neither denies nor confirms that information. Take the freebie, Nadine, and run with it. That's all you get for now."

"I can get out of here in ninety minutes. I'll meet you wherever you want."

"Not tonight. I'll let you know where or when."

"Wait!" If it had been possible, Nadine would have burst through the 'link screen. "Give me something on the suspect. Do you have a description, a name?"

"All avenues of investigation are being vigorously pursued. Blah, blah, blah." Eve broke transmission on Nadine's curse.

Satisfied, she walked into the kitchen, ordered coffee. Then just stood by the window, looking out at the gathering dark.

He was out there now. Somewhere. Did he already have another date? Was he, even now, making himself into some hopeful woman's fantasy?

Tomorrow, the next day, would there be other friends, more family she would have to shatter?

The Lutzes would never fully recover. They'd go on with their lives, and after a while they wouldn't think of it every minute of every day. They'd laugh again, work, shop, breathe in and out. But there would always be a hole. Just a little hollow inside their lives.

They'd been a family. A unit. She'd sensed that unification in the house. In the comfort and clutter of it. In the flowers outside the door, and the easy give of the sofa.

Now rather than parents, they were survivors. Those who survived lived forever with that echo of what was gone sounding inside their heads.

They'd kept her room, Eve thought now while her coffee sat in the AutoChef going cold. When she'd gone through it, looking for something, anything to add to the sum of Grace Lutz, she'd seen the stages of a life, from child to young girl to young woman.

Dolls carefully arranged on a shelf. Decoration now rather than toys, but still treasured. Books, photographs, holograms. Trinket boxes in the shapes of hearts or flowers. The bed had had a canopy the color of sunbeams, and the walls had been virgin white.

Eve couldn't imagine growing up there, in all that sweet, girlish fuss. Ruffled curtains at the windows, the inexpensive minicomputer on the desk that had been decorated with daisies to match the shade on the bedside lamp.

The girl who's slept in that bed, read by that lamplight had been happy, secure, and loved.

Eve had never had a doll, nor curtains at the windows. There'd been no precious little pieces of girlhood to tuck away in heart-shaped boxes. The childhood rooms she remembered were cramped, anonymous boxes in cheap hotels where the walls were thin and often, too often, things skittered in dark corners.

The air smelled stale, and there was no place to hide, no place to run if he came back and wasn't drunk enough to forget you were there.

The girl who had slept in those beds, trembled in those shadows had been terrified, desperate, and lost.

She jolted as a hand touched her shoulder, and instinctively reached for her weapon as she spun around.

"Steady, Lieutenant." Roarke ran his hand down her arm, rested it lightly on her weapon hand as he studied her face. "Where were you?"

"Trying to make a circle." She eased away from him, opened the AutoChef for her coffee. "I didn't know you were home."

"I haven't been for long." He laid his hands on her shoulders now, rubbed at the tension. "Did you have a memory flash?"

She shook her head, sipped the cold coffee, continued to stare out the window into the dark. But she knew if she didn't rid herself of it, it could fester. "When you were gone," she began, "I had a dream. A bad one. He wasn't dead. He was covered with blood, but he wasn't dead. He talked to me. He said I'd never kill him, never get away."

She saw Roarke's reflection in the glass, saw her own merging with it. "He had to punish me. He got up. Blood was pouring out of him, but he stood up. And he came for me."

"He is dead, Eve." Roarke took the cup out of her hand, set it aside, then turned her to face him. "He can't hurt you. Except in dreams."

"He said to remember what he'd told me, but I can't. I don't know what he meant. But I asked him why he hurt me. He said because I was nothing and no one, but most of all he hurt me because he could. I can't seem to take that power away from him. Even now I can't."

"You diminish him every time you stand for a victim. Maybe the further away you get from him in reality, the harder it is to pull back in dreams. I don't know." He skimmed his fingers through her hair. "Will you talk to Mira?"

"I don't know. No," she corrected. "She can't tell me anything I don't know."

Are ready to know, Roarke thought, and let it be.

"Anyway, I need her for a consult on the murders."

"Another?"

"Yeah. So I've got to put more hours in."

"Was it the same man?"

She didn't answer, but wandered back into her office. She didn't want the coffee after all. Instead she kept moving, let it all play through her head as she gave him the basic details of the second murder.

"If there's a local source for the illegals used, I could track it for you."

She looked at him, elegant in his dark business suit. It didn't pay to forget there was a dangerous man inside it, one who had once trafficked with other dangerous men.

Roarke Industries might have been the most powerful conglomerate in the world, but it had been born, like its owner, in the dark alleys and grim streets of Dublin's slums.

"I don't want you to do that," she told him. "Not yet. If Charles and Feeney both crap out, I may tag you. But I'd as soon you didn't make a connection with that particular area."

"My connection would be no different than yours, only quicker."

"Yeah, it's different. I'm the one with a badge. You know a lot of women."

"Lieutenant. That portion of my past is a closed book."

"Yeah, right. What I'm saying is, in my experience, most guys generally go for a type. Maybe they like brainy women, or subservient women, or jocks, whatever."

He moved in on her. "What type do you suppose I go for?"

"You just scooped them up as they fell at your feet, so you went for the variety pack."

"I definitely don't recall you falling at my feet."

"And don't hold your breath on that one. You don't count so much because you'd never have to go fishing in the cyber-pool for a date or sex or anything."

"You're not making that sound complimentary."

"But what I'm saying is, people generally have expectations, or fantasy types. Date number one. Savvy, sophisticated, urban female with a romantic bent. Slick dresser, sharp looker. Snappy apartment, sexually active when she can get it. Outgoing, friendly. She likes fashion, poetry, and music. Spends her money on clothes, good restaurants, salons. May or may not be looking for Mr. Right, but would really enjoy a Mr. Right Now."

"And," Roarke put in, "is adventurous enough to audition a candidate over drinks."

"Exactly. Date number two, solid middle-class suburban background. Shy, quiet, intellectual. Hoards what money she has to buy books, pay the rent on an efficiency apartment. Rarely eats out, and spends fifteen or twenty minutes every morning with a female neighbor old enough to be her grandmother. She has no other close friends in the city. She's very young and still a virgin. She's looking for a soul mate. The one man she's saved herself for."

"And is naive enough to believe she's found him without ever having met him."

"One is introverted, the other extroverted. Physically they are nothing alike. In the first case, the murder appeared to have been unplanned, and the killer panicked. There were no signs of violence on the body that were inflicted premortem. Sexual activity was vaginal only."

She picked up a disc from her file, slid it into her computer. "In the second case, the murder appeared to have been premeditated, and the killer was deliberate in the execution. There were signs of violence, bruises, small bites. The victim was repeatedly and roughly raped, and sodomized. It could be theorized that he became . . . encouraged, aroused, intrigued by the first murder and decided to have the experience again, purposefully, more aggressively this time as the act excited him."

With a nod, Roarke walked over to stand with her. "It could be."

"Image on wall screen," Eve ordered. "I've done a split screen with the security cam feed from the entrance of each victim's building. That's Bankhead on the right.

We know the killer is wearing a wig, face putty, and makeup. With this look he goes by the name Dante. On the left is Lutz, and there he goes by Dorian. The face jobs are good. Body type, height, more or less the same. Each can be altered easily enough—lifts, padding in the shoulders."

She'd already studied the images, over and over. She knew what she was seeing now.

"Note how Dante holds her hand, kisses her fingers, holds the door open for her. The perfect dream date. Dorian's got his arm around her waist. She's looking up at him, starry-eyed as they approach the door. He's not looking at her, no eye contact. It doesn't matter to him who she is. She's already dead."

She switched images. "Here, Dante's coming out. You can see the panic, the sweat. Christ, he's thinking, how did this happen? How will I get out of it? But you see here, the exit from Grace's place. The way he strolls out, almost a swagger, the way he looks back and smirks. He's thinking: That was fun. When can I do it again?"

"The first theory would hold," Roarke commented. "He's building confidence and need and pleasure. A second would be he has different personalities for different looks, for different women. But you've a third theory." Roarke looked away from the screen, looked at Eve. "You think you're after two men."

"Maybe it's too simple. Maybe it's what he wants me to think." She sat, stared at the split screen again. "I can't get inside him. I ran a probability on two killers. It came in just over forty-three percent."

"Computers don't have instincts." He came over to sit on the edge of the desk. "What do you see?"

"Different body language, different styles, different types. But it could be role-playing. Maybe he's an actor. Drinks at an expensive, romantic location, then the return to the victim's apartment. He doesn't dirty his own nest.

Candles, wine, music, roses. So he uses the same staging. I haven't got the results back on DNA, but the sweepers didn't find any fingerprints but the victim's and her neighbor's in Grace Lutz's apartment. Not on the wine bottle or the glasses, and not on her body. He sealed this time. Why is that, when he knew we'd have prints from the first murder?"

"If there are two—in reality or by personality split— they know each other intimately. Brothers of a sort," Roarke said when Eve looked over. "Partners. And this is a game."

"And they'd keep score. One each. They'd need a tie-breaker. I'm going to set up here to monitor some of the chat rooms where one of the screen names popped before."

"Do it from my office. My equipment's faster, and there's more of it. Plus," he added, knowing she was trying to think of a reason to refuse, "I can give you the list of the wine purchases."

"Can you cross-reference that with purchases of Castillo di Vechio Cabernet, forty-three?"

"I can," he agreed, pulling her to her feet. "If somebody keeps me company and has a glass of wine with me."

"One glass," she said and moved over into his office with him. "I may be at this for a while."

"Just plug in the locations you want to monitor on this unit."

She skirted the long black console, stood for a moment in front of one of his several sleek units. "I have to get them from the file."

"Computer. Access Unit Six, Eve." He perused the wine bottles in the rack behind his office bar. "Just enter the file name you want," he told Eve, "and request copy."

"Is there any point in saying that I keep official NYPSD data on my home unit, and you have no authorization to access that data?"

"None whatsoever. Something light, I think. Ah,

this." He drew out a bottle, turned, chuckled at her scowling face. "Why don't we have a bite to eat while we're at it?"

"Remind me to rag on you later."

He opened the bottle. "I'll make a note of it."

Chapter 7

She sipped wine, nibbled on caviar, and tried not to think how ridiculous it was. If anyone from Central caught wind of it, she'd never live it down.

Roarke did the same, and prepared to enjoy it. "Key in the screen names you want to watch for."

"DanteNYC," she said. "DorianNYC. Feeney's running names ending with NYC, but—"

"Yes, we can run another search. You'll end up with millions, I imagine, but we might get lucky."

"What about the account name? He may cruise with other screen names, or ditch the old ones when he's done."

"Here, nudge over." He scooted her chair a few inches to the left, then sat beside her. "Computer, run continuous search for all activity under account name La Belle Dame."

BEGINNING SEARCH . . .

"Feeney said you had to go through the privacy blocks and account protocol in order to . . ." She trailed off, lifted her glass when Roarke merely quirked his eyebrows in her direction. "Never mind."

"Computer, notify if and when activity under said account takes place, and locate source of activity."

SEARCH IN PROCESS. NOTIFICATION WILL BE GIVEN. WORKING . . .

"It can't be that simple."

"Not usually, no." He leaned over and kissed her. "Aren't you lucky to have me? A rhetorical question, darling," he said and stuffed caviar into her mouth. "Just let me put that consumer list on-screen."

He did so manually, with a few deft taps on a keyboard. Eve watched them scroll on, blew out a breath.

"It could be worse," she decided. "It could have been cheap wine, then we'd have, oh, a hundred times as many names."

"More than that, I imagine. We can break these down into individual sales and restaurant orders. Now we'll see what we can find on the Cabernet."

"Is that your label, too?"

"No, a competitor's. But there are ways. This will take a few minutes."

Because she thought it slightly tacky for a member of the NYPSD to sit and watch a civilian severely bend the law, she rose and wandered closer to the wall screen. "Computer, display single male consumers on screen four."

That whittled it down some more, she noted. She couldn't and wouldn't discount the restaurant, the female, and the joint accounts, but she'd start with the two hundred recorded sales to single men.

"Computer. Display, screen five, multiple purchases of product by single men. Better," she mumbled as the number went down by another eighty-six.

"You got that data yet?"

"Patience, Lieutenant." He glanced up, then just

looked at her in a way that made her skin tingle and her thigh muscles go loose.

"What?"

"You're such a study, standing there—all cop. Cool-eyed and grim with your weapon strapped on. It makes my mouth water." With a half laugh he went back to work. "Baffles me. Here you are, split on screen three."

"Do you say that sort of thing to get me stirred up?"

"No, but it's a pleasant side benefit. You're also quite a study when you're stirred up. My red edged out the competition's red by a few hundred sales in the area over the past twelve months."

"Big surprise," she said sourly, and turned around to repeat the same breakdown. "Computer, cross and match, all consumer purchases of both brands in given time period. Less than thirty." She pursed her lips. "I figured more."

"Label loyalty."

"We'll start with these. Standard run, eliminate males over fifty for a start. Our guy, or guys, are younger. Then I have to refactor. Could be daddy who buys the wine, or uncle, or big brother. Or," she added, glancing back at the screen with joint accounts. "Mom and Dad. But I don't think so." She began to pace. "I need Mira's profile, but I just don't think so. Seems to me it's not romantic, it's not sexual if your parent or parents buy the wine. Then you're a child again and you're, by Christ, a man and you can prove it.

"You can pluck a woman right out of the pack," she continued. "Pick of the litter, and your choice. Women are merciless, from the poem. They'll crush you if you give them the chance. So you won't. You're in charge this time."

She stared at the names, moved away from them, then back again. "Women. Bitches, whores, goddesses. You desire them, sexually, but more than that, you want power. Absolute power over them. So you plan, hunt, select. You've seen her, but she hasn't seen you. You have to see her, have to make absolutely certain she is attractive enough, that she hasn't created the fantasy of herself the same way you've created yourself. She has to be real. She has to be worthy. You wouldn't waste your time on anyone or anything that's less than you deserve."

Fascinated, Roarke sat back. "What does he do?"

"He selects. He arranges. He seduces with words, with images. Then he prepares. The wine. One that suits his taste, his mood. No one else's. Candles, scented to please his senses. The illegals, so that he has control. He won't be refused. More, he'll be desired. Desperately desired."

"Is it about sex?"

She shook her head, still studying names. "Desire. That's different. To be desired by his choice. That's as vital as his control over her. She *must* want him. He goes to too much trouble to make himself an object of desire for it to be only about control and power. He has a need to be the focus, the center because it's his moment. His game. His victory."

"His pleasure," Roarke added.

"Yes, his pleasure. But he needs her to think it's hers as well. He stands at the mirror and makes himself into what he'd like to be, and what he believes a woman wants. Dashing, sexy, stunningly handsome, but elegant. The kind of man who quotes poetry and woos with roses. The kind who makes that woman believe she's the only woman. Maybe he believes it. Or did, with the first one. Maybe he deluded himself into believing it was romance. But under it's calculation. He's a predator."

"Men are."

She glanced back. "That's right. Humans are, but sexually men are more basic. Sex is more easily viewed as a function where women, in general, prefer an emotional rush along with it. These women did, and he was aware of it. He took the time to know them first, to discover their weaknesses and their fantasies so he could play on both. Then he controlled them. Like a droid, only they were flesh and blood. They were real, so the thrill was real.

When it was over, they were spoiled. He'd made them whores again, so they stopped being worthy. He'll need to find the next."

"You were wrong when you said you couldn't get inside him. I wonder how you can be so much what you are and still look so clearly, so coldly, through the eyes of the mad and the vicious."

"Because I won't lose. I can't lose or they all win. Right back to my father."

"I know it." He rose, walked to her. Wrapped his arms tight around her. "I've never been sure if you did."

NOTIFICATION OF ACTIVITY, ACCOUNT LA BELLE DAME . . .

Eve jerked her body free, whirled. "Screen name of user and location of activity."

USER NAME OBERONNYC, LOCATION CYBER PERKS, FIFTH AVENUE AT FIFTY-EIGHTH . . .

She was running for the door when Roarke pulled it open. "I'll drive," he told her.

She didn't bother to argue. Any one of his vehicles would be faster than hers. She grabbed her communicator on the race down the steps.

"Dispatch, this is Dallas, Lieutenant Eve."

Detailing orders, she snagged her jacket and headed out the front door.

It took them six minutes and twenty-eight seconds from the notification to Roarke's swing to the curb in front of Cyber Perks. She timed it. And she was leaping out of the car before the brakes stopped squealing.

At a run, she spotted the black-and-white and the uniforms she'd ordered.

"No one leaves," she snapped, flipping out her badge, then sliding it shield out into the waistband of her trousers.

The noise blasted her the instant she walked through the doors. Cyber-punk rolled like a tidal wave, swamping the voices of patrons and beating violently against eardrums.

It was a world she'd yet to explore, and it was jammed elbow to groin with a motley throng who sat at counters, tables, cubes or airskated between stations. But even in the stupendous confusion, she saw the order.

Freaks with their painted hair and tongue rings were strewn across a section of color-coded table space. The geeks, earnest faces and sloppy shirts, were huddled in cubes. Giggly teenage girls skated in herds and pretended not to notice the packs of teenage boys they sought to allure.

There were students, most of whom were gathered in the café area trying to look sophisticated and world weary. Pocketed with them were a smatter of the standard urban revolutionaries, uniformed in sleek black, which students worshiped.

Scattered throughout were the tourists, the travelers, the casual clientele who sought the atmosphere, the experience, or were simply scoping out the place as a possible fresh hangout.

Where would her man fit?

Tracking the room, she strode to the glass kiosk marked Data Center. Three drones in red uniforms sat on swivel chairs in the center of the tower and worked consoles. They kept up what appeared to be a running conversation through headphones.

Eve zoned in on one, tapped on the glass. The boy, with a smattering of fresh pimples on his chin, looked up. He shook his head, attempted to look stern and authoritative, and gestured to the headphones on Eve's side of the glass.

She shoved them on.

"Don't touch the tower," he ordered in a voice that was just waiting to crack. "Stay behind the green line at all times. There are open units in the café. If you prefer,

there is currently one cube available. If you wish to re-
serve a unit for—"

"Kill the music."

"What?" His eyes darted like nervous birds. "Stay behind the green line or I'll call security."

"Kill the music," Eve repeated, then slapped her badge
on the glass. "Now."

"But—but I can't. I'm not allowed. Whatzamatter?
Charlie?" He whipped around in his chair. And all hell
broke loose.

The roar that burst out of the crowd outdid even the
computer-generated ferocity of the music. People leaped
off stools, out of cubes, screaming, shouting, cursing. A
wave of them charged the data kiosk like peasants
storming the king's palace. Full of fear and fury and
blood lust.

Even as she reached for her weapon, she took a way-
ward elbow on the chin that rapped her head back against
the kiosk and exploded a fountain of white, sizzling stars
in front of her eyes.

And that seriously pissed her off.

She kneed a green-haired freak in the groin, stomped
hard on the instep of a wailing geek, then fired three
blasts at the ceiling.

It served to stop most of the momentum, though several bodies tumbled or were simply flung in the general
direction of the kiosk.

"NYPSD!" She shouted it, holding up badge and
weapon. "Kill that fucking music. Now! Everybody back
off, go back to your seats or stations immediately or
you'll be charged with rioting, assault, and creating a
public hazard."

Not all of it got through, and some of her orders were
lost in the swarm of voices and threats. But the more
civic minded, or cowardly, slunk back.

One of the teenage girls lay sprawled at Eve's feet,
airskates tangled. She was bleeding from the nose and
weeping in jerky hiccoughs.

"You're okay." Eve nudged her as gently as she could with her foot. "Sit up now."

The shouts from various sections were gaining strength again. Civic duty and cowardice wouldn't hold on for long against mob passion.

"Nothing will be resolved until I have order, until I have quiet."

"This is a guaranteed virus-free zone," someone shouted. "I want to know what happened. I want to know who's responsible."

So, apparently, did a number of other people.

Roarke cleaved his way through the crowd. *Like,* Eve thought as she watched him, *a sleek blade slicing through a jumble of rock.*

"A virus was uploaded into the system," he said softly. "Corrupted the units. All of them, and from all appearances, simultaneously. You've got a couple hundred very angry people on your hands."

"Yeah, I got that part. Get out of here. Call for backup."

"I'm not leaving you in here, and don't waste your breath. Let me talk to them while you call in the troops."

Before she could argue, he began to speak. He didn't raise his voice. It was a good technique, Eve thought as she slipped out her communicator. A lot of people stopped yelling to try to hear what he was saying.

She could hear him fine, but she didn't understand half the cyber-speak he was rattling off.

"Lieutenant Dallas. I have a situation at Cyber Perks, Fifth Avenue, and require immediate assistance."

As she detailed the circumstances, she watched another portion of the mob quiet, slip back to tables. By her head count they were down to about fifty hard cases, spearheaded by the revolutionaries who were blathering about conspiracies and cyber-wars and communication terrorists.

It was time, she decided, to change tactics again. She

zeroed in on one man. Black shirt, black jeans, black boots, with a shock of gilded, deliberately disordered hair.

Eve stepped up in his face. "Maybe you didn't hear me tell you to go back to your table or station."

"This is a public place. It's my civil right to stand and speak."

"And it's within my authority to deny you that right when you use it to incite a riot. When you or anyone claiming that right is responsible for bodily harm or property damage." She gestured to the young girl who sat up, still weeping quietly as a friend mopped at the blood on her face. "They look like terrorists to you? Or him?" She jerked a thumb back to where the boy she'd spoken to had his terrified white face pressed against the kiosk glass.

"Pawns are used and discarded."

"Yeah, and kids get hurt because people like you want to masturbate your ego in public."

"The NYPSD is nothing but a soiled tool used by the hands of the right-wing bureaucrats and demigods to crush the will and freedom of the common man."

"Come on, stay on target. Is it communication terrorists and cyber-war or is it bureaucratic demigods? You can't cover all the bases at one time. Tell you what. You go sit down and I'll have somebody come over to listen to all your fascinating theories. But right now there are some people in here who require medical assistance. You're hampering that, and my investigation of what transpired here tonight."

He smirked at her. Always a mistake. "Why don't you finish violating my civil rights and arrest me?"

"Okay." She'd already planned her move, and had him cuffed before he could think to resist. "Next?" she asked, very pleasantly even as backup streamed in the door. He was shouting again as she passed him to a uniform.

"Not bad," Roarke commented. "For the soiled tool of right-wing demigods."

"Thanks. I need time to re-establish some order." She scanned the faces. "He's not here anymore."

"No," Roarke agreed. "He's not here. I'd say he was out before your uniforms arrived. Why don't I talk to the data crunchers? See what I can find out for you?"

"Appreciate it."

She interviewed and released the injured first, then sprang the under-twenty and over-fifty crowd. Out-of-towners came next, then the remaining women. Even as she took data, formed impressions, listed names, she was certain her bird had flown.

Left with staff, she set them in the café and joined Roarke at a private cube. The monitor of the unit was, like every other she'd seen, swimming with chaotic colors and strange symbols. Beside it was a tall mug of some fancy coffee mixture.

"Is this the source?" she asked him.

"It is, yes. I'll need to—"

"Don't touch anything!" She grabbed his wrist. "Don't—touch—anything," she repeated, then signalled a uniform. "I need a CS kit."

"We've only got minis in the patrols."

"That'll do. Then, Officer Rinksy," she added scanning his nameplate, "you can inform the guy in charge around here that this joint is closed by order of the NYPSD until further notice."

"Won't that be fun?" With surprising cheer, Rinksy walked off to get the kit.

"I wasn't," Roarke said when she turned back to him, "going to touch anything. This is hardly my first day on the job, Lieutenant."

"Don't get pissy. And it's my job, not yours. How do you know this is the source?"

He circled his fingers, examined his manicure. "I'm sorry." He smiled absently. "Did you say something? I'm just biding time, waiting to take my lovely wife home when she finishes work."

"Jeez. Okay, okay, sorry I jumped on you. I'm a little tense. Would you tell me, since you're so brave and strong and smart, how you know this is the source?"

"That would've sounded better if you hadn't had your lip curled, but it'll do. I know this is the source because by tracking through the central system, I traced the virus to its starting point. This unit was the first infected, and the virus was programmed to self-clone and, I suspect, slither into central, spread to all interfaced units, then erupt in a nearly simultaneous burst. It's very clever."

"Great."

Rinsky stepped up beside her again. "Your kit, Lieutenant."

"Thanks." She took the kit, opened it. She coated her hands with Seal-It first, then passed the can to Roarke. "Don't touch anything yet." She took out a wand, shined its pencil-thin beam and washed cool blue light over the coffee mug. "Gotta good thumbprint. Yeah, partial index finger. You got your palm unit on you?"

"Always."

"Can you access the casefile? I need to compare these latents."

While he did as she asked, Eve shined the light over the table surface. Too many prints, she mused, most of them smeared.

"Lieutenant?" Roarke held out a small printout of the casefile prints.

She grunted, then held the printed copy against the latent on the mug. "That's our boy. Hold on." Using the wand she picked up the mug, balanced it with a sealed finger on the base, then poured the coffee mixture into an evidence bag. "Why do people screw up perfectly good coffee with all that froth and flavors?" She sealed the bag, then tipped the cup into a second, sealed that. "Question."

"Ask it."

"How did he know we were coming? He had to know. That's why he uploaded the virus. We were here minutes after notification, but he tagged us, dumped the germ and danced. How?"

"I have a theory, but I'd prefer exploring it a bit first."

She shifted her weight. "Exploring how?"

"I need to open this unit."

She debated. Strict procedure meant she could, and likely should, roust either Feeney or McNab and haul them over to check out the unit on site. Or she could call in another EDD tech.

But Roarke was here.

If he'd been a cop, he'd have been commanding EDD by this time.

"Consider yourself field drafted as an expert consultant, civilian."

"I've always liked the ring of that." He slid a small case out of his inside pocket, then wiggled his sealed fingers. "I'm touching things now."

He used a microdrill and had the casing removed in seconds. Then he let out a little *hmmm* and began to probe. "There are three system levels in this club," he said conversationally. "This is the highest level and costs from one to ten dollars a minute depending on the number of functions utilized."

Her stomach sank. "Is this your club?"

"It is, yes." He continued to work, hooking his PPC to the unit with a hair-thin cable. "But that's neither here nor there. Unless you consider that you'll have no bitching and moaning from the owner about tonight's little adventure—or the impounding of this unit as evidence." He glanced up once, just a sweep of her face with those amused blue eyes. "Less paperwork for you."

"You know how those right-wing bureaucratic demigods are. They feed on paperwork."

"You've a bruise gathering on your jaw."

"Yeah." She rubbed her thumb over the ache. "Shit."

"Hurt?"

"I bit my tongue. That hurts more. You?"

"Nothing major. This system is corrupted, and very thoroughly. Clever boy," he reflected. "Clever, clever boy. You'll need to run a full diagnostic, but it appears you have a top-level tech on your hands, and one who believes in being prepared. It isn't a simple matter to rig a public unit to notify a user of a search on his account. He had a portable scanner, highly sensitive, I'd say, interfaced it. Very cautious, very smart."

"Can you get around it?"

"Eventually. The units in this club are designed quite well to shut down and lock at any attempt at contamination. There's an internal detector and filtering system as backup. Despite that, he managed to upload a virus that wiped this unit, and every other in here. And it did it in minutes, after detecting a shield notification."

She leaned back. "You sound impressed."

"Oh, I am. Considerably impressed. Your man has a brilliant talent. A pity, really, that he's as corrupt and worthless as this unit."

"Yeah. Breaks my heart." She stood up. "I'm going to spring the staff, have the unit impounded and sent to EDD. Once we're cleared out, I want a look at security. Let's see what he looked like tonight."

He looked, Eve decided, smug. She caught it in the way his eyes drifted over the crowd—dismissing, smirking even while he kept a pleasant, inoffensive smile on his face.

He walked through the crowd, kept himself removed from them. No contact, no casual greetings. And moved directly to the cube that put his back to the wall, and kept his view of the room unobstructed.

"He's been here before," Eve noted.

None of the staff had been able to confirm that. Then again, the manager had been so flustered—not by the police intervention, not even by the near-riot, but, she remembered, by the realization that Roarke was in the club—that he'd had a hard time sputtering out his own name.

The unit and cube had been reserved under the name R. W. Emerson. An alias, she had no doubt, and the name, she'd learned after a quick run, of a long-dead poet.

His hair was a smooth, warm brown mane tonight, and he wore square-framed glasses of tinted amber. She supposed his attire was casual trendy with the dark pegged pants, the ankle boots, the long, hip-swishing shirt in the same amber hue as his lenses. There was a gold cuff bracelet on his right wrist and a curve of winking studs along the shell of his ear.

He ordered the coffee first, made a call on his pocket 'link. Then he drank a little while he continued to watch the room.

"He's making sure the environment's stable," Eve said. "And he's hunting. Tracking the women, considering them. You can message to any other unit in the club, right? Isn't that one of the deals why people go instead of just staying home and scoping the 'net in peace?"

"Another way of socializing," Roarke confirmed. "Excitingly anonymous, even voyeuristic. You message a unit across the room, can watch their reaction, decide if you want to take it to the next step and make personal contact. Units are equipped with a standard privacy shield for those who don't want to be disturbed. Or hit on."

She watched her suspect log on, and choose manual instead of voice mode.

"There." Roarke touched her arm, then ordered the screen to zoom in, to enlarge a sector. "The scanner."

She saw what looked like a small, slim, silver business card case. He drew a thin, retractable cable out of the corner, plugged it into the side port of the unit.

"Oh, he is very, very good. I've never seen one that compact," Roarke told her. "Odds are he made it himself. I wonder—"

"Think about your research-and-development potential later," she ordered. "Bang. He's made us."

His body went rigid, his face slack. He didn't look so smug and superior in that instant. He looked shocked, and he looked scared. The eyes behind the fashionable lenses were jittery as they darted around the room.

He pulled the scanner out, then curled over the keyboard with the earnest devotion and intensity of the classic compugeek.

"Coding in the virus," Roarke said quietly. "He's sweating, but he knows what he's doing. Uploading it."

He was shaking. He rubbed the back of his hand repeatedly over his lips. But he sat where he was, his gaze glued to the monitor. Then he was up, leaving his barely touched coffee, and hurrying for the door recklessly enough to run into tables, bump into people.

He was nearly running by the time he made the door. Eve saw him swing his body to the right before he disappeared and the door closed behind him.

"Out. Out and gone in what, under two minutes. Bolted a good minute before the uniforms responded and arrived on scene."

"Ninety-eight seconds by the clock," Roarke concurred. "He's fast. He's very fast."

"Yeah, he's fast, but he's shook. He was heading uptown. And he was running scared—for home."

Chapter 8

It took him nearly an hour to stop shaking. An hour, two whiskeys, and the calmer Lucias added to the second drink.

"It shouldn't have happened. It shouldn't have been possible."

"Pull yourself together, Kevin." Lucias took out a cigarette he'd laced with just a whiff of Zoner. He lighted it, crossed his ankles. "And think. How did it happen?"

"They managed to dig under to the account name. The shielded account name."

Irritably, Lucias pulled in smoke. "You told me that would take them weeks."

"I underestimated them, obviously." Annoyance shimmered over nerves. "It can't be traced back to us in any case. But even having the account name, how could they trace me to that location, and so quickly? The police don't have the facilities, the manpower, the equipment to surveil every cyber-club in the city, and every unit in them. Then there are the matters of the privacy blocks, the standard one and the ones I implemented."

Lucias drew in smoke, then expelled it in a lazy stream. "What are the odds they just got lucky?"

"Nil," Kevin said between his teeth. "They used both superior equipment and a superior tech." He shook his head. "Why in God's name would anybody with those skills settle for a cop's salary? In the private sector, he or she could name any price."

"It takes all kinds, doesn't it? Well, this is exciting."

"Exciting? I might have been caught. Arrested. Charged with murder."

The Zoner, as always, was doing the job. "But you weren't." Willing to placate, Lucias leaned over, patted Kevin's knee. "However smart and skilled they are, we're more so. You'd anticipated this sort of possibility, and prepared for it. You infected an entire club. Very sweet. You'll be headlined in the media again." He sighed. "More points for you."

"They'll have me on security cam." Kevin inhaled slowly, exhaled slowly. In many ways, Lucias was his drug of choice, and his approval smoothed over the worst of the nerves. "I might not have altered my look if I hadn't been using a club so close by."

"Fate." Lucias began to laugh, and drew an answering grin from his friend. "It's really just fate, isn't it? And all on our side. Really, Kev, it just gets better and better. You'll take care of the account? Generate another?"

"Yes. Yes, that's no problem." Kevin shrugged that off. There was nothing he couldn't do with electronics. "They've made a great many details public, Lucias. The chat rooms, the setup. We may want to stop for a time."

"Just when it's getting interesting? I don't think so. The higher the risk, the greater the thrill. Now, at least, we know we've pitted ourselves against an adversary or adversaries that are worthy of our efforts. It adds such a flavor. Savory."

"I could keep the account open," Kevin mused. "Send out some decoys."

"Ah!" Lucias slapped a hand on the arm of his chair.

"Now you're in the game. Just think of it. Think of when you have your rendezvous tomorrow night. Why, you and the lovely lady can discuss this recent horror over drinks. She shivers, delicately, over the fate of her doomed sisters. Never knowing she's fated to join them. God, it's delicious."

"Yes." The whiskey and the drug cruised inside him, turned the air he breathed into soft liquid. "It does add to the thrill."

"One thing for certain, we're not bored."

Amused now, Kevin reached over to take a hit from the laced cigarette. "And unlikely to be for some time. I know just what I'll wear tomorrow. Just how I'll look. She's so sexy. Moniqua. Even her name reeks of sex." He hesitated, hating to disappoint. "I don't know if I can go through to the end of it, Lucias. I don't know if I can kill her."

"You can. You will. One doesn't drop back a level of achievement." He smiled when he spoke. "Think of it, Kevin. You'll know, the whole time you're touching her naked body, while you bury yourself in her, that you'll be the last one to do so. That your dick pumping inside her is the last thing she'll ever know."

Kevin went hard thinking of it. "I suppose there's something to be said for the fact she'll die happy."

Lucias's laughter bounced cold around the room.

Since she was always trying to lose weight, Peabody got off the subway six blocks down from the stop nearest Eve's home. She was feeling pretty peppy about meeting at the home office site again, where the AutoChef was a treasure trove of wonders.

Another reason, she admitted, for the hike. Sort of penance before the sin. It was a solution that appealed to her Free-Ager's sensibilities. Of course in the tenants of Free-Agism there was no sin and penance, but imbalance and balance.

But that was really just semantics.

She'd grown up in a big, unwieldy family who'd believed in self-expression, had a reverence for the earth and the arts and a responsibility to be true to oneself.

She had known, it seemed she'd almost always known, that to be true to herself she needed to be an urban cop who tried to maintain . . . well, balance, she supposed.

She was sort of missing her family right now though. The bursts of love and surprise. And hell, the simplicity of it all. Maybe she needed to take a few days and go sit in her mother's kitchen, eat sugar cookies, and soak up some uncomplicated affection.

Because she didn't know what in God's name was *wrong* with her. Why she felt so sad and unsettled and dissatisfied. She had the one thing she'd wanted most in life. She was a cop, a damn good cop, under the direct command of a woman she considered the ultimate in examples.

She'd learned so much in the past year. Not just about technique, not just about procedure, but about what made the difference between that good cop and a brilliant one.

About what separated the ones who wanted to close a case from the ones who took it a level deeper, and cared about the victim. Who remembered them.

She knew she was getting better at the job every day, and she could take pride in that. She loved living in New York, seeing its face change and shift as you moved from block to block.

The city was so *full*, she thought. Of people, of energy, of action. While she could go back and sit in that homey kitchen, she'd never be content living there again. She needed New York.

She was happy in her little apartment, where the space was all her own. She had steady comrades, good friends, a worthy and satisfying career.

She was dating, well, sort of dating, one of the most incredibly handsome, considerate, sophisticated men she'd ever known. He took her to galleries, to the opera, to amazing restaurants. Through Charles, she'd been exposed to not just another side of the city, but of life.

And she lay in bed at night, staring at the ceiling and wondering why she felt so lonely.

She needed to pull out of it. Depression did *not* run in her family, and she wasn't going to be the first to spiral down into it.

Maybe she needed a hobby. Like glass painting or container gardening. Holographic photography. Macrame.

Fuck it.

It was just that thought in her head when McNab popped out of the subway glide and all but collided with her.

"Hey." He took a jerky step back even as she did. Stuck his hands in his pockets.

"Hey." Could her timing have been worse? she wondered. She couldn't have walked a little faster, a little slower? Left home five minutes earlier, two minutes later?

They frowned at each other for a moment, then had to move or be mowed down by the commuters flooding off the glide and onto the sidewalk.

"So." He pulled his hands out of his pockets to adjust the fit of the tiny, round sunshades with aqua blue lenses. "Dallas called for the home office deal."

"I got the update."

"Sounds like she got some action last night," he continued, struggling to keep it all mild and easy. "Too bad that creep didn't drop into Cyber Perk the other night when we were there. We might've made him."

"Unlikely."

"Try a little optimism, She-Body."

"Try a little reality, jerk-face."

"Wake up on the wrong side of slick-boy's bed?"

She heard her own teeth grind. "There is no wrong

side of Charles's bed," she said sweetly. "It's a big, soft, round playpen."

"Oh yeah?" Half the circuits in his brains fried at the image of Peabody romping naked in some plush, sexy bed. With someone else.

"That's just the sort of quick repartee I've come to expect from you. You must be sharpening your wits on all those bimbos you're bouncing on these days."

"The last bimbo had a doctorate from MIT, the body of a goddess, and the face of an angel. We didn't spend much time on wit-sharpening."

"Pig."

"Bitch." He grabbed her arm as she swung toward Roarke's gate. "I'm getting fed up with the way you slap at me every time I get within striking distance, Peabody. You're the one who put the brakes on."

"Not soon enough." She tugged, but his grip stayed firm. She always underestimated those skinny arms of his. It was mortifying to realize the strength in them had her stomach doing cartwheels. "And as usual you're wrong and you're stupid. You're the one who ended things because you couldn't have everything your way."

"Right. Excuse me for objecting to the fact you'd roll out of my bed and roll into the whore's."

She rammed a fist into his chest. "Don't call him that. You don't know anything about it, and if you had one tenth of Charles's class, his charm, his consideration, you'd crawl up to subhuman. But since you don't I should thank you for putting the skids on what was a ridiculous, embarrassing, and revolting mistake on my part by ever letting you lay a hand on me. So thanks!"

"You're welcome."

They were panting, wild-eyed and nose to nose. Then they were moaning and mouth to mouth. They jerked apart, still wild-eyed.

"That didn't mean anything," she managed between gasps.

"Right. It didn't mean anything. So let's do it again."

He yanked her back, sank his teeth greedily into her bottom lip. It was, she thought, dizzying, like being shot out of a cannon. Her ears were ringing, her breath and balance gone. And all she wanted was to run her hands all over his long, bony body.

She settled for his butt, digging her fingers in as if she could twist off a nice little chunk to keep in her pocket.

He spun her around, struggling to get his hands under the stiff, starched jacket of her uniform. Under it, he knew her body was a wonder of curves and soft, yielding flesh. Desperate for it, he shoved her back, through the gate sensors and rapped her smartly against the iron bars.

"Ow."

"Sorry. Let me—God." He buried his mouth against her neck and wondered if he could just slurp her up like ice cream.

"I beg your pardon." The voice came from nowhere, from everywhere, and had them both goggling at each other.

"Did you say something?" she asked.

"No? Did you?"

"Officer. Detective."

Still in midgrope, they both slid their eyes to the right and stared at the security panel on the stone pillar. Summerset, his face expressionless, stared back out from the view screen.

"I believe the lieutenant is expecting you," he said, coolly polite. "If you take a step back from the gate, you're less likely to fall through them when they're opened."

Peabody felt her own face flame like a scorched tomato. "Oh man. Oh shit." She shoved McNab, stepped clear, then began to tug her uniform back into place. "That was just stupid."

"Felt good though." Somehow his kneecaps had become detached so that the first steps he took through the open gate were wobbly and disjointed. "What the hell, Peabody."

"Just because we've got this . . . chemical reaction, doesn't mean we have to act on it. It just screws things up."

He danced in front of her, walking backward. His long, sleek ponytail bobbed from side to side. His thin jacket billowed to his knees and was the color of field poppies. Despite all her good intentions, her lips twitched into a smile.

"You're so damn goofy."

"Why don't we get a pizza tonight? See where it goes."

"We know where it went," she reminded him. "We don't have time to do this now, McNab. We don't have time to think about it."

"I think about you all the time."

That stopped her, dead in her tracks. It was tough to walk when your heart had bounced to your shoes. "You're messing me up."

"That's the plan. A pizza, She-Body? I know how you are for pizza."

"I'm on a diet."

"What for?"

The fact that he could ask, sincerely, had always charmed and baffled her. "Because my ass is approaching the same mass as Pluto."

He circled around her as they hiked up the long curve of the drive. "Come on. You've got a great ass. It's *there*. A guy doesn't have to spend half his time looking for it."

He gave it an affectionate squeeze, earned a narrowed, warning look, and grinned. He knew when he was making headway. "We'll just eat and talk. No sex."

"Maybe. I'll think about it."

He remembered what Roarke had advised him about romance. In a quick dash, he loped around the lawn, snapped a blossom from an ornamental pear. He caught up with Peabody at the steps, and slid the flower through the top buttonhole of her jacket.

"Jeez," she muttered, but she strode into the house without taking the flower out.

She was very careful to avoid direct eye contact with Summerset. And very aware of the heat creeping up her neck as he invited them to go straight up to Eve's office.

Eve stood in the center of the room, rocking lightly on her heels as she watched the security tape again. The man was smug, she thought. And aloof. He enjoyed casting that amused glance over the crowd in the cyber-café, thinking everyone in there was less than he. Knowing he had a secret.

But he also dressed to draw attention. Admiration and envy. So those who saw him understood he was more.

He thought ahead. Was so cocksure nothing and no one could touch him. But when things had gone wrong, there was fear and panic.

She watched the sweat dew on his face as he stared at the monitor in his cube. And she could see him, easily see him, heaving the lifeless body of Bryna Bankhead off the balcony. *Get rid of the problem,* she mused. *The inconvenience, the threat. Then run away.*

She couldn't see him following through the very next night with another woman. With deliberate intent and cold blood.

She turned as Peabody and McNab came in. "Run this guy's image front, back, and sideways," she ordered. "Concentrate on the facial structure, the eyes—shape, not color—and body type. Forget the hair, odds are it's not his."

"You have a bruise on your jaw, sir."

"Yeah, and you have a flower in your buttonhole. So we both look stupid. Dickhead came through on the wigs and enhancements. I've got the brand names. You chase down outlets on them, Peabody, get me a consumer list.

Cross-reference it with the one I've got on the wine. Roarke's getting me a list of the top shops for men in the city."

"Roarke has got it for you." He stepped into the office, held out a disc. "Good morning, class."

"Thanks." She passed it off to Peabody. "Our guy likes the good stuff. Designer shoes, tailored wardrobe. What do you call it?"

"Bespoke," Roarke supplied. "While he may purchase directly from London or Milan, the first suit was definitely British cut," he added. "The second certainly Italian, he'd· be likely to patronize some of the high-end shops here in New York."

"Taking our fashion advisor at his word," Eve said dryly, "we run it through, see if anything pops. Unless he's got his own greenhouse, he's buying those pink roses from somewhere. Probability's high it's in his own neighborhood, and I'm betting that neighborhood is either Upper West Side or Upper East Side, so we look there first."

She glanced over, momentarily surprised when Roarke gave her a mug of fresh, hot coffee. "I've got a consult with Mira here in an hour. Feeney's at Central, directing the exam of the unit we impounded from Cyber Perks. I want answers, I want a trail, and I want it today. Because he's going to move again tonight. He has to."

She turned back to the screen where the killer's face sneered out at the crowd. "He's already got his next target."

She walked over to a board where she'd pinned photographs of both victims, the computer images of the killer as he'd looked before and after each murder.

"She'll be young," Eve said. "Early- to mid-twenties. She'll live alone. She'll be attractive and intelligent with an affection for poetry. She'll be romantic, and not currently in any serious relationship. She lives in the city. Works in the city. He's already seen her, studied her on the street or at her job. She may have spoken to him and not known he was the man who's been seducing her. She's probably thinking about tonight, about this date she has with a man who's exactly what she's waited for. In a few hours, she thinks, I'll meet him. And maybe, just maybe . . ."

She turned away from the board. "Let's keep her alive. I don't want to see another face on this board."

"A moment of your time, Lieutenant?" Roarke gestured to his office, stepped out himself before she could put him off.

"Look, I'm on the clock here."

"Then why waste time." He shut the door behind her. "I can get you those consumer lists, have them cross-referenced and complete in a fraction of the time it would take Peabody."

"Haven't you got work?"

"Considerable, yes. It would still take me less time." He skimmed a fingertip over the bruise on her jaw, then lightly along the shallow dent in her chin. "I find I prefer having my mind fully occupied just now. And," he added. "I'd rather not see another face on your murder board either. I intend to do it anyway, but I thought you might feel less annoyed if I made the pretense of asking."

She scowled at him, folded her arms. "Pretense?"

"Yes, darling." He kissed the bruise. "And this way, as you know what I'm up to, it frees you to have Peabody along with you in the field, wherever that might be." His in-house communication panel beeped. "Yes?"

"A Dr. Dimatto is here to see Lieutenant Dallas."

"Send her up," Eve ordered. "Do what you're going to do," she told Roarke. "But for right now I'm going with the pretense that I don't know about it."

"Whatever works for you. I'm just going to take a minute to set some things up. Then I'd like to say hello to Louise."

"Suit yourself." She opened the door, glanced back. "You generally do."

"That's what makes me such a contented man."

She gave a rude snort and crossed into her office to greet Louise.

She came in fast, but Eve had rarely seen her move another way. She took one look at the coffee in Eve's hand and smiled. "Yes, I'd love some, thanks."

"Peabody, coffee for Dr. Dimatto. Anything else we can get you?"

Louise stared at the danish McNab was currently trying to swallow whole. "Is that an apple danish?"

With his mouth stuffed, he made some sound, a mixture of affirmation, pleasure, and guilt.

"Love one, too, thanks again."

Eve swept a glance over Louise's snappy red suit. "You don't look dressed for seeing patients, Doc."

"I have a meeting. Fund-raiser." Diamonds twinkled at her ears when she tilted her head. "You tend to squeeze out more money when you look like you don't need it. Go figure. In any case . . . thank you, Peabody. Mind if I sit?" She did, crossing her legs, balancing the plate with the danish expertly on her knee as she took her first sip of coffee.

She heaved a long sigh before she sipped again. "Where do you get this stuff? It has to be illegal."

"Roarke."

"Naturally." She broke off a tidy corner of the danish.

"Have you got a reason for dropping by, Louise, other than a little coffee break? We're a little busy here."

"I'm sure you are." She nodded toward the board. "I asked about Bryna Bankhead in my building. She knew everyone on her floor, and several others. She was very well liked. She'd lived there three years. She dated fairly regularly, but no one serious."

"I know all that. Thinking of giving up medicine for police work?"

"She lived there for three years," Louise repeated, and the humor had died from her voice. "I've lived there for two. She fell on the sidewalk at my feet. I'd never had a conversation with her."

"Feeling guilty over that won't change what happened to her."

"No." Louise broke off another bite. "But it made me think. And it made me more inclined to work harder to get any information for you that might help your investigation. There was a research project at J. Forrester. That's a private, fairly exclusive clinic that specializes in sexual dysfunctions, relations, fertility issues. Nearly twenty-five years ago, J. Forrester formed a partnership with Allegany Pharmaceuticals to research, study, and develop various chemical products that could alleviate dysfunction and enhance performance, sexually speaking. Many top chemists and R and D people were involved or associated with the project."

"Testing with elements found in the controlled substances known as Whore and Wild Rabbit."

"Those, others, combinations. They did, in fact, develop the drug trademarked as Matigol, which has helped extend sexual performance ability in men well past the century mark, and the fertility drug Compax, which allows women to safely conceive and give birth into their fifties should they desire it."

She nibbled on the danish. "Both these drugs have a very high success rate, but are extremely expensive and therefore largely inaccessible to your average consumer. But for those who can afford it, they're a miracle."

"Do you have the names of the players?"

"I'm not finished." She turned her head, shot out a sunny smile as Roarke walked in. "Good morning."

"Louise." He went to her, lifted her hand to his lips. "You look lovely, as always."

"Yeah, yeah, blah blah. What?" Eve demanded. "What else?"

"Your wife is rude and impatient."

"That's why I love her. By the way, Lieutenant, Charles Monroe is on his way upstairs."

"What is this? A convention?" But as she spoke she aimed one hard, warning look at McNab. His eyes glittered back at her, and he managed to hold the look for a good five seconds before he dropped his gaze, sulkily. "You, get me some data on J. Forrester and Allegany Pharmaceuticals."

She clenched her jaw, which sent it throbbing as she caught the interest flicker over Roarke's face. "Damn it."

"I bought out Allegany, eight, no, I believe it was ten months ago. What's the connection?"

"I don't know precisely, because the doc here's being coy."

"I'm never coy," Louise corrected, then her eyes blurred almost as they had when she'd taken her first sip of coffee. "Oh, well," she said as Charles walked in. "My, my."

"I guess you want coffee, too," Eve said.

He nodded. "I wouldn't say no."

"I'll get it." Flustered, flushing, floundering, Peabody escaped into the kitchen.

"Roarke. McNab." With the second greeting, Charles's practiced smile dimmed slightly. Then it polished right up again when he aimed it at Louise. "I don't believe we've met."

"Louise. Louise Dimatto." She offered a hand.

"Don't tell me you're a cop."

"Doctor. You?"

If he heard McNab's muttered opinion, Charles ignored it. "Professional companion."

"How interesting."

"Can we save the social hour for later? We'll have a damn party. Everybody's invited," Eve snapped. "I'll get to you," she said to Charles. "Finish it out, Louise."

"Where was I? Oh yes. Despite the success in development, the project and the partnership were dissolved some twenty years ago. Lack of funds, lack of interest, and a number of unfortunate side effects from other experimental drugs during that period. It was decided that further research using forms of those particular chemicals was both cost-prohibitive and potentially financially risky due to threats of legal action. The decision was largely influenced by Dr. Theodore McNamara, who, in essence, headed the project and is credited for the discovery of both Compax and Matigol. There were unsubstantiated rumors of abuse and pilfering during the project. Talk of experimentation not only in the lab, but out of it. Gossip is that some of the suits filed were internal, female staff who claimed to have been given drugs without their knowledge or consent and were sexually molested, perhaps impregnated, while under the influence. If it's true," Louise concluded, "nobody in the know is naming names."

"Good work. I'll follow it up. If you've got a meeting—"

"I've got a little time. I'll just finish my coffee, if it's all the same to you. In fact, I'll just help myself to another half cup."

She breezed into the kitchen.

"Okay, Charles. You're up."

He nodded at Eve, grinned intimately at Peabody when she brought him his coffee. "My client believes I wanted this information for another client. I'd like to keep it that way."

"I protect my sources, Charles."

"And I believe in protecting my clients," he returned. "I need your word that no action will be taken against her if what I tell you ends up exposing her."

"She doesn't interest me. And if all she's doing is making herself horny, I'll make sure she doesn't interest Illegals. Fair enough?"

"Sex isn't easy for everyone, Dallas."

"If people didn't want to get off," McNab shot out, "you'd be out of work."

Charles smirked at McNab. "True enough. If people didn't want to steal, cheat, maim, and kill, so would you be, Detective. Aren't we all lucky human nature keeps us in business?"

Eve stepped between the chair where Charles sat and the desk where McNab worked, effectively blocking their view of each other. "Give me the dealer, Charles. Nobody wants to bust your client."

"Carlo. They don't use last names. She met him in a chat room, one on sexual experimentation."

Eve eased onto the corner of the desk. "Is that so?"

"About a year ago. She said he's changed her life."

"How do the buys work?"

"Initially, she'd e-mail him, place an order. She'd pay with an electronic transfer of funds into his account, then pick up the delivery at a mail drop at Grand Central."

"No personal contact?"

"None. Now she's on what she calls a subscription service and receives a regular monthly supply. The payment, with the subscription discount, is automatically transferred from her account to his. Five thousand a month for a quarter ounce."

"I need to talk to her."

"Dallas—"

"And here's why. I need his account data, and anything else she can tell me. She does regular business with him, so she'd have a feel. More than that, she needs to be put on guard. She could be a target."

"She's not." He rose as Eve came off the desk. "Those are your victims?" He gestured to the board. "What are they, twenty, twenty-five? This woman is over fifty. She's attractive, she takes care of herself, but she doesn't have that bloom. Media reports said they were single, lived alone. She's married. Her association with me is a perk. Like a day at the salon. She lives with her husband and

her teenage son. And being questioned by you on this
will embarrass and humiliate her, and her family."

"It may also damage her sexual ego," Louise put in.
She stood across the room, sipping her second cup of
coffee. "The use of the drug and a professional companion have most likely shorn some dysfunction in this area.
Exposing her need for them to an authority who could
deny and punish her for the first, and smirk at her for the
second, isn't advisable from a medical or psychological
standpoint."

"Protecting her from that exposure runs the risk of
slapping another dead woman on that board."

"Let me talk to her again," Charles asked. "I'll get the
information you need. Better, I'll open an account with
him, at my own expense. He's only got to do a standard
background to verify my license. An LC's a reasonable
client for sexual illegals."

"Get me the data by three o'clock," Eve decided.
"Don't do anything else. I don't want him to have your
name."

"You don't have to worry about me, Lieutenant
Sugar."

"Just the data, Charles. Now go away."

"I need to get along myself. Thanks for the coffee."
Louise set the cup down, glanced at Charles. "Want to
share a cab?"

"Perfect." He trailed a fingertip over the flower in
Peabody's buttonhole as he turned for the door. "I'll see
you later, Delia."

"Keep it zipped, McNab," Eve warned. "Peabody,
Roarke is generating some data. You'll assist in his office." Which should, she hoped, keep the peace for a
while. She glanced at her wrist unit, thought of Mira.
"I've got a meeting."

Chapter 9

She set up in the library because it was quiet and in another section of the house. Mostly, unless it related to a case, she liked to remain as oblivious as possible to emotional vibrations. But there'd been so many of them winging around in her office, she'd been tempted to duck and cover.

Here, the air was smooth and placid. She settled down at one of the desks, input the fresh data into the file.

"Computer, factoring new data, run probability scan on subject Carlo as alias for suspect."

WORKING . . . PROBABILITY SUBJECT CARLO AS ALIAS FOR SUSPECT IS NINETY-SIX-POINT-TWO PERCENT.

"Yeah, that's what I think. Second run. Probability subject Carlo manufactures illegals he subsequently sells."

WORKING . . . INSUFFICIENT DATA FOR SCAN. REQUEST FURTHER INPUT TO COMPLETE.

"That's where you're wrong." She pushed away from the desk to pace on the faded roses on the antique rug. "He makes it, he bottles it, he sells it, he uses it. Control. It's all about control. Sixty thousand a year from one client for what, three ounces of that shit? Troll the 'net, hook a couple dozen rich marks, and you're rolling. But it's not about the money."

She stalked to one of the rows of tall, arched windows, flipped the drape, and stared out over the vast blooming estate. Even for Roarke, who'd been desperately poor, achingly hungry, it wasn't about the money so much as it was about the game of compiling it, *having* it, using it to make more of it.

And wielding the power of it.

But this was about neither greed nor need.

"Twenty k an ounce, and you slip a quarter of that into the first victim, *after* she's alone with you, helpless and naked in her apartment. *After* you've already poured more than two ounces of Whore into her. Computer, street value, illegal Whore."

WORKING . . . HORMONIBITAL-SIX, COMMONLY KNOWN AS WHORE, STREET VALUE SIXTY-FIVE-THOUSAND USD PER FLUID OUNCE. KNOWN STREET USE OF THIS SUBSTANCE IS NEGLIGIBLE. DERIVATIVE, EXOTICA, IS COMMON. STREET VALUE EXOTICA, FIFTY USD PER FLUID OUNCE. DO YOU REQUIRE LISTING OF OTHER COMMON DERIVATIVES?

"Negative. Derivatives aren't good enough for this guy. No clones, no substitutes, no weak sisters. Date cost him about a hundred and fifty thousand. You could buy ten of the best LCs in New York for that and have a hell of a party. But it's not about money, and it's not about sex. They're only factors in the game."

"I wonder why you think you need me," Mira said from the doorway.

Eve turned. "Thinking out loud."

"So I heard."

"I appreciate you coming out here," Eve began. "I know you're busy."

"And so are you. I always love coming into this room." Mira glanced around at the walls of books that dominated the two-level room. "Civilized luxury," she commented. "You've hurt your face."

"Oh." Eve rubbed her knuckles along her jaw. "It's nothing."

Mira's face was, Eve always thought, perfect. Serene and lovely, framed by a smooth sweep of sable hair. She wore one of her quiet and elegant suits that looked like it had been formed out of cool, fresh limes. The long gold chain around her neck was as thick as Eve's pinky and enhanced with a single cream-colored pearl.

She smelled of apricots and her skin was baby smooth as she brushed her lips lightly over Eve's jaw.

"Habit," she said, and her blue eyes smiled easily at the line that formed between Eve's. "Kissing hurts to make them better. Shall we sit?"

"Yeah. Sure." She never quite knew how to handle Mira's maternal attitude toward her. Mothers were a mystery with too many of the pieces missing to attempt to form a picture. "You'll want tea."

"I'd love some."

Because she knew Mira's habits, she programmed for a cup of the fragrant herbal brew Mira favored. And because she was in her own space, Eve programmed the second cup for coffee.

"How are you, Eve?"

"I'm okay."

"Still not getting enough sleep," Mira commented when Eve brought her tea.

"I get by."

"On caffeine and nerves. How is Roarke?"

"He's—" She started to pass it off. But this was Mira. "What happened with Mick Connelly's still weighing on him some. He's dealing with it, but it's, I don't know. . . . It's knocked him off stride some."

"Grief levels us. We go on, we do what's necessary, but there's a shadow on the heart. Knowing you're there for him lightens the shadow."

"He's horned in on the investigation, and I haven't given him as hard a time about it as I probably would have otherwise."

"You're a good team, in a number of areas." Mira sampled the tea, approved it. "I imagine he has some concerns about you standing as primary in this type of investigation."

"Sexual homicides. I've done them before, I'll do them again. I know how to handle it."

"I agree. And from your reports, from the thinking aloud I overheard, you've already formed your own profile." Mira slipped a disc out of her bag. "And now you have mine."

Eve turned the disc in her hand. "One profile?"

Mira sat back, watching Eve as she sipped her tea. "Two. There are two, whether individuals or personalities I can't tell you with absolute certainty. While multiple personality syndrome is rare, except in fiction, it does exist."

"I don't think this is MPS. I read up on it last night," she explained when Mira looked surprised. "The same basic method, the same basic motivation, the same staging. But two different styles, two different target types. He used a condom or spermicide, sealed his hands with the second victim, but left DNA and latents with the first. If it was MPS there'd be more distinction. One personality to hunt, another to kill. One to hunt and kill, the other to function normally. This is two guys, two, working together and taking turns at bat."

"I'm inclined to agree, but I can't rule out MPS." She crossed her legs, settling in comfortably to the talk of murder and madness. "The first murder appears to be accidental, or consciously unplanned. There is the possibility that the thrill and fear of the first triggered the more deliberate and more violent tone of the second. 'Turns at bat' is an accurate analogy. He, or they, are game players. There's a need here to dominate women, to debase them, but to do so with what is perceived as style and charm. Romance and seduction. The sexual act is wholly selfish, but would be rationalized as mutually satisfying as with the drug the victims would be eager and aggressive."

"More punch because as it happens she's looking at him as a sexual creature, a desire. Because, at the core of it, he's the focus."

"Precisely," Mira agreed. "It's not rape in the traditional sense, which uses force, violence, or intimidation. He doesn't look for fear, but for surrender. He's smart, patient. He spends time getting to know them—their fantasies, their hopes, their weaknesses. Then plays on them and fashions himself into those fantasies. Pink roses. Not red for passion, not white for purity. Pink for romance."

"We're dealing with two very specific, very technical skills. Computer technology and chemistry. I have new data and have run a probability on it. It's very likely that a third alias is in use, for the purpose of selling sexual illegals. High-end illegals. One of these guys knows his drugs. How to get them, more, in my opinion, how to create them. Maybe he risks selling them because it's how he makes his living. But I think it's more. I think he feeds on risk."

"Agreed." Mira inclined her head. "He likes to take chances. Calculated ones."

"The computer technology is ace. When Roarke's impressed, you can be damn sure the skill's earned it. Is MPS going to give one guy two highly developed skills in different areas?"

"Again, not impossible." Noting the impatience that crossed Eve's face, Mira gestured. "You want a yes or no, and I can't oblige you. I could give you case studies, Eve, but they wouldn't hold up against your instincts. We'll say two, for the sake of argument. Two individuals. One is fanciful, lives in his head a great deal. His female ideal is sharp and sexy and sophisticated. He wants to enthrall her as much as he wants to dominate and conquer her. He's a man who can and does become caught up in the moment."

"He sent roses to Bankhead at work," Eve pointed out. "Grace Lutz received no roses."

"The second is more calculating, more deliberate, and potentially more violent. He doesn't delude himself to the same extent as the first that this is romance. He knows it's rape. Accepts that. He wants youth and innocence because he wants to possess then destroy them."

"The second would be the dominant partner."

"Yes, almost certainly. But they do have a symbiotic relationship. They need each other, not only for the details and the skills, but for the reinforcement of ego. Male to male approval, as when Arena Ball players slap each other on the ass, or catch each other in headlocks after a score."

"Teamwork. I pass, you kick, and we make the goal."

"Yes. This is a great game to them." Mira set her tea aside, toyed absently with the pearl on the end of her chain. "And they need the competition. They are defective and brilliant minds with young, spoiled boys' egos. Manipulators who didn't learn to be that way overnight. They come from money and privilege, are used to demanding or taking what they want as they want it, and with impunity. They *deserve* it."

"They'd have played games before," Eve put in. "Nothing to this level. They've worked up to this."

"Oh yes. One mind or two, they've known each other a very long time and shared a great deal. There's a lack of maturity that leads me to believe they may very well be in the same age bracket as their victims. Early twenties. Mid-twenties at best. They don't simply enjoy the finer things. They must have them."

"Outward appearances," Eve added. "The snazzy

clothes, the status of the wine labels, the exclusive venues for the dates."

"Mmm. Status and exclusivity are vital. And what's more, I think, what they're accustomed to. To deny themselves or be denied is intolerable. Under the sheen of romance is a fear and a hatred for women. Look for a mother figure who was either dominant and abusive or weak and abused. Neglectful or overly protective. A man, particularly in his youth, most usually forms opinions and images of women based on his opinion and image of the woman who raised him."

She thought of Roarke and of herself. Motherless child. "What if he doesn't know her?"

"Then he forms them another way. But a man who seeks to exploit and hurt and abuse women will certainly have some female figure in his life who these represent to him."

"If I stop one, do I stop both?"

"If you stop one, the other will self-destruct. But he may very well kill on his way down."

She did what she did when there was too much data, too many threads, too many angles to all mix and match and tangle.

She went back to the victim.

When she used her master to uncode the police seal and unlock Bryna Bankhead's apartment, she blanked her mind of facts, and opened it to impressions.

The air was stuffy. There was no scent of candlewax or roses now, but the faint, dusty odor left behind by the sweepers.

No music. No softly glowing light.

She ordered the lights on full, checked that the privacy screen was in place, then wandered the room while an airbus rattled across the graying sky beyond the glass.

Strong colors, contemporary art, and still essentially female. The attractive nest of a single woman of very defined style and taste who enjoyed her life and her work.

A woman young enough that she had yet to form any serious or permanent sexual relationships. And confident enough to experiment. Adventurous enough to form a fanciful attachment with a faceless man over the 'net.

She'd lived alone, both tidily and fashionably, but was friendly with her neighbors.

Very eclectic music library, Eve mused as she flipped through the discs filed orderly in the entertainment unit. She came across *Mavis: Live and Kicking*, and despite the grim task felt the grin stretch over her face.

Her friend, Mavis Freestone, nearly always made her grin.

But it had been classical that night, Eve remembered. His choice or hers? His, she decided. It had all been his choice.

His fingerprints on the wine bottle. He'd brought it with him, opened it, poured. His fingerprints along with hers on one wineglass, only his on the second.

Handed her the wine. Perfect gentleman.

She walked into the bedroom. The sweepers had bagged the rose petals. The bed had been stripped down to bare mattress. Ignoring it, Eve opened the balcony doors, stepped out.

The wind lifted the choppy ends of her hair, streamed it back away from her face. It was starting to rain, soft, thin drops that fell soundlessly.

Her stomach pitched but she made herself step to the rail, made herself look down. *A long drop*, she thought. *Long last step.*

What had made him think of the balcony? There was no indication he'd been to the apartment before.

She replayed the security disc in her head and watched Bryna and her killer approach the front door of the building from the street. No, he hadn't looked up at the building, New Yorkers never did anyway. They'd been completely absorbed in each other.

Why had he thought of the balcony?

Why hadn't he just run in panic as he had in the cyber-café? Because part of his brain had stayed cool enough to click into survival mode both times. Had he thought the chemicals wouldn't show on a tox screen? Had he thought that far ahead?

Or just the first desperate step? He lives in the moment, Mira had said. And the moment had been shocking.

She's dead, and I'm in such trouble. What should I do?

Self-termination ploy. Toss her away. Out of sight, out of mind. But why not clean up evidence and leave it as a potential self-overdose and buy more time to escape?

To cause confusion, she decided, *as he had in the café.* He could have uploaded a virus in the single unit, but programmed it to spread. And was knowledgeable enough about those who frequented such places to be sure a riot would result.

A woman splats on the sidewalk, witnesses are shocked, stunned, afraid. They might run to the body or away from it, but they don't rush into the building looking for a killer—and the killer gains time to rush out and away.

But how did he think of the balcony?

As the rain thickened and began to plop, as her stomach churned at the height, she scanned the street, the neighboring buildings.

"Son of a bitch," she cursed softly as she read the sign:

COFFEE AND A BYTE.

It was hardly more than a hole in the wall. Ten tables fitted with low-end units. Counter service for six. But the coffee smelled fresh and the floors were clean.

The counter was manned by a droid of the fresh-faced, geek variety. His hair was styled to fall in a pointed brown flap across his forehead.

Two of the tables were occupied by the same type in human form, and the waitress was young and too perky not to be another automation.

"Hi! Welcome to Coffee and a Byte. Would you like a table?"

She had poofy blonde hair and lips the color of bubblegum. Her breasts were like two ripe melons that peeked rosily out of the bodice of her snug white top.

Eve imagined the geeks had nightly wet dreams with her name on them.

"I need to ask you some questions. Both of you."

The waitress, Bitsy according to her name tag, replied, "Everything's on the menu, including specials, but either Tad or I will be really happy to explain anything."

Bitsy and Tad. Eve shook her head. *Jesus, who thought of this shit?*

"Sit down, Bitsy."

"I'm sorry, but I'm not supposed to sit. Would you like to hear about today's coffee beverage?"

"No." Eve pulled out her badge. "This is a police investigation, and I have to ask you some questions."

"We're programmed to cooperate fully with the police and security, the fire, the health, and the emergency medical departments." This was from Tad, who whisked his flap of hair back with his fingers.

"That's good." She sensed movement and shifted to point at the thin-shouldered man who was trying to slide invisibly from behind his table. "There's no trouble here," she told him. "Just questions. Why don't you sit back down, relax? You might be able to answer some of them."

"I didn't do anything."

"Good. Keep not doing anything," she advised.

She turned back to the droids, but kept her body angled so the tables knew she had them in her scope. "You know what happened across the street? The woman who died?"

"Oh yeah." Tad brightened, a student with the answer for the teacher. "She got tossed out the window."

"There you go." Eve took the photo of Bryna Bankhead, laid it on the counter. "Did she ever come in here?"

"No, ma'am."

"Don't call me ma'am."

He blinked rapidly at that, trying to process. "I'm supposed to call female customers ma'am."

"I'm a cop, not a customer." Except . . . She sniffed the air. "Is that real coffee?"

"Oh yes . . ." His face underwent several expressions, ended up baffled.

"Lieutenant," Eve said helpfully.

"Oh yes, Lieutenant. We serve only genuine soy products, with or without caffeine additives."

"Never mind." She held up the photo so both men at the tables could see it. "Either of you ever see this woman?"

The one who'd tried to slither out the door shifted in his seat. "I guess I did. I didn't do anything."

"We got that part. Where'd you see her?"

"Around. I live a couple blocks down. That's why I come here. It's close and it's not all crowded and noisy and full of freaks and slicks."

"Slicks?"

"You know, the ones who cruise cyber-houses to pick up dates. I do serious work here."

"You ever talk to her?"

"Nah. Women like that don't talk to guys like me. I just saw her sometimes is all. Around the neighborhood. She was really pretty, so I looked at her. I didn't do anything."

"What's your name?"

"Milo. Milo Horndecker."

Doomed, she thought, *from birth to geekdom*. "Milo, you keep telling me you didn't do anything, I'm going to start thinking you did." She pulled out the three stills of the three faces the killer had used. "Do you know any of these men?" She laid them on the counter first for Tad and Bitsy. And got simultaneous head shakes out of them.

"But they're really pretty, too," Bitsy added.

The negative responses from the customers had Eve re-evaluating. "Okay. You have anyone in here the past few weeks. Somebody who just started coming in recently, hasn't been in since the murder? He'd want to sit near the front window. He'd come around in the mornings, but not after ten. Or in the evenings, but not before six."

She had to shuffle through the files in her head to come up with Bryna's regular work schedule. "If he came in otherwise, it would be on Tuesdays. He'd order fancy coffee. Slim latte grande with chestnut flavoring."

"He came in two Tuesdays in a row." Bitsy bounced on the toes of her pink slippers. "He sat in the front and he always had two lattes while he worked. And then he left."

"Which table?"

"He always used station one. Always." She pursed her bubblegum lips. "It has a nice view of the street."

And Bryna Bankhead's building, Eve thought.

She pulled out her communicator and tagged Feeney. "I'm at a cyber-club across from Bankhead's building. I'm looking at a unit he used. I need an impound warrant and an image tech."

Sitting at station one, Eve drank the genuine soy product with caffeine additives. Beggars couldn't be choosers.

She had only to angle her head to see the twelfth floor of the apartment building across the street. Bryna's apartment windows. The little terraces.

"He likes to be thorough," she said to Feeney. "He's a data addict and needs his input fix. She told him in her e-mails what she usually did on her days off. How she liked to open the windows first thing to see what sort of day it was."

I love to take that first breath of New York in the morning, she'd written. *I know what people say about city air, but I think it's so full, so exciting and romantic. All the scents and flavors and colors. I have them all, and on my day off, I bask in them.*

"He probably watched her step out on the terrace. Maybe she'd have a cup of coffee out there, standing by the rail. Being a creature of order, she'd tidy up the apartment, get dressed, probably go out shopping awhile. Meet a friend. He would have tailed her, just to make sure what she told him in e-mail clicked with her habits. Want to make sure she lived alone, that there was no boyfriend or whatever to cramp his style. More, he wanted to see how she behaved, how she *looked* when she was unaware of him. She had to be good enough to fuck after all."

She looked back at Feeney, who with his magic fingers and droopy eyes was giving the unit its first check. "He's a creature of habit, too," she said. "And the habits are a trail. Can you find him on this?"

"He used it, we can find out when and how. Gonna take time to filter through all the data and find his. But what he put in, we can get out."

With a nod, she pushed away from the table and walked back to where the image tech worked with the droids. The one thing about droids, she thought, was no matter how annoying they might be, their eyes were a reliable camera.

Already she could see the face and features coming to life on the tech's comp-canvas.

Soft face, bland features. A hairline starting to recede from a wide dome of brow and left to shag messily over the ears. The kind of face that passed through a crowd unnoticed, that blended to the point where it was a faint smear on the memory.

Except for the eyes. They were sharp and cold.

Whatever he did to his face, Eve knew when she looked into those eyes, she would know him.

There was no cyber-joint within view of Grace Lutz's building. No coffee shop or little diner. There was a small, walk-in deli with one long narrow aisle, but Eve's morning run of luck ran out there.

She'd sent for Peabody, and her aide walked in just as she was buying a candy bar.

"That's a very childish lunch," Peabody said, craving it. "Is that veggie hash fresh?"

"What have you got for me?"

"A big, gaping pit where my stomach used to be," Peabody told her, and ordered a take-out serving of the hash. "I'm trying this new diet where you eat only the white of a hardboiled egg for breakfast. Then—"

"Peabody." Cruelly, Eve unwrapped the candy, took a slow, deliberate bite. "Have you somehow mistaken me for someone who has an interest in dietary matters?"

"That's really mean. You're got a mean temperament because you're spending your caloric intake on processed sugar and . . . is that caramel?"

"Bet your ass." Eve licked a glossy string of it off her index finger while Peabody enviously followed the move. "Outside. I need to walk."

"Oh well, if we're going to exercise give me one of what she's got," Peabody demanded, and dug for more money.

On the street, she scooped up forksful of hash slowly to make it last and matched her stride to Eve's.

"If you can manage to swallow, Peabody, I'd like your report."

"It's pretty good. I think they used dill. We listed sixteen possibles," she said quickly. "Roarke, well, I don't have to tell you, but he's one mag tech. So fast and smooth. And when he does manual searches . . . Have you ever noticed his hands?" She ate more hash at Eve's steely stare. "Yeah, guess you have. Anyway, we've had sixteen names that jibed with the purchases, and we factored them down to ten, deleting two guys who got married in the last two weeks. May and June, still big months for weddings. Another who got run over by a maxibus a couple days ago. Did you read about that? This guy, he's walking along doing his stock checks on his PPC, and steps right off the curb in front of the bus. Blap."

"Peabody."

"Okay, well. We narrowed it down to ten most-likelies, going with the outlets McNab came up with in-city for the enhancements. The wigs are taking longer because he's got to target the manufacturer, and he says there's about two hundred who use that high-grade human material—then hit the brand, then the product name. The style used in the first murder is a pretty popular hair alternative, and goes by several names, depending on the brand and material used."

She flipped her empty take-out carton into a recycler, and began to peel the wrapper off her candy bar with the slow precision and intense concentration of a woman stripping her lover.

"He wants to have pizza tonight."

"What? Roarke wants pizza?"

"No, McNab. McNab wants to have pizza with me tonight. He says he wants to talk and stuff, but this morning we broke a couple of public moral codes outside your gates."

"Shit. Shit." Eve pressed her fingers under her eye where a muscle began to tic wildly. "There it goes again. Why do you tell me this stuff? It makes me spasm."

"If we have pizza, we're going to have sex. What does that mean?"

"It's more than a spasm. I think it's an embolism. One of those brain bombs, and you have your finger twitching on the button."

"I don't want to get messed up again. But I feel messed up anyway."

Eve sighed. "What do I know about this kind of stuff, Peabody? It's taken me more than a year to find my rhythm with Roarke, and I still screw it up half the time. Cops are bad bets."

She turned, jamming her hands in her pockets. The street was dirty, the traffic loud, and the smoke that belched from the glide-cart they passed stank of fried re-hydrated onions. She could see an illegals deal in the making a half block down and across the street.

"Trying to have a life off the job is work. Two of you trying to have a life off it, I don't know. Damn it." Her heart might have been going soft for her aide, but her eyes were still hard and clear. "That's going bad. Call for the beat cops, then back me up."

She pulled out her badge, pulled out her weapon, and was already zagging across the street when one of the men on the opposite sidewalk drew a blade.

There was a swipe, a dodge, then the second man flashed out a knife of his own.

They jabbed, circling each other. Bystanders scattered.

"Police! Drop your weapons."

They ignored her, and she could see one was jonesing, the other high. That made both of them dangerous.

"Lose the stickers, or I drop you both."

As one, they turned on her. The man desperate for his fix lunged wildly. She heard one of the pedestrians screaming. As the knife arched up, she took her man down with a stun across the knees.

He fell toward her. She pivoted, blocked, then brought the heel of her boot down hard on his knife hand.

While he wailed, flopped, she saw the second man had moved fast. He had the side of his blade lodged at the throat of the screaming pedestrian. And he had Zeus in his eyes, that elixir that made gods of men.

"Drop it. Let her go and drop it."

"Fuck you. Fuck her. This is my goddamn corner!"

"You cut her, you'll die on this goddamn corner." The man on the ground was weeping now. She could smell the piss leaking onto the sidewalk where his bladder had let go.

"You put your piece down or I cut her from ear to ear." He leaned in, running his tongue over the terrified woman's cheek. "And drink the blood."

"Okay. Looks like you've got me." She lowered her weapon, watching his eyes follow it down. Then watching them jitter as Peabody stepped in from behind and laid her stunner against the back of his neck.

Eve sprang forward, grabbing his knife hand, twisting it. The civilian slid to the ground like an empty sack. "Stun him again!" Eve shouted as the drug-induced strength had the knife jamming toward her throat. She felt the prick, that hot sting of metal against flesh.

And both of them scented her blood.

His body jerked, then lifted when Eve plowed her knee into his groin. She shifted her weight, sliced her heel into his instep, then curled to use the momentum to flip him over her back.

He landed like a felled tree, flat out, and with a solid crack of skull on concrete.

Eve scooped up the knife, and wheezing, stayed bent over.

"Dallas? You okay? Did he cut you?"

"Yes, damn it. Get that one." She pointed at the first man, still weeping, trying to crawl away.

She heaved the second man over, clapped on restraints. The hostage was on the ground as well, and still screaming.

Eve wiped the blood off her throat with the back of her hand and glanced over. "Somebody shut her up."

Chapter 10

She had a long, shallow cut from just under her right ear to just above the jugular. A little more pressure, the MT Peabody had summoned behind her back had cheerfully noted, a little more depth, and she'd have pumped herself dry quick, fast, and in a hurry.

As it was, it wasn't so bad. Though she had blood on her shirt.

"They've got stuff that'll take the blood right out," Peabody assured her as they drove uptown. "My mother always used salt and cold water though. Does the job. Mostly."

"So does chucking it in the rag pile." Though she imagined Summerset would pluck it out again, work some sort of household voodoo, and it would end up back in her closet. Good as new.

"See if you can put a hook in McNamara. I'd like to work him into my day, see what he has to say about the partnership, scandal, and sex drugs."

While Peabody made the call, Eve checked in for messages, grumbling when there was nothing new from Feeney or McNab.

"Dr. McNamara's off planet, sir. Isn't expected back for a couple days. I've left a request that he contact you with his admin, and on his voice mail."

"Okay, we'll shuffle him down in the pile for now. Give me the run on this first guy. Lawrence Q. Hardley."

"Thirty-two. Single, white male. Family hit it big in the late twentieth in the Silicon Valley explosion. No marriage or cohabitation on record. No criminal or military record."

"And no prints on file."

"None. NYC resident since forty-nine. Assists in running family business, NY branch, and holds title of exec vp in charge of marketing. Reported income—salary, investments, dividends, expense quota, approximately five million two annually."

Peabody studied the image alongside the data. "Looks pretty good, too. Maybe he'll fall in love with me and beg me to marry him, thereby providing me with the style of living to which I would be willing to become accustomed."

It didn't work out that way. Hardley showed no particular interest in Peabody, but he did toward his pretty male admin. Things had looked hopeful when he'd become flustered and annoyed at the questioning, had refused to answer without his attorney present.

It took twenty minutes to arrange for the consult, and another twenty to wade through standard questions with the addition of the attorney through holo-projection.

An hour wasted, Eve thought as she slid back into her car, ticking Hardley off the list.

"Why didn't he just tell us he was gay?" Peabody wondered. "And had an alibi for both nights in question?"

"Some people are still uncomfortable with alternative sexuality, even when it's theirs. Run number two."

They eliminated three out of the ten before Eve cut Peabody loose for the day. Because she knew her job—

she didn't have to like it—she swung to the curb in front of Peabody's building and asked the question.

"So, are you having pizza or what?"

"I don't know." Peabody's shoulders rose and fell. "I think probably not. It'll just get all weird and screwed-up again. He's really an asshole." But she said it wistfully. "He really got hyped and looney about Charles."

Eve shifted in her seat, wishing she could stem the thin trickle of sympathy for McNab. "I guess it could be rough on a guy to figure he was competing with someone like Charles."

"We never said we were exclusive. And he can't go around trying to direct my life. He can't just start telling me who I can see, who I can be friends with." Heating up, Peabody turned the glare on Eve. "And if I had been having sex with Charles, which I wasn't, it wouldn't be any of his damn business."

Whoops, Eve thought. *Forget your job for one little minute and take a blast right in the forehead.* "Right. Absolutely right. Once an asshole, always an asshole. Good to remember that."

"So screw him." Peabody huffed out a breath and felt righteous. "He didn't even bother to tag me during the day to see if I was up for it anyway. So screw him."

"Sideways. We'll interview the last names on the list tomorrow."

"What?" Peabody brought herself back. "Right. Yes, sir. Tomorrow."

Thinking she'd done a reasonably decent job of it, Eve shoved the car into crosstown traffic. With luck, she could be home in thirty minutes.

While she fought her way across and uptown, Roarke sipped a beer, and did his job.

"I think the pizza's a good approach," McNab said. "She's got a weakness for it. And it keeps it casual-like. Friendly."

"I'd pick up a bottle of red. Nothing fancy."

"That's good." McNab's face brightened. "But no flowers or anything."

"Not this time. If you want to put things back as they were, you need to take her off guard. Keep her guessing."

"Yeah." Roarke, in McNab's estimation, was the guru of romance. Anybody who could make Dallas soft was a veritable genius in affairs of the heart.

"But this deal with Charles," he began.

"Forget it."

"Forget it? But—" McNab stuttered in shock.

"Set it aside, Ian. At least for now. She's fond of him, and whatever their relationship might be, it's important to her. Every time you take a jab at him, you push her away."

They were sitting, sharing beer, in some sort of den area McNab hadn't even known existed. There was a pool table, an old-fashioned bar, view screens on opposing walls, and deep leather sofas and chairs the color of good red wine.

The art on the remaining walls were nudes. But they were classy nudes—long, streamlined female bodies that looked somehow foreign and refined.

It was, McNab thought, a real guy room. Away from the work stations, away from the 'links, where the only women were stylized art that didn't drive you crazy. Here there were acres of wood, the smell of leather and tobacco.

Back to class, McNab thought.

Charles had class.

If that was what Peabody was after, he was sunk before he floated.

"We had some good times, you know? Not just good naked times, I mean. I was sort of getting into that stuff you suggested before. You know, taking her out places, coming up with flowers and shit some times. But when we busted up . . . It was bad." He gulped beer. "Really bad. I figured the hell with her. But we work together a lot so you've got to have some level, right? Maybe I should just leave it like that, before it gets messed up again."

"That's an option." Roarke took out a cigarette, lighted it, blew out smoke thoughtfully. "From what I've seen, you're a good detective, Ian. And an interesting man of interesting tastes. If you didn't have a good brain neither Feeney nor Eve would be working with you. However, despite being a good detective with a good brain, and an interesting man of interesting tastes, you're leaving one vital factor out of this current equation."

"What?"

Roarke leaned forward, gently patted McNab's knee. "You're in love with her."

His jaw dropped. The beer in the pilsner slid danger-ously toward the edge as it tipped. Roarke righted it.

"I am?"

"I'm afraid so."

McNab stared at Roarke with the expression of a man who'd just been told he had a fatal disease. "Well, hell."

Fifty minutes, two stops, and a long subway ride later, McNab knocked on Peabody's door. Dressed in her ratti-est sweatpants, an NYPSD T-shirt, and a new seaweed face pack guaranteed to give the skin a clear, youthful glow, she opened to see him holding a pizza box and a bottle of cheap Chianti.

"Thought you might be hungry."

She looked at him—the pretty face, the silly clothes—and caught the siren's whiff of spicy sauce. "I guess I am."

It seemed to be the night for dating. In the posh and fra-grant Royal Bar of the Roarke Palace, where a trio in evening dress played Bach, Charles lifted a shimmering flute of champagne.

"To the moment," he said.

Louise clinked her glass musically to his. "And to the next."

"Dr. Dimatto." He skimmed a finger lightly over her hand as he drank. "Isn't it a happy coincidence we both had the evening off?"

"Isn't it? And an interesting one that we'd meet this morning at Dallas's. You said you'd known her more than a year."

"Yes. We brushed together on another of her cases."

"That must be why she lets you get away with calling her Lieutenant Sugar."

He laughed, topped a small blini with caviar, and offered it. "She intrigued me right from the start, I admit. I'm attracted to strong-willed, intelligent, and dedicated women. What are you attracted to, Louise?"

"Men who know who they are and don't pretend otherwise. I grew up with pretense, with role-playing. And I shook it off as soon as I could manage. I stuck with medicine, because it's my passion, but I practice it my way. My way didn't please my family."

"Tell me more about your clinic."

She shook her head. "Not yet. You're too good at drawing out personal information without giving any in return. I'll tell you I became a doctor because I have a need, and a talent, to heal. Why did you become an LC?"

"I have a need, and a talent, for giving pleasure. Not just sexually," he added. "That's often the simplest and most elemental part of the job. Spending time with someone, discovering what it is they need or want, even if they don't know themselves. Then providing it. If you do, the satisfaction's more than physical for both parties."

"And sometimes it's just about fun."

She made him laugh. She'd been making him laugh, he realized, since he first met her. "Sometimes. If you were a client—"

"But I'm not." She didn't say it with a sting, but with a slow, very warm smile.

"If you were, I might have suggested drinks just like this. Giving us time to relax, to flirt, to get to know each other."

The server topped off their glasses, but neither of them noticed. "And then?" Louise prompted.

"Then, we might dance a little, so you'd grow used to the way I held you. And I to the way you want to be held."

"I'd love to dance with you." She set her glass down.

He rose, took her hand. On the way to the dance floor they passed a shadowy booth where a couple ignored their own bottle of champagne and kissed passionately.

He turned, slid his arms around Louise. Fit her body to his with the easy skill of a man who knew, perfectly, how a woman fit against a man. There was a delicacy about her that stirred him. A directness that aroused and appealed.

In the cab that morning, she had handed him a card and suggested he call her sometime—when he wasn't working.

Very direct, he thought again as he drew in the scent of her hair. Very clear. She was attracted, interested. But not as a client.

He'd been attracted, interested, and had suggested they have drinks that same evening.

"Louise?"

"Mmm."

"I wasn't free tonight. I broke an engagement to be here."

She tipped back her head. "So did I." She laid her head on his shoulder again. "I like the way you hold me."

"I felt something as soon as I saw you this morning."

"I know." She relaxed, drifted on the music. On the moment. "I don't have time for a relationship. They're so messy and take so much effort. I'm selfish, Charles, about my work and often, very often, resent anything that gets in the way of it."

Her fingers trailed into his hair. "But I felt something, too. I think I could make time to find out what it's about."

"I haven't had much luck with relationships. My work

usually gets in the way." He turned his face into her hair, breathed in the scent. "I'd like to take time to find out."

"Tell me." She brushed her cheek against his. Smooth, she thought, with just enough friction to make her skin shiver. "If I were a client, what would we do after we dance?"

"Depending on what you wanted, we might go upstairs, to the suite I'd have reserved. I'd undress you." He skimmed his palm over the warm, bare skin of her back. "Slowly. I'd tell you how beautiful you are as I took you to bed. How your skin's like silk. I'd show you how much I want you as I made love to you."

"Maybe next time." She drew away, just a little, so she could look at him. "And it sounds nearly perfect. But if the next time comes, Charles, we'll take each other to bed. And I'll make love with you."

His fingers tightened on hers. "It doesn't matter to you, what I do?"

"Why should it?" She had to rise on her toes to touch her mouth to his, and left it at merely a whisper. "Anymore than it should matter to you what I do. Excuse me a minute? I want to freshen up."

She walked to the women's lounge and when she was sure she was out of sight, pressed a hand to her jittery stomach. She'd never had a reaction like this to a man.

To want a man, of course. To enjoy his company, to feel desire and interest and humor, affection. But never all at once, never so much of all on such short acquaintance.

She needed a minute to settle down.

She stepped inside the opulent lounge, moved directly to one of the deeply cushioned chairs in front of its individual triple mirror.

She took out her compact, then simply sat, staring at her own reflection. She'd said no more than the truth. She didn't have time for a relationship. Particularly one that was bound to be intense and complex and complicated. She had so much she wanted to accomplish.

It was one thing to socialize now and then. A date, a

party. Particularly if she could use the time to garner interest in the clinic, or the abuse shelter, or the expansion of the free med-van units she was working on.

But a relationship with Charles would be pure indulgence.

She'd had no idea how much she'd want to indulge.

She opened and closed her compact a few times, then began to powder her nose while lecturing herself to be a grown-up. As she fussed with her hair, a long, slim brunette in a clingy black gown came out of the stall area.

She was humming, a quick, jumpy tune that suited her quick, jumpy moves when she plopped into a chair and took out her lipstick.

"Ooh," she said and snagged one of the cut-glass bottles of scent. "Do Me." She spritzed it on lavishly, then to Louise's surprised amusement, tucked the bottle in her evening bag. "That's just the idea."

She scooped back her long mane of curls, sent Louise a glittery smile. "Congratulate me." Moniqua rose, skimmed her hands over her breasts, down her hips. "I'm about to get really lucky."

"Congratulations," Louise told her, and laughed a little as Moniqua slithered out of the room.

She slithered right up to the booth where the man she knew as Byron was already standing, holding out a hand. "Ready?"

She took his hand, leaned in, and rubbed her body provocatively over his. "Want to hear what I'm ready for?"

Though she whispered as they walked, they skirted close enough to where Charles sat that he caught one very imaginative suggestion. Idly, he glanced after them and wondered because of the man's subtle detachment, if he was an LC on the job.

Then he looked over, saw Louise walking back. And couldn't think of anything but her.

Moniqua Cline worked hard as a paralegal in one of the city's midlevel firms. She had aspirations and ambitions, most of which were oriented toward career. But she had more intimate ones as well, which involved fantasies about the perfect mate who would share her love of neo-classic art, tropical get-aways, and poetry.

A man, in her dreams, with a sophisticated edge, a toned body, a romantic mind, and some good urban polish.

It seemed she'd found him in Byron.

He was so handsome, with his shoulder-sweeping bronze hair, his golden tan. Her nervous pulse had jumped like dice in a cup when she'd seen him waiting in the booth they'd agreed upon.

He'd already had champagne poured and ready.

When he'd spoken her name, the warmth, the faintest of British accents in his voice had made her want to melt.

The first glass of champagne had gone to her head. She'd been so hot, so itchy. When she'd slid across the booth, she hadn't been able to stop herself from getting her hands on him. Her mouth on him, she'd felt drunk and happy.

Now they were alone in her apartment, and everything seemed soft and fluid. As if she were looking through a thin veil of warm, rippling water.

There was music playing, sweeping rainbow arches of music. And more champagne to dance in her head and sweeten her tongue.

His mouth was silky as it skimmed over hers. His hands so skilled that everywhere he touched her throbbed and ached. Unbearably. He said lovely things to her, though it was hard to understand them through the dizziness, the arousal that bloomed inside her like roses.

Then he drew away and made her moan in protest.

"I want to prepare." He took her hands, traced kisses over the backs. "Set the stage. You want romance, Moni-qua. I'm going to give it to you. Wait here for me."

Her head spun as she watched him get to his feet, pick up his bag. She couldn't quite . . . think.

"I want—I need to . . ." She got shakily to her feet, gestured toward the bathroom. "Freshen up. For you."

"Of course. Don't be long. I want to be with you. I want to take you places you've never been."

"I won't." She strained against him, lifting an eager mouth to his. "It's so perfect, Byron."

"Yes." He led her to the bathroom door, nudged her gently inside. "It's perfect."

He lighted the candles. He turned down the bed, sprinkled rose petals on the sheets, plumped the pillows.

He'd chosen well, he decided, as he studied the bedroom. He approved the art, the colors, the good fabric of the spread. She was a woman of taste. He touched the slim, old volume of poetry on her bedside table. And intellect.

He might have loved her. If love existed.

He set two fresh flutes of champagne on the table. Added three drops of the drug to one. He would dilute it this time, extend the experience. Lucias had told him she could live for two hours, perhaps a bit more, with the combination of drugs in this proportion in her bloodstream.

He could do a great deal with her in two hours.

He turned when she came to the bedroom door. He held out a hand.

"Beautiful, Moniqua. My love. Let's discover each other."

It was better this time. Even better. Lucias was right. He was always right. The excitement of knowing this experience would be her last, that he would be the last thing she saw, felt, smelled, even tasted was almost unbearably erotic.

Oh, she responded to him, tirelessly. Her heart stormed against his. And still she pleaded with him for more.

She gave him two hours. Two magnificent hours.

When he felt her dying, he watched her almost tenderly. "Say my name," he whispered.

"Byron."

"No. Kevin. I want to hear you say it. Kevin. I want to hear you scream it."

He rammed himself into her, plunging toward the end. And when she screamed his name, he knew the most perfect pleasure of his life.

Because of it, he drew the sheet gently over her body, laid his lips on her brow in a soft kiss before he walked out of her apartment.

He couldn't wait to get home and tell Lucias everything.

It was an hour later when she moved. Her fingers scraped over the sheet, the eyes behind her closed lids twitched. There was a numbness in her chest, and under it a kind of terrifying, unspeakable pain. Her head burned like the sun.

Tears leaked out, trickled down her cheek as she struggled to lift her arm. It felt dead, and the effort had small, strangled sounds trembling on her lips.

Her fingers brushed a glass on the table, knocked it to the floor where it shattered. And the sound of it was dim, like glass breaking under a pillow.

Her fingers crawled over the table, bumped the 'link. Sweat sheathed her as she forced those fingers up, forced her confused mind to count. Slot by slot until she reached the top key on memory.

She pushed it, then her hand fell limp and her body lay drenched in exhaustion.

"What is your emergency, Miss Cline?"

"Help me." Her lips tripped over the words as if they were some exotic foreign language. "Please. Help me," she managed to whisper before she fell back into unconsciousness.

Eve woke when the world started to sway. She opened gritty eyes and stared into Roarke's.

"Why are you carrying me?"

"Because, Lieutenant, you need to sleep. Not at your desk," he added as he stepped into the elevator in her home office. "In a bed."

"I was just resting my eyes."

"Rest them in bed."

She should, on principle, insist he set her back on her feet. But it was kind of nice to get carted around, especially when she only had to turn her head to sniff his neck. "What time is it?"

"Just after one." He carried her into the bedroom, climbed the short steps to the platform, then sat, cradling her, on the side of the bed.

"Do you know what I was thinking?"

She snuggled in. "I've got a pretty good idea."

He laughed, ran a hand over her hair. "I can put my mind to that as well. But I was thinking when I walked into your office and saw you with your head on your desk and your face pale the way it gets when you're finally too exhausted to take another step, that in a matter of weeks we'll have been married a full year. And I'm still fascinated by you."

"We're doing okay, huh?"

"Yes, we're doing just fine." He tugged on the chain she wore around her neck, slid the diamond pendant he'd once given her out from under her shirt where she most often wore it. "You were angry with me when I gave you this. Yet you wear it more often than anything I've ever given you but your wedding ring."

"You told me you loved me when you gave it to me. It pissed me off. And it scared me. I guess maybe I wear it because it doesn't piss me off anymore. But it still scares me sometimes."

Though his cheek rested on the top of her head, he traced a finger unerringly along the mark the knife had left on her throat. "Love's a scary business."

She turned into him. "Why don't we terrify each other?"

Her lips were a breath from his when the 'link beeped.

"Ah, damn it, damn it." She crawled over the bed to answer it.

Eve burst out of the elevator into ICU, strode down the deathly quiet corridor. She hated hospitals more than morgues. She slapped her badge on the counter at the nurses' station. "I need to see whoever's in charge. I need to see Moniqua Cline."

"Dr. Michaels is in with her now. If you'd just wait—"

"In there?" Eve jabbed a finger toward a set of thick glass doors. She was through them before the nurse could do more than let out a piping sound of protest.

She knew who she was looking for. She'd gotten a solid description from the med-tech who'd helped transport the victim into the ER.

She passed a glass-walled room, scanned the bed inside. The woman lying on it looked a hundred and fifty and was tethered to so many machines she no longer looked human.

Give me a full blast, right in the heart, Eve thought, *and end my time clean.*

In the next room the man was much younger, and cocooned in a thin transparent tent.

She found Moniqua one door down, with the doctor scanning the readout on a monitor while his patient lay white as death and still as stone.

He glanced over with annoyance, and a frown marred the face set off by a natty beard and mustache the color of paprika.

"You're not allowed in here."

"Lieutenant Dallas, NYPSD." She offered her badge. "She's mine."

"On the contrary, Lieutenant. She's mine."

"Is she going to make it?"

"I can't say. We're doing all that can be done."

"Look, I don't want the company line. Two other

women haven't made it to the hospital. They went straight to the morgue. MT told me she had a cardiac incident, a bp that hit the cellar, and complications from the OD. I need to know if she's going to come out of it enough to tell me who put her here."

"And I can't tell you. Her heart was damaged. We're unable to determine as yet if there was brain damage as well. Her vitals are low and weak. She's in a coma. Her system's been so compromised by the drugs it's a minor miracle she was aware enough to call nine-eleven."

"But she did, and I say that makes her tough." She looked down at Moniqua, willed her to consciousness. "The drugs were administered without her knowledge. Are you aware of that?"

"That hasn't been confirmed, but I've heard the media reports on the two murders."

"He doused her with the two illegals, then he raped her. I need someone in here with a rape kit."

"I'll have one of the physician's assistants take care of it."

"I need a police rep, too, to collect whatever evidence she's got in her."

"I know the drill," Michaels said with a snap of impatience in his voice. "Get your rep, get your evidence. That's not my concern. Keeping her alive is."

"And mine is pinning the son of a bitch who put her here. That doesn't make her less to me. You've examined her? Personally?"

He opened his mouth again, then whatever he read on Eve's face had him nodding. "I have."

"Any trauma? Bruises, bites, cuts?"

"No, none. Nor any sign of forced sexual activity."

"Was she sodomized?"

"No." He laid a hand, almost protectively over Moniqua's. "What are we dealing with, Lieutenant?"

"Don Juan, with an attitude. Who'll know he didn't finish the job once this hits the media. I'm putting a guard on her, twenty-four–seven and I don't want any visitors. None. No one gets into this room except authorized staff and cops."

"Her family—"

"You clear them through me first. Me personally," she added. "I need to know if and when there's any change in her condition. I need to know the instant she wakes up. And I don't need any bullshit about her not being able to answer questions. He meant her to die, and she didn't. Two others have. He's having too much fun to stop now."

"You wanted to know her chances? Less than fifty percent."

"Well, I'm betting on her." Eve leaned over the bed, spoke quietly, spoke firmly. "Moniqua? You hear that? I'm betting on you. If you give up, he wins. So you're not going to give up. Let's kick this bastard in the balls."

She stepped back, nodded at Michaels. "You contact me when she wakes up."

Chapter 11

By the time she left Central it was nearly four A.M., and exhaustion was wrapped around her like a damp blanket that smothered the senses. Rather than trust her reflexes, she programmed for auto. And hoped the jokers down in Maintenance hadn't played any pranks with the mechanism.

Still, she was too tired to care if she ended up in Hoboken. There were bound to be beds in Hoboken.

The recycle trucks were already out, limping along with their monotonous *whoosh-bang-thump*, and their teams moving like shadows to dump contents of sidewalk receptacles and bins and prepare the city for another day's garbage.

A utility crew in their ghostly white reflector suits was tearing up a half block section along Tenth. The nasty, tooth-drilling buzz of their hydrojack competed with the headache spiking into her left temple.

A couple of the guys gave her the once-over from behind their safety goggles as she idled at the light. One smooth customer grabbed at his crotch, grinning with

˙what she imagined passed for charm in his limited world
while he jerked his hips.

The pantomime had several of his cronies laughing
uproariously.

She knew she was past her personal threshold when she
couldn't drum up the irritation to step out of the car and
bust their balls while she cited them for sexual harassment.

Instead, she let her head lay against the seat, closed
her eyes as the sensors picked up the light change and the
car cruised through.

Mentally, she took herself through Moniqua's apartment again. Champagne this time. Eve had recognized
the label as one of Roarke's and knew the bubbly could
go for upwards of a grand a bottle. A hell of an outlay, in
her opinion, for some pop and fizz.

He'd taken glasses into the bedroom this time, but the
rest of the setup was identical to the others.

Creatures of habit, she thought, drifting a little. *Taking
turns.*

Keeping score? Most games were competitions,
weren't they? The goal hadn't been reached with Moniqua. Would they try to finish it? Or just sit back and hope
she did the job for them and coded out?

She shifted in the seat, seeking comfort.

Call Michaels in the morning, check status. Brief
guards at change of shift. She'd put the dependable Trueheart on the first shift. He'd be solid. Process data on Allegany and J. Forrester. Follow through with Dr. Theodore
McNamara. Nag Feeney re cutting through blocks on the
account number Charles had provided. Continue to nag re
data search on unit impounded from cyber-joint.

So far, she'd gotten nowhere on the roses. Take another push at the flowers.

Take dose of goddamn Awake, and swallow a stupid
pain blocker before your head explodes.

She hated drugs. They made her feel stupid or weak or
overcharged.

Drugs would be trickling into Moniqua's system now. Sliding inside her, working to bolster her heart, clear brain channels, and God knew. If the tide turned the right way, she'd wake up. And remember.

She'd be scared, confused, disoriented. Her mind would feel detached from her body, at least at first. There'd be blank spots, and the questions that had to be asked would drop into some of them.

The mind, she knew, protected itself from horror when it could.

To wake in the hospital, with the machines, the pain, the strange faces. What could the mind do but hide?

What's your name?

They'd asked her that. It was the first thing they'd asked her. Doctors and cops, standing over the gurney while she'd stared up at them.

What's your name, little girl?

The phrase sent her heart racing, made her try to curl up into herself. Little girl. Terrible things happened to little girls.

They'd thought at first she was mute, either physically or psychologically. But she could speak. She just didn't know the answers.

The cop hadn't looked mean. He'd come after the doctors and the others in flapping white coats or pale green smocks.

She'd learned later that it had been the police who'd brought her out of the alley where she'd hidden. She didn't remember it, but she had been told.

Her first memory was of the light over her head, burning into her eyes. And the dull, detached pressure of her broken arm being set.

She was filthy with sweat, dirt, and dried blood.

They spoke gently to her, those strangers, as they poked and prodded. But like the cop, the smiles didn't reach their eyes. Those were grim or aloof, filled with pity or questions.

When they went down, down to where she'd been torn, she fought like an animal. Teeth, nails, with the howling screams of a wounded animal.

That's when the nurse had cried. A tear sliding down her cheek as she helped hold her down until the calmer in the pressure syringe could be administered.

What's your name? the cop had asked her when she'd drifted back. *Where do you live? Who hurt you?*

She didn't know. She didn't want to know. She closed her eyes and tried to go away again.

Sometimes the drugs let her slip under. But if they took her too deep the air was cold, cold, cold and smeared dirty red. She was afraid, more afraid down there than of the strangers with their quiet questions.

Sometimes, when she was in that cold place, someone was with her. Candy breath and fingers that skittered over her skin like the roaches that skittered across the floor when the lights came on.

When those fingers were on her, even the drug couldn't stop her screams.

They thought she couldn't hear them, couldn't understand when they spoke in their hushed murmurs.

Beaten, raped. Long-term sexual and physical abuse. Suffering from malnutrition, dehydration, severe physical and emotional trauma.

She's lucky to have survived.

Bastard who did this ought to be cut into little pieces. One more victim. World's full of them.

No identity records. We're calling her Eve. Eve Dallas.

She woke with a jolt when the car stopped, stared blankly at the dark stone of the house, the glow of lights against the glass.

Her hands were shaking.

Fatigue, she told herself. Just fatigue. If she related to Moniqua Cline, it was only natural. One more tool, she thought as she climbed out of the car, in the investigation.

She knew who she was now. She'd become Eve Dallas, and it was more than a name the system had labeled her with. Who she'd been before, what had come before, couldn't be changed.

If that broken, frightened child still lived inside her, that was okay.

They'd both survived.

She dragged herself upstairs, stripping off her jacket, releasing her weapon harness. Stumbling and peeling off her clothes as she headed for the bed. She tumbled in, curling under warm, smooth sheets and willing the voices that still echoed in her head to quiet.

In the dark, Roarke's arm came around her, drew her back against him. She shuddered once. She knew who she was.

She felt his heart, the steady beat of it, against her back. His arm, the comforting weight of it, over her waist.

The tears that stung her throat shocked and appalled her. Where had they been hiding? The sudden wave of cold warned her the shakes would follow.

She turned to him, into him. "I need you," she said as her mouth found him. "Need you."

Desperate for warmth, for him, she fisted her hands in his hair.

She knew him in the dark—taste, scent, texture. Here, with him, there were no questions. Just answers. All the answers. She felt his heart that had been so steady against her back leap against her breast.

He was there for her as no one else had ever been.

"Say my name."

"Eve." His lips ran warm over the bruise on her face, took the ache away. "My Eve."

So strong, he thought. So tired. Whatever images that were playing in her brain she sought to fight, he'd fight with her. It wasn't tenderness she sought, but a kind of ruthless comfort. He slid a hand down her body, used his mouth and fingers to bring her that first sharp release.

She trembled, but no longer from cold. The aches that ravaged her body were no longer from fatigue. She arched against him when he found her breast. Quick little bites that shot flashes of pleasure into her. A busy tongue that laved heat over heat.

She rolled with him, her breath ragged as they tangled in the sheets. Her body was a rage of wants and grew slick under the hands that met them.

He loved the long, lean length of her, craved it with a hunger that was never quite sated. Her skin, always a surprise of delicacy, was damp and hot so that it slid like wet silk over his as they moved together. Her mouth came back to his, burning like a fever, and drenched them both in madness.

"Inside me." She rolled, crawling, clawing over him. Straddling him. "Inside me." And took him hard, fast, deep.

Her hips pistoned, a speed that blurred his brain. He could see the shape of her over him, the gleam of her eyes against the dark as she drove them both, brutally.

Battered, he rocked in the pleasure, let her take and take until her head fell back, until he felt the orgasm punch through her like a fist through glass.

Until she shattered.

Then he reared up, dragged her still shuddering body against him. And let go.

She fell into sleep like it was a pit and stayed there, sprawled facedown, for three hours.

She felt considerably better when she woke. She told herself the headache was gone, and it was so deeply buried under denial, it was nearly the same thing.

And a couple of catnaps during the day, she was sure, would do more for her than some chemical.

She didn't even make it out of bed before Roarke was sitting beside her, fully dressed. He had his morning stock reports on screen, muted, a pot of coffee still seductively steaming on the table in the sitting area.

And he held a pill in one hand, a suspicious-looking glass of liquid on the bedside table.

"Open up," he ordered.

"Uh-uh."

"I hate to give you more bruises, but if I must, I must."

They both knew he'd enjoy using brute force. "I don't need anything. You're nothing but a chemi-head pusher."

"Darling, you say the sweetest things." In a move too fast to evade, he had her earlobe pinched between his thumb and forefinger. One flick of his wrist and the shock of the twist had her mouth dropping open.

He popped the pill in. "Phase one."

She swung at him, but since she was choking her aim was off. The next thing she knew he was yanking her head back by her hair and pouring the liquid down her throat.

She swallowed twice in self-defense before she managed to shove at him.

"I'll kill you."

"All of it." With grim efficiency, he pinned her and forced the rest of the booster into her. "Phase two."

"You're a dead man, Roarke." She swiped the back of her hand over her chin where some of the booster had dripped. "You don't know it, but you've already stopped breathing. The walking dead."

"I wouldn't have to put us both through that if you'd take reasonable care of yourself."

"And when you finally realize you're dead, and drop to the ground—"

"Feeling better?"

"—and you're laying there, I'm going to step over your cold, lifeless body, open the doors of that department store you call a closet, and I torch it."

"Really, darling. No need to get nasty. Yes, better," he decided with a nod.

"I hate you."

"I know." He leaned in to give her a light kiss. "I hate you, too. I'm in the mood for eggs Benedict. Why don't you have your shower, then you can update me over breakfast?"

"I'm not talking to you."

His grin flashed as he rose. "Such a clichéd and female weapon." He turned, started down the stairs. And wasn't the least surprised when she landed on his back.

"That's more like it," he managed as she squeezed his windpipe with her crooked arm.

"Just be careful who you call a female, ace."

She dropped off, strode naked into the bath. Watching the indignant twitch of her ass, Roarke chuckled. "I don't know what I was thinking."

She only ate because there was no point in wasting the food. She only updated him because it helped her sort through data when she relayed events out loud.

He listened, idly stroking the cat.

"Between the hospital and MT staff," he commented, "the media will have been fed by now. That could work in your favor."

"I'm figuring. These two, they're not the type to go into the wind. Too much ego on the line for them to stop cold. I've got a lot of data on them. Maybe too much, maybe that's part of the problem. Too much data, not enough focus. You got all these lines to tug, they can get tangled on you."

She got up to strap on her shoulder harness. "I've got to streamline it."

"Why don't you let me take Allegany? It's mine, after all. People would be more likely to tell me things they wouldn't tell a badge. And what they don't tell me," he added, "I can find out in other ways. Ways that would probably be legal, more or less, since I now own the company."

"Your definition of more or less has a wider scope than mine." But it would save her time, and time was essential. "Try to stay close to the line on it."

"Whose line would that be? Yours or mine?"

"Har. I've got a briefing with the team at Central. Pass me anything you pick up."

"Naturally." Bringing the cat with him, he rose and

crossed to her. Kissed her. "Take care of yourself, Lieutenant."

"Why should I?" She headed for the door. "You get such a charge out of doing it for me."

Roarke glanced down at the cat as he listened to his wife's boots click down the hall. "That's a point."

In the conference room she'd booked at Central, Eve played the security disc from Moniqua's building.

"We see here she's more in line with Bryna Bankhead. Similar physical type, more sophisticated appearance and lifestyle. He uses yet another look himself here, which tells me he doesn't like to repeat his character. Keeps it fresh for him. Same pattern, but he can walk through the performance from a new angle. Feeney?"

He picked up the rhythm. "According to the overscan of her home unit, he used the name Byron in correspondence with her. Probability indicates this is from the poet guy. Lord Byron. The e-mail messages go back two weeks."

"Again, follows pattern. He takes his time. With this pattern he'd have studied her in real life. Finding a place near her apartment or her workplace. We check both."

She glanced over as the door opened. Trueheart, young and ridiculously fresh in his uniform, flushed as heads turned in his direction. "Sorry. Excuse me, sir. I'm late."

"No, you're on schedule. Report?"

"Sir, subject Cline's condition remains unchanged. No one without authorization entered her hospital room. I remained on post, inside the room, throughout the shift."

"Were there any calls of inquiry relating to her?"

"Several, Lieutenant, beginning at approximately oh six hundred when the first media report hit. Five inquiries from reporters requesting medical information."

"That jibes as I've had double that on my office 'link. Sign out, Trueheart. Go get some sleep. I want you to resume your post at the hospital at eighteen hundred. I'll clear your duty sheet with your sergeant."

"Yes, sir. Lieutenant? I appreciate you requesting me."

Eve shook her head when he'd closed the door behind him. "Thanking me for sticking him with the most boring duty on or off planet. Okay, Roarke's digging into Allegany. I want all pertinent data on J. Forrester, and this Theodore McNamara who's currently dodging my messages. And we slog away at the online dealer. We concentrate on the chemicals. How, why, and where they get their supply."

"My source in Illegals only came up with one strong possible," Feeney said. "One known local dealer who specialized in the upper-end sex trade and made a profit. Name's Otis Gunn, and he was in the swim about ten years ago. Had a pretty good line going until he got cocky and started cooking and serving his own Rabbit at parties."

"What's he up to now?"

"Year nine of twenty." Feeney pulled a bag of nuts out of one of his sagging pockets. "Rikers."

"Yeah? I haven't visited the old homestead in a while. Wonder if they've missed me?" She broke off as her communicator signalled, paced away to answer. "I just cleared Louise through," she said as she tucked the communicator away again. "She claims to have some information on last night's hit."

She looked at the case board, at the new picture she'd pinned to it. She'd kept Moniqua's face separate from the dead. She wanted it to stay there.

When she turned back she saw something pass between McNab and Peabody. Something with just a little heat, so she looked away fast.

"Peabody, why don't I have any damn coffee?"

"I don't know, sir, but I will rectify that immediately."

Peabody popped up, was actually humming under her breath as she programmed the AutoChef. And there was a bright look in her eyes when she carried the coffee to Eve.

"Eat any good pizza lately?" Eve muttered, and the light in Peabody's eyes turned instantly to embarrassed guilt.

"Maybe. Just a slice . . . or two."

Eve leaned in. "Ate the whole damn pie, didn't you?"

"It was really good pizza. I sort of, you know, missed the taste of it."

"No more humming on duty."

Peabody squared her shoulders. "No, sir. All humming will cease immediately."

"And no sparkly-eye crap either," Eve added and yanked open the door to look for Louise.

"You can look pretty sparkly-eyed after really good pizza, too," Peabody muttered, then decided not to press her luck when Eve snarled.

"Dallas." Louise double-timed it down the corridor. She wasn't wearing a power suit this morning, but the worn jeans and roomy shirt she usually donned for the clinic. "I'm so glad you are here. I didn't want to go into all this over a 'link."

"Sit down." Because Louise was pale despite her rush through Central's labyrinth, Eve took her arm and pulled her to a chair. "Take a breath, then tell me what you've got."

"Last night. I had a date last night. Drinks at The Royal Bar."

"Roarke's place? In The Palace Hotel?"

"Yes. I saw them. Dallas, I saw them sitting in a booth near our table. I spoke with her in the ladies' lounge."

"Slow down. Peabody, some water here."

"I wasn't paying attention," Louise continued. "If I had been I'd have seen . . . I can see her face right now as she sat in front of the mirror. It wasn't just champagne. I'm a doctor, goddamn it, I should have seen she was drugged. I can see it now."

"We see all kinds of things after. Here." She shoved the water into Louise's hands. "Drink, then suck it in, Louise. Suck it in and tell me everything you remember."

"Sorry." She sipped once. "When I saw the media report this morning, I recognized her. Realized." She drank again. "I called and checked on her condition on the way over. There's been no improvement. None. Her chances decrease every hour."

"Last night. Concentrate on last night. You're having drinks in the bar."

"Yes." She drew in a breath. Steadied. "Champagne, caviar. It was lovely. We were talking. I wasn't paying much attention to anything but him. But I did notice, sort of absently, the couple in the booth. They had champagne and caviar, too. I think, I'm nearly sure, they were already seated when we got there. They were sitting very close together. Very intimate. They were a very attractive couple."

"Okay, what next?"

"We danced. I forgot about them. But I went into the lounge, sat down to freshen up, and to get my balance. It was a very intense first date for me. While I was there, she came out of the stalls. She was throwing off all kinds of sexual sparks. Told me to congratulate her, that she was going to get very lucky. I was amused, and half wishing I could be that confident. They were leaving when I came out. They were leaving, and I never gave it a thought."

She sighed. "Her color was too high, her eyes were glassy. I can see it now."

"What do you remember about him?"

"Polished, attractive. They looked right together, and he looked natural in that sort of setting. I wish I'd noticed more. Maybe Charles did."

Eve felt the jolt in her belly, saw it in the quick jerk of her aide's shoulders. "Charles?"

"Yes. Charles Monroe. I tried to reach him this morning, but he has his 'link on message mode only."

"Okay." Oh boy. "I may need to talk to you again."

"You can reach me at the clinic all day." She got to her feet. "I wish I was more help."

"Everything helps."

• • •

Eve said nothing about it as she drove. She intended to say nothing about it ever in this lifetime. But Peabody's absolute silence broke her down.

"You okay about this?"

"I'm thinking about it. It wasn't a job."

"What?"

"They had this vibe going yesterday. It was a date, not a job. I'm okay with it," she decided. "I mean, we're just friends. It was just kind of a shock, that's all."

She glanced over, at the entrance to Charles's building, when Eve pulled to the curb. Apparently, she'd better be all right with it.

He was heading to the elevator as they stepped off. "Dallas. I was just coming in to see you. I just saw—"

"I know. Let's go inside first."

"You know, but . . . Louise. Is she upset? I need to call her."

Eve's eyebrows raised as he fumbled with the keycode of his door. The unflappable Charles was definitely flapped. "Later. She's okay."

"Not thinking straight," he confessed, and ran a hand absently over Peabody's shoulder as they all stepped inside. "I spent an hour in the relaxation tank this morning. Didn't turn on the screen until a few minutes ago. The report hit me in the face. We saw them, just last night. Him and the woman he tried to kill."

"Tell me."

It was almost identical to Louise's statement, save for the interlude in the lounge. But Charles's speculation that the man was an LC interested her.

"Why did you think that?"

"He was detached, just a little. It's hard to explain. He was very solicitous, very smooth, but there was calculation under it. He let her make all the physical advances and let her pay the check. I was preoccupied," he admitted, "but I noticed the way he looked after her when she went into the lounge. Calculation, again. And smugness.

Just a quick impression on my end. Some LCs think of clients that way."

"How about clients?"

"Sorry?"

"Some clients look at LCs that way."

He studied Eve's face, then nodded. "Yes. You're right about that."

She turned for the door. "Check with some of your associates for me, will you, Charles? For a client who likes classical music, pink roses, and candlelight." She tossed a glance over her shoulder. "And poetry. You people keep client files on preferences, right?"

"If we want to stay in business, we do. I'll ask around. Delia? Can I have a minute?"

Eve kept going. "I'll get the elevator."

"I know we'd penciled in dinner this evening," he began.

"Don't worry about it." She found it easy to kiss his cheek. That's what friends were for. "I like her."

"Thanks." He gave Peabody's hand a squeeze. "So do I."

Chapter 12

It usually made employees nervous when Roarke showed up unexpectedly at one of his companies. To his way of thinking, a few nerves helped keep people on their toes.

He paid well, and the working conditions that were found in all his companies, factories, subsidiaries, and offices throughout the world and its satellites were unquestionably high.

He knew what it was to be poor, and to be surrounded by the dingy, the dark, the dirty. For some—himself, for instance—those were motivators to achieve more. By whatever means possible. But for most, a stingy wage and an airless box in which to earn it fostered hopelessness, resentment. And pilfering.

He preferred a higher overhead, which tended to keep those who belonged to him comfortable, loyal, and productive.

He walked through the main level of Allegany, making mental notes on what might need to be adjusted in security, in decor. He found no glitches in communication as within moments of his requesting to speak with the chief chemist he was being escorted to the thirtieth floor. The flustered receptionist who led the way offered him coffee twice and apologized for the delay in locating Dr. Stiles a total of three times before they'd reached the man's office.

"I'm sure he's very busy." Roarke glanced around the large, somewhat disorganized room where the sun and privacy screens were both firmly fixed to the window.

The place was as dim as a cave.

"Oh yes, sir. I'm sure he is, sir. May I bring you some coffee while you wait?"

Three for three, he thought. "No, thank you. If Dr. Stiles is in one of the labs, perhaps—"

He broke off when the man stalked in, all flapping lab coat and scowl. "I'm in the middle of a project."

"So I imagined," Roarke said mildly. "I'm sorry to interrupt you."

"What are you doing in here?" he demanded of the horrified receptionist. "Haven't I told you I don't want people fussing around in my office?"

"Yes, but—"

"Scoot. Scoot." He scooted her personally, waving his hands at her like a farm wife scattering chickens. "What do you want?" he said to Roarke and slammed the office door smartly.

"It's nice to see you again, too, Stiles."

"I don't have time for chitchat and politics. We're working on the new heart regenerative serum."

"How's it going?"

"It has momentum, which you're stopping by calling me out of my lab."

He sat, gracelessly, a beefy man with the shoulders of an Arena Ball fullback. His face was dominated by a nose that sliced down the center of his face like an ax through granite. His eyes were black and brooding, his mouth set in a permanent frown. His hair, a dingy gray he refused to change, sprang up out of his scalp like steel wool.

He was ill-mannered, ill-tempered, surly, and sarcastic.

Roarke liked him very much.

"You worked here when Allegany was associated with J. Forrester."

"Hah." Stiles took out a pipe he hadn't filled in fifteen years and chewed on the stem. "I've worked here since you were still sucking your thumb and drooling on your chin."

"Fortunately I grew out of both distressing habits. The partnership had to do with a particular project."

"Sexual dysfunction. People didn't worry about sex so much, they'd get more done."

"But what would be the point?" Roarke lifted a box filled with what appeared to be a decade's worth of periodical discs, set it on the floor.

"Married now, aren't you? Sex goes out the window."

Roarke thought of Eve rising over him in the dark. "Is that what happened to it?"

The amusement in the tone had Stiles snorting out what might have been a laugh.

"In any case," Roarke continued, "I need information about the partnership, the project, and the players."

"I look like a fucking data bank to you?"

Roarke ignored the question. More, he ignored the delivery, something he wouldn't have done for many. "I've already accessed considerable data, but the personal touch is helpful. Theodore McNamara."

"Asshole."

"As I believe that's your affectionate term for nearly everyone in your acquaintance, and out of it, perhaps you could be more specific."

"More interested in profit than the results. In glory than the big picture. Administrate you to death and back again just for the enjoyment of proving who was pushing the buttons. Wanted a name for himself. He was top dog around here then, and he made sure we all knew it by pissing on everyone as often as possible. Courted the media like a publicity whore."

"I take it you didn't get together for a quick beer after a hard day over the petri dish."

"Couldn't stand the son of a bitch. Can't knock his professional skills. There's a brilliant mind in that puffed up prima donna."

He sucked on his pipe a little, thinking. "He hand-selected most of the teams. Brought his doormat of a daughter in on it. What the hell was her name . . . Hah, who gives a shit? Good brain, worked like a dog, and had nothing to say for herself."

"Can I assume from this the project was primarily Mc-Namara's baby?"

"He made the majority of decisions, made the blue-prints for the direction the work took. It was a corporate project, but McNamara was the figurehead, spokesper-son, main son of a bitch in charge. There was a lot of money riding on the deal. Corporate money, private in-vestors. Sex sells. We had some luck in a couple areas."

"Considerable."

"Guaranteeing a man he can still get a boner when he's a hundred and two and letting a woman keep her bi-ological clock ticking past the half-century mark." Stiles shook his head. "Money and media from that bumped things up. The less snappy stuff we accomplished—in-fertility aids without the risks of multiple births—wasn't as newsworthy. The brass was looking for more, and McNamara put on the pressure for us to give them more. We were working with dangerous elements, unstable ones. Tempting ones. The costs rose, and experiments were pushed too fast to make up the margin. Bad chem-istry. Side effects, unsanctioned use. Recreational, too. Lawsuits started piling up, and they shut the project down."

"And McNamara?"

"Managed to stay out of the stink." Stiles's mouth

turned down in disgust. "He knew what was going on. Nothing ever got by him."

"What about staff? Anyone you remember who had a particular affection for recreational use?"

"Do I look like a weasel?" Stiles barked.

"Actually . . . ah, you meant metaphorically, not literally."

"Give it another fifty years, you won't look so pretty either."

"Just one more thing to look forward to, Stiles." Roarke switched gears, sobered, leaned forward. "This is hardly gossip. Two women murdered, one in a coma. If there's a possibility the source springs back to that project—"

"What women? What murders?"

Roarke nearly sighed. How could he have forgotten who he was talking to? "Get out of the lab occasionally, Stiles."

"Why? There are people out there. Nothing fucks things up faster than people."

"There's a person or persons out there right now drugging women with the very chemicals you and this lab experimented in. Drugging them to death."

"Not bloody likely. Do you know how much it would take to induce death? The cost of the elements involved?"

"I have that data, thank you. The cost in this case doesn't seem to be an issue."

"Hell of a lot of money, even if he's cooking it himself."

"What would it take to cook it himself?"

Stiles thought for a moment. "Good lab, diagnostic and equation units, first-class chemist. Air-seal lock for holding during stabilization process. Has to be privately funded, black market. Any accredited lab or center was working on this, I'd know about it."

"Put your ear to the ground," Roarke told him, "and see if you hear about anything that's not accredited." His pocket-link beeped. "Excuse me."

He engaged privacy mode, flipped on the earpiece. "Roarke."

• • •

Eve hated cooling her heels. She particularly hated it in a space where she was considered as much Roarke's wife, maybe more, than a badge. The Palace was one of those spaces.

She hated it only slightly less after being escorted to Roarke's hotel office where she could interview the waiter who'd served Moniqua and her attacker.

She preferred her visit to Rikers where the facilities were spare, the staff snarly, and the inmates vicious. Even if her interview with Gunn had been a dead end, it had been in more comfortable surroundings.

"I'll have Jamal brought up to you the moment he arrives." The ruthlessly sleek lounge hostess gestured when the elevator doors opened. "If there's anything else I, or any of the Palace staff, can do to aid in your investigation, you've only to ask."

It required both a thumbprint and a code to unlock the office, and this required enlisting the help of the executive office manager.

Security was never taken for granted in a Roarke Industries holding.

"In the meantime"—the hostess smiled warmly—"may I offer you any refreshment?"

"A sparkling mango." Peabody leaped in with the request before Eve could throw up the wall against such niceties. She met Eve's dour look. "I'm kind of thirsty."

"Of course." The hostess glided over to the carved cupboard that held the refreshment center and programmed the AutoChef. "And for you, Lieutenant?"

"Just the waiter."

"He's due in very shortly." She offered Peabody the mango in a tall, fluted glass. "If there's nothing else I can do for you, I'll give you your privacy."

She stepped out, closing the doors discreetly behind her.

"These are really good." Peabody savored each swallow. "You should go for one."

"We're not here to slurp down fancy drinks." Eve wandered the room. Despite the cutting-edge equipment, it was more luxury apartment than office. "I want the waiter's statement before I hit Dr. McNamara. Stop guzzling that and check on Moniqua Cline's condition."

"I can do both."

While she did, Eve contacted Feeney. "Give me something."

"You been to Rikers already?"

"Come and gone. Gunn and I passed a few pleasantries during which he suggested I perform various sexual acts on myself that, however inventive, are either anatomically impossible or illegal."

"Same old Gunn," Feeney said, with some affection.

"Otherwise, he was a washout. He was pissed off enough to find out somebody was out there making money in his area for me to believe he doesn't know a damn thing. So give me something."

"I told you it was gonna take time."

"Time's passing. One of them may have a date tonight."

"Dallas, you know how much crap's passed through this unit? It's a public rental for Christ's sake. I can't just reach in and pluck a single user out like a frigging rabbit out of a hat."

"You've got Cline's unit. Can't you run the cross-check?"

"Do I look like this is my first day on the job? He didn't play with her on this one. Not that I can find. You want me to explain what the hell I'm doing here, or you want me to do it?"

"Do it." She started to cut off, caught herself. "Sorry," she added, then cut off.

"No change," Peabody told her. "She's still critical and comatose."

The door opened. Eve told herself she shouldn't have been the least surprised to see Roarke walk in.

"What are you doing here?"

"I believe this is my office." He glanced around. "Yes, I'm sure it is. Jamal, this is Lieutenant Dallas and Officer Peabody. They're going to ask you some questions, and require your full cooperation."

"Yes, sir."

"Relax, Jamal," Eve told him. "You're not in any trouble."

"No. This is about the woman in the coma. I saw a bulletin, and wondered if I should go to the police station or to work." He glanced at Roarke.

"The surroundings are a bit more comfortable here," Roarke said easily.

"So you say," Eve muttered under her breath.

"Sit down, Jamal," Roarke invited. "Would you like anything to drink?"

"No, sir. Thank you."

"Would you mind," Eve interrupted, "if I conducted this interview?"

"Not at all." Roarke walked over, took a seat behind his desk. "And no, I'm not leaving. Jamal's entitled to have a representative present."

"I would like to help." Jamal sat, his back arrow-straight, and folded his hands neatly on his lap. "Even if I hadn't been instructed to give full cooperation, I would want to help. It's my duty."

"Well, that's a refreshing attitude, Jamal. I'm going to record this. Peabody?"

"Yes, sir. Record on."

"Interview with Jamal Jabar, regarding the attempted murder of Moniqua Cline. Casefile H-78932C. Dallas, Lieutenant Eve, conducting the interview. Also present Peabody, Officer Delia, as aide and Roarke as subject Jabar's chosen representative. Jamal, you're employed as waitstaff in The Royal Bar of the Roarke Palace Hotel. Correct?"

"Yes. I've been serving here for three years."

"And last night, in that capacity, you served a couple in station five of your section."

"I served four couples at that station during my shift."

Eve took out the stills, held them up. "Do you recognize these people?"

"I do. They were in my section last night, at station five. They had a bottle of Dom Perignon '56, beluga caviar with full accompaniments. The gentleman arrived at just before nine o'clock and was very specific in what we wished to be served, and how."

"He arrived first."

"Oh yes, nearly thirty minutes before the lady. But he instructed me to bring the champagne right away, and to open the bottle. He wished to pour himself. The caviar was to be served after she arrived."

"Did he have a bag, black leather, long strap, with him?"

"He did. He didn't wish to check it. He kept it on the booth beside him. He made one call on his 'link. I assumed it was to the lady as he was waiting so long for her. But he didn't seem impatient, and when I stopped by to make certain he was comfortable and inquired if his guest was late, he told me she was not."

"When did he pour the champagne?"

"I didn't notice precisely, but when it was nearly nine-thirty, the glasses were full. She arrived shortly after that. And I realized—thought I realized why he had come so early if indeed she was timely. I assumed he'd been nervous as this was a first date."

"How did you know it was a first date?"

"I would have guessed because there was an excitement, and a slight formality between them at the beginning. But I was sure of it as I heard her say how happy she was to finally meet him face-to-face."

"What did they talk about?"

Jamal turned toward Roarke. "We're not supposed to listen to the guests' conversations."

"You got ears. Hearing isn't the same as listening."

"No, it isn't." Jamal's face registered his appreciation for her distinction. "When I served the caviar, they were speaking of art and literature, the way people do as they look for a comfortable spot to settle with each other. He was very attentive, but gentlemanly. At the beginning."

"But that changed."

"You could say they became very . . . at ease with each other very quickly. They touched, kissed in a way that indicated intimacy, or the willingness for it. If you understand me, Lieutenant."

"Yeah, I follow you."

"When I cleared the caviar, it was the lady who paid. This seemed distasteful to me as he had been the one to order." He looked a little sheepish. "But she gave me a very generous tip. They lingered over the wine. She became, it seemed to me, quite aggressive. At one point . . ." He shifted in his chair, relinked his fingers. "I saw her hand under the table. And, well, in his trousers. As this is against restaurant policy, I debated reporting it to my supervisor. But then she got up and went into the ladies' lounge. When she returned, they left."

"Had you ever seen either of them before last night?"

"I don't remember her, but we see so many people. The Royal Bar is a city landmark, after all. But I remember him."

Eve's head came up, just an inch. "How?"

"He's been in my section before, that same station. Only a week ago, perhaps a little more. With another man. He didn't look the same, but it was him. Last night, his hair was lighter and longer. His face different somehow. I can't really say."

"But you recognized him?"

"His ring. I'd admired it before. My wife is a jeweler, so I tend to notice a good piece when I see it. It's a wide band with alternating ribbons of white and yellow gold with a square stone. A ruby with a dragon's head carved into it. Very distinctive. His companion had one as well, but with a sapphire. I thought at the time they were mates, and these their wedding rings."

"This man last night had on the ruby ring."

"Yes. I nearly remarked on it, but as he looked so different I assumed he didn't wish to be recognized. And he indicated, quite clearly, he didn't wish to speak with his server."

Eve got to her feet, circled the room. "Tell me about the time you saw him before. Him, and the other man."

"I only remember it was about a week ago. I don't remember which evening. But I think it was early in my shift. Near seven o'clock. They had wine and hors d'oeuvres." He smiled thinly. "And didn't tip well."

"How did they pay?"

"Cash."

"What did they talk about?"

"I didn't hear very much. They seemed to be arguing, but good-naturedly, over which of them would start the game. They were in very high spirits. And it amused me when I was taking an order from station six that the gentlemen in five were flipping a coin."

Bryna Bankhead, Eve thought, had died on the flip of a coin. "I need you to work with an imaging tech, Jamal."

"I'm afraid I won't be able to describe him very well."

"Let us worry about that. We appreciate your cooperation. You've been a really big help. Someone will contact you about the imaging."

"All right." He glanced at Roarke, got the nod of approval, and rose. "I hope whatever I've told you helps you stop him from hurting anyone else."

"Jamal." Roarke got to his feet. "I'll speak to your supervisor. You'll be paid for whatever time you need to take off to assist the police. Any lost time won't affect your benefits or salary."

"Thank you, sir."

"We run the ring," Eve snapped the minute the doors closed behind Jamal. "Every jewelry store in New York that does custom work. Order an imaging tech, priority one."

"On it," Peabody replied.

"Lieutenant?" Roarke's voice stopped her before she'd taken two steps toward the door.

"What?"

"Where are you going?"

"Central, to review the security discs. See if I can spot the rings."

"You can do that here. And on this equipment, a great deal faster. Computer, replay security disc, Royal Bar, June six, twenty-two forty-five."

Working . . . Display selection?

"Wait a minute? You've got visual security on the lounge?"

"I believe in being thorough."

She cursed under her breath. "You could've mentioned it."

"Seeing it's so much more effective. Wall screen one."

The lounge spilled onto the screen, all opulence and color. The elegant sat at tables or glided on the dance floor while those who served them moved with seamless efficiency from table to booth, from booth to what she assumed was the kitchen.

The images sped up as Roarke manually ordered fast-forward.

"He should be coming along any . . . Ah." He stopped the progress, froze the screen.

Eve stepped closer, concentrating on his hands. "Can't see the ring from this angle. Play it forward." She waited, watched him speak briefly to the evening hostess. Watched him being led to his reserved booth. His hands were under the table and out of view when Jamal stepped up to greet him.

"Come on, come on, come on," Eve urged. "Scratch your nose or something."

Jamal returned with the bottle of champagne, the

flutes. Completed the setup. But when he offered to pour the wine, he was impatiently waved away.

"Freeze image," Eve ordered, but Roarke already had.

"Increase sector twenty through thirty, fifty percent."

When Roarke repeated her request, Eve realized the unit was set for his voice command only. Any irritation she might have felt was overpowered by the satisfaction of seeing the ruby ring in full detail. "I want a printout of that."

"How many?"

"Give me a dozen. And transfer this disc run to my office unit and Peabody's PPC."

Peabody opened her mouth, then wisely decided not to ask how a civilian could transfer data to an official unit without pass codes and electronic authorization.

"Let's see if we can save some time. Peabody, I want you to do 'link calls to the jewelers. Show them the image of the ring. See if we can tag the shop or craftsman who made it. Is there a place she can set up here, for maybe an hour?" Eve asked Roarke.

"Of course." He contacted his executive assistant on the interoffice communicator. "Ariel, Officer Peabody requires a private workspace. She'll meet you at main."

He glanced at Peabody. "Just go out to the main reception this floor. Ariel will take care of it."

"Great." And with visions of another sparkling mango in her future, Peabody headed out.

"You'll want to see the rest of this," Roarke said, and resumed play at normal speed and range.

On-screen, the killer lined the flutes side by side. He poured a half glass of each, scanning the room as they foamed and bubbled. His hand lifted, hovered over one of the glasses.

"Freeze. Enhance."

She walked to within inches of the screen and saw clearly the trickle of clear liquid spilling from his hand into the glass. "When I get this bastard, the PA's going to do fucking cartwheels over this disc. Resume play, same enhancement, quarter speed. There, there, look at that. He's got a vial palmed in his hand. Premeasured or I'm a monkey's butt."

"And I can attest you're not. Time stamp," Roarke continued, "shows he's given himself a few minutes leeway. In case she's early. He's filled both glasses now, set the spiked one across the table."

"Give me full view again. Look at him. Look at his face. Awful damned pleased with himself. A little private toast. Now he makes the call. His partner. Everything's in place, can't wait to get home and tell you how it went. We'll get a lip reader to study this, see how close I am."

"Here she comes," Roarke commented.

Moniqua stepped into the lounge. Hesitated. Then her lips curved. "There he is, she's thinking," Eve said quietly. "And he's handsome, just as she hoped he would be. Look, perfect gentleman's getting up. Takes her hand, a little peck on the knuckles for that romantic touch.

"Champagne? How delightful. Click glasses. Perfect script. You'd hardly notice that predatory look on his face as she drinks if you didn't know he was a monster. If you didn't know, in his mind, he's killing her right now."

"I'll never know how you do this. Day after day." Roarke spoke from behind her now, laying his hands on her shoulders to rub at the knots of tension.

"Because I know, in my mind, I'll get him. Them. Both of them. They think they've covered all the angles, but you never hit them all. There are always mistakes. Little mistakes. He thinks he's safe, think's he's smart. Anybody looking at them would see she's the one making the moves here. She's the one sliding closer in the booth, touching his arm, his hair, leaning in. Who'd look at that pretty scene and see rape?"

"It hurts you. Don't tell me it doesn't," he said, and

there was an edge in his voice. "You bandage it, but it hurts you."

"It only makes me work harder to stop him. Oh jeez, there's Charles and Louise."

"Is that why you sent Peabody out?"

"I don't need her distracted, and I'm *not* thinking about her weird-ass platonic thing with Charles and her weirder-ass sexual one with McNab because it distracts *me*. What is it, standard seduction plan A: Champagne and caviar?"

"You preferred coffee and red meat as I recall."

"I'll take real cow over a bunch of fish eggs any— There! He's given her a booster. Same little palm deal, new vial. Two doses in her before they get to her place. That's off. Lab found traces of Whore in the living room glass, Rabbit in the bedroom. But her tox screen didn't put that much Whore in her system. That's why she's not dead."

"She's drinking it," Roarke pointed out.

"Yeah, giving him a little hand job under the table and swilling it back. He gives her the third dose at her place. How does her system absorb that much? Because it didn't. She purged. Sicked it up. She's slim, but not skinny," Eve mused. "Doesn't look like the eating disorder type. Probably just got queasy. When she was in the lounge here, or at home. Tossed up some of the wine and fish eggs, and enough of the drug to keep her system from fully overloading.

"Mistake," she said. "He didn't think of that. When he left her she was out cold and he took her for dead. Tells me he's not a doctor or any sort of med-tech. It's the other guy who knows that end. This one's just the computer freak. Run the disc from the second murder. I want to see if I can get a good image of that ring, too."

"Kevin, you really are becoming tedious." There was a mechanical *whoosh* and a fog of cold air as Lucias unsealed the cryo-unit and selected the desired solution in its freezer pack. "The first time you're nearly hysterical because the girl died. Now you're biting your nails because this one didn't."

"I didn't mean to kill the first one."

"And did the second." With tongs, Lucias set the pack in a slot in a treated glass tray. "I'd say, as far as the game goes, old friend, you're in the minus column."

"You're the one doing the cooking." Suspicion, mixed with anger and fear, made Kevin's voice ugly. "What's to stop you from playing around with the mix for my bag?"

"A sense of fair play, of course. Cheating would lessen the satisfaction of winning. We agreed on the honor system, Kev."

"She's very likely to die, so don't mark your score card quite yet."

"That's the spirit. And again in the interest of fair play, I suggest we consider her hospitalization as five points, as we put death at a full ten. If your little playmate dies before I get home from my date tonight, you'll actually be in the lead again. Can't get fairer than that. And if she doesn't . . ." He shrugged, then slid the tray with its various packs into a thin compartment, programmed time and temperature. "I go ahead. We can increase the stakes with some double booking."

"Two in one day?" The horror, and the thrill, of the idea struck Kevin simultaneously.

"If you're man enough."

"We haven't prepared. The schedule calls for three nights off after this evening's round. None of the targets are in line until next week."

"Schedules are for amateurs and drones." Lucias prepared them both a little cocktail. Unblended scotch with a dash of Zoner. "Let's rack them up, Kev. We'll both have impressive American scores before we move the game to France."

"A picnic in the park," Kevin considered. "An afternoon rendezvous. Yes, that might be fun. And, it would be best to start mixing up our methods. Toss the police a sudden curve to screw up their probabilities and profiles."

"Day games. They have their own special panache, don't you think?"

Chapter 13

"No pops on the rings," Eve told her team.

She'd had to pull rank, step on toes, and bribe the scheduling clerk with a block of Swiss chocolate, but she'd managed to hook a conference room.

Roarke was good for the chocolate and would only smirk a little at the bribery angle.

"Best we've got is they're not heirlooms. The jewelers Peabody tapped agree that they're not antiques. If the stones and settings are genuine, the value's estimated at two hundred fifty k each."

"Any guy wears a quarter mil on his finger's a putz" was Feeney's opinion. "And a showoff."

"Agreed. Putz and showoff percentages are high. I want to take the search on them global, so I'm passing that ball to EDD." And she'd tap her own personal source on showoff items. Roarke might not wear baubles himself, but he was sure an expert at buying them and draping them all over her.

"Imaging's working with the waiter, but it's slow. He's a lot clearer on the rings than the guys wearing them. We can access security discs for the last week or two weeks from the Palace, but it'll take time to pick through them, and luck to home in on our men. I'll be doing that run personally, but meanwhile, if nothing jumps by morning, I'm going to request our witness agrees to hypnotherapy."

"There's no guarantee they weren't wearing enhancements when they met for drinks," McNab pointed out and earned a rare nod of approval from Eve.

"That's right, but we detail the image anyway. We keep building the box until we lock them inside. Progress on the rental unit?" She glanced at Feeney. "And don't crawl up my ass."

"Funny you should ask. We cleaned out most of the chatter. You wouldn't believe the shit people send through rentals. Porn sites win ten to one."

"It's so good to have my view of the general citizenship reinforced."

"After that you got your entertainment and amusement sites, then your financials. Personal e-mail comes after. Most promising user name is Wordsworth. All his transmissions are cloaked. You get through one layer of the cloak and the sucker bounces you to another locale. He shot the goods from the cyber-joint to Madrid. Start picking there and it bounces to Delta Colony. Then—"

"I get the picture. What did you find?"

Feeney sulked a little, crunched on nuts. "I uncloaked one transmission so far. Looks like he did three, maybe four more. The one I stripped down went to an account registered to Stefanie Finch. A lot of mushy stuff."

"Shoot the mushy stuff and her address to my units. You're a cyber-wizard, Feeney."

That soothed his ruffles. "Yeah, don't I know it. I gotta take a couple hour's medical, get a quick eye fix. Detective Cyber-Wiz here'll keep on it."

"I'm in the field. Peabody, with me. Peel off," she ordered as she strode out and toward a glide. "Snag me an energy bar or something, meet me in the garage in ten. I need to stop by my office first."

"There's vending right outside the bullpen."

"The vending machines around here hate me. They steal my credits and laugh in my face."

"You've had your vending privileges suspended again for kicking the equipment, haven't you?"

"I didn't kick it, I punched it. And just get me the damn bar." Without waiting for a response, Eve hopped the glide and flipped out her communicator to check in with the imaging tech.

Peabody merely sighed and backtracked to the closest food vender. She was perusing the choices, debating between energy or chemical sweetener for herself when McNab came up behind her.

Since their session the night before, she expected him to go for a little pinch or grab. But he dipped his hands into two of the twelve pockets in his butter yellow trousers and just stood there.

"You doing okay?" he asked her.

"Yeah, just ordering up a few boosts." Figuring Dallas could have them both in the field for hours yet, she went for energy and sweetener.

"I figure you're bent about what happened. You shouldn't be. Stuff like that doesn't mean anything."

Thinking of pizza, and the frantic bout of sex on her living room floor, the second, more thorough session in her bed, she felt her stomach tighten. "Right. Who said it meant anything?"

"I'm just saying you shouldn't be like, embarrassed or upset."

She turned to him, kept her face absolutely stone still. "Do I look embarrassed or upset to you?"

"Look, you don't want to talk about it, fine with me." His personal sense of outrage leaped up, snagged him by the throat. Charles had all but rubbed his new lady in Peabody's face, and she still couldn't see him for what he was. "Everybody knows it was never going anywhere. If you thought otherwise, then you deserve just what you get."

"Thanks for the bulletin. And you can just . . ." She

searched for something, and settled on Eve's favored suggestion. "Bite me." Shoving him aside with her elbow, she marched to the nearest glide.

"Fine." He kicked the vending machine, storming off as it issued the standard warning. If she wanted to get twisted up over having her pet LC trot another woman out under her nose, why the hell should he care?

By the time Peabody made it to the garage she'd eaten her energy bar and started on the candy. And she was steaming. Already in the vehicle, Eve merely held out a hand. Then hissed when Peabody slapped the bar into her palm sharply enough to burn.

"I should have kicked his ass. Just mopped the floor with his skinny, bony ass."

"Christ." In defense, Eve shot out of her slot. "Don't start."

"I'm not starting, I'm finished. Pig bastard wants to stand there and tell me I shouldn't be *embarrassed*, shouldn't be *upset* because last night didn't *mean* anything?"

I will not listen, I will not listen, I will not listen, Eve repeated over and over in her head. "Finch lives on Riverside Drive. Alone. Employed as shuttle pilot for Inter-Commuter Air."

"He's the one who came knocking on *my* door with his pitiful pizza and big sloppy smile."

"She's twenty-four," Eve said desperately. "Single. Perfect fit for target profile of killer number one."

"And who's everyone? Who the hell is everyone?"

"Peabody, if I just agree that McNab is a pig bastard, that you should kick his ass, even give you my solemn word that I will help you kick the pig bastard's ass at the first reasonable opportunity, can we pretend we're focused on this investigation?"

"Yes, sir." Peabody sniffed. "But I'd appreciate it if you would not speak the pig bastard's name in my presence ever again."

"That's a deal. We're going to Finch's. Once I get a

sense of her, we'll see if she can stand up as bait or needs to be removed to protective custody. Next on the list is McNamara. We pin him down today, on or off planet. If McNab . . . the pig bastard," she corrected when Peabody's head snapped around, "manages to uncloak any more target accounts, we move on them immediately. The civilian targets are priority."

"Understood, sir."

"Check in with the officer on duty at the hospital. We're more likely to get word from our own first on any change in the victim's condition than we are from medical staff."

"Yes, sir. Can I say one more thing about the pig bastard? Absolutely the last thing I have to say on the subject."

"The last thing? Well then, I can't wait to hear it."

"I hope his balls shrivel up like overbaked prunes then fall off in useless husks."

"A very pleasant final image. I applaud you. Now tag the guard."

Shuttle pilots, Eve decided, pulled in a fine, fat per annum. The apartment building was swank and silver, a shining spear ringed by glides that allowed residents and guests private exterior access if they were cleared.

As she'd already had her height quota for the next little while, Eve chose the interior access. The electronic greeting station requested her business, her name, and destination in a pleasant and no-nonsense tone.

"Police business. Dallas, Lieutenant Eve, and aide to see Stefanie Finch." She held her badge up to the security screen, listened to the faint hum as it was scanned and verified.

"I'm sorry, Lieutenant Dallas, Ms. Finch is not in residence at this time. You may leave a message for her by requesting visitor voice mail."

"When is she expected back?"

"I'm sorry, Lieutenant Dallas, I am not authorized to give that information without a warrant."

"I bet Roarke owns this place," Peabody commented

as she gazed around the spacious black-and-silver lobby. "It's his style. I bet if you told it you're his wife—"

"No." It irritated her just to think about it. "I want to see the resident or residents in apartment 3026."

"Next-door neighbor. Good thinking."

"One moment, Lieutenant Dallas. Mrs. Hargrove is in residence. I'll submit your request for visitation."

"Yeah, you do that. How do people stand being closed up in these places?" Eve wondered. "Like little ants in a hive."

"I think it's bees in a hive. Ants are—"

"Shut up, Peabody."

"Yes, sir."

"Mrs. Hargrove will allow visitation, Lieutenant Dallas and aide. Please use elevator bank five. Enjoy your visit, and the rest of your day."

Alicanne Hargrove turned out to be not only willing but thrilled at the visit.

"Police." She all but pulled Eve into her apartment. "So exciting. Has there been a robbery?"

"No, ma'am. I'd like to speak to you regarding Stefanie Finch."

"Stef?" The animation on Alicanne's pretty face faded. "Oh my goodness. She's all right, isn't she? She just left this morning for a shuttle run."

"As far as I know she's fine. You and Ms. Finch are friendly?"

"Yes, very. Oh, I'm sorry, sit down."

She gestured to the painfully modern living area with its trio of gel-sofas. To Eve, they looked big enough, squishy enough to swallow any number of household pets. "Thanks, but this won't take long. Can you tell me if you know if Ms. Finch is seeing anyone socially?"

"Men? Stef sees a lot of men. She's a dynamo."

"Anyone named Wordsworth?"

"Oh, the poet. She's been having a romance with him through e-mail. I think they're scheduled to meet when she gets back from her shuttle run. Day after tomorrow.

She'll be based in London until then. It seems to me she said they'd made a tentative date for next week. Drinks at the Top of New York. But the way Stef juggles men, I can't be sure."

"If she gets in touch, or comes back before schedule, ask her to contact me. It's urgent. Card, Peabody."

Peabody dug out one of Eve's cards, passed it over.

"Can I tell her what it's about?"

"Just tell her to contact me. Right away. Thanks for your time."

"Oh, but wouldn't you like some coffee, or—" She trotted hopefully after them as Eve strode out.

"Track her down, Peabody." Her own communicator beeped. "Dallas."

"Lieutenant." Trueheart's earnest face filled the tiny screen. "I think something's going on. Three medical staff just went into the subject's room, including Dr. Michaels, and he came on the run."

"Stand by, Trueheart. I'm on my way."

Since the floor nurse all but threw herself in front of the ICU doors, Eve gave her sixty seconds to produce Dr. Michaels. He whisked out with a swirl of his long white coat and an annoyed expression.

"Lieutenant, this is a hospital, not a police station."

"You can consider it both as long as Moniqua Cline is your patient. What's her status?"

"She's conscious, very disoriented. Her vital signs show improvement, but are still in the dangerous range. She's far from out of the woods."

"I need to question her. Hers isn't the only life at stake."

"Hers is the life under my care."

Because one hard case recognized another, Eve nodded. "Don't you think she'd rest easier knowing the person who did this to her has been put away? Look, I'm not going to interrogate her. I'm not going to browbeat her. I understand the pathology of the victim."

"I appreciate the import of your investigation, Lieutenant, but this woman isn't a tool."

Eve kept her voice steady. "She's not just a tool to me. But to the man who put her here, she's less than that. She's a game piece. Bryna Bankhead and Grace Lutz didn't have a chance to tell anyone what happened to them."

Whatever he saw in her face had him pushing open the door. "Just you," he said. "And I'm staying with her."

"That works for me. Peabody, stand by."

A nurse monitored the machines and spoke in a soothing voice. Though Moniqua didn't respond, Eve thought she heard something. Her eyes traveled back and forth as if measuring the glass box of the room. They flicked over Eve, passed on, then lingered on Michaels's face.

"I'm so tired" was all she said, and her voice fluttered, soft as bird wings.

"You need to rest." He stepped to the bed and covered her hand with his.

In that gesture, Eve's confidence in him solidified. Moniqua wasn't just a patient to him. She was a person.

"This is Lieutenant Dallas. She needs to ask you some questions."

"I don't know . . ."

"I'm going to stay right here."

"Ms. Cline." Eve took the other side of the bed so that Moniqua lay between her and the doctor. "I know you're confused, and you're tired, but anything you can tell me will help."

"I don't remember."

"You corresponded, through e-mail, with an individual you knew as Byron."

"Yes. We met in a chat. Nineteenth-century poets."

"You agreed to meet him last night, for drinks at the Royal Bar in The Palace Hotel."

Her brow, pale as marble, creased. "Yes. At . . . nine-thirty. Was that last night? We'd been talking online for weeks, and . . . I met him. I remember."

"What else do you remember?"

"I—I was a little nervous at first. We'd hit it off so well in cyber, but real life's different. Still, it was just drinks, and in such a lovely setting. If it didn't work out, what was the harm? But it did. He was just as I expected . . . Did I have an accident? Am I dying?"

"You're doing very well," Michaels told her. "You're very strong."

"You had drinks with him," Eve continued, drawing her attention away from Michaels again. "What did you talk about?"

Moniqua's face went vague again. "Talk about?"

"With Byron. When you had drinks with him last night."

"Oh, ah, poetry. And art. Travel. We both like to travel, though he's been so many more places than I have. We had champagne, and caviar. I've never had caviar before. I don't think it agreed with me. I must have gotten ill."

"Were you ill at the hotel?"

"No. I—no, I don't think . . . I must have had too much to drink. I'm usually careful not to have more than one glass. I remember, I remember now. Feeling very strange, but good. Happy. He was so perfect, so attractive. I kissed him. Kept kissing him. I wanted to get a room in the hotel. That's not like me." Her fingers pulled weakly at the sheet. "I must've had too much to drink."

"You suggested getting a room in the hotel?"

"Yes. He laughed. It wasn't a pleasant laugh, but I was so drunk, I didn't care. Why did I drink so much? And he said . . . Take me home with you, and we'll do things the poets write of."

She closed her eyes. "Corny. But it didn't seem corny then. He told me to pay the check. I wasn't offended or surprised that he meant for me to pay, even though he'd made the date. I went in to freshen up, and all I could think was I was going to have amazing sex with this perfect man. And I could hardly wait to get my hands on him. We took a cab. I paid for that, too. And in the cab . . ."

The faintest color washed into her cheeks. "I think I must've dreamed all this. I must have dreamed it. He whispered a suggestion in my ear. What he wanted me to do." She opened her eyes again. "I went down on him, in the cab. I couldn't wait to. It wasn't a dream, was it?"

"No, it wasn't a dream."

"What did he give me?" She groped for Eve's hand, her fingers trying to squeeze, but only twitching. "What was in those drinks?"

Her hand moved, restlessly. Eve covered it. Gripped it. "I wasn't drunk, was I? It was like being hypnotized."

"You weren't drunk, Moniqua, and you're not responsible for anything you did. He drugged you. Tell me what happened when you got to your apartment."

"She needs to rest now." Michaels glanced at the monitors, back at Eve. "She's talked long enough. You have to leave."

"No." Moniqua's fingers moved in Eve's hand. "He gave me something that made me do those things to him, with him, made me let him do those things to me? He nearly killed me, didn't he?"

"Very nearly," Eve agreed. "But you're a hell of a lot stronger than he anticipated. Help me catch him. Tell me what happened in your apartment."

"It's hazy. I was dizzy, queasy. He put on music, lit candles. He had candles in his bag, and another bottle of champagne. I didn't want anymore, but he wanted me to drink. I did exactly what he asked me to do. Every time he touched me, I wanted him to touch me again. He said it needed to be perfect. That he was going to prepare . . . set the stage. I should wait. I felt sick. I didn't want to tell him I felt sick because he might not stay. So when he went into the bedroom, I went into the bath and was sick. After, I felt a little better. Steadier. I went into the bedroom. He had champagne by the bed, and dozens of candles lighted. There were rose petals all over the bed. Pink roses, like the ones he must have sent me at work a few days before. I'd never had anyone go to such trouble."

Tears spilled down her cheeks. "It was so lovely, almost painfully romantic. I actually loved him, in that instant when I walked in and saw him, I was wildly, recklessly in love with him. He undressed me, said I was beautiful. It was all very gentle at first, very sweet and intimate. A fantasy, really. After a while, he handed me the glass. I told him I didn't want more champagne, but he just looked at me, told me to drink it and I did. Then it wasn't gentle. It was outrageous. Like going mad. Like becoming an animal. I couldn't breathe, couldn't think. Burning from the inside out, and my heart beating so fast it felt like it would explode. He was watching me. I can see his eyes now, watching me. He told me to say his name. But it wasn't his name."

"What name was it?"

"Kevin. He told me his name was Kevin. Then it was as if things inside me, my head, my body, ripped. And everything stopped. I couldn't move or see or hear. Buried alive." Now she wept. "He buried me alive."

"No, he didn't." Eve leaned over before Michaels could move in. "You're here and safe and alive. He's never going to touch you again. Moniqua, he's never going to touch you again."

She turned her face weakly to the pillow as the tears flowed. "I let him inside me."

"No, you didn't. He violated you. He forced you."

"No, I let—"

"He forced you," Eve repeated. "Look at me. Listen to me. He took your choice away, and he raped you. His weapon was a drug instead of a knife or his fists, but it was still a weapon. Putting rose petals on the bed doesn't make what he did any less criminal. But you beat him. And I'm going to put him away for you. I know someone you can talk to, who'll help you through this."

"I never told him to stop. I didn't want him to."

"You're not responsible. This wasn't about sex. Rape

never is. This was about him controlling you. You couldn't stop him last night, but you can now. Don't let him control you now."

"He raped me, and then he left me to die. I want him to pay for making me feel like this."

"Leave that part to me."

Eve felt slightly ill when she stepped out again. It was brutal, always brutal, for her to interview rape victims. To look at them and see herself.

She took a moment, bracing a hand against the outer doors, waiting to settle again.

"Lieutenant?"

She straightened, turned to Michaels.

"You did very well with her. I'd expected you to push for more detail."

"I will, next time. I've got to dig out my rubber hose. Can't recall where I left it."

He offered a slow, half smile. "I didn't expect her to live. Medically, her chances were slim to none. But that's one of the rewards of my profession. The small miracles. She still has a rough road ahead, physically and emotionally."

"You can contact Dr. Charlotte Mira."

Impressed, he angled his head. "Dr. Mira?"

"If she can't treat Moniqua personally, she'll give the case to the best rape therapist available. You guys work on giving her back her physical and emotional health. I'll work on giving her justice."

She pushed through the doors, signalled to Peabody, and kept going. She wanted out of the hospital almost as much as she wanted to breathe.

"Sir." Peabody jogged to keep pace. "Everything all right?"

"She's alive, she's talking, and she's given us the bastard's first name. Kevin."

"Solid. But I was talking about you. You look a little whipped."

"I'm fine. I just hate fucking hospitals," she muttered.

"Maintain the guard on Moniqua, and the checks on her condition. Make a note to contact Mira and ask her to consult with Michaels over her therapy."

"I didn't think Mira took private consults."

"Just make a note of it, Peabody." She kept her breathing shallow until she shoved through the hospital doors and strode outside. "Christ! How do people stand being in those places? I've got a personal call to make. Step aside, will you? Call Moniqua's status into the commander and tell him my report will be forthcoming."

"Yes, sir. There's some benches just over there. Why don't you make that call sitting down?" *Because you're white as a sheet*, she wanted to say. But knew better.

Eve walked over to sit in a little area of green the city planners liked to call microparks. The trio of dwarf trees and scatter of flowers were jammed into a narrow island between parking lots. But she supposed it was the thought that counted.

Still, she wished they'd thought to plant something with fragrance. She wanted the stench of hospital out of her system.

She wasn't sure where to tag Roarke. She tried his personal line first, was switched to voice mail so she disconnected. She put the next through to his midtown offices and hit on his admin.

"I need to locate him."

"Of course, Lieutenant. He's on a holo-transmission, if you wouldn't mind waiting a moment. How are you?"

Right, Eve thought. Courtesy and conversation, a duo she often neglected. "Fine, thanks. How are you, Caro?"

"Very well. Delighted the boss is back, though it seems we're busier yet when he's in the cockpit. I'll just beep in and let him know you're on the line."

Waiting, Eve tipped her face back to the sun. It was always cold in hospitals, she thought. The kind of cold that crept into her bones.

"Lieutenant." She focused her attention on Roarke's

voice, on his face on-screen. "What's wrong?" he queried.

"Nothing. Need a favor."

"Eve. What's wrong?"

"Nothing. Really. Moniqua Cline regained consciousness. I just finished questioning her. She's going to tough this out, but it's hard on her."

"And on you."

"I know some of what's going through her head. I know some of what she's going to feel in the middle of the night." She shook it off. "That's not why I called, and you're in the middle of a transmission."

"It can wait. A benefit of being in charge. What can I do for you?"

"Question. Is it possible for you to monitor a standard account, monitor any e-mail, block same?"

"Private citizens who attempt any of the above are in violation of e-privacy laws and subject to fines and/or imprisonment."

"Which means you can."

"Oh. I assumed the question was rhetorical." He smiled at her. "Who do you want me to monitor?"

"Stefanie Finch. She's a potential target. At the moment she's in the air somewhere between the U.S. and England on shuttle runs. When she lands, I want to tell her who and what she's been playing with in hopes I can enlist her help to reel these guys in. But I don't know how she'll react, and she's going to have too much time to fiddle around before I have her under control. I can't chance her going off on a rip and tipping her cyber-pal."

"So you want to block all her transmissions and cyber-activities?"

"That's the ticket. I don't want anything she sends getting through until I'm sure of her cooperation and I have a warrant to put a filter on her transmissions. The warrant's not going to cover us until she's back in New York."

"You know how it excites me whenever you ask me to slip through one of the loops in the law."

"Remind me later why I married a pervert."

"I'll be happy to." His smile spread because color had come back into her face.

"How soon can you have it done?"

"I have some things to finish up here. Best to do this little task at home on the unregistered. Give me two hours. Oh, Lieutenant? I don't suppose this bit of business goes into my report as expert consultant, civilian."

"Kiss ass."

"As long as it's yours, darling."

Chapter 14

When Eve finally ran Theodore McNamara to ground, she was shown into his office by a bird of a woman who chirped about the doctor's demanding schedule and the need to keep the audience brief.

"The doctor really has no time for an extra appointment today. As you know, Dr. McNamara has just returned from a very important consult session on Tarus II."

"He's about to have a very important consult session on Planet Earth," Eve returned. For her own amusement, Eve lengthened her stride so the woman was forced to trot to keep up as they navigated the short breezeway that connected McNamara's office to the main building at J. Forrester. Outside the glass a medi-copter banked left for landing on the heliport of the adjoining hospital facilities.

She saw a half dozen medical personnel waiting for the transport, and imagined the noise was horrendous. But inside the breezeway the air was silent, cool, and faintly floral.

It appeared Dr. McNamara had disconnected himself

from the petty pains and troubles of those his facility served.

The breezeway opened into the office area done in stark white. Walls, rugs, consoles, chairs, even the uniforms of the drones who went silently about their business were unrelieved white.

It was, Eve thought, like walking inside an eggshell.

They passed through a set of glass doors that whisked open silently at their approach, and moved down yet another corridor. At the end loomed a set of glossy white doors. The woman knocked with a kind of fearful reverence.

The doors slid apart, but the woman stood where she was. "Lieutenant Dallas and aide, Dr. McNamara."

"Yes, yes. See that we're not disturbed. Ten minutes. Come in, Lieutenant. My time is very valuable."

He sat in front of a wall of glass at a desk so massive and white it resembled an ice floe. It stood on a platform three steps above the rest of the office so that McNamara peered down, an eagle on his perch, at lesser mortals.

His hair was white—a sleek, close-cut cap that hugged his skull. He had a long, hollowed face dominated by dark, impatient eyes that scowled beneath the white peaks of his brows. His black suit was a slash of power against the frigid white of the room.

"Golly," Peabody said under her breath, "it's the great and powerful Oz."

"State your business," he demanded. "I'm a busy man."

And one who liked to intimidate, Eve mused. They were not invited to sit, but even standing she was forced to look up to meet his gaze.

"You'd have saved us both time if you'd returned the transmissions I sent to you on Tarus II."

"The consult session was my priority. I am not attached as a medical consultant to the NYPSD."

"Which makes you a civilian, and gives me the authority to continue this interview at Cop Central, which I will enforce if necessary. Now, we can continue this pissing contest or you can agree to cooperate."

"You're in my office. It appears I am cooperating."

Annoyed, Eve strode up the steps to the platform. She saw cold fury wash over his face as he was forced to tip his head back. "Peabody. Stills."

Though she knew it was small of her, Peabody enjoyed watching her lieutenant screw up the power structure of the room. "Yes, sir." She passed the photos up.

Eve laid them on the pristine surface of the desk. "Do you recognize any of these women?"

"I do not."

"Bryna Bankhead, Grace Lutz, Moniqua Cline. Ring any bells?"

"No."

"Funny as their names and faces have been all over the media the last few days."

His stare never wavered. "I've been off planet, as you know."

"Last I heard they had media transmissions on Tarus II."

"I don't have time for gossip and media blathering. Nor for guessing games. Now, Miss Dallas, if you'd tell me what it is you wish to discuss—"

"Lieutenant Dallas. You were involved in a research project partnered by J. Forrester and Allegany Pharmaceuticals that involved experimentation with certain controlled substances."

"Research on sexual dysfunction and infertility. Successful research," he added, "that resulted in two landmark medications."

"The project was aborted due to cost overruns, lawsuits, and rumors of substance abuse and sexual misconduct by project staff."

"Your information is flawed. Abuse was never substantiated. The project produced important results and simply ran its course."

"Apparently someone's still experimenting. Two

women are dead, another's in critical condition. They were given fatal doses of the substances commonly known as Whore and Wild Rabbit, in combination. Someone has a substantial supply of both, or the means to create them."

"Drugs used to benefit mankind can and will be abused in the wrong hands. It's not my job to police the masses. It's yours."

"Who on your former research team might have those wrong hands?"

"All doctors and technicians who were involved were thoroughly screened and hand selected."

"And still, there was recreational and criminal use. This isn't gossip or blathering," she said before he could interrupt. "This is a murder investigation. Sex and power, that's a heady temptation."

"We were scientists, not sex mongers."

"Why are all the records sealed? Why are there seals on all the civil cases brought against the project?"

"No civil cases were ever brought to trial. No charges of misconduct were ever pressed. Therefore, it's a matter of privacy to seal records of frivolous suits that impinged upon the names and reputations of those associated with the project. Of maintaining dignity."

Eve pushed the photographs closer. "Someone invaded their privacy, Doctor. Big-time. And didn't leave them with their dignity."

"That has nothing to do with me."

"The project made a lot of money for its top people and its initial investors. It takes a lot of money to play with these particular illegals. I'm looking for two men, men with the means to buy or create substantial quantities of those illegals. Men with expert knowledge of chemistry and electronics. Men who consider women not only fair game, but disposable entertainment. Sexual predators, Dr. McNamara. Who worked with you, who fits that bill?"

"I can't help you. Your problem has nothing to do with the project, nothing to do with me. The project created medication that changed lives. I won't have you besmirch my work or my reputation because you're unable to do your job."

He shoved the stills back toward Eve. "It's more likely these women invited, even encouraged the use of the drugs. Any woman who agrees to meet a man she knows only through mail is soliciting a sexual advance."

"I guess she solicits them just because she was born with tits." Eve scooped up the stills. "It sounds like you caught some blathering after all. I never mentioned how these women met their attackers."

"Your time's up." He pressed a button under the desk and the doors opened. "If you wish to speak with me again, you'll have to contact my attorneys. If I hear any public mention of my name, this facility, or the project in connection with your investigation, they will be contacting you."

She debated hauling him in then and there, then punching her way through the legal uproar. The media would go wild, and the case could potentially be damaged by the exposure. "I always wonder how it is some doctors have such little respect for human life." She stepped off the platform, handed the stills to Peabody. "We'll talk again," she told him and strode out just before the doors clicked shut at her back.

"He's a creep," Peabody said. "A misogynist and a demigod."

"And he knows something. I want a low profile on this, so we play it by the book with him. Contact his reps and arrange a formal interview at Central. We're going to put some pressure on breaking those sealed records. Get yourself back to Central and start the paperwork."

"He'll fight it."

"Yeah, but he'll lose. Eventually. I'm working from home. I'll pass on data as I get it."

• • •

Roarke was already there when she arrived, but she left the door between their offices closed. She sat at her desk and began generating a series of reports. She knew enough about politics and demigods to be certain she'd have to cover her ass as far as McNamara was concerned. Men like him didn't just call lawyers. She had no doubt her commander's, the chief's, the mayor's, even the governor's ears would be ringing with her name in very short order.

She could handle the heat, but she didn't want the fire taken off the case while it was scorching her ass.

When she was satisfied she transmitted copies to all appropriate parties. Next came the pitch to break sealed files for investigatory use in multiple homicides. It was a tricky business, and even if the request went through, it would take precious days.

There was a quicker way. She glanced up at the door that joined her workspace with Roarke's. Quicker, slicker, and virtually undetectable if she gave him the job.

She'd crossed that line before and would again if she had to. But for now, she'd try the system.

"Computer." Absently she rubbed at the back of her neck. "All available data on McNamara, Dr. Theodore, display on wall screen."

Working . . . Data displayed.

She rose, working the tension out of her shoulders as she read the information. The man was eighty-six, and obviously made good use of his face and body sculptors. His education and work records were impressive. He'd had one marriage, and one child from it—a daughter.

Eve pursed her lips and speculated.

When she heard the door behind her open, she spoke without turning. "You've got a man who doesn't particularly like women as a species, considers them inferior.

Well, to be fair, considers everyone inferior, but I got a definite vibe women were lowest on his feeding chain. Called me 'miss,'" she grumbled.

"And lived?" Roarke stepped behind her and began rubbing her shoulders. It passed briefly through her mind that he had some sort of weird psychic ability to hit just the right spot.

"I'd have knocked him around for it, but he's almost ninety. Anyway, a guy like this has one kid and that kid turns out to be a female. That'd be a disappointment, wouldn't it?"

"I suppose it would, if he's an asshole."

"Yeah, he's an asshole. So, why didn't he try again, until he got it right? If the wife was the problem, fertility or otherwise, there are plenty of ways around it. Even forty, fifty years ago, there were ways around it. But maybe he didn't have enough soldiers to do the job. What a pisser."

"Speaking as a man, I can say that finding oneself unable to create a child would be difficult to accept." He brushed his lips over her hair. "And if a child was desired, I'd do whatever could be done to fix the problem."

"Fertility tests . . . they must be really personal, embarrassing. Especially for a guy with a really whopping ego." She glanced over her shoulder.

"Are you asking my opinion as you assume I have a really whopping ego?"

"We could fill Madison Square with your ego, pal. It just runs different than this jerk's. Maybe it explains why he shifted gears from private practice into research—sexual dysfunction and fertility research. Let's take a look at the daughter. Computer, standard background run on Dunwood, Sarah. Née McNamara."

WORKING . . .

"To show how good-natured I am," Roarke began, "I'll ignore that insult and tell you I've just finished my assignment. Transmissions are blocked, and will be diverted to an account I've just created for you."

"I didn't ask you to divert them."

"Two services for the price of one." He whipped her around and crushed his mouth to hers. His hands gripped her butt, squeezed, and molded her body against his. "There. That ought to cover it."

"Stop trying to cloud my brain. I'm on the clock."

DATA ACCESSED . . . DISPLAY OR AUDIO?

"Display," Eve said even as Roarke ordered audio.

CONFLICTING COMMAND. HOLDING . . .

"Cut it out," Eve ordered as he tugged her shirt from her waistband. "What's wrong with you?"

"Apparently not a thing." But he laughed and let her muscle away. "Display data."

"She's fifty-three," Eve said. "Followed in Daddy's footsteps right down the line. Same schools, same training, same hospital residency. And straight into research. One marriage. One child. Carbon copy. Except she got the boy. And look at his DOB. Only a year after the start of the project. She'd already been married eight years. Wouldn't surprise me if she not only worked on the project, but was part of the study."

She blew out a breath. "And what the hell does that have to do with murder? There's a connect. I know there's a connect. Her husband was part of the team, too. But he's too old for these hits. And the son's too young. What is he twenty-one, twenty-two? He was an infant during the heyday of the project. Still . . . Computer, access all available data, Dunwood, Lucias. Display on wall screen."

WORKING . . .

While his data was being accessed a few blocks away, Lucias strolled into the formal parlor of his townhouse. His grandfather rarely paid personal calls, and certainly never spur-of-the-moment visits.

If the king dropped by, there was a reason. Speculating on what it might be had Lucias's palms going damp. He wiped them distractedly on his slacks before he entered the room, smoothed them over his tight red curls, then fixed a pleased and welcoming expression on his face.

"Grandfather, what a wonderful surprise. I didn't realize you were back."

"I arrived last night. Where is Kevin?"

"Oh, at his computers, where else? Shall I arrange for drinks? I have a very nice scotch. I think you'll approve of it."

"This isn't a social call, Lucias. I want to speak with Kevin as well."

"Of course." The sweat that had dampened his palms ran in a thin, nasty line down his back. He gestured casually to the waiting server droid. "Tell Mr. Morano my grandfather's here and wishes to see him."

"Immediately," McNamara added.

"Of course. And how was your trip?" Lucias went to the antique cabinet that held the liquor. His grandfather might not want a drink, but he needed one.

"Productive. A word you've become unfamiliar with since you graduated college."

"With honors," Lucias pointed out and poured scotch neat into heavy crystal. "Just taking a sabbatical after years of study. And actually, I've been doing some work in my lab. A pet project. You know all about pet projects, after all."

McNamara turned away briefly. The boy was a disappointment to him. A severe disappointment. He had helped create him, handpicking the man he'd deemed best suited for his daughter. A man much like himself—intelligent, driven, strong. Ambitious.

Their inability to conceive a child had been a monumental frustration for him, but had helped him launch the project. The project that had advanced his career, created his grandson. And had very nearly ruined everything.

Still, he had risen above it. His name had never been marred. And never would be.

And hadn't he nurtured the child? Educated him, molded him, given him every opportunity to refine and develop the superior mind he'd been born with?

Instead, the boy had been spoiled. His mother's doing, McNamara thought grimly. A woman's weakness. She'd pampered and coddled him. Had ruined him.

Now, he was very much afraid that child had put his name, his career, his reputation in the greatest jeopardy.

"What have you done, Lucias?"

Lucias downed the scotch, poured more. "I'm not prepared to talk about the experiment, though it's coming along quite well, I believe. And how is Grandmother?"

"As ever." He took the glass Lucias offered, studied his grandson's face. And saw what he had always seen. A blank wall. "She misses you. It seems you had no time to visit her, or call, while I was away."

"Well, I've been a busy little bee." The whiskey helped, considerably. "I'll be sure to make time for her very soon. Ah, here comes Kevin."

He went back to pour a drink for his friend, and yet another for himself.

"Dr. McNamara, what a delightful surprise."

"So I just said myself." Lucias handed Kevin the glass. "It isn't often we're so privileged. That will be all," he said to the droid, then dropped into a chair. "Now, what shall we talk about?"

"I want to see your lab," McNamara demanded.

"I'm afraid not." Lucias sipped scotch. "You know how we mad scientists are about our experiments. Hush-hush. Top secret. After all, I learned all about the sacrosanct from you, didn't I?"

"You've been using illegals again."

"No, I haven't. I learned my lesson. Didn't I, Kevin? We both learned our lessons well when you had us tucked quietly away in rehab on Delta last year. Hush-hush," he said again and nearly giggled. "Top secret."

"You're a liar." McNamara exploded, striding to his grandson, knocking the heavy glass from his hand. "Do you think I can't recognize the signs? You're using again. Both of you. Destroying your minds, your futures for a weakness, a temporary indulgence."

"That glass was an heirloom." Lucias's hands wanted to shake, but with anger as much as the innate fear, the bone-deep loathing his grandfather always brought to him. "You should have more respect for family, Grandfather."

"You speak to me of respect? The police came to my office today. They questioned me. I've been ordered into Interview tomorrow, and there's a request being processed to open the sealed files on the project."

"Oh-oh." Lucias's bright blue eyes twinkled, a mischievous boy caught in a prank, as he looked at Kevin. "Now that would be quite the scandal. What do you think, Kevin, about having all those secrets, the grand passions that conceived us both, revealed?"

"I think it would be embarrassing, in some quarters."

"Yes, indeed. Couples, well, coupling, under the fierce scrutiny of the exalted Dr. Theodore McNamara. No candlelight and music to romanticize the exercise. No indeed. No muss, no fuss. Just a clinical process hyped by sexual enhancement drugs with one purpose. Us."

He laughed now and swilled back scotch. "And a rousing success it was."

"Medical advancement. Procreation of the species." McNamara's voice trembled with rage. "I had assumed, incorrectly it seems, that both of you were mature enough to understand the scope of what you were part of."

"But then we weren't really part of it, were we?" Lucias countered. "We were simply part of the results. I don't believe we were given a choice in the matter. I don't believe a number of the participants were, either. Isn't that what we discovered, Kev, when we read through the files?"

"Those files are sealed," McNamara said.

"Seals were made to be broken." Lucias continued. "Just like rules. You broke a number of rules, Grandfather, in the name of science. Why shouldn't Kevin and I do the same, in the name of . . . entertainment?"

"What have you done?" McNamara demanded.

"Nothing to concern you."

"It concerns me when I'm ordered into Interview. And it best concern you as well, as questions will be asked about murdered women that lead to you."

"To us?" Kevin set down his drink. "But that's not possible. How could they know—"

"Shut up." Lucias sprang to his feet. "What did they say about us? What did you tell them?"

"I didn't want to believe it." McNamara braced a hand on the back of a chair, forced himself to stand when he wanted to sink. "You murdered those women."

"Don't be ridiculous. Murder? You've lost your mind. If you're in some sort of trouble with the police—" Lucias's tirade was cut short as McNamara slapped him.

"You disgust me. All of my hopes for you, my dreams, and look at you. You're worthless, you and your pathetic friend. All of your talent, wasted, wasted on games, drugs, and your selfish pursuit of pleasure."

"You created me." Tears, hot with humiliation from the slap, stung Lucias's eyes. "You made me."

"I gave you all that was in my power to give. Every advantage. And it was never enough."

"You gave me orders! Expectations. I've detested you all my life. I live as I choose to live now, and there's nothing you can do."

"You're right. Quite right. And nothing I will do. I won't clean up your mess this time. I won't pay to have you protected, nor will I sacrifice myself to shield you.

When they find you, and they will find you, I won't lift a hand."

"You won't let them take me. I'm all you have."

"Then God help us both."

Changing tacks, Lucias grabbed McNamara's arm, put a plea in his voice. "Grandfather, we mustn't argue like this. I apologize. I was overwrought. Kevin and I have been working very hard."

"Working?" McNamara repeated. "How did you come to be monsters? With so much at your fingertips."

"We're scientists, Dr. McNamara." Kevin ranged himself beside Lucias. "This is all a mistake. That's all. Just a mistake. There was an accident."

"Yes, an accident." Lucias tried to nudge his grandfather into a chair. "And perhaps we got a little carried away. But these things happen when you try to . . . expand the box. You understand that. They were only women. Test subjects."

"Take your hands off me. You'll face this, both of you. You'll pay the price for your actions. If you want my help, you'll come with me to the police tomorrow. I'll arrange for a legal team, and a psychiatric study."

"We're not crazy! You'd let them lock me up? Your own flesh and blood." He leaped, knocking over a table as he fell on top of his grandfather. The priceless lamp that stood on it crashed and showered glass. Enraged, McNamara shoved Lucias aside and tried to regain his feet.

"For years I tried not to see what you were. Allowed myself to see you—both of you—as what I knew you could be." He managed to kneel, braced a hand on the arm of the chair.

"What we've done is no different from what you did a generation ago." Lucias swiped a trembling hand over his mouth. "You dosed test subjects, some with their knowledge, some without, for the purpose of copulation and conception. You did it for procreation, so you say. We're doing it for fun. And with more style."

"You've killed."

"A lab rat is a lab rat and an acceptable sacrifice."

It was horror now that clutched in McNamara's throat. "You've destroyed yourselves. I'm going to the police. The two of you are nothing but an experiment gone wrong."

With a cry of fury, Lucias snatched up the base of the lamp, used it like a club.

"We're men! Men!" Blood sprayed over the chair, the rug as McNamara slumped to the side, flailed out to try to defend himself. "They'll send us to prison. To prison. Stupid old bastard!" He staggered to his feet, screaming as he pounded his grandfather to the floor. "I won't go in a cage because you have no vision."

Breath heaving, Lucias stepped back, tossed the bloodied lamp aside.

"My God." Kevin's voice was soft, almost reverent. "Is he dead?"

McNamara's face was bloody, his mouth agape. Still panting, Lucias crouched down and checked for a pulse. "No, not yet." Then he sat back on his haunches and forced himself to think. "But he will be. He has to be. He'd give us over to the police, give us over like we were nothing."

Though his breathing was shallow, Kevin nodded. "We can't let that happen."

"We'll finish it." Lucias got carefully to his feet. "But not here. We have to take him away from the house, make it look like a robbery."

"You . . . I've never seen anything . . ."

"I've done us both a favor." Staring down at his grandfather, Lucias patted Kevin's arm. He was in control again. Perhaps, he realized, fully in control for the first time in his life. "He's outlived his usefulness. And he's a danger to us. So, we take him out of the equation."

"It has to be done. But, my God, I've never seen so much blood."

"If you're going to be sick, get it over with."

"No, I'm not going to be sick." He couldn't look away. "So much blood. It's . . . fascinating. The others, the women, it was almost gentle, really. But this . . ." He moistened his lips and his face was pale and shining as he looked at his friend. "How did it feel? When you struck him? How did it feel?"

Lucias had to stop and consider. His hands, slick with blood, were steady now. His mind already clearing. "Powerful," he decided. "Extremely. Energizing."

"I want to try it."

"We'll finish him off together then. But not here." Lucias checked his wrist unit. "We have to work quickly. I have a date tonight."

It didn't take long, all things considered.

It was a matter of pulling his grandfather's car into the garage. As a point of pride and control, Dr. McNamara made a habit of driving himself nearly everywhere. He wouldn't, Lucias thought, drive himself to his final destination. With Kevin's help, he wrapped his grandfather's nude body in plastic and folded it into the trunk.

"He might have told someone he was coming here," Kevin pointed out.

"Low probability. He disliked sharing personal business."

"Your grandmother?"

"Her least of all." Lucias tossed the bag of clothes and valuables into the trunk. "It wouldn't have occurred to him to bother, nor would it occur to her to ask if he had any plans. Now." He slammed the trunk closed, brushed his hands together. "You've reprogrammed the droid?"

"Check. They'll be no record we had any company."

"Excellent. We have the location for disposal your computer scan indicated was the best for our purposes.

You follow in your car, we finish it, then dump him and the goodie bag. You did weigh it down enough, didn't you?"

"Absolutely. It'll sink to the bottom of the river."

"And he won't. Perfect. We torch the car, drive back home. And I have plenty of time to dress for my evening out."

"You're a cool one, Lucias. I've always admired that about you."

"Thank you. Well, we'd best be off. You know, this will be a record. Two perfect crimes in one night. I'll have to claim the lion's share of points for the first, though."

"I can't argue about that." Kevin gave him a friendly smack on the shoulder.

"Clean as a whistle," Eve said as she studied Lucias's data. That either makes him a droid or a . . . what's that term Mavis uses? Dweebazoid. No school infractions, no traffic violations. Following right along with the family tradition, too."

"That's why they're called family traditions," Roarke pointed out. "What will ours be, I wonder? Crime, of course, but which side of the spectrum?"

She spared him a look. "He's got his own residence here in the city. I'm going to make time to talk to him. He's rolling in money, so he's a hit there. He's got knowledge of chemistry."

"Attractive young man," Roarke commented, nodding toward the picture beside the written data. "*Young* being the operative word. He's barely been out of university a full year."

"I'm checking him out. And I'll use checking him out to see if it makes his grandfather a little more forthcoming."

"He pissed you off."

"That's affirmative. And I'm going to piss him off right back when I get authority to open the sealeds."

"I can get that data for you."

"I've already had you do an unauthorized and illegal computer block. Let's leave our black marks to a minimum."

"The block may save a life. That's no black mark. And I can get you some of that sealed data by perfectly legal means. A single 'link call to a source at Allegany who worked on the project. If you want names to run, I'll get you names."

"Just a call?"

"Very simple."

"Then do it."

"All right, but it'll cost you."

Because she recognized the gleam in his eye, she narrowed her own. "Get out. I'm not paying for information with sex."

"Consider it taking one for the team," he suggested, and tumbled her into the sleep chair.

By the time she'd paid up, her ears were ringing and every ounce of tension had melted out of her body. It seemed her bones had melted along with it as she discovered when she tried to stand.

She wore only her boots and the diamond pendant he'd once given her.

"You know if you hadn't become a cop, you might have had a future in porn vids. And I mean that in the best possible way. Christ, Eve, you're a picture."

"Don't even think about trying for a second round. I want that data, pal."

"A deal's a deal." He rose, fluidly, wearing nothing but his grin. "Why don't you order us up a meal of some sort," he suggested as he started for his office. "I'm starving."

She watched him go. *Talk about pictures,* she thought. If she didn't consider herself on duty, she'd have been tempted to sprint after him, tackle him, and sink her teeth into his really superior ass.

Instead she'd settle for an AutoChef burger.

She leaned down, scooped up her clothes.

"Catch!"

She straightened and, as her arms were full, took the robe he tossed her in the face.

"Might as well be comfortable," he said. "And oh, darling? I could use a glass of wine."

Chapter 15

A cheeseburger wouldn't have been his first choice, particularly with the Savignon Blanc '55. But it was Eve's show.

"Why didn't you tell me about this guy before?"

He watched Eve shake a blizzard of salt over her fries, and winced. "Had your blood pressure checked lately?"

"Just answer the question."

"You had a lot of irons in the fire, so I took this one. Stiles was bound to be more cooperative with me than with you. As illustrated by the fact that after only minimal grousing, he's digging through his files and his memory. You'll have your data by the time we finish this delightfully adolescent meal. More onion rings?"

"You trust him?"

"I do, yes. Stiles makes a career out of being irritable, but under the rough exterior is an equally rough but honest interior. You'd like him."

It was plain Roarke did, and she trusted his instincts. "What I need is project staff who got a little too involved with the experimentation. People who might have taken it home with them. Their family, friends, associates."

"And so I explained. Relax, Lieutenant, or you'll give

yourself indigestion." He watched her scarf up onion rings. "Though that's pretty much a given in any case."

"You're just sulking because I didn't pick out rack of lamb or something. The murders are connected to the project. It just follows logic. You have to figure supply and intent. You don't pick these particular illegals up on the street. Derivatives, diluted clones, but not the pure goods."

She lifted her wineglass, studied the pale gold liquid. "Just like this stuff. You can't walk into the corner liquor store, a twenty-four–seven and cop a bottle of this. You can get cheap substitutes, inferior, what do you call them, labels, but for the snooty stuff you need a high-end supplier and the wherewithal."

"Or your own vineyard."

"Or your own vineyard," she agreed. "You got that, you can drink it like water. He doesn't settle for substitutes. He's better than that, deserves the very best. The best illegals, the best wines, the best clothes. And the women of his choice. Just another commodity."

"He has the means to indulge himself, in every vice. Isn't it probable he's worked his way up to this ultimate indulgence?"

"Yeah, if you go by percentages, probabilities of profiling. But there's more to it, because there are two of them. Teamwork, competition, mutual dependence. The first one fucked up. He hadn't worked his way up to killing yet, so he panicked. But that upped the stakes. Second guy can't let his pal get ahead of him. He's got more violence in him, and isn't afraid of seeing that part of himself. He enjoys it. Then you bounce back to the first player, and he messes up again. He leaves her alive. He's losing the game."

"You're dismissing multiple personalities?"

"Even if its MPS, we're dealing with two. But I'm more inclined toward the simple route. Two styles, two killers. I wonder if anybody on the project list had two sons. Brothers maybe. It would make sense if . . . or childhood friends." She shifted her attention back to Roarke. "Guys who grew up together. That's like brotherhood, isn't it?"

He thought of Mick. "It is. More so in a way as you don't have the family dynamics, the antagonisms, getting in the way. With Mick and Brian and the rest of us, we were a family we created rather than one we'd been born into. It's a powerful bond."

"Okay, tell me this—from a species that does the majority of its thinking with its penis—"

"I resent that. I don't think with my penis more than twenty-five percent of the time."

"Tell that to somebody you didn't just nail in the sleep chair."

"And I can tell you it took very little thought. But your question is?"

"Guys'll bang anything if they get the chance."

"Yes, and we're proud of it." .

"No offense. That's just the way the machine works. But when they have a choice, a selection, even a fantasy, they tend toward a certain type. Most commonly that fantasy or type is based on a female figure that was or is important to the man. Either the type resembles that figure in some way or opposes it."

"Since I assume in this case you're eliminating basic chemistry, emotion, and relationship, I won't disagree. The female machine runs much the same way."

"Yeah, that's how he gets them. Molding himself into their fantasy. But I'm betting the women he selects are looking for the type he is, or appears to be on the surface. He doesn't have to change much. Why should he? It's his game. I'm going to run some probabilities."

Roarke heard the signal from his office for incoming data. "Stiles came through. I'll transfer that over for you."

"Thanks." She glanced at her wrist unit. "Nine-fifteen," she announced. "Nearly date time."

Her name was Melissa Kotter, and she was from Nebraska. A genuine farm girl who'd fled the fields for the bright lights of the big city. She had hopes, as did thousands of other young women who streamed into New York, of being an actress. A serious actress, of course—one who would remain true to her art, infusing new life into the classic roles played by all the greats who'd trod the board before her.

While she was waiting to light up Broadway, she waited tables, went to auditions, and took whatever work came her way. It was, in her opinion, the way all the great artists began their careers.

At twenty-one, she was full of optimism and innocence. And dreams. She waited tables with tireless cheer, and her farm-fresh looks earned her as many tips as her speedy service.

She was blonde, blue-eyed, and delicate of build.

A sociable creature, Melissa had made a number of friends. She was always eager for friendships, conversation, experiences.

She adored New York with the passion of a new lover, and in the six months she'd lived in the city, her affection hadn't dimmed by a watt.

She'd told her across-the-hall neighbor, Wanda, about her date that night. And had laughed off her friend's concerns. The media reports about the murdered women didn't apply to her. Hadn't Sebastian brought them up himself, hadn't he said he'd understand completely if she didn't feel comfortable meeting him tonight?

As she'd told Wanda, he'd hardly have brought the matter up if he was a dangerous individual.

He was a wonderful man, intelligent, erudite, exciting. And so very different from all the boys back home. Most of them hadn't known Chaucer from Chesterfield. But Sebastian knew all about poetry and plays. He'd traveled all over the world, had attended performances in all the great theaters.

She'd read his e-mails over and over until she could

recite them by heart. No one who could write such lovely things could be anything but wonderful.

And he was meeting her at Jean-Luc's, one of the most exclusive clubs in the city.

She made the dress herself, patterning it after a gown worn by the actress Helena Grey when she'd accepted her Tony the previous year. The deep midnight blue material was synthetic rather than silk, but it had a lovely drape. With it she wore the pearl earrings her grandmother had given her on her twenty-first birthday in November. They looked almost real dripping from her lobes.

The shoes and the bag had been snagged on sale at Macy's.

She did a quick, laughing twirl. "How do I look?"

"You look mag, Mel, but I wish you wouldn't go."

"Stop being such a worrywart, Wanda. Nothing's going to happen to me."

Wanda bit her lip. She looked at Melissa and saw a little woolly lamb who'd bah cheerfully as she was led to the slaughter. "Maybe I'll call in sick, hang out here in your place until you get home."

"Don't be silly. You need the money. Go on, go get ready for work." Melissa draped an arm around Wanda's shoulders and walked her to the door. "If it makes you feel better I'll call you when I get back."

"Promise."

"Scout's honor. I think I'm going to order a martini. I've always wanted to try one. Which do you think is more sophisticated? Gin or vodka? Vodka," she decided before Wanda could weigh in. "A vodka martini, very dry, with a twist."

"You call me, the minute you get back. And don't you bring him up here, no matter what."

"I won't." Melissa twirled herself to the stairs. "Wish me luck."

"I do. Be careful."

Melissa dashed down all three flights, feeling very

glamorous. She called out greetings to neighbors, struck a pose at the wolf whistle delivered by Mr. Tidings in 102. When she rushed out on the sidewalk, her cheeks were flushed and rosy.

She thought about taking a cab, but since she had more time than money thought it best to take the subway uptown.

She joined the hordes on the underground platform, humming to herself as she anticipated the evening. She squeezed on the train and stood, propped up by bodies.

Crowds didn't bother her; she thrived on them. If she hadn't been so busy writing the script for her meeting with Sebastian, she'd have struck up any number of conversations with her fellow passengers.

It was only with one-to-one encounters with men she found herself shy and tongue-tied. But she was sure, she was positive, she'd be neither with Sebastian.

It was as if they were made for each other.

When the train jerked to an abrupt halt, and the lights dimmed, she was tossed unceremoniously against the burly black man wedged in beside her.

"Excuse me."

"That's cool, sister. Ain't enough to you to put a dent in."

"I wonder what's wrong." She tried to see through people, over them in the greenish wash of emergency lighting.

"Always some mess with this uptown train. Don't know why they don't fix the sumbitch." He skimmed his gaze down her and up again. "You got you some date, doncha?"

"Yes. I hope we're not delayed long or I'll be late. I hate being late."

"Look like you, guy's not gonna mind a wait." His friendly face went hard and cold, and sent Melissa's heart bounding to her throat. "Brother, you wanna take your fingers off this lady's purse, or I'm gonna break 'em into little pieces."

Melissa jolted, snatched her purse around to press it to

her belly. She glanced back and caught a glimpse of the small man in a dark trench coat as he slithered back into the jammed bodies.

"Oh. Thank you! Sometimes I forget to be careful."

"Don't pay to forget. You keep that purse close."

"Yes, I will. Thank you again. I'm Melissa. Melissa Kotter."

"Bruno Biggs. They just call me Biggs . . . 'cause I am."

During the ten-minute delay, she chatted with him. She learned he worked in construction, had a wife named Ritz and a baby boy they called B.J. for Bruno, Junior. By the time they'd reached her stop, she'd given him the name of the restaurant where she worked and had invited him to bring his family in for dinner. As people gushed off the train, she waved and let herself be swept along by the current.

Bruno saw her trying to hurry along, her purse once again trailing behind her.

He shook his head and muscled his way off just before the doors closed.

Melissa broke free of the crowd and raced up the stairs. She was going to be late unless she ran the last three blocks. She made a dash for the corner. Something hit her from behind, low on the back, and sent her pitching forward. The strap of her purse snapped clean. She managed one short scream as she tumbled off the curb. There were shrieking brakes, shouts, then a bright, blinding pain as she hit the street.

She heard something else snap.

"Ms. Kotter? Melissa." Bruno bent over her. "God almighty, sister, I thought you'd get yourself run over. Got this back for you." He shook her purse.

"I—I forgot to be careful."

"Okay now, okay. You need the MTs? How bad you hurt?"

"I don't know . . . my arm."

She'd broken the arm. And saved her life.

• • •

"Eight hundred and sixty-eight names." Eve squeezed the bridge of her nose. "Just couldn't be simple."

"That doesn't include building maintenance, or straight clerical."

"This will do for now. We'll focus on the ones your source lists as being reprimanded for recreational use, and those he remembers being named in any lawsuits. But we need to work with all of them. I need to separate them out—medical, administration, e-drones, lab techs. Divide them by age groups. Those with families, and the age of their children. Another list of any who were terminated during the project run."

She looked up at him, the slightest glint in her eye.

"Have I just been demoted to e-drone?"

"You could do it faster."

"Unquestionably, but—"

"Yeah, yeah, it'll cost me. Pervert." She considered, brightened. "Tell you what. We'll do a trade. You give me a hand with this, and I'll consult with you on whatever business deal you're currently wheeling."

He paled a little. "Darling, that's so sweet of you. I couldn't possibly infringe on your valuable time."

"Coward."

"You bet."

"Come on, give me a shot. What have you got cooking?"

"I've a number of pots simmering just now." He dipped his hands in his pockets and tried to think which project or negotiation currently on his plate she could poke into with the least possible damage.

Her desk 'link beeped.

"Saved, so to speak, by the bell."

"We'll get back to this," she warned him.

"I sincerely hope not."

"Dallas."

"Lieutenant Dallas? Stefanie Finch. You've been trying to reach me?"

"That's right. Where are you located?"

"Just got back to New York. Had the last couple runs cancelled. What can I do for you?"

"We need to have a conversation, Ms. Finch. In person. I can be there in twenty minutes."

"Hey, listen. I just walked in the door. Why don't you tell me what this is about?"

"Twenty minutes," Eve repeated. "Stay available."

She cut Stefanie off on an oath, snagged her weapon harness. "You happen to own Inter-Commuter Air?"

He was scanning the data on-screen and didn't look over. "No. Their equipment's old and will cost ten to fifteen hundred million to replace and/or repair. They're operating in the red, and have been for the last three years. Poor customer service record that's heading for a PR nightmare. They'll be finished in a year, eighteen months on the outside." He glanced over now. "Then I'll buy them."

"You wait till they roll over dead." She pursed her lips. "Good plan, but it nixes the idea of taking you along so you can put the elbow on an employee. I'll tag Peabody. The uniform's always a nice touch."

"Agreed, and so's that robe. But you might want to put your boots back on."

She frowned down at herself. "Shit." She grabbed the boots and trotted out. "See you later."

Stefanie didn't pretend to be pleased. She opened the door and led with a scowl. "ID," she snapped.

Eve flipped open her badge, holding it out while Stefanie took a good, long look. "I've heard about you. The cop who hooked Roarke. Nice job."

"Gee, thanks. I'll let him know you said so."

Stefanie merely jerked a thumb toward Peabody. "What's with the uniform?"

"My aide. Do we come in, Stefanie, or do we discuss this in the hallway?"

Stefanie stepped back, closed the door behind them. "I just had two lucrative runs cancelled, my union rep is

talking strike, which is going to put me in a bind. The
shuttle they stuck me with should've been in the fucking
scrap heap, and my gut's telling me I could be out of a job
within the year."

"He never misses," Eve muttered.

"I've got a cop hounding me to Europe and back, so I'm
in a pisser of a mood, Lieutenant. If this is about my bastard ex, I've got one thing to say: He's not my problem."

"I'm not here about your bastard ex. You've been corresponding, via e-mail, with an individual who calls himself Wordsworth."

"How do you know? E-mail's private."

"The individual who calls himself Wordsworth is a
suspect in two murders and one attempted murder.
Now, do you want to do a dance about the violation of
cyber-privacy?"

"You've got to be kidding me."

"Peabody, look at my face. Is this my jokey face?"

"No, sir, Lieutenant."

"Now that we've cleared that up, why don't we sit
down?"

"I've got a date with him tomorrow afternoon," Stefanie said, and hugged her arms as if chilled. "When my
runs were cancelled, I did some e-mail from the pilot's
lounge at Heathrow. He suggested we get together tomorrow for a picnic in Greenpeace Park."

"What time?"

"One o'clock."

He's breaking pattern, Eve thought. *Upping the stakes
again.* "Sit down, Stefanie."

"You're sure about this." Stefanie sat, stared up at Eve.
"Yeah, you're sure. I bet that's your dead-certain face.
Well, I'm embarrassed and I feel like the world's biggest
idiot."

"And you're alive," Eve told her. "I'm going to keep
you that way. Describe Wordsworth for me."

"Physically, I don't have a clue. He's an art dealer. International. Digs opera, ballet, poetry. I was looking for

some class. My ex was an amoeba. If it wasn't Arena Ball it wasn't worth talking about. I supported the worthless bastard the last six months we were together. Bailed him out twice on drunk and disorderlies, then he . . ."

She trailed off. "Apparently, I still have issues. Point is, I was looking for his opposite. Somebody with some polish who could do more than grunt when he wanted another beer. I guess I was looking for a little romance."

"And he said all the right things."

"Bingo. If it's too good to be true, it's probably a big, fat lie. Looks like I forgot that motto. But a picnic in the park, middle of the damn day, you'd think that would be safe. I can handle myself," she added. "I bench-press one twenty. I'm a fifth degree black belt. I'm nobody's victim. No way he'd take me down."

Eve sized her up and agreed. Under most conditions, the woman could probably handle herself just fine. "He plans to drug you, with a very potent sexual illegal. You'd bring him back here because you'd think it's your call. He'd light candles, put on music, give you more laced wine. He'd sprinkle pink rose petals on the bed."

"Bullshit." But she'd gone white. "That's bullshit."

"You wouldn't think of it as rape while it happened. You'd do everything he told you to do. When he gave you the second drug, you'd lap it right up for him. While your system overloaded, your heart would give out; you wouldn't even know you're dead."

"You want to scare me?" Stefanie got to her feet, paced. "You're doing a damn good job."

"That's right. I want to scare you. That's what he plans, that's what might have happened tomorrow afternoon. But it's not going to happen because you're going to do exactly what I tell you."

Stefanie lowered into a chair again. "He doesn't know where I live. Tell me he doesn't know where I live."

"He probably does. He's spent some time watching you. Get any flowers lately?"

"Oh Jesus. Pink roses. The son of a bitch sent me pink

roses yesterday. In my quarters in London. I hauled them home with me. They're in the bedroom."

"Would you like me to dispose of them for you, Pilot Finch?" Peabody asked.

"Dump them in the recycler." Stefanie rubbed her hands over her face. "I'm shaking. I piloted that death trap across the Atlantic, and I'm sitting here shaking. I was feeling pretty pumped about meeting him. Imagined I'd start this really nice, satisfying relationship. The bastard ex is looking better all the time."

"You're not going to speak or contact anyone about this. As far as Wordsworth is concerned, you're meeting him tomorrow. Were there any plans to confirm the date?"

"Only to cancel. I was to let him know by noon if I had to cancel."

"Stand up a minute."

When Stefanie obeyed, Eve rose as well, circled her, judged build, height. "Yeah, two can play the disguise game. When we're done here, you can play it two ways. You can pack what you need and I'll arrange to have you put in a safe house tonight. Or if you want to stay here, I'll have a couple of cops stay over with you. Either way, you'll sleep better."

"Oh yeah, I'll sleep like a baby tonight."

Eve wasn't the only one putting in overtime. McNab was on a mission of his own. He'd fueled himself up for it with two bottles of home brew, which were currently burning at his stomach lining. He wasn't drunk. He'd stopped short of getting drunk. Because he wanted to be clear-headed when he kicked Charles Monroe's pansy ass.

Unaware he'd become the target of a jealous and slightly queasy e-detective, Charles nibbled on Louise's fingers. They were sharing a late supper in his apartment.

"I appreciate you agreeing to start the evening so late."

"We both have odd schedules. It's wonderful wine." She sipped. "Wonderful food. And I like your home very much. More than a restaurant."

"I wanted you to myself. I've wanted you to myself all day."

"I told you I haven't had much luck with relationships, Charles." She rose to wander to the windows. "I'm single-minded, driven, and haven't given any relationship I've been in the attention it needs. Deserves."

"I think your luck's about to change." He turned her to face him. "I know mine has. Louise." He lowered his head, skimmed his lips lightly over hers, once, then twice, drawing her in. He circled her into a dance, deepening the kiss when her arms came around him. Bringing her closer when she trembled.

"Come to bed with me," he whispered. "Let me touch you."

Her head fell back as his mouth trailed along her throat. "Wait. Just . . . wait. Charles." She eased back. "I've thought about this. I spent entirely too much time thinking about this today, and last night. Since I first saw you. Part of my problem is overthinking things."

She stepped away, needing a little distance. "There's such a pull. I haven't felt a pull like this . . . ever," she managed. "But I'm not going to bed with you. I can't."

He kept his eyes on hers, nodded slowly. "I understand. It's difficult for you to accept the idea of being intimate with me."

"Difficult," she said with a half laugh. "No, I wouldn't say difficult."

"You don't need to explain. I know what I am."

She shook her head. "What you are?"

"Licensed companions don't generally have a lot of luck with personal relationships either. Not real ones in any case."

"I'm sorry." She held up a hand. "You think I won't have sex with you because you're a professional? Charles, that insults both of us."

He walked back to the table, picked up his wineglass. "I'm confused."

"I don't want to sleep with you now because it's happening too fast. Because I think what I'm feeling for you goes deeper than that, and I'd like a chance to find out before . . . I'd just like to slow down a bit. I'd like to spend more time getting to know each other. I wouldn't be here now if what you did for a living was a problem for me. And if you think I'm so petty and narrow-minded that I'd—"

"I could fall in love with you."

It stopped her short, stole her breath, just the quiet way he said it. "I know. Oh God, I know. Me, too. It scares me a little."

"Good, because it scares me a lot." He crossed back to her, lifted her hand. "We'll slow down." Kissed it. Then her wrist. Drawing her in again, he brushed his lips over her temple, her cheeks.

Her pulse spiked. "This is slowing down?"

"We won't go any faster than you want." He tipped her face back and smiled. "Trust me, I'm a professional."

And while she laughed, the buzzer sounded.

"Give me ten seconds to get rid of whoever that is. And remember my place."

When he opened the door, McNab shoved him back a step. "Okay, you son of a bitch. We're going a round."

"Detective—"

"Who the hell do you think you are?" McNab shoved him again. "You think you can treat her that way? Rub your next skirt right in her face?"

"Detective, you don't want to lay hands on me again."

"Oh yeah?" *Maybe the second bottle hadn't been such a good idea,* he thought vaguely, but gamely lifted his fists. "Let's try these instead."

"Detective McNab." Calmly, Louise stepped between them. "You're obviously upset. Maybe you should sit down."

"Dr. Dimatto." Flustered, McNab lowered his fists. "I didn't see you over there."

"Charles, why don't you make some coffee. Ian . . . it's Ian, isn't it? Let's sit down."

"Beg your pardon, but I don't want any goddamn coffee and I don't want to sit down. I came to kick his ass." He jabbed a finger at Charles over her shoulder. "I'm sorry you're in the middle. You're a nice woman. But I've got business with this son of a bitch."

"I'm assuming this has to do with Delia."

As Charles stepped away from Louise, McNab rounded on him. "Damn right. You think because you take her to the fucking opera and fancy restaurants you've got a right to toss her over when something more interesting comes along?"

"No, I don't. Delia means a great deal to me."

Literally seeing red, McNab swung out. His punch found its target, had Charles's head snapping back. He followed through with a short-armed jab to the belly before Charles recovered enough to fight back.

While they circled each other, ramming fists, spilling blood, Louise fled the room. They were rolling on the floor, in a sweaty, grunting heap when she came back. And threw a full bucket of ice water over them.

"That's just about enough." She slammed the bucket down, slapped her hands on her hips as both of them gaped up at her. "You should be ashamed. Both of you. Fighting over a woman like she was a juicy piece of meat. If either of you think Peabody would appreciate this, you're very much mistaken. Now, on your feet."

"He's got no right to hurt her," McNab began.

"I wouldn't hurt Delia for anything in the world. And if I have, I'll do everything I can to make it up to her." Charles scooped back his dripping hair. He was getting the picture now. "For Christ's sake, you moron, have you told her you're in love with her?"

"Who said I was?" His bruised face went sheet white. "I'm just looking out for . . . shut up. She wants to roll with you when you're working other skirts, that's her business. But she's not a job." He pointed at Louise.

"That's right. She's not."

"And nobody juggles Peabody that way."

"Look, obviously you're under the impression that Delia and I have been—"

"It just happened, Ian." Louise interrupted quickly, shot Charles a warning look. "It wasn't planned. I'm sorry if I'm responsible for this."

"I'm not blaming you."

"I'm as much to blame. Charles and I . . . we want a chance to make something together. Can you understand?"

"So Peabody's just out of the picture."

"I'm sorry." As the light dawned, Charles got to his feet. "I hope she'll understand. I hope we can still be friends. She's a wonderful woman. More than I deserve."

"You got that part right, pal."

Drenched, aching, and more than a little sick, McNab managed to get up. "You'd better find a way to make it right with her."

"I will. You have my word. Let me get you a towel."

"I don't need a damn towel."

"Then try a piece of advice instead. You've got a clear path. Try not to stumble off of it."

"Yeah, right." He strode out, his exit hampered a bit by squeaking airboots.

"Well." Charles blew out a breath. "That was entertaining."

"Hold still," Louise ordered. "Your lip's bleeding."

As she dabbed at it with a napkin, Charles angled his head. "I'm soaking wet, too."

"Yes, you are."

"I think he bruised my ribs."

"I'll take a look. Come on. Let's get you out of those wet clothes and patch you up. This time," she said, "I'm the professional."

"I love playing doctor, Louise." He stopped her, made her turn and look at him. "Delia and I—She's really very special to me. But we were never lovers."

"Yes, I figured that out." She patted her fingers gently on his bruised cheek. "I can't believe you were about to tell Ian."

"Could be my brain was still rattled from having his bare-knuckled fist slammed into my face. We're friends," he added. "Delia's the best friend I've ever had."

"And you've just done her a lovely favor. Come on now, come with Dr. Louise." She slipped an arm around his waist. "It's sweet, isn't it, the way he leapt to defend her."

"Sweet." Charles wiggled his jaw, and saw a few stars. "He thinks I'm sleeping with her, and that pisses him off. Then he thinks I've stopped sleeping with her, and it pisses him off even more, so he comes over here and punches me in the face. Yes, very sweet."

"It's all point of view. Now, take off your clothes. First house call's free."

Chapter 16

Eve stood on the sidewalk outside Stefanie Finch's apartment building, took a moment to sort through her thoughts. Summer was coming. She could feel the weight of it on the air. "Does it feel like rain to you, Peabody?"

Peabody took a sniff. "No, sir. Humidity's coming in. It's likely to be hot and heavy tomorrow."

"In more ways than one. But I don't want a storm to muck things up."

"Dallas, if we move in on him tomorrow without using bait, we can't be sure of getting him on anything but illegals possession, and that's if he's carrying."

"He'll be carrying. And we've got bait."

Peabody glanced back up at the building. "You didn't say anything to her about keeping the date."

"She won't be keeping it. I will."

"You?" With a shake of her head, Peabody gave Eve a measuring glance. "If he's sticking to pattern we have to figure he knows what she looks like. And you don't look like her. You're close to the same height, but coloring's different, features are different. And she's, well, bustier. No offense."

"By one tomorrow, I'll look enough like her to pass. I'm calling Mavis."

"Oh." Peabody brightened. "Oh, that's iced."

"Easy for you to say. You won't have to listen to lectures from her and Trina on why I haven't had my eyebrows shaped lately, or why I haven't used the butt cream or whatever. And I'll probably have to agree to a full treatment after the op." This was said with undisguised bitterness. "I know how they work."

"You're a true soldier, sir, sacrificing yourself for the cause."

"Wipe that smile off your face, Officer."

"Wiping, sir."

"We've got . . ." She turned her wrist to check the time. "Fourteen hours to put this together. Go home, get some sleep. I want you at my home office at oh six hundred. Wear soft clothes. Contact Feeney and McNab, bring them up to date. I'll have to tag the commander at home." She blew out a breath. "I bet his wife answers."

Eve slid behind the wheel of her vehicle, switched on the autopilot and set it for home. The engine fired, and died.

She sat back, glared at the console. "This is just not right. I'm a ranked officer." She punctuated this by smacking the dash with the heel of her hand. "I deserve a goddamn reliable ride. Computer, run the stinking diagnostic on autopilot."

UNAUTHORIZED USE OF THIS VEHICLE IS AN UN-
LAWFUL ACT PUNISHABLE BY UP TO FIVE YEARS'
IMPRISONMENT AND A MONETARY FINE OF FIVE-
THOUSAND USD. IF YOU ARE NOT AUTHORIZED TO
USE THIS VEHICLE, PLEASE EXIT SAME IMMEDI-
ATELY. IF YOU HAVE AUTHORIZATION, IDENTIFY
YOURSELF. FAILURE TO DO SO WILL AUTOMATI-

CALLY LOCK ALL EXITS AND NOTIFY THE NEAREST
PATROL VEHICLE.

A red haze drifted over her vision. "You want me to
identify myself? I'll identify myself, you demon from
hell. Dallas, Lieutenant Eve. Vehicle authorization code
Zero-Five-Zero-Six-One-Charlie. I am armed and I am
dangerous, and in about five seconds I'm going to draw
my weapon and fry every one of your circuits."

ANY ATTEMPT AT VANDALISM ON THIS VEHICLE
WILL RESULT IN—

"Shut up, shut up, shut up, and run the fucking ID."

POSSESSING . . . YOUR IDENTIFICATION AND CODES
ARE CORRECT, DALLAS, LIEUTENANT EVE.

"Dandy keen, now run the damn diagnostic."

WORKING . . . AUTO-NAVIGATION ON THIS VEHICLE
IS EXPERIENCING SYSTEMIC PROBLEMS. DO YOU
WISH TO NOTIFY MAINTENANCE AT THIS TIME?

"I wish to blow Maintenance and everyone in it to holy
hell. And don't tell me that will result in fine and/or imprisonment because it'd be worth it. Re-engage manual."
The engine rumbled on, and the air conditioning
whirled, filling the cockpit with frigid air. "Disengage climate control."

WORKING . . . CLIMATE CONTROL IS EXPERIENCING
SYSTEMIC PROBLEMS. DO YOU WISH TO NOTIFY
MAINTENANCE AT THIS TIME?

"Oh, fuck you," Eve said and rolled down all windows.
She shot away from the curb, and unwilling to trust
the in-dash 'link, pulled out her own.

Mrs. Whitney answered, looking perfectly groomed and very annoyed.

"I'm sorry to disturb you at home, Mrs. Whitney, but I need to speak with the commander."

"It's after eleven o'clock, Lieutenant. Can't this wait until morning?"

"No, ma'am, it can't."

"One moment," she snapped, and switched Eve to wait mode, complete with canned music. Eve listened to violins and flutes as she drove one-handed through a snarl of traffic.

"Whitney."

"I'm sorry to call you at home, Commander, but there's been a break in the investigation."

"I'm always ready to hear good news."

"I've just come from questioning Stefanie Finch. She has a date with the suspect tomorrow at thirteen hundred, Greenpeace Park."

"He's moved to days?"

"It fits the profile, sir. Upping the risk. Finch is cooperating. She's agreed to remain inside her residence. I have two uniforms with her, round the clock. Unless the suspect hears from her by noon tomorrow, he'll keep the date. I'm making arrangements to go in her place."

"Is there a physical resemblance?"

"We're close in height and build. I'm making arrangements to take care of the rest. I've got more data to study, but I can maintain the cover until he gives me the drug. He puts it in my hand, Commander, and we sew him up."

"What do you need?"

"I'd like six cops, soft clothes, in addition to my team, stationed at strategic areas. I'll go over diagrams tonight and determine placement. I'll go in wired. I'll need Feeney and the e-man of his choice in a surveillance vehicle. Additional vehicular and air backup is advisable, in case he gets past me. I'd like to select the rest of the team and brief them from my home office by oh eight hundred hours. I want everyone in place by eleven."

"You're cleared. Pick your men, and keep me updated. What the hell is that noise?"

"Ah, my climate control's dinky, sir."

"Well, notify Maintenance."

She heard her own teeth grind. "Yes, sir."

When she got home, she marched through her office and into Roarke's.

"Can you get your hands on any explosives?"

He glanced up from his work, picked up the brandy snifter that sat at his elbow. "Probably. What would you like?"

"Anything that will blow that insult, that abomination parked out front into a million tiny little pieces that can never be put back together again."

"Ah." He swirled brandy, sipped. "Vehicular troubles again, Lieutenant?"

"Is that a smirk?" The red haze was gathering again. "Is that a smirk on your face? Because if it is . . ." She shoved up her sleeves.

"Mmm, violence. You know how that arouses me."

She managed a short scream and yanked at her own hair.

"Darling Eve, why don't you let some of my mechanics deal with it? Or better yet, take whatever suits your needs out of the garage."

"Because that's like giving up. Those bastards in Maintenance aren't going to beat me." She huffed out a breath. "Anyway. Mavis and Trina are coming over. Probably Leonardo, too. They're spending the night."

"Are we having a pajama party? Will there be pillow fights?"

"You're just a laugh a minute. You want an update or do you want to fantasize about scantily clad women bashing each other with pillows?"

His grin was quick and wicked. "Guess."

She dropped into a chair and filled him in.

He picked up the cat as she spoke, sat stroking Galahad, watching her. He knew she was doing more than bringing him up to speed. She was refining, checking for holes, firming up the operation as she talked it through. They both knew no matter how meticulously planned the operation, it only took one variable to upset the balance.

"Some men," he said when she'd finished, "lesser men, might object to having their wife picnic in the park with another man."

"I'll bring you back some potato salad."

"That's my girl. You said Feeney will pick his man inside the surveillance vehicle. I believe he could be persuaded to select an expert consultant, civilian."

The circle her mind was taking came to an abrupt halt, then backtracked. "This is an NYPSD op, and there's no need for you to be there. You've got your own work."

"I do, yes, but I so enjoy watching you do yours." He gave the cat's ears a scratch with those long, clever fingers that had Galahad purring in pleasure. "Why don't we let Feeney decide?"

"No bribery."

His eyebrows shot up in amazement. "Really, Lieutenant, you wound me. If I were easily offended, I might not tell you I've separated, cross-filed, and indexed your data."

"Yeah? You're pretty handy to have around. Let's have a look." She got up to walk around to his side of the console. He tapped a single key, then setting the cat down, tugged her onto his lap.

"No funny stuff," she ordered.

"Who's laughing?" He nipped her earlobe. "You see on-screen three of those project personnel with male children who would now be between the ages of twenty and thirty-five. That gives you twenty-eight hits. Adding male siblings and grandchildren, secondary dependents in that same age bracket garners another fifteen."

"So that's, what, forty-three possibles. That's workable."

"However . . ." He kissed the nape of her neck. "Refining and recalculating using those personnel who were reprimanded, cited, terminated or named in civil suits, we decrease those possibles to eighteen. I assumed you'd want to start with them. Screen four."

"Keep this up, the chief's going to offer you a permanent position on the force."

"Now you're trying to scare me, but I'm too strong for that."

"Knock out the overthirties. I'm betting he's younger than that."

He nuzzled her neck and did it manually. "Down to eight."

"Yeah. We start with them. Computer, run background check, all data, on individuals listed on screen four."

WORKING . . .

"It'll take a minute," Roarke told her and worked his way from neck to jaw.

"You're not authorized to attempt to seduce the primary investigator at this time."

"I've vast experience in breaking the law." He found her mouth, sank in.

"Wow. They always look so *hot*."

Mavis Freestone stood in the doorway in four-inch platform boots that rode up to her crotch in shiny, eye-watering pink. Her hair, tinted to match, seemed to burst out of her head in an explosive topknot. With it, she wore a skimmer in dizzying swirls of pink and blue that fluttered down to meet the top of the boots.

She beamed smiles set off by sparkling face studs fixed to the corners of her mouth.

Beside her Trina, her own hair in a foot-high ebony

mountain, snorted. "If this is part of the fringe bennies on cop work, I want a badge."

Eve's fingers dug reflexively into Roarke's arm. "Don't leave me," she whispered. "Whatever you do, don't leave me."

"Be strong. Good evening, ladies."

"Leonardo's bopping over later. He had stuff. Summerset said to come right up." Mavis danced into the room. "We gave thumb's-up to snacks. We've got all kinds of goodies to try out on you, Dallas. This is so ultra mag."

Eve's stomach turned. "Whoopee."

"Where do you want me to set up?" Trina asked and was already studying Eve in a way that made the kick-ass cop want to whimper like a baby.

"In my office. This is an official consult, *not* a personal treatment."

"Whatever." Trina blew an enormous purple bubble, snapped the gum back. "Show me what you want to look like, and I'll make it happen."

In her office, Eve put Stefanie Finch's official ID photo on-screen and managed not to yelp when Trina took her face in her hands. Hands with inch-long sapphire nails.

"Mm-hmm. You know, lip dye isn't a crime in this state. You ought to try it."

"I've been kind of busy."

"You're always kind of busy. You're not using the eye gel I gave you. You can't find a minute twice a day for eye gel? You want bags and wrinkles? You got the finest piece of man-candy on and off planet, and you want him looking at your face with bags and wrinkles? What are you going to do when he dumps you for a woman who takes time to maintain her face?"

"Kill him."

That made Trina laugh and sent the little sapphire she had centered on her left eyetooth winking. "Easier to use the gel. I need a photo of you, put it split screen with the image you want. I need to run some morph programs before we start playing with your face."

"Sure." Grabbing the reprieve, Eve went to her computer.

"Cocktail meatballs! Frigid!" Mavis snagged one from the tray Summerset carried in. "Summerset, you're the summit."

His face transformed. It always surprised Eve that he could smile and his face not crack to pieces. "Enjoy. If you'd like anything else, just let me know. And the AutoChef has been fully restocked."

"You ought to stay and watch." Mavis speared a second meatball. "We're going to make Dallas into someone else."

"That," Summerset said with his smile going thin and sour as a lemon slice when he glanced toward Eve, "is the answer to a prayer. And while tempting, I'll leave you to your work."

"He's such a kidder," Mavis said when he walked out.

"Oh yeah, he really cracks me up. There's your image," Eve told Trina. "I've got to check some data in the other room. Just let me know when you're ready for me."

She went back into Roarke and was met with a cup of coffee. "Though I imagine you could use a stiff drink, I assumed you'd opt for coffee."

"Thanks. She's got three cases, three, filled with her hideous devices of torture." She took a bracing gulp of coffee. "I should put in for hazardous duty pay for this." She turned toward the wall screen. "Let's see who we've got."

She leaned back on Roarke's desk and studied the images and data, one by one.

Doctors, lawyers, students, engineers, she mused. She earmarked one not currently employed with a minor illegals offense on his record.

"He's not a drone," she said, half to herself. "Not somebody who's pulling an eight-hour shift. He needs time for his hobby and he's got money. He's a professional or he's just living on his portfolio. Whoa, wait. Computer, magnify current photographic image."

She stepped closer to the screen as the face filled it. And stared into Kevin Morano's eyes. "This one rings with me. Yeah, I know those eyes. Kevin. Yeah, there you are, Kevin. Let's see . . . So Mama worked on the project. No father listed. She was a PR exec. Owns her own firm now. London based, with offices in New York, Paris, and Milan. He's an only child, and was born thirteen months after the project got off the ground. Interesting. Really interesting how a PR exec files a sexual harassment suit, drops it again within six weeks, agrees to have the records sealed. And walks away with a kid and enough money to start an international firm."

She glanced back at Roarke. "Woman who runs her own public relations firm with that scope, she'd probably need a pretty slick image. Polished, sophisticated."

"It follows."

"Woman has a kid, then after a little scandal in the workplace heads off here and there establishing herself an international company."

"The payoff from McNamara and company must have been considerable."

Eve nodded. "But why'd she go through with the pregnancy? Why have the kid?"

"Perhaps she wanted a child."

"What for? Look at his schooling. She started him full-time at three. All private facilities. Boarding schools. And you can bet your ass someone else was doing the baby thing for the first three years. She didn't found that company while she was changing diapers and carting a kid around."

"Some parents have been known to," Roarke pointed out.

"Beats me how. But if she was into the mother thing, she wouldn't have shipped him off when he was still sucking his thumb."

"I tend to agree with you, though our experience in this particular area's limited. If I were to speculate, I'd wonder if the payoff wasn't linked to her going through with the pregnancy."

"Buy her off, buy the kid," Eve surmised. "It's a continuation of the project in a way. Long-term results. I'm going to have a really fascinating talk with McNamara tomorrow. Look at Morano's educational scope. Very heavy on the computer tech studies. It fits. He's our compugeek. I need the image from the security discs, Moniqua Cline's file."

Behind her, Roarke did the transfer and display, split screen.

"You got a morph program on there?"

"Yes. I know what you want—one minute." Anticipating her, Roarke sat again, went to work. He started with the hair, copying the killer's bronze mane onto Kevin's unobtrusive brown. He altered the shape of the face, defining cheekbones, lengthening the jaw. Then deepened the skin tone to a sun-washed bronze.

"Magic," Eve noted as the two images mirrored each other. "Won't hold up in court. Lawyers'll tear morph ID to shreds. Even with Moniqua testifying about the name, they can wiggle. She was seriously drugged at the time and so on. But it's him. The eyes are the same. He changed the color, but he couldn't change what's in them. Because what's in them is nothing. Nothing at all. Copy and save imagery. Morano, Kevin, data back on the screen. Who are you, Kevin?"

MORANO, KEVIN, DOB 4 APRIL, 2037. HAIR BROWN, EYES BLUE. HEIGHT FIVE FOOT ELEVEN INCHES. WEIGHT ONE HUNDRED FIFTY. CURRENT RESIDENCES: NEW YORK CITY, LONDON, ENGLAND. EMPLOYMENT: FREELANCE COMPUTER PROGRAMMER. EDUCATION: EASTBRIDGE EARLY CHILDHOOD PREPARATORY. MANSVILLE PREPARATORY. ADVANCED EDUCATION: HARVARD TECHNOLOGY.

GRADUATED, SUMMA CUM LAUDE, 2058. NO SIB-
LINGS. MARITAL STATUS: SINGLE. NO CRIMINAL
RECORD.

"He's twenty-two," she stated. "He's only twenty-two.
And so is McNamara's grandson, who also went to East-
bridge, Mansville Prep, then on to Harvard Medical.
Graduated summa cum laude in 2058. No siblings," she
added. "But I bet under the skin, Kevin is his brother.
Give me his data, with image."

"Dallas?" Mavis peeked in the doorway. "We're set in
here."

"Hold it." Eve held up a hand as Lucias's data rolled
on-screen. "Nearly the same height and weight, too. Give
me the image from Grace Lutz's—"

"I'm ahead of you," Roarke told her.

"He's better at it," she said as the images ran side by
side. "Better at hiding what's behind his eyes. Morph him.
It doesn't show on him the same way. He's smarter, more
controlled, more sure of himself. He'd be the dominant."

When Trina came to the door, Mavis shushed her.
"She's working. Frigid to watch."

"I can turn Kevin. Oh yeah, I scoop him up tomorrow,
lock him into Interview, squeeze his balls till they turn
purple. He'll roll on his buddy."

She paced back, studied the faces, considered.
"Maybe I can fast-talk my way into a search and seize
tonight, take them both, take them by surprise. But if they
don't have the lab on premises, if they don't do any of
their work in-house, they could get rid of a lot of evidence before I track it down."

"You have DNA from two of the victims," Roarke reminded her.

"Can't force them to give DNA samples unless I
charge them, can't charge them with what I've got. If I
slide under and get prints or DNA without authorization,
I lose them in court. I'm not losing them. We wait till tomorrow," she decided. "Then we close them down."

"Isn't she the ult?" Mavis asked Trina.

"Yeah, and she'd better get her ultimate butt in the chair."

Eve turned, and the eyes that had been flat and cool showed hints of fear. "This is just, you know, practice. And it's all temporary. You don't do anything permanent to me."

"Right. Strip off the shirt. You need bigger tits."

"Oh God."

While Eve was getting a temporary breast enhancement, Peabody was winding down with a bowl of frozen nondairy dessert some marketing whiz had named Iced Delight. Drenched in chocolate-substitute syrup, it wasn't half bad. Or so Peabody decided as she scraped the bottom of the bowl.

She washed the bowl so that it wouldn't be sitting there in the morning to remind her she had absolutely no willpower. When she heard the knock on her door she was about to turn off the entertainment screen and head to bed.

If it was one of her neighbors again, with a complaint about noise from another apartment, she was telling them to call a cop. She was off duty, damn it, and needed the six hours' sleep she had coming.

A peek in the security screen made her gasp in surprise. She unlocked the door, pulled it open, and stared at McNab. His lip was swollen, his right eye boasted an impressive shiner. And he was wet.

"What the hell happened to you?"

"I had an incident," he snapped. "I want to come in."

"I tried to reach you. You've got your 'links on message only."

"I was busy. I was off duty. Goddamn it."

"Okay, okay." She stepped back before he could plow into her. "We're on at oh six hundred. We caught a break earlier tonight. We've got an op going tomorrow. Dallas—"

"I don't want to hear about it now, okay? I can hear about the damn op tomorrow."

"Suit yourself." A bit miffed, she shut the door. "Your boots are squeaking."

"What, I don't have ears? I can't hear them squeaking?"

"What crawled up your ass and nested?" She sniffed the air. "You reek. What've you been drinking?"

"Whatever I want. Would you get off my back?"

"Look, you're the one who came to my door bunged up, wet, and smelling like the floor of a bar. I was on my way to bed. I've got to get some sleep."

"Fine, go to bed. I don't know why I came here anyway." He stalked to the door, pulled it open. Slammed it shut again. "I went by Monroe's. We got into it."

"What do you mean you . . ." she stammered. "You had a fight with Charles? Are you crazy?"

"Maybe you don't think we've got anything going on, but you're wrong. That's it, you're wrong. And I see him pushing Dr. Blonde in your face, it pisses me off. Best thing could happen to you, in my opinion, but I didn't like the way he tossed you over."

"Tossed me over," she repeated, dumbfounded.

"You break up with somebody, you do it square. He's going to apologize."

"He's going to apologize?"

"What are you, an echo?"

She had to sit. "Charles blackened your eye and split your lip?"

"He got in a couple of shots." Not to mention the gut punch that had him heaving up the homemade brew in the gutter like a common brew head. "His face isn't so perfect tonight either."

"Why are you all wet?"

"Dishy Dimatto was with him. She dumped a bucket of water on us." He shoved his hands in his damp pockets and stomped around the room on his squeaky boots. "I'd've taken him if she hadn't broken it up. He shouldn't have treated you that way."

Peabody opened her mouth to explain she hadn't been mistreated, then wisely closed it again. Her mother hadn't raised a foolish daughter. "It doesn't matter." She cast her eyes down in a sorrowful droop to hide the unholy gleam in them.

McNab and Charles, fighting over her. It was too mag for words.

"Hell it doesn't. If it helps any, I think he was really sorry."

"He's a nice guy, McNab. Not the kind that hurts anyone on purpose."

"Doesn't change the sting." He kneeled down in front of her. "Look, I want us to get back together."

"We got together pretty good last night."

"I don't mean just in the sheets. I want us to pick up the way we were going. But different."

Wary now, she eased back. "Different how?"

"Exclusive this time. And we can, you know, go out to some fancy places. He's not the only one who can get slicked up and take you to . . . wherever. I don't want to go out with anyone else, and I don't want you going out with anyone else either."

Her throat tickled, but she was afraid to swallow. "So, what, you're asking me to go steady?"

His face went hot, his teeth bared, and he shoved to his feet. "Never mind. Put it down to too much to drink." He swung toward the door again, nearly got there.

"Yes." She got up. She wished her knees weren't knocking, but she got up.

He turned back, slowly. "Yes what?"

"I could give it a try. See where it goes."

He took a step back. "Exclusive?"

"Yeah."

And another. "Like a couple."

"Okay."

When she smiled, he leaned in and kissed her. "Oh, shit!" then jolted back when pain exploded in his lip. He blotted at it with the back of his hand, saw fresh blood. "Got anything for this?"

"Sure." She wanted to pet and cuddle him like a puppy. "Let me get the first-aid kit."

When she came back in with it, the bulletin announcement on-screen caught her attention.

The nude body of a man floating in the East River was discovered tonight by dock workers. Though police officials have not released cause of death, the victim has been identified as Dr. Theodore McNamara.

"Holy hell." Peabody dropped the kit with a clatter and raced to her 'link.

Chapter 17

The body had been transported to the morgue and the crime scene cordoned off by the time Eve arrived. Warehouses streamed in a messy ribbon of brick and concrete along the choppy slice between access road and river.

And all had the washed-out, false glare from the police lights.

The media jammed around the barricades and sensors like Saturday night hopefuls vying to gain admission to an exclusive club. And there was just as much chatter from them in the form of shouted questions, demands, and pleas.

Uniformed officers stood in as bouncers. Most were smart enough to ignore the pleas, promises, and bribes for information. But, Eve knew, there would be one who'd weaken and spring the first leak in the data dam.

Accepting it as the natural relationship between cops and media, she hooked her badge on her jacket and started muscling her way through.

"Dallas, hey, Dallas!" Nadine Furst nipped her elbow. "What's the deal? Why were you called in? What's your connection to Theodore McNamara?"

"I'm a cop. He's dead."

"Come on, Dallas." Even in the harsh light, Nadine managed to look vivid and camera-ready. "They don't trot you out for every murder in the city."

She flashed an angry look at Nadine. "Nobody trots me out. Now step back, Nadine, you're in my way."

"All right, okay. But the word is it looks like a robbery/murder. Is that your take?"

"I don't know anything yet. Now friend or not, you move or I bust you for obstruction."

Nadine shifted aside. "Something's up," she whispered to her camera operator. "Something big. Pay attention. I'm going to call my contact at the morgue, see what I can wheedle out. Watch Dallas," she added. "If she's here, she's the center."

Eve pushed her way through reporters and gawkers. She caught a whiff of the river now, a sour smear on the air. The crime scene team was at work, the fluorescent yellow initials on the backs of their jackets searing through the hard white lights. The beam of the powerful portables spilled out onto the pitch-black surface of the river so that it gleamed like oil.

Outdoor, night-time murder, Eve thought, was black and white.

She signalled to a uniform. "Who's primary?"

"Detective Renfrew. Short guy, dark hair, brown suit and tie," she added with just a hint of a sneer in her voice. "That's him. Standing with his hands on his hips looking at the water like the perp's going to swim by doing the backstroke."

Eve studied his back. "Okay. Draw me a picture here."

"Couple of dock hands spotted the floater. Said they were taking their union-sanctioned break, and you have to figure they were using the river for a toilet. Called it in at twenty-two thirty. Nine-eleven caller IDed himself as Deke Jones. Body hadn't been in long or else the fish weren't very interested. Severe head and facial wounds. No clothes, no jewelry, no nothing. IDed him by his prints. Took him off in the dead wagon about fifteen minutes ago."

"This your patrol area . . . Officer Lewis?"

"Yes, sir. My partner and I responded to the nine-eleven. We were on-scene within three minutes. Dock workers were gathered around like a dirt clod, but nobody'd touched the body. And, Lieutenant? I mentioned this to the detective, but he didn't seem interested. There's a report of a car fire about a half mile from here. Late model lux sedan, no passengers. The way this current runs, it could be the dumping point."

"Okay. thanks. Renfrew's going to give me grief, isn't he?"

"Yes, sir." Lewis agreed. "He surely is."

Eve wasn't feeling patient, she wasn't feeling diplomatic, but she told herself she'd have to be both.

Renfrew turned at her approach. His gaze skimmed over her face, dipped briefly down to her badge.

"No one called Cop Central into this." His shoulders went up and back, like a boxer bracing for the first round.

She had a good inch on him in height, and watched as he flexed his body forward on his toes to compensate.

Oh yeah, she thought, noting his combative stance, he was going to give her grief. "I didn't get the tag from Central. I'm not looking to trespass on your turf, Detective Renfrew. Your victim's connected to one of my cases. I think we might be able to help each other out."

"I don't need your help, and I'm not interested in getting the fast shuffle from Central on my case."

"Okay, you can help me out."

"You're on my crime scene, and that makes one too many badges around here. I've got work to do."

"Detective, I need to know what you've got at this point."

"You think you can pull rank on me?" He rocked higher on his toes, jabbed a finger at her. "Waltz in here and take over a high-profile murder so you can get your face splashed all over the screen again? Forget it. I'm primary here."

Eve imagined grabbing the finger he had in her face, bending it back until the bone snapped. But she kept her voice level. "I'm not interested in screen time, in pulling rank, or in taking over your case, Renfrew. I'm interested in finding out why a man I had scheduled for formal interview tomorrow ends up dead in the river. I'm asking you to reach out with some courtesy and cooperation."

"Courtesy and cooperation. Fuck that. How much courtesy and cooperation did you show when you tore into the One-twenty-eight a couple months ago? I don't reach out to cops who turn on cops."

"Sounds like you've got issues, Renfrew. The One-two-eight was a mess, and a cop was killing cops."

He snorted through his nose. "So you say."

"So I say. And right now someone's killing women who think they're going out for a pleasant evening. Your case links to mine, so we can stand here and piss on each other or we can share information that could close both cases quickly."

"This is my crime scene." He jabbed a finger at her again. "I say who comes on it and who doesn't. And I want you out. Remove yourself or I'll have you removed."

Eve stuck her hands in her pockets before she could give in to the urge and punch him. "Have me removed, Renfrew." She dug out her recorder, watched his face go red and tight as she fixed it to her jacket. "Officially and on record have me removed from a crime scene that is potentially linked to an ongoing homicide investigation of which I am primary. Have me removed after I've asked you for the cooperation and courtesy to exchange information that may aid in both investigations."

She stared him down, waited five humming seconds. Around them, crime scene techs had stopped their work to watch. "Have me removed," she said again, "but before you take that step, you'd better think carefully about how such an action will look on the official record, how it's going to play in the media who are standing at the edges of your scene, and how you're going to justify such an act to your superiors."

"Turn that goddamn recorder off."

"It stays on. We're past doing this the easy way. I'm identified as Dallas, Lieutenant Eve, and request from you, Renfrew . . ." She dropped her gaze to his badge. ". . . Detective Matthew, a report on your investigation into the death of Theodore McNamara as this same individual was a potential witness, a potential suspect in a series of homicides of which I am primary investigator."

"You can read my report when I file it. That's all I'm required to give you, Lieutenant. I've got nothing to say to you at this time."

When he stalked off, Eve hissed out a breath. She turned to one of the crime scene techs. "What have you got?"

"We've got nothing here. Body got tangled in some lines, otherwise it would've kept on keeping on. Renfrew, he's a dick. He should have a unit looking up-current for the dump site."

"Time of death?"

"Seventeen-forty."

"Thanks."

"Me, I'm loaded with cooperation and courtesy."

She spotted Peabody and headed over. "With me." She walked away from the crowd, passed through the barricade at its thinnest point. "I want you to check on an automotive torching, late model luxury vehicle. About a half mile from here. Find out who it's registered to."

"Yes, sir."

Eve pulled out her own 'link, then saw McNab. "What happened to you?"

"A slight altercation." He touched fingers gingerly to his bruised eye.

"Peabody, did you pop McNab?"

"No, sir."

"Since you're here and aren't in the middle of an altercation with my aide, you check on the torching. Peabody, cozy up with some of the uniforms, first on-scene was Lewis and her partner. See what else you can get from them. Steer clear of the primary. That's Detective Renfrew, the flaming asshole."

"Did you pop the flaming asshole, sir?"

"No, but it was a close call." She turned away and used her 'link.

When the ME answered, his voice was slurred with sleep.

"Gee, Morris, did I wake you up?"

"What is this, you never sleep so no one else is allowed to? What the hell time is it?"

"Time to do a friend a favor." When he sat up, shifted, Eve winced. "Man, either block video or watch the sheets, will you?"

"Despite male propaganda, I can officially attest that one man's balls are pretty much the same as another's." But he twitched the sheets back up to his waist. "But when you fantasize about me later, and you will, make it good. Now, what do you need?"

"You've got a victim checking into the morgue. McNamara, Theodore."

"Dr. Theodore McNamara?"

"That's the one."

Morris whistled. "Since I'm talking to you, I have to assume the famous doctor didn't buy it from natural causes."

"He's recently been plucked out of the East River, and it doesn't appear he'd decided to take a little swim."

"If you're calling to ask me to flag him priority, you're wasting a favor. High-profile name, high-profile treatment."

"That's not the favor. I'm not primary on this one, but McNamara's connected to my sexual homicides. I had a chat with him this afternoon, and had him booked for formal tomorrow. I need a head's-up on the autopsy. All the data from the body and from the primary's interaction with the pathologist assigned."

"Why doesn't the primary copy you?"

"He doesn't like me. I gotta tell you, my feelings are real hurt over it."

"Who's primary?"

"Renfrew, Detective Matthew."

"Ah." Morris plumped the pillows behind him, laid back. "Territorial little bastard, poor social skills, and a tendency to refuse to broaden his focus."

"In other words, a flaming asshole."

"In other words. I think I'll go in and take a look at the recently departed myself. I'll get back to you."

"Thanks, Morris. I owe you one."

"Yeah, I like that part."

"Morris? What's the tattoo?"

Grinning, Morris tapped a finger on the illustration just under his left nipple. "The Grim Reaper. An equal opportunity employer."

"You're a sick man, Morris." She clicked off. "A sick man."

She'd kept her back to the reporters as she talked, and her radar up. Most of them, with nothing to feed on, were slipping away to do quick live-remotes.

McNab jogged up to her.

"Walk and talk," she ordered. "I want to keep clear of the media. Once they make a connection, we lose whatever advantage we've got."

"It was McNamara's sedan. Good and torched. NYFD's saying there was a chemical accelerant. RD-52. It's a kind of flammable acid. You get a flash, fire burst, and it eats right through the metal while it burns. Really thorough. Witness saw the flash, went to take a look-see, and had the presence of mind to note down the vehicle ID before it evaporated. Five, ten more minutes, we'd have had nothing."

"Smart, but not smart enough. They should've blasted off the ID before they torched it. Little mistakes." She looked back toward the river. "Robbery, my ass. Who rolls a guy, even takes his clothes, then wastes a luxury sedan? What do you bet McNamara paid his killer a visit after I talked to him?"

"I'd put the bank on it."

"If Renfrew was less of a moron, we could wrap this up tonight." Staring into middle distance, she juggled possibilities. "Dunwood doesn't know Renfrew's a moron. Renfrew'll notify next of kin, but that's the wife. No reason for the grandson to come into play there. And no reason for me not to pay him a visit to express my sympathy for his loss and question him. Lucias Dunwood. Get his address. Let's shake him up."

"You got it."

They separated, and Eve made another call. This one to home. "Hi." She tried a smile when Roarke came on. "I guess they're still there, huh?"

As there was music blasting and the sound of half-drunken laughter rolling over it, Roarke just shrugged.

"Look, I'm sorry I dumped it on you. Maybe you should lock yourself in one of the rooms. They'll never find you in that place."

"I'm considering it. I take it you've called to let me know you'll be some time yet."

"I don't know how long. A lot going on. If I can't close it down tonight, I'm still going to need Mavis and Trina tomorrow. Maybe you should lock them in a room."

"Not to worry. I suspect they'll pass out soon enough."

"There's that. Hold on." She turned to McNab. "What?"

"Got an address, but it's bogus."

"What do you mean, bogus?"

"I mean the address listed for Lucias Dunwood is the Fun House, Time's Square. I know because I spend a lot of time there. It's a big e-amusement center. No residences on premises."

"He likes to play games," she replied. "Give me some room here." She stepped away until she was out of earshot. "Listen—"

"You'd like me to find Dunwood's actual address."

"McNamara would've had it. I'm not going to be able to access his files from here because the primary on this is playing big stud dog with the investigation."

"I see." Roarke was already moving away from the music.

"I could call Whitney and get clearance, but that's messy. Plus, it makes me feel like a tattlettale or something."

"Mm-hmm."

"I could tag Feeney, and he'd wangle authorization through EDD, but I've already gotten one person out of bed tonight." She glanced back at McNab. "Maybe more."

"And I'm already up."

"Yeah. Technically . . . well, just skimming the technicalities, I'm authorized to access some data because he's a suspect. Whether this data includes his address files or personal data is debatable, but I'd have clearance for it in the morning anyway so . . ."

"Why wait? Would you like that address now, or would you like to keep rationalizing a bit longer?"

She blew out a breath, noting that he'd gone up to his office while she'd been talking. "I'll just take the address."

He gave it to her. "Oh, Lieutenant? Since that's only a few blocks from here, perhaps you'll make it home while I still have my sanity."

"I'll do my best. Guess I owe you one, too."

"Be sure I'll collect."

She broke transmission, signalled McNab. "Get Peabody. We're moving."

She was nearly to her vehicle when she saw Nadine, leaning on the hood and examining her nails.

"That's city property you're resting your ass on."

"Why do they go out of their way to make official vehicles so ugly?"

"I don't know, but I'm taking it up with my Congressman first chance I get."

"Rumor is you and Detective Renfrew got into a little power tussle."

"Rumors are your department."

"Then you wouldn't be interested that rumor continues that he's a jerk and you cut him down bloodlessly." Nadine tossed her streaky blonde hair. "But you may be interested in a deduction, since deductions are your department. I deduce that Dr. Theodore McNamara plays into the sexual homicides you're investigating, that robbery had nothing to do with his ending up in the river, and that you have a very good idea who bashed him about the head and face earlier this evening. And whoever that may be has a starring role in your homicides."

"That's a lot of deducing, Nadine."

"Will you confirm?"

Eve merely crooked a finger, walked away. When the camera operator fell into step behind Nadine, Eve stopped her with one steely stare.

"Wait for me," Nadine told her. "She's just doing her job, Dallas."

"We're all just doing our jobs. Turn the recorder off."

"Recorder?"

"Don't waste my time. We go off record, or you get nothing."

Nadine sighed, heavily and strictly for form, then disconnected the recorder worked into her gold lapel pin. "Off record."

"You don't go on the air with anything until I tell you."

"Do I get a one-on-one?"

"Nadine, I don't have time to negotiate with you. For all I know there's another woman dead tonight and no one's found her yet. You go on air with your deductions and there could be another one dead tomorrow."

"Okay. It stays in holding until you say."

"McNamara's connected. I talked to him this afternoon. He wasn't cooperative. I believe he knew or suspected the identity of the killer. I believe he confronted that individual after our conversation, and as a result ended up a floater."

"That only confirms my deductions."

"I'm not finished. I believe the root of these murders goes back to a project partnered by J. Forrester and Allegany Pharmaceuticals nearly twenty-five years ago. Sex, scandals, illegals abuse, payoffs, and coverups. Dig there for your background and you'll be several steps ahead of the other networks."

"Was McNamara directly involved in the killings?"

"Years ago he spent a lot of time, energy, and money making sure that facts, actions, and criminal activities that should have been part of the public record were sealed. He refused to cooperate by volunteering information pertinent to the investigation of the murder of two women and the attack on another, instead opting to withhold that information. Did he kill them? No. Is he responsible? That's a moral call. That's not my department either."

Nadine touched her arm as Eve turned away. "I have a contact at the morgue. McNamara was struck several blows on the head and face nearly an hour before he died. One defensive wound, right wrist. While the initial injuries came from a blunt instrument about eight inches wide, the killing blow was delivered by a different weapon. A long, slim metal object such as a crowbar or tire iron that might be found in the tool kit of a car."

She paused. "I believe in the courtesy and cooperation of shared information."

"I really hate knowing that phrase is going to follow me around for the next six weeks."

Eve walked back to the car. "Backseat, McNab."

"How come I can't sit in front? I outrank her. And my legs're longer."

"She's my aide, you're ballast." She climbed in, and didn't speak again until McNab had stopped grumbling and arranged himself on the backseat. "We're going to pay a visit to Lucias Dunwood."

"How'd you get the address?"

She glanced at McNab in the rearview mirror. "I have my ways of ascertaining data. Peabody, you'll go in with me. McNab, you'll stay in the vehicle."

"But—"

"I go in with a uniform, not a uniform and a detective. And not a detective who looks like he spent his evening brawling in the streets. You'll stay behind, with your communicator open as mine will be. If we run into any trouble, you call for backup, then, using your judgment, decide whether you wait for that backup or come in and assist. Now I want you to get me another address. Kevin Morano."

Making the best of things he pulled out his PPC and stretched his length out on the backseat. "Hey, there's a candy bar taped to the back of the passenger's seat."

Even as Peabody swiveled around to try to look, Eve bared her teeth. "First one who touches it gets their fingers ripped off and stuffed up their nose."

Peabody sprang back into position. "You're hoarding candy."

"It's not a hoard. It's an emergency supply, which the sneaking candy thief who keeps raiding my office hasn't found yet. And if he or she does find it, I'll know why." She paused significantly. "And you will pay."

"I'm on a diet anyway."

"You don't need to diet, She-Body. You are a just-right female."

"McNab?" Eve said.

"Yes, sir."

"Shut up."

"It's all right, Dallas. We're a couple."

"A couple of what? No, don't tell me. Don't talk to me. Don't talk to each other. Let there be silence across the land."

Peabody managed to muffle a snicker, then tried to adjust the climate control manually.

"It's busted. Shut up."

Saying nothing, Peabody rolled down her window.

McNab shifted in the back. "Permission to speak on official business, sir?"

"What?"

"Kevin Morano's address. Yankee Stadium. Do you want me to contact Roarke and have him . . . I mean," he amended when she glared in the rearview, "do you want to implement your ways of ascertaining data?"

"No. I know where he lives."

When she stopped in front of the grand old brownstone, it was after one A.M. The house was dark but for the red pinprick of light on the armed security system.

"Are you armed, McNab?"

"My off-duty stunner."

"Keep it set on low, keep your communicator open. Don't approach the house unless I signal you to do so. Come on, Peabody, let's go wake this prick up."

She crossed the sidewalk. When she stepped onto the first stone stair, the security system went into a warning hum. She pressed the bell. Instantly light washed down from overhead and the security system went on first alert.

YOU ARE CURRENTLY UNDER SURVEILLANCE. PLEASE STATE YOUR NAME AND YOUR BUSINESS. ANY ATTEMPT TO ENTER THE PREMISES OR CAUSE DAMAGE TO SAME, AND THIS SYSTEM WILL IMMEDIATELY NOTIFY THE POLICE AND THE NEIGHBORHOOD WATCH.

"Lieutenant Dallas, NYPSD." She held her badge up to the view screen. "I need to speak with Lucias Dunwood regarding a police matter."

ONE MOMENT, PLEASE, WHILE YOUR IDENTIFICATION IS PROCESSED AND VERIFIED . . . PLEASE WAIT WHILE MR. DUNWOOD IS INFORMED OF YOUR REQUEST . . .

"Lieutenant, do you think—"

Eve shifted her body subtly, and stepped on Peabody's foot under camera range. "I think it's difficult having to wake Mr. Dunwood up to tell him about his grandfather's death. But there's never a good time for hard news, and no point in waiting for morning to give it."

"No, sir." Peabody cleared her throat, fixed a sober expression on her face as she realized she was being told they were likely under audio as well as video surveillance.

It took several minutes before the light in the first floor windows flashed on. She didn't hear locks being disengaged, which told her the door was fully soundproofed. It opened silently, and she got her first look at Lucias.

His bright red hair was disheveled. He wore a long white nightrobe belted loosely at the waist. And gave every appearance of a young man just roused out of sleep, and puzzled as to the reason why.

"I'm sorry." He blinked owlishly. "You're the police?"

"Yes." She offered her badge again. "Are you Lucias Dunwood?"

"That's right. What's this about? Is there some trouble in the neighborhood?"

"Not that I'm aware of. May we come in and speak to you, Mr. Dunwood?"

"All right. Sorry, I'm a little punchy." He stepped back, gestured them into a wide foyer with marble floors glowing under the lights from a three-tiered silver chandelier. "I've been in bed a couple of hours. I'm not used to having the police come to my door."

"I'm sorry to disturb you so late. I have some difficult news. It might be better if we sat down."

"What kind of news? What's wrong?"

"Mr. Dunwood, I'm sorry to tell you that your grandfather is dead."

"My grandfather?"

Eve watched with reluctant admiration as he paled, lifted a hand that trembled very slightly to his lips. "Dead? My grandfather's dead? Was there an accident?"

"No, he was murdered."

"Murdered? Oh God, oh my God. I do need to sit

down." He made it as far as a long silver bench in the foyer, then collapsed on it. "I can't believe this. It's like I'm dreaming. What happened? What happened to him?"

"Your grandfather was found in the East River earlier tonight. The investigation into his death is underway. I'm sorry for your loss, Mr. Dunwood, but it would help us if you'd answer some questions."

"Of course. Of course I will."

"Are you here alone?"

"Alone?" His head came up and she saw suspicion pass quickly over his face before he lowered it again.

"If you're alone, perhaps there's someone you'd like my aide to call. To stay with you."

"No. No, I'm all right. I'll be all right."

"When's the last time you saw your grandfather?"

"He's been away, some consult business off planet. I suppose it's been several weeks."

"Did he at that time express to you any concerns, any fears for his safety?"

"Why no." Lucias looked up again. "I don't understand."

"There's a possibility your grandfather was killed by someone he knew. A car registered in his name was set on fire only hours before his body was found. The car was parked near the ground-shuttle tracks off East One-forty-three. Are you aware of any business that would take him to that area?"

"None whatsoever. His car was set on fire? That sounds like—like some sort of vendetta. But Grandfather was, he was a humanitarian, a great man who dedicated his life to medicine and research. This has to be some terrible mistake."

"Are you studying to be a doctor?"

"I'm taking a leave from schooling just now." He pressed his fingers to his temple, covering most of his face. And Eve studied the dragon's head carved into the sapphire in the blended gold ring on his right hand.

"I wanted time to think, to explore, to decide what

area of medicine would suit me best. My grandfather . . ." His voice broke, he looked away. "He leaves big footprints to fill. He was my mentor, my inspiration."

"I'm sure he was very proud of you. You were close then?"

"I think so. He was larger than life, a man who drove himself to excel. I hope to be worthy of his memory. To end like this, thrown in the river like . . . sewage. My God, to have been stripped of his dignity at the end of his life. How he would hate that. You have to find who did this to him, Lieutenant. They have to pay for what they did."

"We'll find them, and they'll pay. I'm sorry, but I have to ask, it's standard procedure. Can you account for your whereabouts tonight, between the hours of seven and midnight?"

"My . . . Christ. I hadn't thought . . . I'd be a kind of suspect. I was home here until about eight-thirty. Then I went out to a club. I didn't actually talk to anyone. Didn't see anyone very interesting. I'd been hoping . . . Okay, I confess. I'd thought I might pick up a girl for the evening, but it didn't work out. I came home early. Ten-thirty, I'd say. My security system would verify that."

"So you were alone, essentially?"

"I have a house droid." He got to his feet. "I can get it. You can question it as to when I left, when I came back. Oh, and I have a cash receipt for drinks. I'm sure they're time and date stamped. Will that help?"

"Very much. We'll just clear this up so we can move on in the investigation."

"Anything I can do. Anything to help. I'll get the droid. And while you're doing the questioning, I'll get the receipt. I'm sure I stuck it in my pocket."

"Appreciate it. Oh, I should tell you your address is mislisted in the city files."

"Excuse me?"

"Your address, there's an error. I got your correct location from your grandfather's files. You might want to see to that, when you get the chance."

"How odd. Yes, I'll take care of it. Excuse me just a minute."

He got the droid, having no doubt Kevin's careful reprogramming and falsified input would hold. But his fists were clenched when he strode into his bedroom. Kevin rushed in behind him.

"You said they'd never identify the car."

"Well, they did," Lucias shot back. "But it doesn't matter. Everything's fine. Looks like it's just as well that stupid bitch didn't show up at Jean-Luc's tonight. I wouldn't have this." He tugged the receipt out of his trouser pocket. "Alibied all around, and playing the shocked and grieving grandson."

"What about me?"

"They don't know about you, and there's no reason they should. There's no connection between this and the project as far as the cops are concerned. And no connection that can be proved between me and my grandfather's death. Just stay up here and be quiet. I'm handling this."

He hurried down again. "Lieutenant, in my pocket, just as I thought." He handed Eve the receipt.

"Fine. I'd like my aide to make a copy of this for the files."

"Of course."

He waited while Peabody scanned the receipt. "Is there anything else I can do? Anything at all?"

"Not at this time. We'll be in touch."

"You'll let me know if you—when you find who did this."

"You'll be the first," Eve promised.

She walked back to the car, slid behind the wheel. "Cold-blooded son of a bitch. He was enjoying that."

"Droid could've been reprogrammed," McNab said from the backseat. "Same for the security. The guy who's been doing the e-work could've done both. It'd be cake."

"Still, we didn't get much out of him," Peabody complained.

"Didn't we?" Eve tapped her fingers on the wheel. "I never said his grandfather's name and he never asked. He has the requisite two, both New York City residents. But he never asked which one was dead. Didn't have to ask. And that bit about being stripped of his dignity at the end of his life. That's just what he'd done. What he'd intended to do. And he out-thought himself by not just saying his pal and housemate Kevin was with him part of the evening. Didn't want to share the spotlight."

"I guess we got more out of him than I thought."

"That's right. Little mistakes."

Chapter 18

Roarke met them at the door. It only took one look at Eve's face to confirm his suspicion that she was running on fumes. At that moment, he'd have preferred closing the door in Peabody's and McNab's faces, scooping his wife up, and pouring her into bed.

Because she read something of his thoughts, Eve nudged everyone inside. "It was quicker to bring them here."

"We can catch a cab downtown," Peabody said, sacrificing the delights of lolling in one of the magnificent beds for a few hours.

"Don't be silly." Roarke skimmed a hand over Eve's hair, a subtle gesture of reassurance. "We've plenty of room. Whose fist did you run into, Ian?"

"Monroe's." He smirked and sent his sore lip throbbing. "We ran into each other's."

"It's nothing to brag about." Eve stripped off her jacket. "Crash here. The briefing's at oh six hundred anyway. Pick a couple of bedrooms on opposite sides of the house."

"Aw" was all Peabody said.

Laughing, Roarke patted her arm. "She doesn't mean it."

"Do, too," Eve replied. "Mavis and Trina?"

"In the pool, along with Leonardo, who arrived about two hours ago. I bowed out when they decided it was time for nude relay races."

"They're naked?" McNab perked right up. "Wet and naked? You know, a quick swim would be good. Just a passing thought," he murmured when Peabody curled her lip.

"Playtime's over. Bed." Eve pointed up the stairs. "We've got a major op tomorrow, and I want you both fresh. Where are the mermaids and friend bunking?"

"Oh, here and there," Roarke said easily. "Why don't you go up? I'll settle our company in."

"Good. I've got some things left to run before I turn in." She started up the stairs. "And I don't want to hear the patter of little feet sneaking around the corridors."

"She's so strict," Peabody said under her breath.

"Tired and cross is what she is. Now, why don't we take the elevator." Roarke gestured. "I think you'll like the accommodations I have in mind. Plenty of room for two."

Eve went to his office first, brought up a diagram of Greenpeace Park. After highlighting the picnic site, she let the computer select the most strategic locations for her men. She'd see if she agreed—after a few hours of sleep.

She listed the men she wanted for the operation, transmitted the order, and copied Whitney.

A shower, she decided when her vision blurred. Maybe a shower would wash some of the fog out of her brain so she could put another hour in.

She was staggering into the bedroom when her pocket-link beeped. "Dallas."

"Figured I'd tag you on the portable." Morris yawned hugely. "Our guest this evening departed this plane of existence at seven-forty. Previously, he had an unpleasant altercation with a blunt object. This altercation would have resulted in death within an hour, perhaps a tad less. The medical term would be having one's brains bashed in."

"Got it." Too tired to stand, she sat on the arm of the sofa in the sitting area. "I hate to be the one to break this to you, Morris, but I already got the data from a media source. You've got a gossip in your house."

"No! Why, I'm shocked and amazed. A city official leaking information to the media. What is the world coming to?"

"You're a fucking jolly soul."

"Love your work, love the world. I don't imagine your media contact had quite everything, as I've just gotten the tox results."

She shook her head clear as Roarke came into the room. "He was drugged?"

"Between the initial insults and the coup de grâce, the doctor was given a stimulant."

"They tried to revive him?" Her thoughts jumbled, then cleared before Morris could answer. "No, that doesn't make sense. They wanted to keep him alive a little longer."

"Give the lady a stuffed panda. The substance used stimulates the heart, and it's quickly absorbed. If we'd gotten him in here twenty, thirty minutes later, we wouldn't have found a trace of it."

"They kept him alive so they could get him to a dumping site and kill him there. He'd have died anyway, right, from the initial beating?"

"Without immediate medical attention, yes. And even then his chances were minimal. He'd certainly have drowned without that final blow."

"So they wanted to give him that last shot. When he was unconscious, helpless. Stripped of his dignity."

"You've got yourself mighty nasty customers, Dallas. I'm sending the data to our mutual friend Renfrew. His robbery theory doesn't cut the mustard."

"Thanks. I appreciate you handling this yourself."

"Just part of our luxury package. Get some sleep, for

sweet Christ's sake, Dallas. I've got customers in here who look perkier than you."

"Yeah, I'll do that." She broke transmission, then just sat, staring down at her 'link. She blinked back when Roarke released her weapon harness. "You put them in a room together, didn't you?"

"Haven't you more to worry about than the sexual activities of your subordinates?"

"My subordinates come dragging their asses into the briefing because they've spent what's left of the night playing hide the salami . . . what're you doing?"

"Taking off your boots. You're going to bed."

She stared down at the top of his head. Jesus, the man had the most incredible hair . . . All black and silky, she thought as her head started to loll. So you just wanted to bury your hands in it. Your face in it and . . .

She snapped back. "I'm going to grab a shower and get another hour in."

"No, Eve, you're not." Temper simmered in his voice as he tossed her boots aside with just enough force to have them bounce and skitter. "I'm not standing here watching while you make yourself sick. You go to bed on your own, or I knock you out and put you there."

She frowned at him. It wasn't often the rage showed, that hot and bubbling violence they both knew lived inside him. Seeing it leap, she knew she must look every bit as ragged as Morris indicated.

"I saw his face. I looked in his face." She spoke quietly. "I can't sleep, Roarke, because I'll see it." She pressed her fingers to her eyes, then rose. "I looked at him, and if I hadn't known what he was, I wouldn't have seen it."

She walked away, dragged open a window. Breathed. "He's young. His face is still a little soft around the edges. His hair's all red and curly like, I don't know, a pretty kid's doll or something. He'd killed tonight, taken a life—a life connected to him by blood—with deliberation and forethought and extreme violence. And he sat there talking to me. Teary. Remorseful. He played it perfectly, and I wouldn't have seen it. I wouldn't have seen what's in him."

He hated to hear the fatigue in her voice, and more the discouragement that ghosted through it. "Why should you?"

"Because I was watching for it, and it wasn't there." She whirled back. "He enjoyed it. I know that, in my gut, but I didn't see it on his face, didn't see it in his eyes. He was . . . entertained. I'd upped the stakes for him again. Same game, new level.

"I wanted to hurt him," she continued. "Personally. I wanted to ram my fist into his face until I erased it. Erased him."

"Instead you walked away." He crossed to her, certain she was unaware that her cheeks were wet. "Because you'll erase him by stopping him, by putting him in a cage for the rest of his life. Eve." He framed her face in his hands, brushed at the damp with his thumbs. "Darling Eve, you're exhausted, right down to the bone. If you don't rest, who'll stand for those women?"

She lifted her hands to his wrists. "The dream I had, the last one, with my father standing there bleeding from dozens of holes I'd put in him. He said I'd never be rid of him. He was right. You take one down and another one's right there. Right there waiting. I can't sleep, because I'll see them."

"Not tonight." He drew her in. "We won't let them come in tonight. If you won't sleep . . ." He brushed his lips over her temple. ". . . you'll rest."

He picked her up, carried her back to the sofa.

"What are we doing?"

"We'll watch a movie," he told her.

"A movie. Roarke—"

"It's something you don't do enough of." He laid her down, selected a film disc. "Go outside yourself and into make-believe. Dramas or comedies, joys and sorrows that pull you away from your own for a bit of time."

He came back, slid behind her, and tucked her head on his shoulder. "I've told you about this one, Magda Lane. It took me out of my own miseries once."

It felt so good to lie with him, to have his arm hooked cozily around her waist. The opening music swept into the room, color and costume swirled on-screen. "How many times have you seen this?" she asked him.

"Oh, dozens, I suppose. Shh. You'll miss the opening lines."

She watched, and when her lids drooped, she listened. Then she slept.

When she woke, it was quiet, and it was dark, and his arm was still around her. Fatigue wanted to drag her back under, but she willed it back and turned her wrist up to check the time.

Already after five, she thought. She'd had a solid three hours' sleep, and it would have to be enough. But when she started to move, Roarke's arm tightened.

"Take a few minutes more."

"Can't. It's going to take a half hour in the shower to beat my brain back into shape. I wonder if I can take a shower lying down."

"It's called a bath."

"Not the same."

"Why are you whispering?"

"I'm not whispering." She cleared her throat. And felt as if she'd swallowed splinters of glass. "Just a little hoarse."

"Lights on, ten percent." In the dim glow he nudged her onto her back. "Pale as a ghost, too," he said and laid a hand on her brow. Something like panic ran over his face. "I think you're running a fever."

"I am not." If he could feel panic at the thought of illness, she could feel fear. "I'm not sick. I don't get sick."

"You don't sleep more than a handful of hours in a week and live on coffee, you get sick. Damn it, Eve, you've sabotaged your immune system once too often."

"I have not." She started to sit up, then plopped back when the room spun. "I'm just getting my bearings."

"I ought to strap you in bed for the next month. You need a bloody keeper." He rolled off the sofa, strode to the house 'link.

"I don't know what you're so pissed off about." Her voice was perilously close to a whine, and appalled her. "I'm just a little muggy yet."

"You set a single toe off that sofa, and I'm hauling you to the doctor."

"You just try it, pal, and we'll see who needs medical attention." Since the threat came out in a wheeze, it wasn't particularly effective.

Roarke simply glared at her, and snapped into the 'link. "Summerset. Eve's ill. I need you up here."

"What? What are you doing?" She shoved herself up, nearly gained her feet before Roarke stalked back and held her down. "He's not touching me. He lays one hand on me and I'm beating you both bloody. Where's my weapon?"

"It's him or the health center."

She sucked in air. "You are not the boss here."

"Prove it," he challenged. "Take me down."

She pushed up, he shoved her back. She reared again, and this time pumped her fist into his belly.

"It's gratifying to see you have some strength left, even if that was a girl punch."

The insult nearly rendered her speechless. "The first chance, the very first chance I get, I'm tying your dick into a knot."

"Won't that be fun?" He looked over as Summerset came in. "She's running a fever."

"I am not. Don't you touch me. Don't lay a hand—" She cursed, struggled, when Roarke straddled her and pinned her arms.

"Such childishness." Summerset clucked his tongue, laid a hand on her brow. "Temperature's slightly elevated." He danced his long fingers under her jaw, along her throat. "Stick out your tongue."

"Eve." Roarke's single word was drenched in warning as she pressed her lips tightly together. She stuck out her tongue.

"Do you have any pain?" Summerset asked her.

"Yeah, in my ass. I call it Summerset."

"I see your droll wit hasn't suffered. Just a bit of a bug," he said to Roarke. "Due, I imagine, to exhaustion, stress, and juvenile eating habits. We can ward it off, and treat the symptoms. I'll go get what she needs. She'll do best with a day or two in bed."

"Get off me," she said in a low, clear voice when Summerset went out. "Right now."

"No." Her arms were trembling under his grip, and he didn't think it was all from temper. "Not until we've dealt with this. Are you cold?"

"No." She was freezing. And the pitiful struggle she'd put up had awakened aches everywhere.

"Then why are you shivering?" He bit off an oath, snagged a throw from the back of the couch and had it flung over her before she could push the order from brain to body to move.

"Damn it, Roarke, he's going to come back and poke at me, and try to make me drink one of his weird brews. I just need a hot shower. Let me up. Have a heart."

"I do, and it's yours." He lowered his brow to hers. "That's the problem."

"I'm feeling better. Really." It was a lie, poorly executed as her voice was beginning to tremble. "And when I close this case, I'll take a day off. I'll sleep for twenty hours. I'll eat vegetables."

He had to smile. "I love you, Eve."

"Then don't let him back in here." Her eyes wheeled as she heard the elevator doors open. "He's coming," she whispered. "In the name of everything holy, save me."

"She needs to sit up." Summerset set a tray on the table. On it was a glass of milky liquid, a trio of white tablets, and a pressure syringe.

Eve let herself go limp, and when Roarke eased back,

she sprang. It was a sweaty battle, but a short one. Without batting a lash, Summerset stepped over, pinched her nose closed, dropped the tablets in her mouth, and chased them down her throat with the liquid.

He smiled at Roarke while she sputtered. "I recall having to do that to you a time or two."

"That's where I learned it."

"Get her shirt off. The vitamin booster will work fastest this way."

To save time, and his own skin, Roarke simply ripped off her sleeve. "How's that?"

"Good enough."

She'd gone past anger into weeping, humiliating herself. Everything hurt—head, body, pride. When the syringe pressed against her arm, she barely felt it.

"Shh, baby. Shh." Shaken, Roarke stroked her hair and rocked her. "It's all over now. Don't cry."

"Go away," she said even as she clung to him. "Just go away."

"Leave me alone with her." Summerset touched Roarke's shoulder, felt a pang when he saw the naked emotion on his face. "Give us a few minutes."

"All right." Roarke held her tight another minute. "I'll be in the gym."

When he set her aside, she curled into a ball. Summerset sat beside her, saying nothing until she'd sniffled herself into silence.

"What he feels for you overwhelms him," Summerset began. "There was never anyone else. The women who came and went before you were diversions, temporary interests. He might care, because despite everything that was done to him, he's a man with a large capacity for caring. And still, there was no one before you. Don't you see how he worries?"

She uncurled herself, rubbed her hands over her wet face as if she could rub away the embarrassment of the tears. "He shouldn't worry."

"He does and he will. You need rest, Lieutenant, and a

few days without work and worry. And so does he. So very much does he. He won't take his without you."

"I can't. Not now."

"Won't."

She closed her eyes. "Go up to my office, look at the faces of the dead pinned to my board. Then tell me to step away."

"He wouldn't, would he? But to do what you need to do, you require your strength, energies, and wit." He leaned over, picked up the glass. "Finish it."

She frowned at the glass. She hated to admit whatever he'd given her was already working. So she wouldn't. "It's probably poison."

"Poison," he said, amused. "Why didn't I think of that? Perhaps next time."

"Har-har." She took the glass, downed the remaining contents. "There must be a way to make this taste less like sewage."

"Certainly." He set the glass back on the tray, then got to his feet. "But I'm entitled to my small pleasures. I might suggest you try some moderate exercise now."

She didn't have time, but she took it anyway and went down to the gym. He wasn't using the machines, he rarely did, but was steadily, sweatily, working his way through bench presses. He had the screen on, with the audio set to spew out the various stock reports.

She found she didn't understand the words any more than she did the symbols.

She went to him, knelt by his head. "I'm sorry."

He continued to lift, set, lower. "Feeling better?"

"Yeah. Roarke, I'm sorry. I was an idiot. Don't be mad at me. I don't think I could handle it right now."

"I'm not mad at you." He lifted the bar into the safety, then slid out from under. "The situation occasionally rips my throat out."

"I can't do anything else. I can't be anything else."

He reached down for his towel, rubbed it over his face. "I wouldn't want you to do or be anything else. It's beyond my capabilities not to react as I do when you run yourself into the ground."

"You usually drag me back out before the ground closes over my head."

He looked at her face. Still so pale, he thought. Nearly transparent. "Doesn't seem I was quite quick enough this time."

"Let's go to Mexico."

"Excuse me?"

"The house in Mexico." She figured if she could surprise him, she was still in reasonable shape. "It's been a while. Why don't we take a long weekend once this is over?"

Considering her, he drew the towel between his hands, then hooked it behind her head to bring her closer. "Who's dragging who back out now?"

"Let's drag each other. Give me time to close this down, and you do whatever it is you do to clear a few days. Then we'll run away. We'll lie on the beach, we'll get drunk and have monkey sex. We'll watch film discs until our eyes fall out."

"Go back to the monkey sex."

She laid her hands on his cheeks. "I've got to get ready for the briefing. We've got a deal, right?"

"Yes." He pressed his lips to her forehead, relieved to find it cool again. "We definitely have a deal."

She got up, but when she reached the door, turned back to look at him. He still sat on the bench, lean and sweaty in a black muscle shirt. He'd tied his hair back and had yet to bother with shoes.

And he watched her through eyes so brilliantly blue, it seemed she could dive through them, and into him.

"There was never anybody before you," she said. "I just wanted to say that. And when I did what I do, and it opened a crack in me like it did last night, there was nobody there to hold on to me. I didn't want anyone to hold on to me. Until you. And I got through and I got by, and it was okay. But I think, maybe, if I'd just kept getting through and getting by, I'd have come to a point where I couldn't do it anymore. And if I couldn't do it anymore, it'd be the end of me, Roarke."

She took a steadying breath. "So when you hold on to me, you're helping me stand up, one more time. And the dead, you're standing for them, too. I just wanted to say that."

She went out quickly, and left him staring after her.

When she strode into her office at six minutes after six, she was heavy-eyed, pale, but clear-headed. She found McNab and Peabody had already raided the AutoChef. And Feeney, just arrived, was helping himself to the spread set out across her desk.

"What the hell do you think this is, the Breakfast Barn?"

"Gotta have fuel." Feeney munched into a strip of bacon. "Mother Mary, it's pig meat. Know how long it's been since I had a slice of real pig?"

She nipped it out of his fingers, ate it herself. "Then get a damn plate. You can eat while I bring you up to speed. Peabody, it appears there's no cup of coffee in my hand. I can only assume I've somehow stepped into an alternate universe."

Peabody swallowed a heaping forkful of ham and eggs. "Maybe in this one I'm the lieutenant, and you're . . ." She hopped up, propelled by Eve's frightening look. "Let me get you a cup of coffee, Lieutenant. Sir."

"You do that. The rest of the team are due here by oh eight hundred. I've already got the diagram of the target area on-screen, with computer-generated selections for personnel placement. We'll consider those and adjust if warranted. Feeney, I'd suggest you take McNab into the surveillance vehicle."

"I'd prefer a spot in the park, sir, and a chance to be in on the takedown."

Eve angled her head at McNab and copped another slice of bacon from the plate Feeney had just fixed. "You should have thought of that before you picked a fight and got your pretty face all banged up. Which will only draw attention to you in a place where children play and birds sing merrily in the trees."

"Gotcha there," Feeney said to McNab. "You're with me."

"You'll want another e-man as point," Eve continued. "You know your men better than I do, so I leave it to you."

"Good, because I've already picked him. Roarke," he said, and wagged a finger at the doorway as the man in question strode in.

"Good morning." He was still in black, and though the shirt and trousers were elegant, he managed to look every bit as lean and dangerous as he had in the muscle shirt. "Sorry. Am I late?"

"You think you're sneaky, don't you?"

He snatched the bacon Eve had snatched out of her hand. "Not at all, Lieutenant. I know I am. Which is why I'm very suited for this op."

"You want in, it's up to him." She jerked a thumb at Feeney. "But remember, this is my op."

He bit into the bacon, handed it back to her. "How could I forget?"

By eight-thirty, the full team was briefed. She began assigning roles and positions.

"Hey, hey." Detective Baxter waved a hand. "How come I have to be a sidewalk sleeper?"

"Because you make such a good one," Eve told him. "And you look so sexy with a beggar's license around your neck."

"Trueheart ought to be the sleeper," Baxter insisted. "He's the rookie."

"I don't mind, Lieutenant."

Eve glanced at Trueheart. "You're too young, too wholesome. Baxter's got some miles on him. Peabody, you and Roarke will do the couple's stroll through this area." Eve used her laser pointer to highlight the diagram on-screen. Trueheart, you're park maintenance staff, and you'll cover this sector."

"I've got the best gig," Peabody told McNab.

"Nobody approaches the suspect," Eve continued. "That time of the afternoon, spring day, the park's going to have a lot of traffic. People taking their lunch in the open air, kids running around. The park's open daily to botany clubs, bird-watching clubs, school field trips. The area the suspect selected is fairly secluded, but there will be civilians. Weapons are not to be drawn without extreme need. I don't want to see little Johnny stunned off the swing set because somebody got jumpy."

She sat on the edge of her desk. "You'll also be on the lookout for the second suspect. We have no way of knowing if they work in tandem during their setup stage. If you spot him, if you think you've spotted him, you relay that data to Feeney. You do not, repeat, do not, move on him. If he shows, he's to be kept under surveillance."

She scanned the room. "To lock this cage tight, I have to wait for this asshole to spike the drink and offer it to me. When that occurs, we take him—possibly both of them—quick, quiet, clean. Questions?"

Chapter 19

The last question was asked and answered, and the troops dispersed. Surveillance and placement in the park would begin at eleven hundred hours.

"The entire op will be recorded. Every man will be wired, audio and video. We'll have all the angles." Still she paced her office, searching for any holes in her plan.

"You'll have him in hand in a matter of hours," Roarke told her.

"Yeah, I'll have him." She stopped, peered out the window. It was a beautiful day, full of flowers and warmth and white puffy clouds. Springtime in New York. Come out and play.

The park would be full of people. That's what he wanted, she thought. He liked crowds. They added to the thrill, the risk, the satisfaction.

Kill in plain sight.

"I'll have him," she repeated. "But I want it quick and clean. Carrying the illegals isn't enough. Mixing it with a drink isn't enough. But once he hands it to me, he's done."

She turned, looked at the board. Looked at the faces.

"Finch make any transmissions I should know about?"

"None whatsoever."

"Good. I thought she was smart enough to be scared."

The others, she wondered, had they been frightened? Had there been a moment, one instant when they'd understood enough to have the fear leaping into their throats, clawing toward a scream?

"You saved her, Eve. But for you, her face would be on that board."

"It doesn't feel like enough." Peabody had said that, Eve remembered, right at the beginning. "I have a lot of questions for Kevin Morano."

"It's unlikely the answers will satisfy you."

"Having them is sometimes the only satisfaction you get." And she'd have to make it enough. "I don't want you taking a weapon," she said as she turned to Roarke.

"A weapon?" he asked innocently. "Why, Lieutenant, an expert consultant, civilian, isn't issued a weapon."

"Issued, my ass. You've got a fucking arsenal in your museum upstairs. Leave them there."

"Of course. I give you my word I won't take anything out of my fully registered and legal collection."

"Roarke—I'm warning you . . ."

"It sounds like your other consultants are on their way." Giggles bounced into the room. "Be sure to remind them about the weapon policy."

"You want me to have you searched before the op?"

"Only if you do it, darling." His voice was oh-so-warm, and very Irish. "I'm shy."

Her pithy response was drowned out as Mavis and company piled into the room.

"Hey, Dallas, you missed the party."

"So I hear."

"We were supposed to have a practice session," Trina reminded her.

"I was, you know, unavoidably detained." She had to order herself to stand her ground when Trina came up to stare at her face. "What?"

"You look crappy."

"Thanks. That's just the look I was going for."

"When this is over, you're in for a full treatment, including relaxation therapy."

"Actually," Eve said, "I'm going out of town right after—"

"You can go wherever the hell you like *after* the treatment. How am I supposed to use you to drum up new clients when you go around looking like you spent a week in a cave? You trying to ruin my reputation?"

"Yes. Actually that's been my central goal since we met."

"Funny. Let's get started."

"I'll just leave you to it," Roarke said.

"Where are you going?" Eve made a grab for him, much like a drowning man would grab at a dangling rope.

He evaded her hand. "I have work." And he turned his back on the love of his life, deserting her without a backward glance.

"Now, you're mine." Trina smiled with lips dyed a summer grass green. "Strip."

"Leonardo's whipping up an outfit for you," Mavis said sometime later. "He said you don't have anything in your wardrobe that suits this look."

"It just gets better and better." Eve kept reminding herself that she'd vowed to protect and serve whatever the cost. Even if that was ninety minutes of allowing a crazy woman to smooth, pack, and tuck God knew what all over her face and body.

"Coming along." With her green skinsuit covered with a bright pink smock, Trina smoothed at the face putty she'd used to redefine Eve's chin. "How you holding up?"

"Boobs feel funny. Heavy."

"That's because you have some now. I know a guy who can do that permanent for you—at cost."

"I'll keep my own, thanks just the same."

"Up to you. Hold still. This needs a minute to set."

"Why is it taking so long? I can't believe those ass-holes spent hours a day prepping for these dates."

"Probably not. Change your appearance that way in under an hour if you know what you're doing. But we're not just changing yours. We're replicating as close as we can somebody else's image." Trina snapped the kiwi-scented gum she was chewing. "It's lots trickier."

"It's really working, too." In a smock of dizzying neon swirls of blue and yellow, Mavis stood in as first assistant. "The whole shape of your face is different, Dallas. You've lost the chin dent, the edge of your cheekbones. You look softer. Wanna see?"

"No. Not till it's done. How much longer? I've got to get in the field."

"Final inning's coming up. I've gotta blend this color, do the surface enhancements." Trina rubbed a bit of color into the back of Eve's hand, pursed her lips, studied the computer image of Stefanie Finch. "What do you think?" she asked Mavis.

"Need to pink it up just a little."

"Yeah." She added a dab to a testing bowl, blended. "Yeah, yeah, this is it. I'm a fucking genius. Mav, better call Leonardo and tell him to hustle it with the outfit. I need to know how much of her to cover with this."

"As little as possible." Eve begged.

"Relax your face. I'm going to start there. This is a nice face," she added as she went to work. "Pretty and all. Yours is actually the more interesting of the two, though."

"Golly, Trina, I'm all atingle."

"If you took basic care of it, it would last you another fifty–sixty years without serious sculpting. 'Cause you got good bones."

Across the room, Mavis was cooing into the house 'link. It seemed to Eve she and Leonardo couldn't have a conversation with each other without cooing.

"White skinsuit, red swish," Mavis announced. "Elbow sleeves, scooped neck to midboobs. He'll have it down in five."

"What the hell's a swish?" Eve wanted to know.

"No talking till I finish the lip area. Very sexy," Trina said to Mavis. "Good choice with this coloring. Can you do the extremities?"

"Frigid! I just love playing with the goop. I have to take your wedding ring, Dallas. I'll give it to Roarke."

Instinctively, Eve curled her fingers in protest, a gesture that made Mavis's romantic heart sigh. "Don't worry." She gave Eve's hand a part. "I remember when he put this on you the first time. Almost a year ago. It was the best wedding."

Eve relaxed again, listened to Mavis's chatter with half an ear.

She knew Leonardo came in by Mavis's purr of greeting. Then there was cooing and kissy sounds.

"Wonderful job, Trina." His rich voice sounded very close to Eve's head, which told her he'd bent down to study the work. "I wouldn't have recognized her. Did you decide on the silitrex or the plastisinal base?"

"Silitrex. More pliable, and she doesn't need it to last that long."

Eve opened one eye when a finger poked at her cheek. And saw Leonardo's wide, golden face looming in front of hers. "Am I done yet?" she asked him.

He smiled, eyes warming, teeth flashing white and gold. "Almost. You're going to be pleased. What about the eyes?" he asked Trina.

"Temp gels. We'll get them close. She'll wear some amber sunshades, too." She peered at something over Eve's shoulder. "Great outfit. I've got a lip dye that matches that red, and we'll use crisp tones on the cheeks and eyes. Can you guys handle doing her nails?"

"I don't need my nails done."

"Woman goes on a hot date, she does her nails. Fingers and toes," Trina added. "Fifteen more minutes," she promised.

It took nearly twice that, and Eve was considering making a break for it. But since she was surrounded, she stayed put and nearly wept with relief when Trina fixed on the wig she'd dyed and styled the night before.

Eve sat while her three keepers took several steps back and studied her.

"I've got one thing to say," Trina began. "I am good." She snapped a finger. "Wardrobe and accessories."

Two hours after the transformation began, Eve stood in front of the mirror Leonardo hauled in. After the first jolt, she settled down to study and critique.

She knew what a swish was now. It was exactly that— a swish of material that swirled down in a kind of open-fronted skirt. This one was murderous red and fell to midcalf. It did nothing, as far as she could see, to make the skinsuit more modest. Nothing could. They were called skinsuits for a reason, the same reason she never wore the damn things.

Might as well walk around naked.

The body she was walking around in was curvier than her own. Despite the fact the breasts weren't hers, she felt uncomfortable having them so prominently displayed. Another inch of flesh, and she'd have had to cite herself for indecent exposure.

Her hair was lighter, longer. Sort of a subtle blonde that scooped into points at her chin. A rounded, undented chin, with soft and rounded cheeks. Her mouth didn't look quite so wide with those cheeks, that chin. Still, with the rich red dye, it practically popped off the face.

Her eyes were hazel with hints of green. But the expression in them was all Eve.

"Okay." She nodded, watched Stefanie's face nod back at her. "You are good. But let's give it the big test."

She crossed the room, walked into Roarke's office.

He was on the 'link, had a laser fax coming in and a holo-blueprint of a building hovering over his desk. "I'll approve the changes to the first level. Yes. But I'll need to see . . ." He trailed off, stared for a full five seconds. "Sorry, Jansen, I'll have to get back to you." He ended transmission, tapped something that had the holo evaporating.

He rose, walked to her, around her. "Amazing. Truly. Are you in there?" he murmured then looked into her eyes. "Ah yes. There you are."

"What tips it?"

"Trina may be a miracle worker, but she can't do anything about those cop's eyes." When she frowned, Roarke lifted her chin with his hand. "Feels very natural," he added with a gentle rub of his thumb.

"Check the boobs," Trina invited from behind Eve. "They're the latest temps. Can't tell them from Godmade. Go ahead. Take a squeeze."

"Well, if you insist." Ignoring Eve's growl of warning, he cupped the breasts. "You feel very . . . healthy."

"They come off the minute I take him down. So don't get any sick ideas."

"They taste real, too," Trina assured him.

Roarke's eyebrow arched. "Really?"

"Don't even think about it." She slapped his hands away. "Give me the verdict. Will he buy it?"

"Hook and line, Lieutenant. You might want to adjust your gait a bit. Saunter rather than stride."

"Saunter. Check."

"And try not to look at him as though you already had him in Interview. You're going to a picnic in the park. Try to remember what that's like."

"I've never had a picnic in the park."

He skimmed a finger down her chin, just where the dent would be. "We'll have to fix that. Soon."

She rode to the north end of the park in the surveillance vehicle, leaning over Feeney's shoulder as he did the checks.

"Running sweeps. Baxter."

The first of Feeney's screens showed a fountain fed by a leaping dolphin. She could hear the tinkle of water against water, snatches of conversations as people strolled, and Baxter's whiny plea for contributions. The screen jumped slightly as he circled.

"Doing your gimp routine, Baxter?" Eve demanded.

"Roger that," he replied.

"Just remember, whatever you take in from the suckers goes in the Greenpeace fund."

As Feeney moved from man to man, she gauged the situation. As she'd predicted, the park was a popular place on a bright June afternoon. She watched a trio of teachers herding a school group like woolly sheep through the botanical gardens.

"Possible sighting." Peabody's voice came over the speakers. "Male, Caucasian, shoulder-length black hair, wearing tan trousers, light blue shirt. Carrying wicker picnic basket and black leather bag. Heading east on path, Endangered Species section."

"I see him." Eve studied the man on-screen. Now that was sauntering, she decided, watching the way he swung the basket gently at his side. And on his hand was a bicolored gold ring set with a ruby. "Go in on the ring," she told Feeney.

He blocked, magnified. And she saw the dragon's head carved into the stone.

"That's a positive ID. We got our man. Keep him in sight. Baxter, he'll be moving into your sector."

"Copy that. I'm on him."

"Peabody, you and Roarke maintain your distance. He's thirty minutes early," she said. "Needs time to get set up. Let's give it to him."

"Trueheart's got a visual," McNab said from his bank of screens. "Possible suspect moving south now. He's heading toward the arranged area. Looks like we've got him."

"Maintain distance," Eve warned. "Trueheart, angle a little to your left. Perfect. Let's watch the show."

He moved off the path onto the grassy area designated for picnics. Two other couples were there before him, as well as a trio of women, obviously taking a long lunch break from work. One lone male lay flat on his back, sun-bathing. At Eve's order, he rolled lazily to his side, propped an e-book by his elbow and gave her a new angle on Kevin Morano.

Kevin paused, turning his head right and left as he studied the area. He opted for shade, turning for the largest tree where sun dappled softly on the grass. There he set down basket and bag.

"I want all available eyes on him," Eve announced. Then she hissed as she saw the visual from Peabody's recorder. "Peabody, Roarke, not too close."

"Lovely spot for a picnic." Roarke's voice was warm and cheerful. "Just let me spread this blanket, darling. I wouldn't want you to get grass stains on that lovely outfit."

"Blanket? I didn't clear that," Eve began.

"This sure is a surprise." Peabody gave what Eve recognized as an uneasy laugh. "I wasn't expecting a picnic."

"What's life without some surprise?"

She saw Roarke's face and the amused look on it as he spread a blanket on the ground.

Several feet away, Kevin mirrored the move.

"Such a pretty spot," Roarke continued, then lowered his voice as he sat. "We can enjoy the view without getting in anyone's way."

"I want no interference from any location. No one, re-peat no one, moves in without my signal."

"Naturally. Champagne, sweetheart?"

"Peabody, you take one sip and you're busted to Traffic."

Even as she spoke, she watched Kevin. He opened the basket, removed three pink roses, and laid them on the blanket. He lifted wineglasses, held them to the sunlight to watch them sparkle. He opened a bottle of white. Poured a glass.

"Okay, okay, add the chaser, you son of a bitch."

But instead he raised the glass in a kind of self-toast and sipped.

Then he turned his wrist, checked the time. Taking out his pocket-link, he made a call.

"Up your audio, Peabody," Eve ordered. "Let's see if we can get an ear on him."

She heard birds, conversations, giggles, a child's war hoop. Before she could demand it, Feeney was filtering.

Kevin's voice came clearly. "Couldn't be better. Ten people in the immediate area, so that's a point for public venue. I suspect we'll have to pass some park police on the way out, bonus points there." He paused, laughed. A very young, very happy sound. "Yes, having her do that to me in broad daylight in a public park would certainly shoot me into the lead. I'll let you know."

He tucked the 'link away, then sat a moment, breathing deep, admiring the view.

"Just a game," Eve murmured. "It's going to be a pleasure taking these bastards down."

He continued his preparations, moving a bit faster now, taking out a cold pack, opening it to a presentation of caviar. He set out toast points and the accompaniments. Foie gras, cold lobster, fresh berries.

"Gotta admit, the guy knows how to set out a spread."

"Shut up, McNab," Eve muttered.

He sampled a berry, then another. As he nibbled, she saw his eyes change. There, she thought. There it was. The coolness, the calculation. It remained steady as he poured the second glass of wine.

He watched and watched carefully as he opened the black bag. He reached in, brought his hand out again with the palm facing his body. And casually, he held his hand over the second glass, tipped.

She saw, in Roarke's recorder, a thin trickle of liquid.

"Bingo. He's ready for her. I'm coming in. Take third stage positions. Report any possible sightings of alternate target."

She moved to the rear doors. "I'm under."

"Take him down, kid," Feeney said and kept his eyes glued to the screens.

She stepped out into the sun and warmth. When she caught herself striding, she did her best to saunter. She was barely into the park when a lunch-hour jogger trotted up to her.

"Hey, beautiful. How about a little run?"

"How about you back off before I knock you on your pudgy ass?"

"That's my cop," Roarke said softly in her ear as she kept walking.

She spotted Baxter under a stringy tangle of dirt-colored hair, a torn T-shirt, and drooping trousers that were both smeared with what looked like egg substitute and ketchup.

Most park patrons were giving him a wide berth. As she neared him, she caught the whiff of old sweat and stale brew mixed with urine.

The man really got into character, she thought.

When she passed him she got a wheezy wolf whistle.

"Bite me."

"I dream of it," he said behind his hand. "Night and day."

In the five minutes it took her to move through the park, she was approached with propositions four times.

"You might want to take the I'll-kick-your-ass-then-eat-it look off your face, Lieutenant," McNab suggested. "Most guys'd be a little put off by it."

"I've never been," Roarke commented. "Caviar?" he said to Peabody.

"Well . . . I guess."

Eve fixed what she hoped was a pleasant expression on her face, and thought about the nice little chat she'd be having with her personnel, including her expert consultant, civilian.

Then the view opened; she saw Kevin. Everything else was set aside.

He saw her as well. A slow, boyish smile crossed his face, just a little shy at the edges. He got to his feet, hesitated, then walked to her.

"Make my dreams come true and tell me you're Stefanie."

"I'm Stefanie. And you're . . ."

"Wordsworth." He took her hand, lifted it to his lips. "You're even lovelier than I imagined. Than I hoped."

"And you're everything I thought you'd be." She left her hand in his. Dating had never been one of her strong suits, but she'd planned carefully how she would behave, what she would say. "I hope I'm not late."

"Not at all. I was early. I wanted . . ." He gestured toward the picnic. "I wanted everything to be perfect."

"Oh. It looks wonderful. You've gone to so much trouble."

"I've looked forward to this for a long time." He led her to the blanket. She passed within a foot of Roarke. "Caviar!" she said as she sat. "You certainly know how to throw a picnic."

She leaned over, turned the bottle of wine around so she could see the label. The same he'd used with Bryna Bankhead. "My favorite." She made her lips curve. "It's as if you could read my mind."

"I've felt that way, ever since we first corresponded. Getting to know you online, I felt as if I *knew* you. Had always known you. Was somehow meant to."

"This guy is *good*," McNab breathed in her ear.

"I felt the connection, too," Eve said, using Stefanie's words to her as a guide. "The letters, the poetry we shared. All the fabulous stories about your travels."

"I think . . . it's fate. 'It is he that saith not Kismet.'"

Oh, shit, Eve thought. Mind scrambling, she opened her mouth. And Roarke whispered the rest of the quote in her ear. "'It is he who knows not fate,'" she repeated. "What do you think fate has in store for us, Wordsworth?"

"Who can say? But I can't wait to find out."

Give me the damn wine, you worthless, murdering bastard. But instead, he handed her the roses.

"They're lovely." She made herself sniff them.

"Somehow I knew they'd suit you best. Pink rosebuds. Soft, warm. Romantic." He lifted his own glass, toyed with the stem. "I've looked forward to giving them to you, to having this time with you. Shall we have a toast?"

"Yes." She continued to look into his eyes, while she willed him to pick up the glass, to put it into her hand. Trying for flirtatious, she brushed the rosebuds against her cheek.

And he picked up the glass. He put it into her hand.

"To fateful beginnings."

"And even better," she said, "to destined endings." She brought the glass to her lips, saw his gaze greedily follow it. And the shadow of irritation smoke over them as she lowered it again without drinking.

"Oh, just one second." She let out a quick laugh, set the wine aside, and opened her purse. "There's just one thing I want to do first."

With her free hand, she took his, then pulling out the restraints, snapped them on. "Kevin Morano, you're under arrest—"

"What? What the hell is this?" When he tried to yank away she had the pleasure of knocking him flat, rolling him, and with her knee in the small of his back, securing the restraints.

"For the murder of Bryna Bankhead, the attempted murder of Moniqua Cline, and accessory in the murder of Grace Lutz."

"What the hell are you talking about? What are you doing?" When he tried to buck she simply held her weapon to his head. "Who the hell are you?"

"I'm Lieutenant Eve Dallas. Remember it. I'm your goddamn fate. My name is Dallas, Lieutenant Eve," she repeated because her gorge wanted to rise into her throat. "And I've stopped you."

So what? a voice whispered in her ear. Her father's voice. *Another's coming. Another always is.*

For an instant, just an instant, her finger twitched on her weapon. Tempted.

She heard the voices behind and above her—the alarmed buzzing of civilians, the clipped orders from her team. And she felt Roarke there, just there at her side.

Rising, she dragged Kevin up. "Looks like this wasn't such a fucking picnic after all. You have the right to remain silent," she began.

She escorted him to transport herself. She needed to. He wasn't remaining silent. Instead he babbled about mistaken identity, miscarriages of justice, and his influential family.

He wasn't yet babbling for his lawyer, but he would. Eve was sure of it. She'd be lucky to have fifteen minutes in Interview with him before his terror and shock settled back into calculation.

"I've got to go in, get started on him right away."

"Eve—"

She shook her head at Roarke. "I'm all right. I'm okay." But she wasn't. There were drums banging inside her skull. In defense she dragged off the wig, scooped her hand through her hair. "I've got to get this crap off me. They should be finished booking him by the time I get back to normal."

"Trina's going to meet you at Central, give you a hand with it."

"Good. I guess. I'll see you at home."

"I'm coming in with you."

"There's no point—"

"In discussing it," he finished. Nor in telling her he was going to administer the next round of meds Summerset had given him. "Why don't I drive you? We'll get there faster."

It took forty minutes to get back into her own skin. Eve could only think Roarke had said something to Trina. The woman didn't utter a single complaint about dismantling her masterpiece so soon, nor did she launch into a lecture on face and body maintenance.

When Eve was blissfully rinsing her face in cold water, Trina shuffled her feet. "I helped do something really important, right?"

Face dripping, Eve turned her head. "Yeah, you did. We couldn't have brought this down today without you."

"Gives me a rush." She blushed. "Guess you get that a lot. You going to go squeeze his balls now?"

"Yeah, I'm going to go squeeze his balls."

"Give them an extra twist for me." She opened the door, surprised at seeing Roarke walk into the bathroom. Trina tapped the sign on the door. "You definitely ain't no woman, sweet buns." With a wink, she headed out.

"She's right, you definitely ain't no woman. Even at Central, we have certain standards of behavior, and guys don't come into the women's toilet facilities."

"I thought you'd prefer a little privacy for this." He took a packet, pills, and the dreaded pressure syringe out of the small bag he carried.

"What?" She backed up. "Stay away from me, you sadist."

"Eve, you need your next dose."

"I do not."

"Tell me—look at me—tell me you don't have a massive headache, in addition to body aches, and that your own sweet buns aren't starting to drag. Lying to me," he continued before she could speak, "is just going to piss me off enough so I gain twisted pleasure in forcing the meds on you. Which we both know from experience I can do."

She gauged the distance to the door. She'd never make it. "I don't want the shot."

"Well, that's a pity, as you're getting it. Don't put us through another round like this morning. Be a brave little soldier now, and roll up your sleeve."

"I hate you."

"Yes, I know. We've added a bit of flavoring to the liquid packet. Raspberry."

"Gee. My mouth's just watering."

Chapter 20

She was rolling up her other sleeve as she walked toward Interview Room A. Apparently, it wasn't just her car that was having an electronic rebellion. Climate control was on the fritz in this section, and the air was hot, stuffy, and violently scented with bad coffee.

Peabody was waiting outside the door, perspiring lightly in full uniform.

"He whining for a lawyer yet?"

"Not yet. Sticking to the mistaken identity story."

"Beautiful. He's going to be an idiot."

"Sir, in my opinion, he thinks we're the idiots."

"Better and better. Come on, let's do this."

Eve pushed open the door. Kevin sat at the single table at one of the two chairs. He was sweating as well, and not so delicately. He looked over as Eve came in, and his lips trembled.

"Thank God. I was afraid I'd just been left here and forgotten. There's been some horrible mistake, ma'am. I was having a picnic with a woman I met online, a woman I knew only as Stefanie. Suddenly, she went crazy. She said she was the police, and then I was brought here."

He spread his hand, a gesture of reason and puzzlement. "I don't know what's going on."

"I'll just bring you up to speed." She drew out a chair, straddled it. "But calling me crazy isn't going to endear you to me, Kevin."

He stared. "I'm sorry? I don't even know you."

"Now, Kevin, what a thing to say after you gave me those pretty flowers and quoted poetry to me. Men, Peabody, what are you going to do?"

"Can't live with them, can't beat them with a stick."

Kevin's eyes darted from one face to the other. "You? It was you in the park? I don't understand."

"I told you to remember my name. Engage recorder," she said. "Interview with suspect Kevin Morano, regarding charges of murder in the first in the case of Bryna Bankhead, accessory to murder in the case of Grace Lutz, attempted murder in the cases of Moniqua Cline and Stefanie Finch. Additional charges of sexual assault, rape, illegals possession, administering illegals to persons without consent, also filed. Interview conducted by Dallas, Lieutenant Eve. Also present, Peabody, Officer Delia. Mr. Morano has been informed of his rights. Isn't that so, Kevin?"

"I don't—"

"Did you receive the Revised Miranda warning, Kevin?"

"Yes, but—"

"Do you understand your rights and obligations as contained in that warning?"

"Of course, but—"

She made a mildly impatient sound, held up a finger. "Don't be in such a hurry." She stared at him, went silent. When he licked his lips, opened them, she wagged a finger at him again. And watched a single line of sweat drip down his temple. "Hot in here," she said conversationally. "They're working on the climate control. Must be pretty miserable under that wig and face putty. You want to ditch them?"

"I don't know what you—"

She merely reached over, gave the wig a quick jerk, then tossed it to Peabody. "I bet that feels cooler."

"It's not a crime to wear hair alternatives." He raked unsteady fingers through his short-cropped hair.

"You wore a different one the night you killed Bryna Bankhead. Another still the night you tried to kill Moniqua Cline."

He looked Eve dead in the eyes. "I don't know those women."

"No, you didn't know them. They were nothing to you. Just toys. Did it amuse you to seduce them with poetry and flowers, with candlelight and wine, Kevin? Did it make you feel sexy? Manly? Maybe you can't get it up unless the woman's drugged and helpless. You can't get a boner unless it's rape."

"That's ridiculous." A ripple of anger passed over his face. "Insulting."

"Well, pardon the hell out of me. But when a guy has to rape a woman to get off, it tells me he can't do the job otherwise."

His chin lifted a fraction. "I have never raped a woman in my life."

"I bet you believe that. They wanted it, didn't they? Once you slipped a little Whore into their wine, they were practically begging you for it. But you only did it to loosen them up." Eve rose, walked around the table. "Just priming the pump. Guy like you doesn't have to rape women. You're young, handsome, rich, sophisticated. Educated."

She leaned over from behind him, put her mouth close to his ear. "But it's boring, isn't it? Guy's entitled to a little extra zip. And women? Hell, they're all whores under the skin. Like your mother, for instance."

He cringed away from her. "What are you talking about? My mother is a highly regarded and highly successful businesswoman."

"Who got knocked up in a lab. Did she even know

your father, I wonder? Did it matter to her once she was
revved to go? How much did they pay her to drop the suit
and complete the pregnancy? She ever tell you?"

"You have no right to speak to me this way." His voice
was thick with tears.

"Were you looking for Mommy in those women,
Kevin? Did you want to fuck her, punish her, or both?"

"That's disgusting."

"There, I knew we'd hit a point of agreement. In the
end she sold herself, didn't she? No difference, really, between her and those other women. And all you did was
bring out their true natures. They were cruising for it on
the web. Got what they asked for. And then some. Is that
what you and Lucias figured?"

He jerked, and his breath hitched. "I don't know what
you're talking about. I'm not going to listen to any more
of this. I want to see your superior."

"Whose idea was it to kill them? It was his, wasn't it?
You're not a violent man, are you? Bryna, that was an accident, wasn't it? Just bad luck. That might help you out
some, Kevin. Might help you out a little with Bryna being
accidental. But you'll have to work with me on that."

"I told you. I don't know any Bryna."

She whirled until her face was pushed into his. "Your
pants are on fire, asshole. Look at me. We've got you cold.
All the goodies in your little black bag, the illegal substance you slipped into the wine. We had you under surveillance, fully recorded from the time you stepped into
the park. Heard you talking to your pal about the points
you were going to rack up. And you're real photogenic,
Kevin. I bet the jury thinks so, too, when they see the disc
of you slipping the illegal into the wine. I bet they'll be so
goddamn impressed they'll give you, oh, I'd say three life
sentences—no possibility of parole—on an off planet
penal colony. A nice concrete cage to call your own."

She hammered it at him while he stared at her with
horror creeping over his face. "Three squares a day. Oh
not the squares you're used to," she added, fingering the

material of his shirt. "But they'll keep you alive. A long, long time. And you know what happens to rapists in prison? Especially pretty ones. They'll all try you out, then they'll fight over you and try you out some more. They'll fuck you half to death, Kevin. And the more you beg them to stop, the more you plead, the harder they'll ram into you."

She straightened, stared into the two-way glass, into the nightmare that lived in her own eyes. That crawled in her own belly.

"If you're lucky," she said, "somebody named Big Willy will make you his bitch and keep the others off you. Feeling lucky, Kevin?"

"This is harassment. This is intimidation."

"This is reality," she snapped. "This is fate, this is destiny. This is your goddamn kismet, pal. You trolled for women in online chats. Poetry chats. That's where you found Bryna Bankhead. You developed a relationship with her while using the name Dante. And working with your friend and fellow creep, Lucias Dunwood, you arranged to meet her."

She paused, let it sink in. "You sent her flowers, pink roses, at work. You spent some time watching her on her day off. You used a unit in the cyber-joint across the street. We got you nailed there. You know, we've got a whole frigging division of cyber-geeks on the payroll, Kev. I'll tell you a little secret."

She eased in again, dropped her voice to a conspirator's whisper. "You're not as good as you think you are. Not there, not at the joint on Fifth either. You left prints."

She watched his lips tremble like a child about to cry. "Anyway," she said, "back to Bryna Bankhead. You met her at the Rainbow Room. Coming back to you yet, Kevin? She was a pretty woman. You had drinks. Or you did, and she had Whore you mixed with her wine. When she was primed with it, you went back to her place. Gave her a little more, just in case."

She slapped her hands on the table, leaned in. "You

turned on music, you lit the candles, you tossed fucking pink rose petals on the bed. And you raped her. To give it all a little more kick, you fed her some Wild Rabbit. Her system couldn't take it, and she died. Died right there in the bed of roses. Scared you, didn't it? Pissed you off. What the hell did she mean by dying and messing up your plans? You threw her off the terrace, threw her out on the street like she was garbage."

"No."

"Did you watch her fall, Kevin? I don't think so. You were done with her. Had to cover your ass, didn't you? Run home to Lucias and ask him what to do."

She straightened, turned away, strolled over and got herself a cup of water. "He runs you, doesn't he? You haven't got the spine to run yourself."

"No one runs me. Not Lucias, not you, not anyone. I'm a man. My own man."

"Then it was your idea."

"No, it was—I have nothing to say. I want my lawyer."

"Good." She eased a hip down on the table. "I was hoping you'd say that because once you bring the lawyers in, I don't have to work with you toward any sort of deal. I've got to tell you, Kevin, just the idea of making a deal with you was making me sick to my stomach. And I've got a really strong stomach, right, Peabody?"

"Titanium steel, sir."

"Yep, that's me." Eve gave her stomach a little pat. "But you managed to churn it. Now I'm all steady again picturing you spending the rest of your pitiful life in a cage, without your pretty suits, all snuggled up with Big Willy." She pushed off the table. "When I have Lucias sitting where you're sitting now, I'll get a little sick again, working with him. Because he's going to go for a deal and roll right over on you. What are the current odds on that in the pool, Peabody?"

"Three to five, on Dunwood, sir."

"I better place my bet. Let's get you that lawyer,

Kevin. Break in Interview, due to suspect's request for representation." She turned for the door.

"Wait."

Her eyes, January ice, met Peabody's. "Something on your mind, Kevin?"

"I just wondered . . . strictly out of curiosity, what you mean by a deal."

"Sorry, I can't get into that as you've called for your lawyer."

"The lawyer can wait."

Gotcha, Eve thought, and turned back. "Record on. Continuation of Interview, same subjects. Please repeat that, Kevin, for the record."

"The lawyer can wait. I'd like to know what you mean by a deal."

"I'm going to need a nausea pill." She sighed, sat again. "Okay. You know what you've got to do, Kevin? You've got to come clean, tell me how it all happened. I need chapter and verse. And you're going to have to show me some good faith and some sincere remorse. You pull that off, and I'll go to bat for you. Recommend that you're given better facilities, separated from the general population of butt-fuckers."

"I don't understand? What sort of deal is that? You think I'm going to go to jail?"

"Oh, Kevin, Kevin." She sighed. "I *know* you're going over. What happens to you after you're there is up to you."

"I want immunity."

"And I want to sing show tunes on Broadway. Neither one of us have a chance in hell of realizing those precious dreams. We got your DNA, you stupid putz. You didn't suit up for your parties. We got your juice, your prints. And you know that little sample they took from you at Booking? They're running it right now. It's going to match, Kevin, we both know it's going to match what you left behind in Bryna and Moniqua. Once it does, once I have the DNA match in my hot little hand, play time's over. I'll put you down like a sick dog, and all the lawyers in all the land won't be able to help you."

"You have to give me something. A plea bargain, a way out. I have money—"

Her hand whipped out, snatched his shirtfront. "Was that a bribe, Kevin? Am I adding bribing a cop to your list of credits?"

"No, no, I just . . . I need some help here." He tried to calm himself, to sound reasonable, cooperative. "I can't go to prison. I don't belong in prison. It was just a game. A contest. It was all Lucias's idea. It was an accident."

"A game, a contest, someone else's idea, an accident." She shook her head. "Is this multiple choice?"

"We were bored, that's all. We were bored and needed something to do! We were just having a little fun, a kind of re-enactment of his bastard grandfather's great experiment. Then it went wrong. It was an accident. She wasn't supposed to die."

"Who wasn't supposed to die, Kevin?"

"That first woman. Bryna. I didn't kill her. It just happened."

She leaned back now. "Tell me how it happened, Kevin. Tell me how it just happened."

An hour later, Eve stepped out of Interview. "A miserable, pusboil on the ass of humanity."

"Yes, sir, he is. You wrapped him up tight," Peabody added. "A platoon of lawyers won't be able to poke so much as a pinhole in that confession. He's gone."

"Yeah. The other boil won't break so easy. Alert the team, Peabody. Same personnel as the park. I'm getting a warrant for Dunwood. They deserve to be in on act two."

"You got it. Dallas?"

"What?"

"Do you really want to sing show tunes on Broadway?"

"Doesn't everyone?" She pulled out her communicator, prepared to request her warrant. It beeped in her hand. "Dallas."

"My office," Whitney ordered. "Now."

"Yes, sir. What is he, psychic? Round up the crew, Peabody. I want to move on Dunwood within the hour."

With the interview on her mind and the anticipation of getting her hands on Lucias hot in her blood, she walked into Whitney's office. She'd been prepared to give him her report orally. Her plans changed when she saw Renfrew and another man in Whitney's office.

Face impassive, Whitney remained behind his desk. "Lieutenant, Captain Hayes. I believe you and Detective Renfrew have already met."

"Yes, sir."

"Detective Renfrew is here with his captain. He's considering filing a formal complaint re your conduct in the Theodore McNamara investigation, of which he is primary of record. In hopes to avoid any such action, I've asked you to come here so that the matter can be discussed."

There was a dull roar inside her head, a low burn deep in her gut. "Let him file."

"Lieutenant, neither I nor this department have a desire to wade through the mess of a complaint if it can be avoided."

"I don't give a damn what you or the department wants." Her tone bit and had something unidentifiable flashing in Whitney's eyes. "You file your complaint, Renfrew. File it, and I'll finish you."

"I told you how it was." Renfrew bared his teeth. "Got no respect for the badge, no respect for fellow officers. She comes onto my crime scene throwing her weight around, pulling rank, undermining my investigation. Questioned my crime scene unit after I requested her to remove herself before she contaminated the scene. Goes behind my back to the ME getting data on a body that's not hers."

Whitney held up a hand to halt Renfrew's tirade. "Your response to this, Lieutenant?"

"You want my response to this? I'll give it to you." Furious, she yanked a disc out of her pocket, slapped it onto the desk. "There's my response to this. On record. You idiot," she said to Renfrew. "I was going to let it slide. That was my mistake. Nobody should let cops like you slide. You think the badge is some sort of protection for you? Some sort of hammer you can toss around? It's your fucking responsibility, your goddamn duty, not your cushion and not your weapon."

Hayes made a move to speak. Whitney silenced him by lifting a single finger.

"Don't you tell me about duty." Renfrew braced his hands on his thighs, leaned his body forward. "Everybody knows you're out for other cops, Dallas. You're in IAB's pocket. The rat squad's poster girl."

"I don't have to justify what I did about the One-two-eight to you. It seems you've forgotten cops were dying. Want their names, because I've got them in my head. I stood over them, Renfrew, you didn't. You want a piece of me over that, you should've taken it outside the department, off a homicide investigation. You want a shot at me, you don't take it over the dead we're supposed to stand up for. I asked you to reach out, I asked you to share information vital to both our investigations so we could do the damn job."

"My robbery-homicide hasn't been connected to your sex whacks. And you've got no business on my scene without authority. You've got no right recording on that scene, and anything in such a recording is bogus."

"You pompous, egotistical, ignorant fuckhead. You don't have a robbery-homicide. I've got one half of your murder team in the tank. I've got a full confession, on record, that includes the murder of Theodore McNamara."

Renfrew leaped out of his chair. "You go around me to bring my suspect into interview?"

"My suspect, brought in for questioning re my investigation, which as I told you, asshole, is connected with yours. If you hadn't been so busy taking the easy way, so tight-assed about cooperating, you'd have been part of the op that brought him in. Get out of my face, and get out of it now, or I'll take that badge you don't deserve and make you eat it."

"That's enough, Lieutenant."

"It's not enough." She whirled back to Whitney. "It's not enough. I just listened to a twenty-two-year-old boy tell me how he and his sick friend were bored and made up a game. A dollar a point, a goddamn dollar a point for the one who bagged the most women in the most inventive ways. They drugged them, raped them, killed them, for the satisfaction of being the top stud. And when McNamara realized what his grandson and his playmate were doing, when he confronted them, they bashed his brains in, kept him alive with a stimulant, stripped him naked, bashed him again, and tossed him in the river where he had the bad luck to be assigned to this disgrace.

"Three people are dead, and one's in the hospital fighting to come back. Because one cop decides to take a personal dislike to another, there might have been more. So it's not enough. It's never going to be enough."

"You think you can hang your screwups on me," Renfrew began.

"Stand down, Detective." Hayes got slowly to his feet.

"Captain—"

"I said stand down. Now. There will be no complaint filed from my house. If Lieutenant Dallas wishes to file—"

"I have no wish to file."

Hayes inclined his head. "Then you're a better man than I. I'd like to request a copy of that disc, Commander."

"Request granted."

"I'll consider the contents of the recording and take such actions as are deemed appropriate. Open your mouth, Renfrew, and I'll be filing myself. I want you to step outside. That's an order."

The insult went deep enough to have him vibrating. "Yes, sir, but under protest."

"So noted." Hayes waited until the door slammed.

"My apologies, Commander Whitney, for bringing this
mess to your door, and for the unbecoming behavior of
my officer."

"Your officer needs discipline, Captain."

"He needs a kick in the ass, sir, and I can promise you
he'll get one. My apologies to you as well, Lieutenant."

"Unnecessary, Captain."

"That's the first thing you've said I disagree with
since you walked in. Renfrew is a problem child, but he
is, for the moment, my problem child. I run a clean
house, Lieutenant, and take responsibility for any untidi-
ness that works its way in. Thank you for your time,
Commander."

He started for the door, paused, and turned. "Lieutenant, Sergeant Clooney and I rookied together. I went
to see him after the events of last May came to light. He
said you were an untarnished badge and he was grateful
you were the one to bring him in. I don't know if that
makes any difference to you, but it did to him."

He nodded again, stepped out, and closed the door
quietly at his back.

When they were alone, Whitney rose and walked to
his AutoChef. "Coffee, Lieutenant?"

"No, sir. Thank you."

"Sit down, Dallas."

"Commander, I apologize for my disrespect and in-
subordination. My behavior was—"

"Impressive," Whitney interrupted. "Don't spoil it by
remembering who's in charge in this room now."

She winced and searched for something to say. "I have
no excuse."

"I didn't ask for one." He brought his coffee back to
his desk. "But if I required one I might start by asking
how much sleep you got last night."

"I don't—"

"Answer the question."

"A couple."

"And the night before?"

"I don't . . . I can't say."

"I told you to sit down," he reminded her. "Shall I make it an order?"

She sat.

"I've never been a witness to you dressing down an officer—heard rumors," he added. "Now I can safely say you've earned your rep. You did what had to be done with Clooney and the One-twenty-eight. That doesn't mean you won't take flak for it."

"Understood, sir."

He studied her face, and because he could see hints of fatigue, grief, anger, knew she was running thin. "The badge doesn't make the man, Eve, it's the other way around."

She blinked, off balance by his use of her first name. "Yes, sir. I know."

"You're high-profile, professionally and personally. That kind of exposure and shine causes jealousy and resentment in certain types. Renfrew's a prime example."

"He doesn't concern me, personally, Commander."

"Glad to hear it. You have Kevin Morano's confession."

"Yes, sir." She started to rise, to give her oral, but Whitney gestured her back down.

"I don't require a formal report at this time. I got the gist from your rant. Has the warrant for Lucias Dunwood been issued?"

"Requested. It should be waiting for me in my office."

"Then go get him, Lieutenant." Whitney sipped his coffee as she got to her feet. "Contact me when you've wrapped him up. We'll need to schedule a press conference after which you're ordered to go home and use whatever method you choose to guarantee you eight full hours' sleep."

When she left, Whitney picked up the disc, turned it in his hand. Light glinted from it.

An untarnished badge, he thought. It was a good description of her. Watching the light play, he contacted Chief Tibble to make his own report.

• • •

It was tempting to blow the doors on the brownstone and blast in with a full squad of cops armed with riot guns and body armor. The circumstances of the case and the weight of the charges gave her the option to do just that.

It would make a splash, a blistering statement.

And it would be completely self-indulgent.

Eve let the fantasy fly away, and with only Peabody beside her, approached the door.

"All stations manned and ready?"

"That's affirmative," Feeney said through her earpiece. "He tries to rabbit and gets past you, we'll scoop him up."

"Copy that." She glanced at Peabody. "He's not getting past us."

"Not in this life."

Eve pressed the bell, counted off seconds as she rocked on the balls of her feet. She'd reached ten when the house droid opened the door.

"Remember me?" She gave him a toothy smile. "I need to speak with Mr. Dunwood."

"Yes, Lieutenant. Please come in. I'll tell Mr. Dunwood you're here. May I offer you some refreshment while you wait?"

"No, we're set, thanks."

"Very well. Please make yourself comfortable."

He walked away, stiff and formal in his classic black uniform.

"Now if Roarke would ditch Summerset and get a droid, I could be treated politely like that every day."

"Yeah." Peabody grinned. "You'd really hate it."

"Who says?"

"Those who know you best, sir."

"I think I know me best," she countered. "What makes you say . . . hold that thought," she said when she saw Lucias turn into the foyer. "Mr. Dunwood."

"Lieutenant." He'd dressed in black as well, had used just a hint of makeup to give his face a grieving pallor. It had worked wonders on his mother that morning, and he had no doubt it would set just the right tone with the cops. "You have some news about my grandfather? I spent the morning with my mother, and she . . ."

He trailed off, looked away as if composing himself. "We'd both be grateful for any news. Anything at all to help us make some sense out of our loss."

"I think I can help you with that. We already have someone in custody."

He looked back at her, an instant of surprise before it was masked. "I can't tell you what this means to us. To have his killer brought to justice quickly."

"Brightens my day, too." *Indulgent,* she told herself. She was being indulgent after all. But what the hell. "Actually, there were two people responsible. One has been charged, and an arrest of the second is imminent."

"Two? Two against a helpless old man." He worked rage into his voice. "I want them to suffer. I want them to pay."

"We're riding the same wave on that one. So let's get started. Lucias Dunwood, you're under arrest."

She whipped out her weapon when he took a quick step back. "Oh, please," she invited. "Keep going. I didn't have the opportunity to use this on your pal, Kevin, and it's made me twitchy."

"You stupid bitch."

"I'll take the bitch, but hey, which one of us is going into a cage? Stupid is as stupid does. Hands up and behind your head. Now."

He raised his hands, and when she turned him to face the wall, made him move.

Maybe she let him. Eve wasn't going to lie awake at night debating the point. But when he shoved, she let her body flow back, gave him room to swing. And ducking under the arch of his fist, rammed her own, twice, into his gut.

"Resisting arrest," she said when he fell to his hands and knees, retching. "Another mark on your permanent record." She nudged him flat with her foot, then put her

boot lightly on the back of his neck. "I won't add assault-
ing an officer because you missed. Restrain this clown,
Peabody, while I finish stating the charges against him
and read him his rights."

He was demanding a lawyer before she'd finished.

Chapter 21

The sky was still blue, a deep, dreamy evening blue, when she walked up the steps to her own front door. For the first time in days her mind was clear enough to let the sound of birdsong and the soft drift of flowers register.

She considered just sitting down on the steps and drawing it in, all those sweet and simple pleasures the world could offer. Remembering, taking the time to remember there was more than death, more than blood and those who spilled it with the selfishness of spoiled children made the difference between living and sinking.

Instead she pinched off a sprig of the purple flower spilling out of an urn and went inside. There was something she wanted more than fresh air.

Summerset took one look at the blossom in her hand and scowled. "Lieutenant, the arrangements in the urns are not cutting flowers."

"I didn't cut it. I snapped it off. Is he home?"

"In his office. If you want a display of verbena, you can order one from one of the greenhouses."

"Blah, blah, blah," she said as she walked up the stairs. "Yak, yak, yak."

Summerset nodded with approval. It seemed the medications had put her back to normal.

Roarke was at the window, holding a conversation on his headset. It seemed to be something about a revision to the prototype of some new communication/data system, but there was too much e-jargon for her to decipher. So she tuned out the words themselves, and just listened to the flow of his voice.

The Irish in it occasionally gave her a strange thrill, along with misty images of warriors and fragrant fires. And poetry, she supposed. Maybe the female of the species was just hardwired to react to certain stimuli.

Maybe in ten or twenty years, she'd actually get used to it. To him.

The sun, sinking in the sky, spilled in the window and drenched him in shimmering gold. He'd tied back his hair, which made her think he'd been at something that had required his hands and no distractions.

The light made a halo around him they both knew he didn't deserve, but that looked incredibly right.

He had the screen on, and a news report was humming. His desk 'link beeped and was ignored.

There was a scent to the room that was money, that was power. That was Roarke. Inside her rose a need basic as breath.

And he turned to her.

With her eyes locked on his she crossed the room, jerked him to her by his shirtfront, and captured his mouth with hers.

In the headset a voice continued to buzz in his ear, dim under the stirring of his own blood. He caught her hips, pressed heat against heat.

"Later," he muttered into the headset, then pulled it off, tossed it aside. "Welcome home, Lieutenant, and congratulations." He lifted a hand to brush it over her hair. "I caught your press conference on Seventy-five."

"Then you know it's over." She offered the verbena. "Thanks for your help."

"You're welcome." He sniffed the flower. "Anything else I can do for you?"

"As a matter of fact." She tugged the band out of his hair. "I've got another assignment for you."

"Really? My schedule's a bit tight right now, but I want to do my civic duty." He tucked the little flower behind her ear. "What sort of assignment is it? And be specific."

"You want me to be specific?"

"I do, yes. Very . . . very specific."

With a laugh, she boosted herself up so she could wrap her legs around his waist. "I want you to get naked."

"Ah, an undercover assignment." Bracing her hips, he started toward his office elevator. "Is it dangerous?"

"It's deadly. Neither of us may make it out alive."

Inside the elevator, he pressed her back against the wall. Felt the strength of her—and the yielding. "Master bedroom," he ordered, then ravaged her mouth. "I live for danger. Tell me more."

"It involves a lot of physical exertion. Timing . . ." Her breath clogged when his teeth found her throat. "Rhythm, coordination has to be perfect."

"Working on it," he managed and swung her out of the elevator into the bedroom.

The cat, stretched across the bed like a fat, furry rag, leaped up with a hissing complaint when they dropped onto the mattress beside him. Roarke reached out, gave him a light shove that sent him jumping down with a thud.

"This is no place for civilians."

With a snort of laughter, Eve locked her arms tight around him. "Naked." She raced kisses over his face. "Get naked. I want to sink my teeth into you."

Tugging at clothes, they rolled over the bed. Her shirt tangled in her weapon harness, making her curse breathlessly as she fought free of both. Their mouths met again, a frantic mating of lips, teeth, tongues that had the blood rushing hot through her veins and her body plunging under his.

She tugged at his shirt, yanking it down from his

shoulders so she could dig her fingers into that hard ripple of muscle and test strength to strength.

But he caught her hands in his, drew her arms over her head. Stared down at her with those depthless blue eyes until her own muscles began to quake.

"I love you. Darling Eve. Mine." He lowered his mouth to hers in a soft, soft kiss that turned those trembling muscles to water.

His mouth left hers to skim along her jaw, down the column of her throat. He would know, she thought as her heart shuddered. He would know she needed more than the flash and the fire. She needed the sweet and the simple.

She relaxed and drew it in.

He felt her open, surrender herself. There was, for him, no more powerful seduction than the yielding of her to him, and to herself. When she accepted the tenderness inside him, he found himself filled with bottomless wells of it.

Gently, his lips slid over her skin, savoring the flavor. Gently, his hands played over her body, cherishing the shape. Her heart beat thick under the glide of his tongue. And she reached down to cradle his head against her when he nuzzled lazily at her breast.

She smelled of her shower at Central, of the practical soap available to her there. It made him want to pamper her, to smooth away the harshness she was too accustomed to. So his lips were like a balm over her flesh, teasing out the warmth before the heat.

She drifted on a cushion of sensation, sliding into pleasure so subtle, so soft, it wrapped around her like mists. Her fingers threaded through his hair as the mists became a river, and the river a quiet sea of bliss. With a sigh, she let herself sink into it.

She heard him murmur as he moved down her body, the Gaelic he used when he was most stirred. It sounded like music, both exotic and romantic.

"What does it mean?" Her voice was sleepy.

"My heart. You're my heart."

He traced a line of kisses down her torso fascinated, always fascinated by the long, lean line of her. So much strength and courage lived inside that whip-tight body. In the heart, he thought as his hands whispered over her breasts. In the gut. He rubbed his lips over her belly.

The muscles quivered, and he heard the first unsteady catch of her breath.

Still he took his time, his slow and torturous time until that catch of breath became a moan, until that tough, toned body trembled.

When he took her over, he felt her release spill through her, and into him.

And the sea where she was drifting turned restless. Bliss became a craving and pleasure, a deep and throbbing ache that pulsed through her like a hunger. She arched against his busy mouth, crying out as her system erupted.

Desperate now, he worked his way up her body, inciting a dozen fires, a riot of the pulses. Maddening himself even as he maddened her. "Go up. Go up." Breath heaving, he drove his fingers into her, into the drenched heat. "I want to watch you. Again."

"God!" Her eyes went wide and blind as the orgasm ripped through her.

As she shuddered over the crest, he closed his mouth over hers, danced his tongue over hers until her breath, his breath slowed. Thickened. Slid slowly, slowly inside her.

Her eyes cleared, deepened, held his. Love, like silvered velvet, shimmered over the red haze of passion. She lifted a hand to his cheek as they moved together. The rise and fall of lovers who loved. The sweet and the simple.

When her pleasure peaked this time, it was like grace. He lowered his head, kissed away the tear that spilled down her cheek.

"My heart," he said again, then pressed his face into her hair and poured himself into her.

She lay with her body curled against his side. The light was going. The end of a long day. "Roarke."

"Hmm? You should sleep for a bit."

"I don't have the words the way you do. I can never seem to find them when they matter most."

"I know what they are." He toyed with the ends of her hair. "Turn your mind off, Eve, and rest a while."

She shook her head, pushed up so she could look down at him. How could he be so perfect, she thought, and still be hers?

"Say what you said before again. The Irish thing. I want to say it back to you."

He smiled. Took her hand. "You'll never pronounce it."

"Yes, I will."

Still smiling, he said it slowly, waited for her to fumble through. But her eyes stayed steady and serious as she brought his hand to her heart, laid hers on his, and repeated the words.

She saw emotion move over his face. His heart leaped hard against her hand. "You undo me, Eve."

He sat up, dropped his brow against hers. "Thank God for you," he murmured in a voice gone raw. "Thank God for you."

She refused to sleep, so he talked her into sharing a meal in bed. She sat crosslegged on the sheets, plowing her way through a plate of spaghetti and meatballs.

The combination of sex, food, and a blistering shower had done the job.

"Morano broke down in interview," she began.

"I'd put it that you broke him down," Roarke corrected. "I watched you." And had seen the way she'd stared into the glass. Into herself. "He wouldn't have known how difficult it was for you."

"Not so difficult, because I knew I'd break him. I didn't know you were there."

"I was part of the operational team." He twirled a bit of her pasta onto his fork. "And I enjoy watching you work."

"It was a contest to them, and the women game pieces.

All I had to do was box Morano into a corner, and game over. The way he sees it, it was Dunwood's fault, and he was just trying to keep up. Bankhead was an accident, Cline didn't die, and McNamara, well that was, in his view, a kind of self-defense. I looked at him, and I didn't see anything calculating or particularly vicious. He's just empty, weak and empty. A kind of—it sounds hokey—void of evil."

"It sounds accurate. Dunwood's a different kettle, isn't he?"

"And then some." She picked up her wineglass, sipped, then leaned over to sample some of Roarke's linguini with clam sauce. "Mine's better," she decided, pleased. "After the session with Renfrew in Whitney's office—"

"What session?"

"Forgot. I didn't tell you."

So, between mouthfuls of spaghetti and the herbed bread he offered, she did. "I can't believe I practically told Whitney to shut up. He should've slapped me down for it."

"He's a smart man. And a good cop. Renfrew now, he's just the type of cop who made things relatively easy for me. During a past, and regrettable period of my life," he added soberly when she frowned at him. "More ambitious than clever, narrow of view and focus. Lazy."

He scooped up another forkful of her pasta. She was right; hers was better. "And," he continued, "he epitomizes my previous view of the species. The view I held of badges before I got to know one more intimately."

"His kind pisses me off, but his captain . . . He's solid. He'll deal with it. Anyway. Anyway." She let out a long breath. She was stuffed, but still wanted more. "I took the team, minus our civilian consultant, to his place to bring him in. He lawyered straight off, and kept his mouth shut. He's not stupid, and he's not weak. His mistake is believing everyone else is. That's what'll take him under."

"No, you're what will take him under."

His absolute confidence in her warmed as much as any words of love. "Really stuck on me, aren't you?"

"Apparently. How about letting me have what's left of that meatball?"

She nudged the plate in his direction. "Dunwood had three lawyers in tow before we finished booking him. He claims to know nothing about nothing, except he did notice his good friend and companion Kevin's been acting a bit strange, coming in at odd hours, dressing up in strange getups to go out."

"Friendship's a beautiful thing."

"You bet. We've got no DNA on him, and he knows it. He's playing the innocent victim, the outraged citizen, and letting his reps do all the talking. He didn't even blink when we brought up the home lab, and the samples we're testing from it. Didn't even get a shrug out of him when I pointed out we'd found the wig and the suit worn in the Lutz security disc in his bedroom closet. That his bathroom vanity contained the brand of face putty and enhancements found on her body and her sheets. His story is Kevin used them, planted them. Same thing with the Carlo account," she added. "The illegals operation. He doesn't know a thing. It must've been Kevin."

"Where do you go from here?"

"Feeney's doing his e-thing with all the 'links and computers we confiscated from the townhouse. He'll find something. Dunwood was meeting someone on the night he killed his grandfather, and my take is she didn't show. We find her, verify the correspondence and the meeting scheduled that night for the club where he bought drinks, and we add more layers. The samples from the lab are going to test out for Whore and Rabbit. His lawyers can try to dance around that experimenting isn't illegal, and we have to prove use and/or distribution for sale. But it adds the next tier. We dig until we connect him to the distribution of those illegals as Carlo, through Charles Monroe's client. Crime Scene's fluoroscoping the house, and they'll find blood. We've got Morano's point-by-point confession. We've got plenty for an indictment. When we add up everything we'll lock in over the next couple days, we'll wrap him up in it."

More due to a need to move around than a sense of tidiness, she cleared the plates off the bed. "I'll sic Mira on him," she added. "But even she's going to have a tough time chipping at that shell. In the end, we'll dump all the evidence—physical, circumstantial, forensic, the psych profiles, the statements—into a box and wrap it up for the lawyers. He won't walk away."

"Will you? Can you?"

"If you'd asked me that twenty-four hours ago, I'd have said no. Unless I lied." She turned around to face him. "But yeah, after I finish putting the case together, take a couple more shots at him in Interview, I'll pass it to the PA. And I'll walk away. There's always another, Roarke, and if I don't walk away, I can't face the next."

"I need time with you, Eve. Alone, away. No ghosts, no obligations, no grief."

"We're going to Mexico, right?"

"To start, anyway. I want two weeks."

She opened her mouth, a dozen reasons why she couldn't take that much time ready to trip off her tongue. And looking at him found the reason, the one that mattered, why she would. "When do you want to leave?"

"As soon as you're able. I've dealt with my schedule."

"Give me a couple days to tie the ends together. Meanwhile, I've got a direct order from my commander I have to follow. I'm ordered to use whatever method guarantees me eight hours' sleep."

"And have you chosen your method, darling Eve?"

"Yeah, and it's foolproof." She dived onto him.

She had his robe off and her hands full when the interhouse 'link beeped.

"What the hell does he want?" she demanded. "Doesn't he know we're busy?"

"Don't forget your place." Roarke blocked video, answered. "Summerset, unless the house is on fire or under massive enemy attack, I don't want to hear from you until morning."

"I'm sorry to disturb you, but the lieutenant's commander is here to see her. Shall I tell him she's unavailable?"

"No. Shit." She was already scrambling up. "I'll be right down."

"Have Commander Whitney wait in the main parlor," Roarke said. "We'll join him in a moment."

"This isn't good, this can't be good." She yanked open a drawer and grabbed the first items that came to hand. "Whitney doesn't drop in for drinks and an after-work chat. Goddamn it."

Without bothering with underwear, she pulled on ancient jeans, dragged a faded NYPSD T-shirt with the sleeves ripped off over her head. Still cursing, she hopped into her boots.

In the same amount of time Roarke had managed to dress in pleated black trousers and a pristine black T-shirt. He slipped into loafers while she caught her breath.

"You know, if I wasn't in a real hurry, that would make me sick."

"What would that be?"

"How you can put yourself together like some fashion plate in under two minutes," she complained and hurried out of the room.

In the main parlor, amid the gleaming wood and glinting glass, Whitney and Galahad studied each other with cautious and mutual respect. When Eve strode in, Whitney looked relieved.

"Lieutenant, Roarke, I'm sorry to intrude on your evening."

"It's not a problem, Commander," Eve said quickly. "Is something wrong?"

"I wanted to tell you personally, and face-to-face rather than have you hear it second-hand. Lucias Dunwood's attorney's asked and received an immediate bond hearing."

Eve read the results of it on his face. "They let him out," she said flatly. "What kind of judge sets bail for a man charged with multiple first-degrees?"

"A judge who, as a friend of the Dunwood and McNamara families, should have excused himself from the hearing. It was argued that there's no physical evidence against Dunwood."

"There will be in a matter of hours," Eve began.

"And further argued," Whitney continued, "that the heaviest weight in the charges stems from the confession of Kevin Morano, which implicates Dunwood. That Dunwood has no priors, is a member of a respected family, a man who only last night was informed of his grandfather's tragic death."

"Murder," Eve snapped out. "One he committed."

"His mother attended the hearing. Made a personal plea that bail be granted so that her only son could assist her in memorializing and burying her father. Bail was set at five million, paid, and Dunwood was released into his mother's custody."

"Think." Roarke laid a hand on Eve's shoulder before she could speak. "Will he run?"

She drew herself in, forced herself to see through the rage. "No. It's still a contest. Just a different game. He intends to win. But he's pissed because I changed the board on him, so he's likely to do something rash. He's spoiled, and he's angry. We need to put a flag on the lab work. We need positive identification of the chemical samples taken from the townhouse."

"Already done," Whitney told her. "I spoke with Dickhead—Berenski," he corrected, "on the way here. You have a positive match for the illegals found in the victims. Using that evidence and the judge's relationship to the accused, the PA has filed for immediate revocation of bond."

"Will he get it?"

"We'll know within the hour. Regretfully, I'm going to have to countermand my order for you to get eight hours' sleep, Lieutenant. Your day isn't finished. Nor is mine," he added. "I'll go back to Central and stand by. With any luck, you'll be picking Dunwood back up tonight. I intend to go with you."

"With me? But . . ." She caught herself in time, swallowed the words back. "Yes, sir."

"I put my time in on the streets, Lieutenant. I can assure you, desk jockey or not, I'm not dead weight."

"No, sir. No disrespect intended. With your permission, Commander, I'll tag Feeney, have him snatch up McNab so they can put in time tonight on the electronics we have in Evidence."

"It remains your case. Plug the holes. I'll contact you as soon as I have word from the prosecutor."

"Commander." Roarke kept his hand on Eve's shoulder. He could feel her vibrating under it—revving to act, to do. "Have you had dinner?"

"Not as yet. I'll catch something at my desk."

It took two squeezes of Roarke's hand on her shoulder for Eve to clue in. "Um. Why don't you have something here, Commander? Save yourself some travel time."

"I don't want to put you out."

"It's no trouble at all," Roarke assured him. "I'll keep you company while Eve makes her calls." He gestured to the doorway. "Your family's well, I hope."

Eve took a deep breath and watched them leave the room. She wasn't sure which was weirder—her commander settling down to have dinner in her house or him settling down to have that meal in the company of a man who'd spent the majority of his life successfully breaking every law on the books. And some that hadn't even been written.

"All-around weird," she said to Galahad. And leaving the socializing to Roarke, she headed up to her office to get back to work.

Chapter 22

Because she understood his feelings exactly—and his way with words when riled was even more inventive than she was—Eve let Feeney rant, rave, and spew.

And didn't mention the fact that he'd answered the 'link wearing pajamas with little red hearts on them and that the music in the background was some bass-voiced singer crooning about making sweet love to his woman.

It seemed she wasn't the only one who'd had seduction in the plans for the evening.

"We'll get him back," she said when Feeney ran down to sputters. "I'm going to order surveillance on the mother's place and his townhouse. I don't think he'll rabbit, but I don't want to risk it. Get me something on those electronics, Feeney. Find me something to add to the pile."

"Judge oughta be stripped down, dragged through the streets, with a big sign that says BRAIN-DEAD FUCKFACE tied to his dick."

"Yeah, well, that's a pleasant and satisfying image, but I'll settle for a quick overturn on the bail. You'll tag McNab."

"Probably bouncing on Peabody," Feeney barked. "Talk about rabbits."

Eve decided it showed great restraint and sterling character for her not to mention the heart pajamas at such a prime opening. "If he is, I don't want to know about it, but you can tell Peabody to stand by for data. You pull anything out, she can follow it through."

"You don't want her with you on the take-down?"

"No, I've got another cop coming along. Whitney."

"Jack?" Feeney's drooping face brightened like a boy's. "No shit?"

"No shit. What do I do with him, Feeney? If we run into anything hinky, am I supposed to give him orders?"

"You're primary."

"Yeah, yeah." She pinched the bridge of her nose. "I'll play it by ear. Get me something. Oh, and Feeney? Love the pjs."

She broke transmission. Okay, maybe she didn't have such a sterling character.

She called in, requested surveillance on the two locations, then got up to pace off the time.

What was taking the PA so long? She should probably go downstairs. And play hostess. She was better at it than she'd been a year ago. Not good at it, but better. Still, she usually did that duty when there were groups, business dinners, or parties where there were so many people, giving anyone a lot of personal attention wasn't necessary.

Casual conversation and small talk were Roarke's strengths not hers. She took the coward's way and stalled by going back to the bedroom for her weapon harness.

The minute she strapped it on, she felt more in control.

Lucias felt the same way. In control. The rage, the *insult*, was a black, bubbling brew beneath the ice. And if from time to time it burned a hole through, he was still in control.

He'd known his mother would whine and beg and weep for him. She was so predictable. Women were, to his way of thinking. They were, by nature, weak and sub-missive. They required direction and a firm hand. His grandfather, then his father, had always given his mother a firm hand.

He was simply carrying on the McNamara-Dunwood tradition.

Dunwood men ran the show. Dunwood men were winners.

Dunwood men deserved respect, obedience, and un-questioning loyalty. They were not to be treated like com-mon criminals, to be pushed around, locked in a cage, *questioned*.

And they were never, never to be betrayed.

Naturally they'd let him go. He'd never doubted he'd be released. He'd never go to prison, never allow himself to be locked away like an animal.

He would, one way or the other, come out of this the winner.

But that didn't make up for the humiliation of being dragged behind bars, taken into a courtroom. Deprived of his rights.

He'd deal with Eve Dallas. Under it all she was just a woman. God knew women should never be put in posi-tions of authority or power. That, at least, had been something he and his late unlamented grandparent had agreed on.

He'd bide his time with her, plan carefully. Pick his time and place. When he was ready he'd pay her back for laying hands on him, for spoiling the game. For the pub-lic embarrassment she'd caused him.

A quiet place, a private interlude. Oh yes, he intended to have a very hot date with Lieutenant Dallas. This time she'd be the one in restraints. When she was loaded with Whore, begging for the one thing women truly wanted, he wouldn't even fuck her.

He'd hurt her. Oh yes, he'd give her pain—exquisite pain—but he'd deny her that final, glorious release.

She'd die desperate, just another bitch in heat.

The idea made him hard, and the hardening only proved he was a man.

But Dallas and her punishment would wait. There was, he knew, a natural order to things.

And first there was Kevin.

A lifetime friendship was no buffer against the sin of disloyalty. Kevin had to pay, and in paying would essentially ensure Lucias's own vindication.

He'd groomed himself carefully for this particular task. His hair was a gleaming copper, worn like a snug helmet over his skull. His complexion milk-white. His name was Terrance Blackburn, as his identification would verify. And he was Kevin Morano's attorney of record.

There were flaws. Lucias could admit there were flaws in the disguise. But the need to hurry outweighed the need to polish every small detail.

In any case, he knew people generally saw what they expected to see. He looked a great deal like Blackburn, would identify himself as such. He wore the sharp, conservative suit of a successful criminal attorney. Carried the expensive leather briefcase. Fixed the sober and aloof expression on his face.

He passed through the levels of security at Central without trouble. When he demanded a consultation with his client, he elicited annoyance more than interest from the duty cop.

He submitted coolly to the cursory pat-down, to having the contents of his briefcase x-rayed once again. And when he was shown into a consultation room, he sat, folded his hands, and waited for his client.

Seeing Kevin escorted in wearing a baggy fluorescent orange jumpsuit, put a nice, chilly scrim over Lucias's bubble of rage. His friend's face appeared gray and drawn above the hideous prison clothes. But he looked momentarily hopeful when he spotted Lucias.

"Mr. Blackburn, I wasn't expecting you to come back tonight. You said you were arranging for me to go into

Testing tomorrow, to show my emotional and mental dependence. Is there something new, something better?"

"We'll discuss it." When Kevin sat, Lucias waved the guard away with an absent gesture and opened the briefcase. The door closed with a satisfying snick. "How are you feeling?"

"Terrible." He linked and unlinked his fingers. "I'm in a cell alone. Lieutenant Dallas, she kept her word on that. But it's dark, and it—it smells. And there's no privacy, none at all. I really don't think I can go to prison, Mr. Blackburn. It just isn't possible. There must be a way to arrange Testing so that it comes out in my favor. I could spend some time in a private rehabilitation facility, or—or accept at-home incarceration. But I can't possibly go to prison."

"We'll just have to find a way to avoid that."

"Really?" Relieved, Kevin leaned forward. "But before you said . . . well, it doesn't matter. Thank you. Thank you. I feel so much better knowing you'll make some arrangements."

"I'll need more money. To smooth the path."

"Anything. Anything you need." Kevin buried his face in his hands. "I can't stay in this place. I don't know how I'll make it through even one night."

"You need to stay calm. Let me get you some water." He rose, crossed over to the water cooler in the corner. And as he filled a cup, added the contents of the vial he wore on a chain under his shirt.

"Your confession," Lucias added as he brought the cup back, "clearly states that Lucias Dunwood was to blame. It was his game, and one he was winning."

"I feel terrible about that. What else could I do? The things Dallas said would happen to me." He gulped at the water. "And it's not my fault. Anyone can see it's not my fault. I'd never have gone so far without Lucias egging me on."

"He's smarter than you. Stronger."

"No. No, he's not. He's just . . . Lucias. He's competitive. Inventive. I can't help it if it came down to him or me. Anyway . . ." Kevin worked up a weak smile. "I guess, at this point, I won the game."

"Do you think so? You couldn't be more wrong."

"I don't know what you . . ." His vision swam, went gray at the edges. "I don't feel very well."

"You'll pass out first," Lucias said softly. "Just slide under. You'll be dead before they get you to the infirmary. You should've been loyal, Kev."

"Lucias?" Panicked, he tried to rise, but his legs buckled. "Help me. Somebody help me."

"It's much too late." Lucias got to his feet, slid the chain from around his neck and looped it around Kevin's. Tucked it neatly under the jumpsuit.

"You can't mean to do this." Kevin gripped Lucias's arm weakly. "Lucias, you can't mean to kill me."

"I have killed you. But painlessly, Kev, for old times' sake. They'll think self-termination at first. It'll take them a while to figure out your visitor wasn't Blackburn. And since I'm at home with Mother, it couldn't have been me. One consolation," he added as Kevin crumbled to the floor, "you won't go to prison."

He reached over, closed the briefcase, brushed at his suit jacket. "Our game's over," he mumbled. "I win." He hit the panic button under the table, then crouched down, began tapping Kevin's cheeks with his hand.

"He passed out," he told the guard. "Went into a rant about not being able to stand the thought of prison, then collapsed. He needs medical attention."

And while his dying friend was being carried to medical, Lucias Dunwood walked briskly out of Cop Central.

Whitney and Roarke were sharing after-dinner coffee and cigars when Eve walked in. She actually heard Whitney laugh—not the low rumbling chuckle she'd occasionally heard out of him—but a big, rollicking belly laugh that stopped her in her tracks.

He was still grinning from it when she managed to unstick her feet and continue into the dining room.

"I don't know how the pair of you stay so fit with the menu to choose from in this place."

Amusement slid slyly over Roarke's face as he lifted his cup. "We . . . work out a lot. Isn't that right, darling?"

"Yeah, exercise is the key to good health. I'm glad you enjoyed your meal, sir. Feeney's on the electronics. I've arranged for surveillance on Dunwood's townhouse and his mother's home. Peabody's standing by to run any new data as it comes in. I goosed CSU, and they report they found blood on the living room floor and rug that matches McNamara's type. O Neg. Dunwood's also O Neg, but with some pressure on the tech on duty at the lab I had him run the full DNA. Early indications are it's McNamara's, sir. We'll confirm that before morning."

Whitney puffed on the cigar, a small luxury his wife denied him. "Do you ever wind down, Dallas?" At her blank look, he shook his head. "Sit down. Have some coffee. Everything's being done that can be done. We can't move until the PA reports in."

"She won't argue if it's an order," Roarke pointed out.

"I hate to, in her own house. Please." Whitney pointed to a chair. "Roarke tells me you're off to Mexico for two weeks. Have you put in for the time?"

"No, sir." Restless and reluctant, she sat. "I'll take care of it in the morning."

"Consider it taken care of. You're an exceptional cop, Lieutenant. Exceptional cops burn out faster than mediocre ones. A good marriage helps. I can attest to that. Children," he added, then laughed at her expression of sheer horror. "When the time comes. Friendships. Family. In other words, a life. Outside the job. Without it, you can forget why you do what you do. Why it matters that every time you close a case and put one down, there's one less."

"Yes, sir."

"I think since I've sat here eating your food, smoking your man's very excellent cigar, you could call me Jack."

She thought about it for about three seconds. "No, sir. I'm sorry. I can't."

He leaned back, blew a lazy smoke ring. "Ah well," he said, and his communicator beeped.

He went from relaxed to command in a single heartbeat. "Whitney."

"Bail is hereby revoked," the PA announced. "Lucias Dunwood is to be remanded into custody, all charges holding, immediately. Copies of the revocation order and new warrant transmitting now."

Whitney waited while they spit out of the data slot. "Good work." He shoved the communicator away. "Lieutenant. Let's go do the job."

When Roarke rose as well, Whitney inclined his head. "The civilian consultant on this case has requested permission to accompany us, and that request has been granted." He handed her the paperwork. "Do you have a problem with that, Lieutenant? As primary."

She sucked in a breath as Roarke gave her an easy smile. "A lot of good it would do me, so no, sir, I have no problem with it."

Sarah Dunwood lived in a two-level apartment in a quiet building only blocks from her son. Security pissed around with the usual "retired for the evening," "not receiving visitors," until Eve drilled through the muck with badge, warrant, and bitter threats.

"Impressive," Whitney commented as they stepped on the elevator. "But tell me, is it technologically possible to rip out a mother board and stuff it up a computer's ass?"

"I've never had to follow through, sir. The threat's usually sufficient. Dunwood's likely to resist," she continued. "He won't like being thwarted this way, and his instinct will be to attack before his control snaps back."

She hesitated. "Commander, I'd like to arm the consultant. For his own protection."

"That's your call, Lieutenant."

Nodding, she bent down, released her clutch piece from its ankle grip. "It's on low stun, and it stays there. It doesn't come into your hand, it is not deployed unless you're in immediate physical jeopardy. Clear?"

"Crystal, Lieutenant." Roarke slid the weapon into his pocket as they stepped out on the Dunwoods' floor.

"I'm at point," she continued. "We do this fast. Go in, locate, and restrain. I want you to clear any and all civilians out of the area."

She buzzed, and the instant the door opened, pushed inside. "Police. Bail for Lucias Dunwood has been revoked. He's ordered to turn himself over to my authority immediately."

"You can't come in this way! Miss Sarah! Miss Sarah!"

Roarke drew the shrieking maid aside, clearing Eve's path. "You'll want to sit down now, before you get hurt."

Scanning entries and exits, Eve strode into the living area. Her fingers twitched toward her weapon, then away again as a woman came rushing down the stairs.

"What is it? What's the matter? Who are you?"

She was a small, rail-thin woman with a gleam of curly red hair, disordered now, and a mildly pretty face spoiled by bruising under her left eye and along the soft curve of her jaw.

"Mrs. Dunwood?"

"Yes, I'm Mrs. Dunwood. You're the police. You're the woman who arrested my son."

"I'm Lieutenant Dallas, NYPSD." She offered her badge, but her eyes tracked for any movement and her ears were pricked for any sound. "Lucias Dunwood's bail has been revoked. I'm here to take him into custody."

"You can't. I paid. The judge—"

"I have the revocation order and the warrant. Mrs. Dunwood, is your son upstairs?"

"He's not here. You can't have him."

"Did he do that to your face?"

There was terror now in the pitch of her voice. "I fell. Why won't you leave him alone?" She began to cry. "He's just a boy."

"That boy killed your father."

"That's not true. That can't be true." She covered her face with her hands and broke into wild sobs.

"Commander?"

"Go. Mrs. Dunwood, you need to sit down."

Leaving the men to deal with the hysteria, Eve laid her hand on her weapon and started her search. She went upstairs first, trusting Lucias could be dealt with if he made any move on the lower level. She swept each room, entered, searched. When she came to a locked door, she drew out her master, bypassed the locks.

He'd kept a room here, she noted as she stepped inside. A pampered, indulged boy's room full of high-class toys. The entertainment unit spread over an entire wall— video, audio, screen, game components. The data and communication center took up most of an L-shaped counter. Shelves were stocked tight with discs, books, mementos.

There was a minilab, fully equipped, set up in the adjoining room.

In both areas, the drapes were drawn tight over the windows, the doors locked to the outside hallways. It was a little world of secrets, she thought.

She searched the closets first, found more wigs stored in clear boxes along with what she assumed he considered his secondary wardrobe.

In the bath she found traces of face putty and face base on the counter.

No, he wasn't here, she thought. And he hadn't walked out as himself.

Holstering her weapon, she walked back to the data center.

"Computer, display last opened file, image or data."

CANNOT COMPLY WITHOUT PASSWORD . . .

"We'll see about that." She hurried out, went to the top of the stairs. "Roarke, I need you a minute."

She walked back through the bedroom into the lab and helped herself to a can of Seal-It.

"The maid claims Dunwood and his mother had a shouting match," Roarke told her as he came in. "Or rather, Dunwood did the shouting. She heard his mother crying, heard the sound of blows. That's when she ran out of the kitchen area. She heard him slam out, and found Mrs. Dunwood on the floor. Apparently, it's not the first time he's used his fists on her. Like his grandfather and father before him. The father's in Seattle on business. He doesn't spend much time here."

"Big, happy family. I want whatever you can get me out of this, last work first. It's passcoded. If you have to touch anything, use this."

She tossed him the sealant. "I'll be back in a minute."

She left him to it, went downstairs. "He's not on the premises," she told the commander. "Mrs. Dunwood, where did Lucias go?"

"For a walk. He just went out for a walk. His mind's troubled."

I'll say, Eve thought, but crouched down. "Mrs. Dunwood, you're not helping him. You're not helping yourself. The longer it takes to find him, the harder it's going to go on him. Tell me where he is."

"I don't know. He was upset and angry."

"How was he dressed when he left?"

"I don't know what you mean."

"Yes, you do. He disguised himself again. And you knew when you saw him that way, you knew in some part of yourself that he'd done everything he's been accused of."

"I don't. I don't believe it."

Eve turned away when her communicator signaled. She strode out of earshot, listened. Then she gave the order for an APB.

"Kevin Morano's dead." She said it flatly, watched shock and horror pale Mrs. Dunwood's face.

"Kevin? No. No."

"He was poisoned. He had a visitor this evening in a consultation room. You know what that visitor looked like, don't you, Mrs. Dunwood? Your son went to visit his friend, and he killed him. Then he walked away."

"How the hell did he get through security?" Whitney demanded to know.

"By looking like this." Roarke came back in, held out a hard copy of an image. "This data was the last work on his computer."

"Blackburn," Eve said, without looking at the printout. "Morano's attorney of record. They'd have passed him through with minimal checks. He's a well-known criminal attorney."

"There's something else." Roarke offered her another printout. "The rules of the game."

SEDUCE AND CONQUER, Eve read, *a contest of romantic and sexual exploits between Lucias Dunwood and Kevin Morano.*

And scanned the rest.

It was all there, meticulously organized and detailed. The setup, the rules, the payoff system, the goals.

Disgust tightened her belly as she whirled back. "Look at this," she ordered Sarah Dunwood. "Read this. This is what he's done. This is what he is." She pushed the sheet under Mrs. Dunwood's face.

"Do you want to leave me with nothing?" Tears spilled down her cheeks as she stared at Eve rather than the printout. "I carried him in my body. After months of tests and treatments, of grief and hope, I made him inside me. Will you leave me with nothing?"

"I'm not the one leaving you with nothing, Mrs. Dunwood. He's taken care of that himself." She turned away again, and ordered two uniforms up to the apartment.

"He needs a place to remove the disguise," she said as they left the apartment. "He'll come back here eventually, but he doesn't have all his things here. He'll want more of his toys. Clothes."

She tried to put herself in his head. "Gotta ditch the disguise first. He'll know we'll come around to him with Morano's death. He can't afford to leave any trace of that around. But he thinks we're slow and stupid. He's so much smarter. He'll hurry, but he won't rush. He'll go home, take off the face and hair. Clean up. Spend some time gloating, packing some things up, destroying anything he thinks might be incriminating."

"You put men on the house," Whitney reminded her. "They'll spot him."

"Maybe, maybe not. Because he'll expect them to be there. Will you drive, sir?" she asked as they stepped outside. "I need the civilian to draw me a picture."

He drove fast, and without sirens. Whitney's eyebrows lifted, but he said nothing when at Eve's request Roarke quickly called up blueprints of the townhouse on his PPC.

"You got holo-features on there?"

"Naturally. Display data holographically." The image spilled out into Eve's lap.

She studied it. And planned. "We'll move the surveillance team to the rear. One man in, one man out. Additional men entering here, and here. We go in the front. Roarke, you'll go left, and up the stairs. The commander right to sweep the main level. I'll take the steps down. He's got full security, with video, so if he's paying attention, and he pays attention, he'll know we're coming. Watch each other's backs because at the core, he's a coward."

While she committed the holo to memory, she called for additional backup.

When they pulled up behind the surveillance vehicle, she hopped out, demanded status. She detailed the situation, gave her orders quickly.

"Seal hasn't been breached," Whitney commented as they approached the front.

"He wouldn't use the main door. There are three other entrances, twelve first-story windows." She detoured at a jog to the side of the house farthest away from the surveillance. "Broken glass," she reported. "He's in there."

Both she and Whitney pulled out masters. "I beg your pardon, sir."

"No. Forgot myself. Go." He replaced the master with his weapon.

She uncoded the seal. "On three."

"She likes to go in low," Roarke told Whitney, and on Eve's count went in the door with her, high.

They speared off, three arrows. Eve called out the required warning as she took the stairs to the lower level with her back to the wall.

The droid met her at the bottom.

"I am programmed to deflect, restrain, or impede any and all unauthorized intruders on these premises. If you attempt to come any farther, I will be forced to cause you physical harm."

"Back off. We're the police, fully authorized and warranted to enter these premises and remand Lucias Dunwood into custody."

"I am programmed to deflect, restrain, or impede," he began, moving toward her.

"Fuck this," she muttered, and blasted him.

While he sparked and shuddered, she kicked him aside. "Lights on," she ordered, and didn't bother to swear when her order was ignored. She moved in the dark, leading with her weapon each time she approached a doorway.

At the soft sound of footsteps behind her, she whirled, finger twitching. "Goddamn it, Roarke."

"You have two men covering the first level. Additional backup on the way. This'll go faster with two of us down here. And," he continued, moving up to guard her back, "down here is where he is."

Her instincts told her the same. Which was why she'd taken the area personally.

"Lab's going to be straight back," she said quietly, though she'd already picked up the security cameras tucked into the corners of the ceiling. "He's boxed in, but he's ready for us."

The door was locked.

"I'm going to bypass," she whispered in Roarke's ear. "He'll expect us to rush. That's what he's ready for. Don't go through the door until I give the signal."

She slipped the locks, kicked the door, then spun away.

The move saved her. Something crashed in the dark near the toes of her boots. She saw the smoke, heard the hiss, and was forced to sidestep before the acid eating into the floor hit leather.

There was a flash from inside. She felt a bright, shocking pain in her left shoulder. "Shit!"

"You're hit." Roarke dived across the open doorway, blocked her body with his as another series of blasts shot through like lightning bolts.

"Just glanced me." Her arm was numb now, shoulder to fingertip. "Get my communicator out of my pocket. My left hand's dead."

He pulled it out. "Lowest level, east end," he said into it. "Dunwood's armed. The lieutenant's been hit."

"Minimal damage," she snapped, irritated. "I'm not down. Repeat, I am not down. Security panel's over there." She jerked her head. "Bypass the damn voice command and get the lights on. Dunwood!" she shouted, duck-walking to the doorway with her left arm hanging useless and her weapon in her right hand. "It's over. The house is surrounded. You've got nowhere to go. Throw out your weapon, and come out with your hands up."

"It's not over until I *say* it's over! I'm not finished." He fired again. "Do you think I'm losing to a *woman*?"

The lights went on, and gave her a good look at the blackened hole in the floor only inches from her feet. "Seduce and conquer. We accessed your game, Lucias. Not too smart of you to write it all down so nice and tidy for us. We know you did Kevin. That was slick, but you don't know as much about law as you do about chemistry. His confession stands. And you were stupid enough to leave traces of putty and base in your bathroom. Really losing points fast."

Glass crashed inside the room, and his voice raged as temper lashed out. "It's my game, you bitch. My rules."

She held up her gun hand, signaling the men back as she heard them rushing down the stairs.

"New game, new rules, and you'll never beat me, Lucias. I'm better than you are. Throw out the weapon and come out or I'm going to hurt you."

"You won't win." He was weeping now, a spoiled boy choked by a tantrum. "Nobody beats me. I'm undefeated. I'm a Dunwood."

"Cover me." She drew in a breath, tucked and rolled into the room. The stunner blasts jolted over her head, shot along the floor by her hip as she dived for cover.

"Not smart, Lucias." She pressed her back into a wide cupboard. "Nope, not so smart. You keep missing. Aiming wild. You buy that off the street? Did they tell you it was fully charged? They lie. I bet if you check the discharge rate, you're more than half out already. I've got a full load. And I don't miss. I won the game. And my prize is locking you into a cage for the rest of your life. A woman's going to lock you away, Lucias."

She angled herself, signaled to Roarke to lay down fire to her right. On the blast, she leaped up. She swore, fired a stun shot. But was already too late.

The vial he held slid out of his hand as he shuddered and collapsed.

"Call for MTs," she shouted, and leaped over the broken glass. She kicked his weapon away, crouched. "What did you take?"

"What I gave Kevin." He smiled, coldly. "Double the dose for speed. No woman's locking me away. I end the game my way, so I win. I *always* win. You lose, bitch."

She watched him die, and felt nothing. "No. Everybody wins."

Epilogue

She stood outside, breathing in the night air, cradling her now tingling left arm in the palm of her right hand.

Sarah Dunwood would be burying both her father and her son. Daughter and mother, trapped in loves and loyalties that made no sense.

Maybe they weren't meant to.

"Do you want medical attention, Lieutenant?"

She glanced over at Whitney. "No, sir." Flexed her fingers. "It's coming back."

"You played him as well as anyone could." Together, they watched the black bag that held Lucias Dunwood, twenty-two, boy genius, beloved son and predator, being carried out of the house. "You couldn't guess he'd self-terminate rather than surrender to you."

But she had, Eve thought. A part of her had known exactly what she was doing—and had done it, had goaded him to it, with cold calculation.

Had they carried her father out of that freezing, filthy room in a black bag?

Then she closed her eyes because she was a cop—and

the badge stood for . . . Everything. "I knew it was a risk, Commander. I pushed his buttons fully aware there was a probability he'd take himself out rather than lose when we had him cornered. I could have ordered the room rushed. Potentially he'd be on his way to lockup instead of the morgue."

"He was armed, dangerous, and had already fired on you with a black market weapon set on full. Men might have been lost, certainly injured, who are going home to their families tonight. You played him as well as anyone could," he repeated. "File your report, then go get some sleep."

"Yes, sir. Thank you."

Rolling her awakening shoulder, she crossed the street to where Roarke waited. "I have to go in, write and file my report."

"How's your arm?"

"It feels like there are about six million hot needles sticking in it." She wiggled her fingers again. "Should be back to normal in a couple hours, which is about what it'll take to do the paperwork."

Because he knew her, and what she was thinking he said, "The world's better off with him out of it, Eve."

"Maybe, but that wasn't my decision to make."

"You didn't make it. He did. He had only to give up. You'd have taken him in, turned him into the system, and been satisfied."

"Yeah." Because it was true, she settled again. "I'm sending a police counselor to his mother. She doesn't need to hear about this from me, and she'll need someone who has the right words."

"Later, when her grief's not so raw, we might send someone from the abuse shelter to talk to her." He took her good hand in his. "Walk away, Eve."

She nodded. "Let's go tonight," she said as they walked to the car.

"Go?"

"Yeah, to Mexico. As soon as I've closed this, let's just head out, take one of those snappy transpos of yours and get the hell out of town."

He kissed her fingers before opening the door for her. "I'll make the arrangements."

NORA ROBERTS

MIDNIGHT BAYOU

PUTNAM